"Whether writing crime, mystery, or fantasy, a writer has two main functions: to transport and elucidate. A little weird also doesn't hurt. In *The Crack in the Crystal*, author Barak Engel takes the reader far away, with the wildest tale you'll find this side of Misty Mountain. An enchanting out-of-this-world experience guaranteed to keep your heart racing."

—**JOE CLIFFORD**, author, The Jay Porter Thriller series

"As a new player in the fantasy genre, Barak Engel has certainly made a strong impression with *The Crack in the Crystal*. His ability to create a compelling story with multi-dimensional characters and a richly detailed world suggests that he has a bright future ahead of him in the literary world. I eagerly anticipate his next work and hope to see more of his unique voice and imaginative storytelling in future books."

—**RJ WINDHAM**, global activist and author of *Inside the Mind of a Cancer Patient*, RJWindham.com

"The weaving of a world is a long, arduous task filled with self-doubt and disappointment. But on rare occasions, a rich tapestry such as *The Crack in the Crystal* by Barak Engel is woven. Each painstakingly crafted detail stands out in sharp relief, yet they create a tactile harmony. The gold and silver threads that wind their way through this wondrous story are the instantly intriguing, beautifully flawed, and gloriously realized characters. This is not a tale to be missed."

—**BILL ROPER**, legendary video game creative (including Diablo, Starcarft & Warcraft series), musician, actor, and epic nerd

"The adventure drew me in quickly and I wanted to find out what would happen next . . . **it's a fantasy novel that doesn't suck!**"

—**MICHAEL MECHANIC**, author, *Jackpot*

The
CRACK
IN THE
Crystal

ASCENDANCE

The CRACK IN THE Crystal

BARAK ENGEL

GREENLEAF
BOOK GROUP PRESS

Published by Greenleaf Book Group Press
Austin, Texas
www.gbgpress.com

Distributed by Greenleaf Book Group

For ordering information or special discounts for bulk purchases, please contact Greenleaf Book Group at PO Box 91869, Austin, TX 78709, 512.891.6100.

Design and composition by Greenleaf Book Group
Cover design by Greenleaf Book Group
Cover Image: alexkoral/stock.adobe.com

Publisher's Cataloging-in-Publication data is available.

Print ISBN: 979-8-88645-244-0

eBook ISBN: 979-8-88645-245-7

To offset the number of trees consumed in the printing of our books, Greenleaf donates a portion of the proceeds from each printing to the Arbor Day Foundation. Greenleaf Book Group has replaced over 50,000 trees since 2007.

Printed in the United States of America on acid-free paper

24 25 26 27 28 29 30 31   10 9 8 7 6 5 4 3 2 1

First Edition

To Mia, my love; Josh and Karms, my heart; Ziggy, Dingo, Gidget, and Pippa, the barks of my days.

To Willow, Shayan, Lauren, Dan, and Corey.

And to all those who struggle with emotions.

XLTL

Pronunciation: /Sh*uh*-LUHT/
Meaning: Precious Twin

THE
Book
OF
Stories

SPARK

It lived there for a long time.

Right until the world ended.

It had a good enough awareness of itself to know that it was formless. It was also genderless. He—or she, or perhaps they—wasn't sure. Not that it was something that occupied its mind, which it couldn't do anyway because it didn't have a mind, at least not in the classical sense.

Then again, what was "sense," exactly? And what did it mean for it to be classical?

For this time-moment, it decided it would be *They*. *They* sometimes played around with words this way, just to feel what it would be like.

They certainly had thoughts. These were long thoughts, slow ones, the kind that can take much time to think through. Or maybe they were fleeting, and their sense of time was warped? *They* pondered this question several times. Perhaps many times. *They* didn't exactly remember.

Memory was definitely a problem.

How *They* ended up on the inside of the big shiny rock was also a mystery, but *They* remembered that something happened. Something big, important, so important that it was the meaning of creation and of life itself. Which was odd because *They* clearly never had a life.

At least not in the classical sense.

They kept feeling guilty for some reason, but the reason was shrouded in darkness. The kind of darkness that only the gods themselves can place inside a person's mind. Or a thing's mind. Or any mind, really. But *They* weren't overly bothered by the darkness. It was the guilt that bothered them, and a sense that *They* might be able to do something about it. But when and how and where were another mystery.

A classical one, *They* amused themselves thinking.

They did know some things. *They* knew, for example, that the rock was pretty on the inside. *Might be on the outside too*, *They* thought to themselves, even while acknowledging that they couldn't leave and could, therefore, never see it from that vantage point. The rock had (Has? Will have had?) a strange and beautiful color, a sort of yellowish-blue that, after all these millennia—*They* didn't know it was millennia but assumed it because millennia was a cool word that *They* seemed to know, and it described a very long time indeed—became warm and comforting, an intimately familiar color. So much so that it had become more than a hue.

It became something *They* could taste, feed on, and become satiated and happy.

And because there was so much of it around, *They* were always happy, or at least *They* thought they were. *They* weren't sure what not being happy might be, but there was another memory of being sad, and when *They* thought about it, the feeling was exactly unlike that of being happy, so *They* assumed it was the opposite feeling. *They* also remembered having other feelings: the feeling of being in love, and of being torn, and even (while *They* tried to avoid it) of being punished.

That feeling sucked. But it was in the before times—the times before being in the rock—and *They* assumed those were bad times because they ended in such a feeling. Now must be the good times, because *They* were in the rock, and the rock was this color, and it tasted so, so good.

They also figured out at some point that the rock was a kind of crystal, and eventually, *They* decided to call the color by the truly clever name of "crystal color." It made sense.

Perhaps even classically so.

· · · · ·

When the calling came, it did so without warning, and *They* weren't ready for it at all.

One moment, *They* were sitting there basking in the warmth of the crystal, thinking idle thoughts about places that made no sense— of tall buildings made of metal and liquid stone, of impossibly large towers floating in the skies, of massive lands full of grazing sheep with coats so soft and so perfect that to lay one's head (were one to have a head) against one of them would mean to instantly fall into the most comfortable and refreshing sleep ever imagined.

Even the mere image of those sheep was enough to fall into precisely such a slumber.

Suddenly, rudely, with no right for it to happen at all, *They* were awoken by a terrible sound. A sound that nothing could ever make, should never make, a torment so immense that it would instantly crush every soul that would be unfortunate enough to hear it. A sound so obscene that it was impossible.

It was the sound of the fabric of the world itself tearing apart.

And then the world died, and *They* died with it.

SOLLIS (ONE)

"It's a girl!"

The midwife held the baby up to the beaming father. His face was covered in tears as he gingerly picked up the wriggling infant, and he entirely missed the midwife's look of concern. He hugged the baby girl before moving around the makeshift bed, placing her on her exhausted mother's chest.

"She's here, honey. She's finally here," he whispered, holding her hand. "She is so beautiful . . . she looks just like you!"

The mother opened her eyes, a tired smile on her face.

The baby cooed. It appeared to be taking in its surroundings, but nobody noticed. Nobody except the midwife, who made a quick warding sign behind her back. Then she spoke: "Congratulations. She's a . . . lovely baby. It seems like everyone is healthy and happy, so I will take my leave now."

The father turned his head in surprise toward the midwife. After a moment, he nodded, and she turned and left the room. He shifted back to admiring his wife. His hands moved to caress the baby's head, and, as his fingers touched her ears, he froze for a mere instant in confusion. Then the baby cooed again, and his face cleared before he leaned over the mother.

"She's perfect, honey. Absolutely perfect. What shall we name her?"

• • • • •

When Sollis blasted through four feet tall at the age of five, nobody was concerned. Sure, she was a head taller than her peers—at least the human ones—but if anyone thought anything of it, they kept it to themselves. She wasn't any taller than the elven children, anyway.

When she hit five feet shortly after her eighth birthday, her parents still didn't think that there was anything unusual about her. Other people did notice but only spoke behind her back. "That little girl . . . with the funny name . . . Sollis? You sure she's only eight?" And sometimes, in a hushed tone, "Did you see her ears?"

Sollis heard them. She could pick out the remotest of whispers from across a room or even through a wall.

So she took to hats. That was unusual, and kids could act cruel about anything unusual. Yet with Sollis being so much taller than anyone else in her age group, and her demeanor so detached, nobody messed with her. The one time somebody did try, he ended up in a corner, breathing heavily with light smoke coming out of his clothes.

Sollis was nine at the time.

When asked what happened, the boy was too terrified to answer at first. But the story got around that when he pushed her, her eyes lit up in a strange color ("mix of blue and yellow," he said). Then she raised her fingers, and he was zapped off his feet and slammed into the nearest wall,

"He must be exaggerating because he's embarrassed" was the consensus.

While wizards existed, it took a lot of money to become one, and a significant amount of formal education. Neither of these were available to people in the Shallows, so there were no wizards there, only diviners who got their powers from a deity who took favor upon them. Diviners like Rajiv in his Church of Tranquility.

If you asked Sollis about the incident, she would say she didn't remember. But she knew exactly what had happened. She told her parents that she was trying to defend herself against this older and much stronger boy. When he raised his fist, she became scared, and something had happened. She felt a strange power coalesce around her, course through her body, and then blast outward like it was a shockwave—and then the boy was lying a few feet away against a wall.

Sollis would never tell you the last part: ever since it happened, she had been seeking. Not the power; although, over the next few years, she learned how to summon it. To do that, Sollis placed herself in ever riskier situations until she triggered it again. This time, it was in a dead-end tunnel, with a couple of huge dire rats aiming to make her into their next few meals. She learned that the power could do other things, and she suspected it was the reason she could project her hearing.

But what she was seeking was a scent. An unnatural one. It had come with the shockwave, and again with the dire rats, and every other time when she managed to invoke the strange power. It was so faint and so unlike anything else that, try as she might, she couldn't describe it, even to herself.

All she could think of was that it smelled like wet pebbles.

When Sollis hit six feet at the age of twelve, people were no longer keeping their opinions to themselves. They would point, gawk at her, and giggle at her pointy ears, calling her a half-breed. Of course, she couldn't be half-elven; she was growing old at the same rate as the humans did. Half-elves lived a lot longer and took their sweet time to get there. They had a special celebration, the Thriceteen, which entailed a ceremony upon their reaching the tender age of thirty-nine. Regardless, by then, the story of the boy and the shockwave had made the rounds, and nobody wanted to mess with her. Thus, despite her frail exterior, she was never threatened again.

It also meant she had no friends.

Sollis found that perfectly acceptable.

By the time she was fifteen, Sollis stopped growing, but her six-foot-eight frame made her tower over everybody else, even the elves. She had kept to herself for so long that most people ignored her, in that way people ignore somebody who was badly disfigured. They certainly noted her—how could you not?—but they kept their distance.

Her isolation deepened.

· · · · ·

It happened shortly before her sixteenth birthday. She was walking toward her house, deep in thought. Her mother had taken ill, and her father was tending her bedside and didn't pay attention to Sollis, so she had left. It was another opportunity to test her power. As she got nearer to home, it slowly dawned on her that something was wrong; people were shouting and running back and forth, and when she raised her head, she could see the smoke.

By the time she arrived, there was nothing much left. She found her parents' grotesque, blackened figures still hugging each other over the smoldering bed frame. She took in the charred smell of their burnt bodies, lying there with bits of ash floating lazily in the air over them. The few people who were there to make sure there were no embers remaining (anything of value had already been swiped) noticed her. One of them even managed to overcome his fear long enough to murmur some words of comfort. But Sollis ignored him and the rest of them, then walked away.

She would never admit that she had felt nothing inside.

Isolating yourself when you have a place to rest your head at night and a meal in the morning is all well and good. Being isolated when you no longer have a home nor a family to take care of you is less comfortable.

Thankfully, by the time the fire happened, Sollis had learned how to use her powers to her advantage. She had long ago stopped listening to the whispers, not giving a damn what people thought of her. They were all boring simpletons anyway.

Instead, she would listen in on hushed conversations when plans would be made. Like once, she heard two thugs preparing to beat up a rival thug whom she happened to know. She found their intended mark and warned him of the attack. When the assailants showed up later, they discovered they had become the targets. The irony was lost on them; by the time they could conclude their plans had been disrupted, they were unconscious and missing all their valuables, as well as a couple of teeth.

Sollis, watching from a safe position, accepted her reward from a grateful ruffian. He tried sweet-talking her into staying with him, promising protection and more payouts, but she ignored him.

She liked being a free agent.

Loitering one afternoon outside the Steadfast Inn, she overheard two thieves planning to break into the safe of a petty officer from a docked merchant vessel. Their plan was poor and would have failed, but they never got the chance. Sollis preempted them and executed an improved heist. By the time they arrived, the safe had been cleaned out, and she was gone. She later traded the jewel for enough money to provide weeks of food and shelter, and she learned a powerful lesson: this was a much easier way to survive.

The Steadfast Inn became her primary place of business.

Otherwise, Sollis spent her days honing her craft and learning what else she could do and for how long before she became exhausted. That was one of her earliest discoveries; whenever she evoked the power, she would tire and require plenty of rest. Another recent discovery was exciting. By twisting her fingers just so, a ghostly flaming dart would materialize and shoot with uncanny accuracy from her outstretched hand. Its fire was cold, except when it hit living flesh. Then it burned, badly. Enough to instantly kill a small animal.

And no matter how tired she became, it was the whiff of otherworldly scent that lingered afterward that made everything worthwhile.

Sollis had no idea what it all meant.

Then she got caught.

• • • • •

Grabbing the jewel tightly, Sollis made her way to her regular fence.

She was deep in thought about a new magical effect when she entered the underground warehouse, which is why she didn't see the archers. Nor that Willie, her fence, had a couple of extra bodyguards. She also stepped unknowingly under a net hanging from the rafters, one that would have escaped her attention anyway because what did she know about warehouses?

She came to the desk where they always did business.

"Oh, hey, Sollis! Good to see you." Willie's tone was unusually ebullient. "What have you got for me?"

He was grinning. Willie never grinned.

Why was he grinning?

Sollis opened her palm, the realization that something was amiss slowly encroaching on her attention. She hesitantly brought the jewel up to the light, and her eyes locked on the additional bodyguards.

"Ohhh . . . now look at that! That is a beauty . . . you got it off the first officer of the Marinda, right? I heard about it. Some say it goes all the way back to the battle of Stormbridge."

"Yeah, Willie. I don't care. Just need my payout." Her eyes were scanning the room, and she noticed the archers. "What's with the extra security?"

"Ah, that." Willie's grin broadened. "Weeelllll . . . you see, Sollis, truth is that while I have my little domain here, which I run pretty well even if I say so myself . . ." Willie winced slightly and coughed.

Sollis focused her eyes on him, her fingers moving into the shock-wave position.

"Truth is, you know, the Thieves' Guild has its own interests here, and sometimes they override mine. So, you know, I have to do what I have to do."

He was grinning again.

"Whatever, man. Just give me my money."

"Right. Yes. Here we are . . ." Willie pulled out his purse.

"Think you can pay me in gold this time, Willie? This one's special, like you said." Sollis was becoming impatient. "I want to work with some new materials and they're expensive."

"Sure. Here, let me get it for you . . ."

Willie shook a few coins onto his palm and picked two shiny golden ones. Sollis, satisfied that whatever was going on wasn't related to her, relaxed her fingers. As she moved a step closer and put out her hand for payment, she resumed thinking about the new magical effect. Which is why, by the time she realized this actually had everything to do with her after all, she was ensnared in a net that had mysteriously dropped from the ceiling.

With all that isolation, she never was very good at reading people.

• • • • •

The next day, Sollis found herself standing by the Steadfast Inn. This time, however, she had a new purpose.

The bodyguards held her fingers tightly so she couldn't use her powers—Willie knew her better than she realized. Then some fellow from the Thieves' Guild stepped forward, sheathing a knife he had held at Willie's back. He told Sollis that her skills were appreciated and that their own agents had missed out on several acquisitions because a mysterious expert pilferer got them first, often using variations of his agents' very own tactics.

That wouldn't do.

"It's not the money," he said. There were principles involved. Even in the Shallows, the Guild wanted to ensure they were held in proper respect. They figured that Willie fenced these items, and capturing Sollis from there was merely a matter of waiting for her to show up.

Then he made her a proposal. She could choose to be stripped of everything she owned, roughed up a bit, and then tossed out on the road a couple of miles outside of Kyber, never to return. Or she could accept a simple, paid mission from the Guild, and in return, they would forgive all of her indiscretions. "Plus," he added, "you might find that having an arrangement with us isn't necessarily bad."

It took Sollis all of half a second to accept.

He told her his name was Bradd, and he even paid her the two gold. He said it was as much a token of appreciation for the jewel as it was a birthday gift for turning eighteen earlier in the week. It was something he had no right to know.

Sollis admired him for that. After all, for all of the district's faults, she liked living in the Shallows, where she had established a sort of street cred.

And she still needed to eat.

ARRIVAL

I t was an atypically slow day at the Shallows docks, but this happened occasionally in late summer when winds were unpredictable, and ships didn't quite arrive on schedule. Only half of the berths were occupied with different vessels, the biggest of which was the Marinda, a midsized ship that usually dealt in spices and high-end jewelry from the Far East.

Lormek moseyed over toward the Steadfast Inn. He shifted his gaze upward; Tradebay was a bit fuller. Across the shallow bay that served as the floor of Port Kyber, a small merchant ship crawled toward the Elevator, and if you looked out to sea, you could see a few straggling trawlers headed back with the morning's catch.

As he neared the inn, Lormek was surprised that the foot traffic was so slow for midday. He bobbed his head and grinned at a couple of locals who recognized him from his father's church and then kept moving. The note said to be there at high noon, and the sun had already begun to crest the viewing platform across the top of the Gash.

He would be there in good time.

When he got closer to the entrance, he couldn't overlook the incredibly tall, thin woman who stood deep in thought some distance in front of the swinging doors. Not wishing to alarm her, he changed direction so he would approach her from the side.

"Are you looking for something, ma'am?" he called as he got nearer.

The woman didn't seem to notice him. He stepped closer and spoke again.

"Ma'am, are you in search of something? Perhaps I can offer some assistance?"

Startled, Sollis snapped her head lower and met his eyes. Her yellow hair was tucked inside a straw hat, which was wide of brim and pulled down tightly enough to cover the top half of her ears. The hat's movement caused the shadows over her face to shift rapidly. It seemed like her eyes changed colors momentarily.

Fetching, Lormek couldn't help but think as he looked at her face. *Truly fetching.*

He stopped a couple of steps away from Sollis and smiled reassuringly. "I know most of everything there is to know around these parts," he offered. Then he pointed at the inn. "If you're in need of lodging, this is a great place to stay."

She shook her head. "No," she said in a quiet tone, adding after a second, "I have a meeting here." Her intonation was very precise and a bit awkward.

"Well, how funny is that! So do I!" he exclaimed. After a moment, he pointed toward the doors. "Shall we?"

Sollis considered him briefly, then nodded. As they started walking toward the inn, they missed the gnome who had just slipped inside after stepping nimbly and almost invisibly in the shadows along the side of the inn.

• • • • •

Once inside, the two of them moved toward the bar, Lormek's purposeful stride matched by Sollis's longer steps.

The bartender, who knew both of them, raised her head and grinned.

"I don't see ya here often, Lormek . . . your dad okay?"

"Yeah, he's good," he replied. "A little busy. Lots of hungry people, you know."

"Bless his heart! I don't know what the Shallows would be without him, my boy." The bartender turned her head. "As for you, young lady . . . you still owe me for your breakfast yesterday!" She winked and grinned. "You ran out of here so quickly I would have thought you'd stolen something!"

Sollis blushed as she took a coin out of a hidden pocket and handed it to the bartender.

Quite fetching, indeed, Lormek thought again as he snuck a sideways glance at her. Then he turned back to the bartender.

"Listen, Treena, I am supposed to be meeting someone, but I don't know for sure where or even who they are . . . do you know, maybe?" he asked.

Treena's eyes lost their twinkle, and her smile vanished. "Truth is I do. You have a meeting too, don't you, Sollis?" she asked.

Sollis nodded.

"All right, they said to head over downstairs. It's the room at the end of the hallway, you know, the one right at the edge of the dock."

Lormek and Sollis looked at each other in surprise, then back at the bartender.

"Wait," they both said at once, which startled them.

A second passed, then Lormek grinned and spoke up. "You mean we are both invited to the *same* meeting?"

"Seems that way!" Treena responded cheerfully. She turned her head back to the large, muscular brute sitting in front of a back door next to the kitchen. "Yo! Stinky! Check 'em and tag 'em and let 'em through!" Looking back at Lormek and Sollis, she added, "Go along now. The other two are already here."

"What other two?" Lormek asked in confusion. Sollis seemed puzzled as well.

Treena said nothing and pointed at the door. As Sollis and Lormek eyed each other, she went back to arranging glasses.

The huge bouncer stood up, flashing a hideous grin that could have easily given most anyone a heart attack. His intimidating posture and the slight protrusions on his broad forehead hinted at orkin blood. His muscles rippled all over his half-naked body, and his large, calloused hands flexed in the dim light, making it clear that one should remain on their best behavior around him to avoid having the daylights punched out of them. Particularly unruly patrons of the bar would learn that painful lesson from experience.

"Come here," the bouncer instructed them in a voice that was deep, smooth, and surprisingly pleasant.

Somewhat hesitantly, they made their way over to the door.

The bouncer sprang into action. His hands moved quickly and efficiently, removing the almost foot-long dagger Lormek always carried at his side and putting it on the table. Then he turned to Sollis, whose thin frame nevertheless towered over the massive half-orc. He frisked her as well, locating and removing the knife she had hidden in her boot.

"I'll keep 'em safe for ya," Stinky said, grinning again. Then he moved sideways, pushed open the door, and gestured for them to move through. The door's spring-loaded hinges were already causing it to shut slowly.

They continued into the hallway beyond, and Stinky turned back and sat in his chair.

As he did so, the door closed quietly, but the shadows around it seemed to move in a way that—had anyone seen it—would have seemed unnatural and, perhaps, aroused their curiosity.

In reality, nobody saw it nor paid any attention to it.

CHILD

"Hey, Ma! Are we there yet?"

The young dwarf hopped up the stairs as fast as his stubby legs could carry him. But the ship, like all ships, was built for taller races, so stairs posed a constant challenge. Dwarves had little use for ships. "We are made of earth and stone," his father always reminded him. "And too much water can wash it all away."

They sailed anyway.

· · · · ·

It was important to take the trip, although he didn't know why. His father had done something remarkable—spoke to humans or something—instead of just ignoring or insulting them. Turned out these humans were a delegation who had gotten lost and were worried for their lives, and they were grateful for the help.

Humans were funny like that. They seemed to appreciate their short lives in a way that belied their willingness to waste them on frivolities like war. Dwarves went to war too, but only to protect themselves or to ensure that their hill remained theirs. They preferred to stick to those hills, or tend to their tunnels, depending on the clan.

These humans followed his father's directions and left, but a bit later came back with wagons full of offerings. Then they had a council for three days and three nights with the clan elders. When the event concluded, his father was given the most important of tasks: sail to the human lands to meet with a clan elder called King.

While he had no idea who King was, judging by the content of the carts, even a youngster like him understood that King was very rich.

To get there, they would have to sail by boat across the Big Water that met the coastline, which they had all sort of assumed was the end of the world.

Naturally, not a single dwarf knew how to swim. The idea was preposterous. Why would anyone want to do that? So it was something they never really considered.

The humans promised that their ships were strong, and that they had made trips back and forth many times. It was on one of those trips when their guide, an elven scout, fell ill and lost her mind from the sting of an arphyd. The group had taken a few wrong turns as a result, and that's how they ended up at the foothill of Clan Tallgrass.

By the time the trade council ended, the elf had regained her clarity and could resume her guiding duties. After they first departed, no one expected that they should be back, seeing as humans were fickle by nature. But several moons later, there they were, asking for his father and whether he was all set to join them.

Only then did his father finally admit that he didn't really want to take the trip.

The clan elders impressed upon him that this was an opportunity to rise above his station—to become an elder himself. He would be the clan's first "diplomat." This was a word the humans taught them that loosely meant "a dwarf who would make trade with other clans and peoples without upsetting anybody," which was a sentiment that the dwarves appreciated.

So his father collected his family, and when the time came to depart, they flattened themselves with all their might against the center floor of the deck as the anchor was lifted and the big ship rocked gently and started to glide off shore. It took nearly two full days for them to finally be nudged away from that spot, and even then, it was more because their bladders were at their bursting point than anything the humans said or did.

He was first to adjust. Being the youngest, he was less afraid, and the least nauseated. On request from the tribe elders, who sympathized well with his parents' fear of water, let alone the Big Water (the humans called it an "ocean" and implied, inconceivably, that there was more than one), they were given room in the center of the hold. This, they were told, would be the best place to travel, as it would move the least even if the waters turned a little rough.

"Which is not going to happen," the humans added hastily. "Because we are going to sail in high summer, see, and the water is always very, very calm in high summer."

His parents were suspicious, but the humans told the truth. The sun had come up and fallen eleven times since they set sail, and other than a bit of rocking, mostly at night, the ship was as stable as a gentle creep of rocks after a spring shower. He would never tell his parents, but after the fear had passed, he found himself enjoying the trip. Eventually, he became familiar with all parts of the upper deck and even spent some time next to the captain where he stood looking out to sea behind the massive wheel that turned the ship.

The wheel was as big as he himself was tall, and he remembered thinking that it was only appropriate that you needed such a big wheel to navigate an ocean.

In truth, there wasn't much to see. Mostly the sun's reflection on the surface of the water, which stretched endlessly in all directions. Occasionally, he would catch sight of big fish playing and swimming, but after the first few times, he stopped marveling at them. If anything, he admitted to himself, sailing turned out to be a little boring.

Still, no matter how hard he thought about it, he couldn't figure out how the sailors knew where to go.

• • • • •

His mother's kind face warmed up as she opened her arms. She sat against the big post—it was called a "mast"—at the top of the stairs. That was as far as she ever allowed herself to go after they had moved down to the hold.

"Soon, baby, soon. The captain just told us we're within a day of port," she said, smiling.

"Cool!" He started running past her toward the bow.

"Please be careful. We don't know what the water will do . . . you know water is dangerous. It could turn on us at any moment."

"Don't worry, Ma, I'll stay safe!" he shouted over his shoulder.

He reached the short, steep stairs and started climbing, using his hands to help him make it up each step. As he reached the top, he expected that one of the sailors would pull him up the steepest, last stair, as they always did, but this time it didn't happen. He pulled himself up then climbed on a box and stood on his tiptoes against the ledge, raising his head to look.

The first officer was there, paying no attention to him at all, as his eyes stayed fixed toward the distance. He followed the sailor's gaze.

The sky ahead had a strange look to it.

It was dark. In the distance, he could see a flash.

And then he heard it—a distant rumble. Lightning and thunder.

He looked up at the sailor, whose face seemed somber.

"Say," he heard himself speak up, "is there a problem?"

The sailor ignored him.

He looked back at the dark patch of sky, which seemed to be growing visibly. He'd seen storms before, but this one was unusually big and fast. He moved closer to the first officer and repeated his question a little louder.

The sailor looked down at him.

"Not yet, boy. You should get down to the hold, and tell your parents to go with you if they aren't there already." The sailor started to move before stopping and adding, as if remembering his audience, "It could get a little choppy."

• • • • •

They huddled together for what seemed like hours. Still, it couldn't have been much past midday when everything became so much darker. The sunlight, which usually streamed in through the portholes, just . . . disappeared.

Then the ship started rocking.

They tied themselves with a rope to the center mast, which made its way down into the hold. If this was the most stable part of the ship, he thought, he couldn't imagine what being anywhere else would be like.

The ship shook violently. They had the frightening sensation of it jumping in the air, only to crash land with a terrible sound a moment later.

It creaked and it groaned.

Next, they heard the muffled yet still terrifying sound of wood breaking, giving in to forces beyond its power to contain. Water splashed in from above.

His mother screamed.

They hugged closer still, and he could hear his father praying to Thor.

• • • • •

When the end came, it did so without fanfare.

For a very long time, there had been flashes of lightning outside, the sound of rolling thunder, water splashing in every time the ship crashed down, and the sound of feet running above them and of sailors shouting in the darkness.

After a while, he found himself getting used to it.

Clearly, the humans were right; these ships could withstand a big storm. And it sure seemed like they would withstand this one, especially as things started to ease down. The ship sought to right itself in water that was a little less angry. A bit of sunlight came in through the portholes. He heard a sailor shouting for joy and felt reassured that they had made it through safely. Even his parents let their death grip ease ever so much and let out a small sigh of relief.

The explosion, when it came, took them entirely by surprise.

With no warning whatsoever, the hold made an awful groan. *The sound of death*, the thought leapt to his mind unbidden. Then the ship shattered open as if a massive claw was raking it. He wondered if it was a legendary sea monster from his nursery tales, but it soon became clear it was just a huge rock.

As any dwarf will tell you, no wood in the world can withstand the wrath of stone.

The ship split in half.

His last thought was that maybe learning to swim wouldn't have been such a terrible idea.

LORMEK (TWO)

"Goblinface!"

Lormek continued down the alleyway, his face maintaining a neutrality that had the best chance of avoiding a confrontation.

"Undercritter!"

Not that they could hurt him. He was much stronger, even if he was awfully short in comparison. Growing up, being short helped. As he muscled up, developing his robust frame, he enjoyed the relative freedom of being underestimated and then kicking the shit out of them.

At twenty-nine, he could take on anybody in the Shallows. But the bullies knew it too, so they would gang up on him in threes and fours. Rajiv, his adoptive father, always tended to his wounds, so no injury was permanent. That made the bullies beat him even harder, often to within an inch of his losing consciousness.

Sometimes they crossed that line too.

"Shitskin!"

Lormek turned the corner. He could see them huddling together at one of the many makeshift doorways that cluttered the alleys of the Shallows. You needed to handle yourself in the Shallows, or you might be stripped of everything you had . . . if you were lucky. They were taking umbrage from each other as they taunted him. And those taunts inevitably became about the color of his skin.

"Darkmutt!"

Why was he so dark? There weren't many dwarves in the Shallows, but the few who did spend their time in the bottom shelf were all of fair complexion. When compared to them, he stood out like a banana on pizza. Not that Lormek knew what either a banana or a pizza were, but he would have nodded his head vigorously at the comparison.

Other races had darkskins, of course. But most people in the Shallows could never afford to make it high enough to see much of the sun on a regular basis, let alone let it pigment their skin. So he stood out, all four feet of him. Might as well have been two feet taller, like the elves. At least then he wouldn't look so . . . so . . .

Invitingly small.

"Mudder!"

His jaw tightened.

As he grew stronger, he started getting invited to the fighting pits. Father was against it, and Lormek didn't want to upset him. Rajiv always taught kindness, and Lormek wanted to impress his father. But for Rajiv's kindness, he would not be alive today. For this human to adopt a confused, forsaken dwarven child, especially one so dark, then bring him into their home and raise him as their own, was an act of generosity that Lormek could never repay.

So he did all he could to follow in his father's footsteps. He tended to sick animals instead of killing them for a meal. He took care to bring turnip soup to the many beggars who were a fact of life in the Shallows, even the blind or legless ones who were destined to die randomly. Survival was already hard enough if you had your eyesight and all of your limbs. He was coming back from his morning rounds when the bullies saw him.

"You dirty Mudder!"

His jaw clenched even tighter, and he felt his fists clenching involuntarily as well. He kept his pace and started going through his calming routine.

Breathe in. Breathe out.

Six months ago, he had succumbed. The purse on offer was large, and his father could do much good with it. But Lormek knew the truth. He only signed up because he had had enough.

"Mudder scum! Mudder!"

Breathe in. Breathe out.

He turned another corner.

His opponent was human, fair-skinned, and powerful, with the confidence of being superior. The message was reinforced by the shouts of "Mudder! Mudder! Mudder!" from the crowd. Lormek hated that slur, and as it became a chant, then a chorus, his eyes filled with blood and his heart with rage. For the first time in his life, he fought not only to protect himself; instead, he fought for himself.

Breathe deeply. Hold it in. Count to five. Again.

When they finally pulled him off the lifeless pulp underneath, he remembered feeling nothing. Not the pain of his bruised and twisted knuckles, nor the dizziness from losing so much blood. Not even the difficulty of maintaining his balance on a broken ankle or keeping his guts from spilling out of the nasty cut he took from the illegal knife his opponent pulled out. Then, as his eyes rose to see the people surrounding the arena, how disgusted they were and how frightened that he was the winner, he felt a kind of elation, a sense of justice finally being done.

He was going to be a fighter, and none would stand before him. They would never dare to call him Mudder ever again. For the first time in his life, he felt triumphant.

Then his eyes locked on his father, standing quietly in the back of the rabid crowd. The disappointment on Rajiv's face was too much to bear.

• • • • •

The next morning, his wounds healed by Rajiv's divine touch, he woke up consumed with shame. He could not even look directly at his father once he found him preparing for services. He knew he had violated every principle his father had ever taught him, every foundation of kindness and service that he had built.

But what made it worse was that Rajiv simply refused to discuss it.

His father used the prize money, as Lormek had hoped, and stretched it longer than Lormek could have imagined. Somehow, it became another wing of the small church, where the sick and disabled could spend a night safely. He kept tutoring Lormek on how to pray to Freyg so as to bring forth the healing touch. He also continued to preach kindness, and even in a place where such sentiments were usually a precursor to losing your life, the little church continued to thrive and be a safe sanctuary.

But his father wouldn't say another word about the fight, no matter how much Lormek pleaded. Lormek's shame would accompany him for the rest of his life.

• • • • •

Rajiv continued to teach Lormek divinity, insisting that he could become a healer. Indeed, if Lormek prayed hard enough while holding his hands the right way, he could make scratches disappear. But there was no way he could heal a stabbing wound or pull off the miracles his father routinely performed—like making his guts go back into his belly as if they had never spilled out in a fighting pit.

Still, his father was convinced that Lormek had the signs of a healer and that he would eventually be called.

Lormek prayed harder.

• • • • •

After lessons and chores and lunch, Lormek went to the beach. A storm was coming, and he loved the storms. When anyone would seek shelter, Lormek would go outside; when everyone would be hiding, Lormek would stand with his arms raised in joy, his beard soaking in the rain.

This storm was one of the worst. Lightning flashed repeatedly, striking the narrow strip of shore and the tall cliffs behind him, causing small boulders to detach and hurtle down to the beach where he was standing. Some even struck him, but he didn't flinch, because his father could heal any wound. Thunder was rolling constantly. It started to hail.

It wasn't just one of the worst. This storm was the angriest he had ever experienced.

Lormek was elated.

Without warning, words in a language he didn't know came unbidden to his lips. Then a yellowish-blue light surrounded him.

This is unusual.

Lormek spoke the words, louder and louder. Soon enough, he was screaming, his voice lost to the storm. The strange light became brighter, and it emanated from him.

A power filtered through him like he had never experienced before.

It feels so . . . calm.

The storm grew stronger still. Then the lightning found a focus. It stopped striking the beach, or the cliffs. Instead, lightning bolts were pummeling him. Lormek had been struck by lightning before, once. He had almost died from that.

He wasn't dying now. In fact, he felt stronger with every strike.

I am being called.

He should not have been standing. Yet his voice grew louder still. Then everything went silent, the weird color became blinding, and a massive thunder exploded around him. In that very instant, he said one word that he did understand. A name. As he said it, his voice matched the force of the thunder, extending it, overcoming it.

THOR.

• • • • •

Later, Lormek went back through the tunnels. People were milling about, having sought shelter, and one had to be especially careful lest one be mugged, stabbed, or worse.

But Lormek was strong, his stride was confident, and his heart was singing. He had found his calling. He knew his god. And his power to heal had come with a twist; when he treated his own wounds, using more words he couldn't understand, his hands were dimly surrounded by an aura with a faint edge of the color from the storm. He couldn't wait to tell his father about Thor. Lormek was confident that Rajiv would welcome his calling, even if it didn't come from the very kindest of all the gods.

Deep in thought, Lormek turned a corner, and something caught his attention. A woman.

Elven?

She was hunched down in a dead-end alley. There were many such places in the tunnels, and people would get lost in them, especially after the storms. That was another reason why the caves could be so dangerous.

The elf was frightened. As he took a step toward her, she cowered.

"Are you all right, ma'am?" Lormek asked.

He saw her shoulders relax a smidge.

"Are you lost?"

She dipped her head.

"Can I help you?" He reached out his hand. She flinched. Several seconds passed. Then she hesitantly reached out her own hand and stood up shakily.

Is she mute?

"The storm is over. Come. I know the way."

He took her to church, and it turned out that the elven woman was not mute, and that Rajiv was elated to hear Lormek had received his calling. He learned that she could talk when she asked his name.

The way she asked it, Lormek felt as if she genuinely cared, something that had never happened before. She spoke little else and left the next morning, presumably—judging by her clothes—to go back to a higher shelf, and it was only then that he realized she had never even told them her name.

But Lormek never forgot her face, almost childlike both in terror and in kindness, with piercing, slightly slanted green eyes that saw into his very soul. She had smooth, shoulder-length black hair that fell naturally to one side. Lormek had found it enchanting.

• • • • •

When, six double moons later, he received a note, written in the delicate script that bespoke an elven hand and delivered by some random scallywag, he was surprised—and eager. The note stated simply, "Let this be repayment of your kindness toward me," and provided a location.

It wasn't signed.

And so Lormek found himself walking down to the Steadfast Inn. He sensed that this may be a major turning point. He had a premonition that whatever happened next, it would be important, and that his very life may hang in the balance. He felt a thirst for adventure.

But most of all, he was hoping to see her beautiful face.

FIRST CONTACT

ormek followed Sollis down the hall. It had one door, which opened on the office and proprietor's residence of the old and mysterious dwarf Bhaven. The other wall hugged the kitchen and ended in a stair leading to the lower level. At the bottom, the hallway doubled back on itself. That area wasn't well lit, and the way was blocked by a sentry, clearly marking it off-limits.

Instead, they turned into a small alcove set with another door.

Puzzled, Sollis glanced back at Lormek, and he returned her gaze, shrugging his shoulders slightly. "Dunno, ma'am," he said quietly. "Never been down here."

Sollis turned away from him, reached down to the handle, and pushed the door open.

His deeply ingrained tutoring guiding him to protect her, Lormek moved past Sollis to enter first as they stepped inside.

· · · · ·

The room was, in its own way, remarkable.

It was at least twenty-five feet to a side and as richly appointed as it was eclectic. The walls were covered in art, each dramatic painting and sculpture deeply compelling, but without any discernible rhyme or reason. Hanging drapes of velvet and silk were mounted across the room, extending on both sides and away from the door, hinting at multiple configurations.

On the right, a large window overlooked the docks. Facing it was the kind of couch one might find in noble houses. It was heavy and deep with invitingly plush velvet cushions. The couch was too large to fit in either the wide entrance door or the narrower one set at the far end. Indeed, it had been built inside the room hundreds of years ago.

To each of its sides sat a comfortable-looking easy chair; the far one was turned toward the entrance door. It was occupied by an elven woman with a short brown bob and large hazel eyes, who maintained perfect poise. Resting on the chair next to her was a small ornate lute. She slowly raised a glass of red wine to her lips.

On the left, a long serving table ran against the wall. It was covered with breads and rolls, smoked meats, white and yellow cheeses, and different fruits, even exotic ones like bananas and watermelon. Enough of everything was present that a dozen people could share in a feast. Toward the far end were a carafe of red wine, a jug of water, and a bigger one of ale. Next to them were cloth napkins, a small stack of empty wooden plates and cups, and a couple of upturned wine glasses. Leaning against the far wall was a plain man whose bored face, loose clothing, lack of visible weapons, and relaxed posture suggested he was a trained killer.

The floor was almost entirely covered in a thick rug, woven with complicated patterns that bespoke eastern culture. A rug of this size and superb quality would take months to make and fetch a fortune in gold. It had been here for so long that it had set its own barely noticeable groove across the floor to mark its place. Yet the rug kept its appearance throughout its long existence, evidence of preservation magic woven into its seams.

In the center stood an opulent rosewood table. The wood's deep color shone red, the grain catching and reflecting light. Anyone with an appreciation for woodworking would recognize that the table was the pinnacle of craftsmanship. Occupying one of eight matching high-backed chairs was a young man deep in thought as his fingers lightly caressed the wood grain. His otherwise smooth, young face showed a visible scar, running from the left temple to the corner of his mouth. His ears were so heavily mangled that there was no way to tell his race with certainty, but his slightly slanted eyes spoke of elven blood.

At the far end of the table sat a short athletic man of indeterminate age, wearing a sturdy leather tunic covered with pockmarks, betraying a busy past in protecting its wearer's life. His hardened face showed a hint of a smile, while his piercing black eyes missed nothing. In front of him sat a plate with a half-eaten roll, some cheese, and a cup of ale.

• • • • •

Everyone was quietly occupied with their thoughts until the faint sounds of footsteps echoed from outside the room. They were followed a few seconds later by the door opening to reveal an odd couple.

First was a foreign-looking dwarf, his dark complexion unusual in Kyber. His powerful pugilist's physique was mismatched with his kind, cheerful face. He was wearing a light brown cassock over his simple clothes, which did nothing to hide his bulging muscles. He wore an iron chain with a fist-sized symbol of Thor around his neck.

The thin woman who walked in behind him had to duck her head through the doorway. Her light robe was open to show a shirt that left her midriff partly exposed, while her pants barely reached the top of her ankle-high boots. Her light brown eyes peered down suspiciously.

With her right hand, she reached back and closed the door softly behind her.

The man at the head of the table cleared his throat.

"Well, now that everyone's here, we can begin." He raised his head toward the couple, gesturing toward the serving table. "Sollis, Lormek, please grab yourselves something to eat and come sit with us."

He turned to the elven woman and pointed at the table. "Nyelle, why don't you join us?"

The woman looked back at him for a moment, then stood up and moved gracefully to one of the high-backed chairs. She sat across from the scarred man, who had raised his head but whose hands still rested softly on the table in a way that seemed oddly intimate.

Sollis and Lormek filled their plates. He grabbed a cup of ale, while she satisfied herself with water. Then they made their way to the table and sat down.

The man at the head of the table cleared his throat again and opened his mouth.

There was a loud knock on the door.

He closed his mouth, irritation on his face.

There was another knock.

The man rose to his feet and bellowed, "What's going on? We're in a meeting!"

The door opened, and in it stood the sentry who had been guarding the hallway. He was holding up a gnome by the scruff of the neck, his feet dangling in the air.

"Caught this one tailing the other two," the guard said gruffly.

The gnome raised his face toward the man at the far end of the table and giggled. "Sorry, Bradd. I know you said to forget about it." He shifted his gaze momentarily to Sollis. "But she was . . . interesting." His bubbling enthusiasm betrayed his youth.

He giggled again.

Bradd glared at him then chuckled.

"Put him down," he said to the guard, who dropped the gnome

unceremoniously to the floor before turning on his heels and walking back toward his station.

"You know what, Garrett?" Bradd gazed at the gnome. "Why don't you join us? This group could probably use your talents, anyway." Then he looked at the others, and added cheerfully, "Just y'all make sure to hide your valuables!"

WHORE

She liked working at the Classy Lassy.

The name was abhorrent, of course. Who calls any establishment, of ill repute or otherwise, that kind of name? But the owner insisted it was clever. He also owned the Steadfast Inn nearby, and he was a dwarf. Dwarves rarely changed their opinion, so the name stuck.

They held on to it steadfast, she amused herself thinking.

The Lassy was too nice for the Shallows. The merchants who were the primary clientele would say it was business—come on, nobody has business in the Shallows—but considering how busy the Lassy was, it was obvious why so many ships docked at the Shallows.

Follow the money.

The Lassy was indeed classy. The rooms were clean, and the sheets were changed daily, just like at the Steadfast. This was unheard of for a brothel, since sheets were expensive and, in such an environment, especially challenging to clean. But the owners insisted (not always with a straight face) that it was a way to keep customers coming.

And they came, and they came, and they kept on coming.

The hostesses (and a couple of hosts) were paid well too. She had heard many stories, from all over the country, about how in these places you would end up making just enough to live on. At the Lassy, the owner kept only three-quarters of the take for himself and paid the expenses for security and pricey upkeep (like those bedsheets). So not only was the Lassy a high-class—"high lass" the owners sometimes said, again barely keeping a straight face—place to visit, it was a great place of employment.

Whenever an opening became available—perhaps when a girl decided she had earned enough to start a new life somewhere—the next morning they would have twenty girls at the door. The owner could be very picky, and the girls at the Lassy were very pretty. If you were going to spend the mind-boggling sums they charged, then there was no better place to spend them.

• • • • •

During her first stint at the Lassy, she remembered the owner viewing her with a mixture of appreciation and suspicion. It wasn't famous then, and the owner was trying to figure out an edge over the competition. It wasn't too long ago.

Two hundred years perhaps.

"What's yer name again, lass?"

"Leyera," she lied calmly.

He scanned her up and down.

"I have to say, you do look nice . . . how old did you say you were?"

"Two hundred and eighty," she lied. Again.

He squinted.

"Hmm. Well, assuming you are being more or less straight with me, I s'ppose that's old enough for an elf," he said and then added in reflection, "You sure are pretty though."

"Thank you," she responded casually.

He inhaled. "But why would you want to work at a whorehouse?"

She leveled her face at him.

"Looking for new stuff to do," she said and then added, "I'm bored."

• • • • •

That stint lasted fourteen years. Kyber's shelf districts made it an interesting place, and she spent a fair bit of time checking things out. It was then that she helped the owner develop the successful policies that made it a house not of ill but of high repute.

She remembered the evening when she strolled over to his office to tell him she was leaving. Not that any girl could walk over casually to see him.

But she could.

His face was a mixture of sadness, fondness, and concern.

"Oh boy," he said. "You're our anchor piece. You know that, right?"

She agreed.

"What am I going to do without you?" He seemed genuinely worried.

"Don't worry, Bhaven, you'll be fine," she assured him.

"How can you say that? The place might well be called the exotic elven lady!" he exclaimed.

"Mayhaps. But I have some ideas . . ."

And so they entered into a long conversation about how to retain clients and high-quality staff. By the time she left, she held ten gold in her palm from a very grateful dwarf. That was more than enough to gain passage on a caravan heading back to Corrantha City and there to acquire the supplies and expensive gear that she needed to go on a prolonged adventure.

The gift told her something even more important. Dwarves were known for many things, but being generous with their gold was not one of them.

They were friends.

• • • • •

When she came back to Port Kyber some sixty years later, the Lassy was developing its reputation beyond the borders of the burgeoning port city. The city that lay so improbably inside a submerged volcano in the middle of an ocean.

She went to visit him. He maintained the same office at the Steadfast Inn.

And he had kept his promise; the password was relayed to whichever captain was in charge of security, one generation of humans after another. Bhaven liked his guard to be made of short-lived races like humans and half-orcs. "Secrets pass with them," he had told her in confidence.

Learning the password was part of the ritual of becoming captain, but that still didn't make it any less shocking to the current one when she said it to him.

• • • • •

"Leyera!"

Bhaven jumped from his chair and rushed over to hug her, an awkward gesture considering their differing statures. She found it endearing, just like the fact that, in over a century, he had never once challenged her to reveal her real age—or her real name.

He looked much older now.

"You look good, Bhaven. Well-preserved. How are you, old friend?" she said to him after he managed to get his face out of her bosom.

He glanced up at her.

"Well-preserved, indeed! Oh, joy to see you, and blessings be upon you. Have you come for a visit? Tell me of your travels!"

They had dinner and went on with drinks well into the night. She had to admit that the Steadfast had substantially improved its selection of available wines and top-shelf elixirs.

Then she told him that she was looking to spend some time in Kyber.

• • • • •

Her second stint at the Lassy lasted even longer than the first. Bhaven gave her the best room, and she kept her own schedule. They also split the take right down the middle. She knew that he would give her more if she asked, but she liked him and didn't want any resentments.

He still paid for expenses.

A couple of years in, she started training the other girls in the arts of the courtesan. She only hosted when she felt like it and instead managed the Lassy, and Bhaven gave her 10 percent of his own take.

That came out to way more than she had ever made before.

Enough so that she bought a place in Greenpark. It was a beautiful, third-shelf district full of small houses nestled in between branches of the district's tall trees. Her tiny house overlooked the farm extending from the volcano's core where, due to favorable sun exposure, specialty crops were grown. Many elves and half-elves lived in those trees. She was delighted to be part of the community, and nobody cared about what sort of business let her buy her way in.

Elves, after all, lived long enough (a thousand years was common) that if they set their mind to it, they could accumulate enough resources to go anywhere they liked. The only reason this didn't lead to wars of total annihilation by the shorter-lived races was that the elves' massive lifespan was offset by their tremendously low fertility rates, and their resulting tendency to stick to their own.

She loved her life in Greenpark District.

• • • • •

Her wanderlust took her away before she had her third, short, and final stint at the Lassy.

But that is a story for another time.

NYELLE (THREE)

The melancholy tune ended.

As the last note died slowly—on a whim, Nyelle stretched it out even while she was putting away her lute—the small crowd seemed transfixed.

Were transfixed.

It was her acting skill that made her songs so compelling; acting to hide the fact that she could work sound waves to manipulate those around her, even if her audience didn't know why they were so moved. To her, sound was a physical object.

They assumed she was talented. In reality, they had to think exactly that. As she kept practicing, she learned how to influence more than one listener at a time. She would project sound such that each of them would hear what they longed to hear. Had discerning listeners compared notes, they would have realized to their surprise that those experiences were not, in fact, identical. They might get upset, and she would have to race away or risk a beating.

It added a measure of risk to her performances.

She loved it.

• • • • •

Growing up in the Shallows forced a child to realize their talents quickly. Even an elven child like herself would have to find their bearings early in life. Though the other humanoid races had all collectively concluded that killing an elf was a tragic mishap, seeing as so few elves were born every decade, that didn't mean they wouldn't take advantage of you or, sometimes, beat you senseless.

You'd end up not quite dead, but still quite miserable.

The constant racial tension was one reason elves stayed sheltered in their own communities. Another was that their sense of time was so different that living amongst other races could be stressful. How do you explain a dish that needed a month to cook to someone who could try to get pregnant—twice!—in that same period?

Still, there were always strays. And strays needed to grow up quickly, definitely once one was no longer a toddler. As the elven saying went, by the time you were fifty, you needed to know your trees and roots.

When you live in a place like the Shallows, it might as well be forty.

Nyelle remembered when she and her mother moved out of the boarding house and in with the nice man, Yorros. He took a liking to her mom, brought them in, and became her father-for-a-time. She had never known her real father, but Yorros was a pretty good one to have.

Yorros House, which was on the best street in the Shallows and was made of actual bricks and wasn't rickety at all, hosted a small library. That was an astonishing thing to find in a place like this, but he was an educator, and the library wasn't exactly his; it was open to all, but you needed to be vetted to use it.

As his adopted daughter, she didn't need to be vetted.

Nyelle loved the feel of books, the way that each page's unique texture would influence the grains of ink. Only an elf would notice such a thing, which is why many of them had trouble reading; they could get stuck on one page for weeks, studying the beauty of it, absorbing its essence, often forgetting why they were even interested in the book in the first place.

But she lived in the Shallows and didn't have time for that sort of indulgence.

• • • • •

"Mom, look! Look, Mom!" Nyelle ran into the main room. "Mom! Where are you?"

The old swivel chair turned around slowly. Enrielle faced her excited daughter, a kind and gentle smile on her delicate face. She spoke softly.

"What did you find, Ny-ny?"

Nyelle sat down on the low stool next to her mother and thrust the book into Enrielle's lap. Stray hairs from her short brown bob covered half of her face.

"Look! Right there!"

Enrielle saw what seemed like a complicated set of symbols arranged in a chart, and tiny text that was so gorgeous, she found herself admiring it. *That* A *is absolutely remarkable*, she thought, and *is the indentation on top of this* R *truly this deep? Does it mean that the* R *was feeling important?*

"Mom! Stop *looking* at the page and *read* it!" Nyelle woke her up from her reverie.

"Right. So . . . what am I looking at, honey?"

"This!" Nyelle stuck her finger on a group of tightly clustered symbols.

"And?"

"Remember I told you I could see the sound moving?"

Enrielle did remember. Nyelle was a bit more curious than Enrielle could typically handle. But she had started talking about the shape of sound a few years back, insisting that it was real. Enrielle assumed it was an idea that Nyelle picked up from the humans, whose heads always seemed to be filled with crazy ideas, presumably because they died so quickly that their brains were constantly overworked.

"Yes, I remember, honey. But I don't understand what the symbols have to do with it."

Nyelle started rifling through the pages. "See, Mom? This book was written by Zacharias—the bard who wrote the songs they like to sing at the bar by the water."

"The Steadfast Inn, yes." Enrielle took a moment to respond. "I thought they were folk songs."

"Sure, but somebody had to write them first, right? He did," Nyelle said.

Enrielle watched her daughter patiently.

"So in this book, he says that he could see his songs, not just sing them. Like, he could control the sound waves themselves." Nyelle was speaking very rapidly.

"Hold on, dear. I don't understand. Isn't that what singers do? They control their voices to make the songs, don't they?"

"No, Mom, you don't get it. Zacharias could control the sound *after* he sang it!"

"What do you mean? Once sound is made, it lives on its own until it dies, doesn't it?"

"That's what everybody thinks, but . . ." Nyelle opened the page she had shown her mother earlier.

"See? Right here he discusses how he could sing one song, but have each listener hear it differently. The symbols represent the different kinds of sound waves, and he goes on a whole bunch about how each kind could be tuned after it comes alive, like an independent instrument." Nyelle's large hazel eyes were lit brightly, and her face was so full of emotion that she looked almost human. "See? It's what I've been telling you. I think this is what I've been seeing!"

• • • • •

Nyelle read the book multiple times. The explanations were both clear and befuddling, with some instructions written in a way that required a formal musical education. Yorros, who was a sort of principal for the entire Shallows—she heard others refer to him as "superintendent" but never bothered to figure out what the title meant—helped her find a tutor. But her tutor lived on an upper shelf and only came down once every few weeks. Their lessons were also limited because they had to leave enough time to sleep with each other, which was the form of payment he required in exchange for teaching her music.

Still, in only thirty years, she had become an excellent lute player, pretty good with the flute, the harmonica, and the guitar, and could play any folk song on the accordion. Along the way, the book's pages revealed their mysteries to her, and without letting her tutor know, she learned how to shape the sounds.

One night, she made him cry by playing a popular song, and he said it was the most beautiful rendition he had ever heard. She didn't admit how she could see the sound waves, bend them to her will, and have them be suited perfectly for him.

It was her greatest achievement, and she was determined to improve upon it as fast as she could. She had to. Her sickness, her rapid aging, made it urgent.

• • • • •

The book spoke of even greater tomes of knowledge, written by masters that Zacharias had learned from, but she could find no clues as to their location. Zacharias made reference to the great library in the sky, but no one had ever heard of one, and everyone she asked assumed that it was some high tower of learning in a distant land.

Perhaps even a school of wizardry.

But Nyelle knew that Zacharias meant it more literally because he wrote it in a way only a sound-shaper could understand. She swore she'd find it, even as it became clear to her that she was growing old too fast, that she wouldn't even live to see three hundred.

She was ninety-one when the fires came.

· · · · ·

Losing her mother was the worst part. She remembered running out of the house, Yorros slamming the door at their backs, after a horrible shouting match with Enrielle. She remembered the terrible summer storm, with lightning and thunder dancing across the sky. As they left, her mother told her that things should "cool down in a bit," which was ironic seeing as not an hour later, the tremors started, and then the flames came from below.

The volcano didn't quite erupt fully, but the fire blizzard was so fierce that nobody who survived that night would ever see the likes of it again. Everything burned and collapsed, and the Shallows were overrun with screaming people and terrible monsters who were jolted out from their deep caves.

They got separated, and Nyelle found shelter in a narrow tunnel. After the chaos died down many hours later, her mom was nowhere to be found. She was so disoriented, and the Shallows so transfigured by flame, that she couldn't find her way back home. After days of searching, Nyelle concluded her parents died, and she made her way, half-starved, exhausted, with nothing except her lute, to the docks.

Somehow, the Steadfast Inn survived.

· · · · ·

That started her career as a bard, and her real education began. The first time she tried her sound-shaping, she was clumsy, and her listeners caught on. She watched as two of them became irate and started whispering, but she didn't appreciate the danger until later. They were waiting outside. "Witch!" they snarled as they jumped her. The beating she took was bad enough, but they also took her night's meager earnings, meaning she went hungry.

Again.

To earn a living, she found herself spending time in the company of visitors who stayed at the Steadfast Inn. She kept practicing, and her performances improved. Every so often, she would pick out a listener, focus on them, and work the sounds in exactly the right way. If she guessed right, then they would reward her with a big tip.

Once, Nyelle decided on a whim to try it with two people at once, and when they both gave her a silver—exchanging an awkward glance as they reached out to the hat—it was exhilarating. Soon enough, she could do it with three and four, although she then realized that she was stuck. Thoughts of the library in the sky began to haunt her.

As Nyelle's skill grew, so did her choice of bed partners. One human kid, in particular, took a serious liking to her. Darryn, a policeman in the Kyber guard, kept coming to see her perform whenever he could, which was usually on his threeday. Silly as it was, she came to like him too. He was sweet and gentle, and he always paid her well. Sometimes it seemed like he did so as much for her lullabies (which she never shaped for him) as for their lovemaking. Being human, he was always in a great rush, and only a few years after they came to know each other, Darryn told her that he would find a way for her to leave the Shallows.

It had been eighteen years since the fires.

Yesterday, he sent her a note.

• • • • •

It was a small, folded piece of paper, delivered by some street urchin. "You Nielly?" she asked, mispronouncing Nyelle's name in that way that humans often did.

"Yeah?" Nyelle responded.

"Got summin' for ya," she said, then pulled out a little square paper and handed it to Nyelle. "He also said to tell you he hoped you'd come."

"Who said it?" Nyelle asked, but the brat was already running down the street.

"Okay, thank you then," Nyelle muttered and opened the note.

"Keeping my promise," it simply said. Below that, Darryn—it had to be Darryn—added that she should show up to the Steadfast Inn and when. He wrote it in the unsure, functional script of an uneducated human soldier. But because it was from him, she decided to go.

She just wasn't sure what to expect.

9

GROUP FORMATION

"All right, folks. First, thank you for entertaining me by coming here." Bradd looked at Lormek then added, "Some of you, perhaps, more intentionally than others." He shifted his gaze to Nyelle, whose face remained expressionless.

Lormek, meanwhile, stole a glance at Sollis. *Why do I find her so interesting?*

She ignored him.

Bradd raised his glass to his lips. "Let's get down to business, shall we?" He coughed slightly and continued. "So you may have guessed already that I work with the Thieves' Guild," he said, pausing to observe their reactions. The scarred man raised his head to stare at Bradd.

Garrett snickered.

"Garrett, here, is one of my agents," Bradd said, after flashing the gnome a look of mild disapproval. "But he's actually not the only one who has been in my employ . . . just the only one who realizes it." He stopped again, and scanning the faces around the table, satisfied himself that he had everyone's undivided attention.

"Take, for example, Sollis," he said, pointing toward her. "She thinks I only hired her yesterday, but in reality, we have been buying most everything she has been stealing for the last year . . . No, I know I lied to you yesterday, but it was a small lie and only so you would be less nervous coming here," he added hastily as Sollis's face registered surprise and then irritation. "And please rest your fist there, my dear, no harm will come to you. That part wasn't a lie, and you know we could have bound you when you arrived if we wanted."

Sollis stared at him for several long seconds, then slowly relaxed her fingers.

The others exchanged glances. *What was going on here?*

"The rest of you don't know this, but other than being a petty thief, this remarkable young woman represents an extremely rare phenomenon, something that I only heard about but never encountered before in my life. So rare, in fact, that the scribes in Corrantha City say the chances of it happening are one in a million. It certainly hasn't ever happened in Kyber, as far as anyone can tell, at least not since the days of Kenzer."

With everyone's eyes on him, Bradd took another sip, set down his glass, and eased his chair back. Then he crossed his legs, clasped his hands, and focused on Sollis as he addressed the gathering.

"You see . . . Sollis is a wildmage."

Nyelle gasped. Lormek raised his hand instinctively to the symbol of Thor on his chest. Sollis lowered her head slightly, staring at Bradd with a mixture of concern and fear, and her fist balled up again.

"Wait, you mean like she does magic?" Garrett's slightly high-pitched voice was excited. "Like, real magic? Magic magic?"

"Yes, Garrett. Magic magic. And Sollis, look, you've done an excellent job at figuring out this stuff for yourself, but we do know most of what's going on around this town, and . . ."

As he spoke, Sollis's face turned red, and her eyes hardened. She threw her fist contemptuously in Bradd's direction.

They all felt the shockwave, an immense energy released all at once. They could see the vague outlines of it rapidly spreading out from Sollis. They sensed a raw wave of power that should have blasted the room to smithereens.

Yet it didn't.

Instead, the table glowed a faint yellowish-blue color that matched the shockwave. Blasting out of Sollis's fingers, the expanding energy orb collapsed into a flat cone, which hung in the air looking like it had hit an invisible barrier. Then it fell onto the table and dissipated.

The scarred man cried in pain as his hands jerked away. He carefully spread his palms only to find them unharmed, and his anguished look was replaced with one of curiosity. Though Bradd was otherwise unruffled, he nevertheless flinched as the wave was unleashed at him.

"This, people, is a demonstration. Sorry about your hands, Aidan, but I promise you, it would have been much worse if we hadn't arranged to have a—very expensive, by the way—ward in place for exactly this sort of thing. As for you, Sollis . . . as you can see, your magic can be resisted, but if you choose to work with us, we can help you get much better with it."

Sollis, however, was not paying him any attention. Instead, she inhaled slowly, almost in a trance, with her nostrils quivering and her eyes half closed.

• • • • •

"So now that this little bit of excitement is over—don't worry everyone, she won't be able to do it again for a good while, the energy expenditure is significant—we can get back to our reason for being here today." Bradd paused to glance around the table.

"You see, the Guild has always had agents everywhere in Kyber, but the truth is, we may have developed a bit of a blind spot right here in the Shallows. Most of you have grown up here, so you probably know why; there isn't anything particularly interesting going on in the Shallows, except for the docks."

A snort came from the other end of the table. Bradd stared at Garrett as the latter went through several seconds of obvious discomfort trying to get the grin on his face under control. Nyelle, watching this pantomime dispassionately, turned her head back toward Bradd.

"So . . . in the spirit of *transparency*"—she spoke the word with a sneer—"what's he laughing at?"

Bradd sighed.

"I suppose it won't hurt to tell you this, but there is one more area of interest in the Shallows. You wanna tell them, Garrett? Before your face implodes?"

Garrett broke into a grin again. "The prison!"

"Right. The prison. I suspect that none of you knew this?" Bradd let the question hang in the air for a moment.

Lormek tentatively spoke up. "My dad said something like that existed, but that it was well-hidden deep in the Inner Shallows, and I shouldn't worry about it because the town didn't care about wretches like us, and the prison wasn't for us."

"Right he was," Bradd said. "Rajiv, isn't it? That's your dad's name? At the Church of Tranquility?"

Lormek inclined his head slightly.

"Anyway, there's the docks, and the prison, and the Guild has an interest in both. But the rest of the Shallows . . . well, looks like we haven't been paying enough attention. Which is how we missed the miracle that is Sollis—and, for that matter, you." In saying that, he turned to Nyelle.

"Huh?"

"Nyelle, you can do some pretty unusual things with sound, can't you?"

Nyelle's eyes opened wide.

"No, don't worry. Not here to harm you—any of you—but you do have special, extraordinarily rare skills, and you developed them right here in the Shallows, which tells us that something is going on that we need to understand. See, folks, Nyelle can apparently," Bradd paused for a second, "how did he describe it? Shape the sound of her voice. How about a little demonstration?"

Nyelle turned back at him, having regained her composure. "Don't know what you're talking about."

"Oh, I am quite certain that you do, darling." Bradd grinned. "Darryn—that is his name, right? He was quite explicit."

Nyelle stared daggers at him.

"He said . . ." Bradd opened a folded piece of paper he produced from his tunic. "He said, and I quote, that 'she can sing one song to two people at once and each will hear it different.' Sound like you, darling?"

Nyelle's face was frozen.

"Point is . . . the ability to shape sound—to physically manipulate it—is pretty rare too." Bradd opened his arms as he addressed the gathering. "In fact, scholars will tell you that without knowledge gained from writings by the great bard Zacharias, they wouldn't even know this ability existed. Did you know that he was a member of Kenzer's group?"

Nyelle's suspicion was replaced with intense interest. She leaned forward. "Wait, what? You know of him? You have more of his books?"

"Not just books, dear. We have access to scrolls, parchments, notes, and more. Thing is . . . while nobody knows exactly how rare it is, this trait is certainly not a common one. We're not aware of anyone else who has it in Kyber. It's possible that they do, I suppose, since it's not the kind of thing anyone would notice easily. Definitely not like Sollis and her bag of tricks. Our records, which admittedly are only truly comprehensive when it comes to the higher shelves, do not speak of anyone else born in the city with this ability."

Bradd took another sip from his wine glass.

"So now we have two confirmed occurrences of extremely rare talents—both of whom have come from the Shallows at around the same time. We have a saying at the Guild—once is a coincidence, but twice is a pattern. And then we have Aidan."

Aidan's scar shone briefly as he looked at Bradd in surprise. "Me?"

"Yes, you. Show them your bow."

"My bow?"

"Yes, your bow. Come on, show them."

Aidan rose slowly, then reached behind the drapes hanging by the entrance and brought out a longbow. He placed the bow on the table. Everyone examined it. A flicker of interest passed over the face of the forgotten assassin still standing silently at the back wall.

Garrett stood on his chair and leaned over. He whistled in appreciation.

"This bow is unlike any other. It's extremely well-made, isn't it? Even if you don't know anything about bows, look closely, and you will be able to see that the wood grain matches its curves perfectly all over, which you don't usually see in wooden objects." Bradd let them lean closer and examine it. "In fact, there is only one other place in this room where this is true right now."

They raised their heads.

"Take your hands off the table, will you, Aidan? Thank you. Now look, the rest of you . . . look right there!"

They looked. Indeed, where Aidan's hands had been caressing the table, the wood had shifted its grain, as if it were rearranged by some mysterious force. The effect was subtle, and none of them would have noticed on their own, but once you knew where to look, it was plain as day. The wood seemed almost . . . happier, its imperfections all smoothed out. As if it was the one spot where it was no longer in pain from becoming a table.

"He wasn't doing it consciously," Bradd spoke up, "but Aidan has a special relationship with wood. So special that he can heal it with his touch. Word of his unusual talent had reached out all the way to the mainland"—Aidan was plainly surprised at this—"where one of our agents heard about it. So they tracked down one of his bows, bought it, and had it inspected and appraised. The King's master archer said the only thing he had ever seen like it was hanging in the

King's Museum—a bow that was used by Kenzer himself!" Bradd took a breath. "Imagine my surprise to learn that a third Shallows denizen had an unusual mystical skill like that. Forget two being a pattern . . . with three, now it's a story." He sat back, his arms crossed over his chest. "And we have a particular interest in stories," he concluded.

A few seconds passed in silence.

"Anyway . . . seeing as I'm in charge of guild operations down here, I thought, let's put this little group of special people together and see what we can figure out about all of you."

"What about the dwarf and the gnome?" Nyelle asked.

"Right. Well, to be fair, Garrett wasn't supposed to be here at all, but he has been part of our recent push to get some fresh eyes and ears on the ground down here, so it's probably not a bad idea for him to be a part of this. As for Lormek . . . personally, I don't know what's special about him—no offense intended, Lormek—but it seems like someone who matters thinks he's important, and I was told to include him. Maybe he has some special skill that I'm unaware of."

After a moment to let them digest this, Bradd added, "What do you say, folks? Sound interesting? Wanna hear my offer?"

Garrett chuckled and happily raised his thumb. Aidan and Nyelle glanced at each other, and then both nodded. A moment later, Lormek followed suit.

Sollis, who had been studiously ignoring Lormek, smiled at him briefly. Then she turned to Bradd and said, "Okay, whatever man. I don't care, long as I can keep practicing. So what do you want us to do?"

WEREWOLF

Her scent was new.

Not from here, he thought. *Definitely not.*
Wait a second . . . what is this?
Ohh.

New as the scent was, it was also familiar. There wasn't that much difference in how twolegs smelled, except the ones that presented a challenge even in his wolf form. The orcs.

Their blood was spicier. He didn't fancy it and tended to leave them alone. Many of his wolfkin lusted after orc blood, which suited their palates better. This was fine with him because his brothers often let him chase alone the gentler fare that he preferred. It's why he ventured so far up north; fewer orcs that way.

Small ones were sweeter. More to his liking. Plus, they were also a heck of a lot less dangerous on the days when he transitioned from being a wolf and into one of *them*.

He hated those days.

All the werewolves did.

• • • • •

When he picked up the scent, it was on the day after re-wolfing; he was hungry because he had hidden in a cave while he was in twoleg form, and he had eaten unsatisfying things like berries. He had consumed enough to not starve but otherwise avoided everything and tried to sleep it off.

He was surprised once by a pack of twolegs, who came into his cave seeking shelter from the rain. Twolegs did that because they didn't have a thick coat to keep them dry. Or rather they did have them, but the coats soaked up water so badly that they came off their backs. He never understood how they got the coats in the first place, because he never managed to grow one during the moon days, but it didn't really matter, because twoleg coats were useless.

His weakened senses in twoleg form didn't warn him, and he was startled awake to find them surrounding him with pointy sticks. They were making big sounds, but he had no idea what they meant, so he bared his twoleg teeth at them and growled.

It sounded like an argument.

Arguing about him, probably. About what to do with him.

It was the one time in his life that he felt truly scared. He was vulnerable like they were when he was in his were-state.

Eventually, they tied him up and departed, and he guessed they would come back later after figuring out what to do with him. Except his threeday was almost up. A little later, he re-wolfed—in the process, breaking the bonds that held him—and left.

He was hungry, and the easiest thing would have been to hunt them down, but he remembered the pointy sticks and the shine that burned, and he decided to chase down a rabbit. A couple of days later, he got bored and did follow them, but they stayed in a pack. Eventually, he gave up once they went to the path over the white waters.

There was one moment, though, that stuck in his mind.

They were huddled by a fire (unlike many of his brethren, he wasn't afraid of fire). One of the females was lying on the ground, breathing heavily, grunting, and yelping. He couldn't get close enough to see inside the circle—the twolegs had the shiny sticks out, alert to any movement at the edge of the clearing.

Then she screamed out loud, and a new scent hit his nose. She had just given birth. That smell was so fresh, so sweet, and so incredibly, deliciously pure that he was almost compelled to charge toward it, which would have likely gotten him killed.

He had never smelled twoleg cub before.

• • • • •

He sought it for many years after, but while he learned to identify when twoleg bitches were gravid, he never came across a similar opportunity. They always traveled in packs, well-armed and protected, and not once had he witnessed a birth again. The memory of that scent was driving him crazy.

Then he smelled her, and he knew that finally, his time had come.

She was gravid.

She was alone.

All he had to do was bide his time until she gave birth, which was going to be soon. And he had weeks before his next transition. He just had to be patient, track her, and wait. He would strike at exactly the right moment. He might even let her live.

But he had to have the cub.

• • • • •

The sun came and went, and her movement through the fields and forests was fairly slow. He was amazed at how unconcerned she was with her own safety. He wasn't the only wolf around, and there were other dangers. But she carried herself with confidence, the smell of supreme calm.

As a wolf, she would have her own pack.

She was heavy with cub, and he wondered if she was lost. But her movements were purposeful. She was searching. Once, she was excited by something she picked off the ground, something that he couldn't see, yet even at a distance, it made him uncomfortable.

She kept searching.

It interested him, this twoleg who was so unafraid, and he found himself being protective; he even dispatched an orc who'd begun stalking her, intending to strike when she took a rest.

No way are you stealing her cub from me! He jumped on the orc, crunching its neck between his powerful jaws, before hurriedly letting the body go and spitting out the blood. He could never get used to that taste, but he knew his brothers would want it, so he dragged the body away and howled at them to come and grab it.

Later on, he understood why she was so confident.

He had been keeping a safe distance and couldn't stop them from coming at her without ruining his plan. There were two, an orc and a goblin. He watched with dismay and anger at his prey being stolen, his dreams of finally indulging in twoleg cub dashed by the random nature of the wilderness.

He needn't have worried. Heavy as she was, she swiftly drew a beautiful, shining blade and entered into a dance. Moving rapidly, she spun her sword in an intricate pattern that, after it was wet with her first strike, appeared to be drawing blood symbols in the air. He was entranced. He had never seen a twoleg move so eloquently. Every movement she made was perfectly timed with maximum precision to disable and destroy her opponents. It only took her a few seconds to kill them both.

She didn't even break a sweat.

What an exquisite creature, he thought, and then salivated.

Her cub will taste amazing.

When she crossed the path over the white waters, he waited until the darkness fell and the water rose. Then, avoiding all the twoleg guards, he summoned every ounce of courage and swam to the other side. Werewolves were strong and excellent swimmers, but the white waters were dangerous. By the time he made it through the fast stream and sharp rocks, he was so heavily bruised and battered that he was barely alive.

· · · · ·

When the day finally came, he was ready. The goblin, in its dying throes, slashed her calf, giving her a noticeable limp. The cut had an unpleasant smell, the one he knew would make his stomach upset if he ate the flesh around it. She was walking slower than ever. Then she let out a yelp and grabbed her belly. She took several deep breaths, and he could see that her legs had gotten all wet, but he couldn't smell pee.

Soon he recognized the smell for what it was.

She moved toward a clearing. He followed cautiously, his senses aroused by the thought that he might finally get his chance. He had no idea what to expect, except that, in the other time, it had taken several hours for the cub to be born.

She made it to the center of the clearing.

He sat to wait.

It took a good part of the day.

Around when the sun reached the middle of the sky, he let out the first howl. She couldn't move away anymore, and it was time. She heard him and raised her head toward him. Even though she couldn't see him, he could see her, and he noticed that her look of pain was now joined with concern. He could even smell a hint of fear.

His arousal deepened.

He kept howling.

Two of his cousins joined him. They demanded to know why they shouldn't simply go and tear such easy prey apart, but he instructed them to wait. They could have her for themselves. He wanted the cub.

It was a fair deal, so they waited for her to give birth.

As the sun dipped below the treetops, he could see a little head show up between her legs, and moments later, a twoleg cub slid out of her.

The smell of it was wilder than he ever dreamed.

• • • • •

She knew the wolves were there.

One of them had been following her for days, somehow making it across the heavily guarded Stormbridge. She suspected a werewolf, which would complicate things. While she had no idea why a werewolf would stalk her, she knew that they could think more deeply than other wolves. They could plan. She hoped to confront it before the baby came, but the wolf kept its distance.

Then her water broke, and nature had to take its course. She headed toward the clearing she had previously scouted. Perhaps the werewolf would continue to watch her.

Her biggest wish was that the delivery would be quick like it was the last time.

It wasn't to be.

When the howling started, she was no longer able to move. Her sword was at her side, but there was no way she could fend off any wolf while she was in labor, let alone a werewolf. She could see their silhouettes and hear their growls and murmurs as they conversed in Wolftongue. She wondered what held them back.

There was nothing she could do about it, so she focused on breathing and trying to accelerate the process of delivering the baby she had carried through the wilderness.

It finally happened.

The boy shot out of her, landing on the bed of leaves she had made between her legs. Exhausted from the effort, she picked up her sword and stood up shakily on her feet. She ground her teeth against the pain from the infected wound caused by the accursed goblin—and, she admitted bitterly for the hundredth time, her own carelessness. She barely had time to cut off the umbilical cord and place the good luck talisman she had found over her son's chest before the wolves appeared. She uttered a quick prayer, and the talisman flashed briefly.

Her son was cooing.

The wolves were grinning.

She held up her sword, turning it the right way to make it glint, showing the werewolf it was silvered. In her other hand, she held up a mechanical torch, lighting it with an expert flick of her fingers. It burst into flame, and she held it forward. But she had very little hope that it would work.

Turning away one wolf by suggesting there might be easier prey elsewhere was one thing; three were a whole other matter.

Especially when they included a werewolf. Having one present meant that they would act as a unit under the werewolf's command. And these wolves had been talking to each other for hours.

· · · · ·

They moved in sync, spreading to surround her in a half circle. The smell of the cub was so compelling that he found it hard to stay in control.

Then she stood up, shiny blade in one hand, a flaming torch in the other.

His cousins were getting a little anxious.

He bared his fangs and growled, reminding them it was only one twoleg.

After a moment, they continued their careful advance.

His mouth filled with saliva at the smell of the cub and the blood from the birthing.

She started dancing.

He had seen her dance before, but his kin had not. They didn't expect it, although he had warned them. She flowed like a whirlwind, and he could not help but admire the graceful precision of her gestures.

• • • • •

Glad for her experience from the wars, ignoring the bolts of pain shooting from her shin, she mustered her strength and executed a complex series of steps that, in a flash, took her near one of the smaller wolves. As it tried unsuccessfully to snap at her, fooled by the movement of her sword, she touched the torch to his side, then rapidly positioned herself back above her newborn son. She hoped it would serve as a warning.

The wolf yelped, then rolled on the ground to put out the fire before standing up and growling in anger. She guessed that they were reassessing the threat, inquiring with their leader. At least for the moment, she had checked their advance.

She quickly scanned her flanks, then locked her gaze on the one in the middle, the one that had been following her. The biggest of the three.

The werewolf.

It was more determined than the others. It was staring back at her, calculating and reflecting the intelligence that made it much more dangerous than any other wolf.

It was eyeing her baby.

• • • • •

The scent was so strong he could taste it.

His kin were nervous now. She had singed one of them badly, and they all knew that the shiny blade would hurt them—him most of all. He snarled at them to press the attack. They didn't budge. He took a step forward, causing her to swiftly point the torch at him. That was good because he wasn't as afraid of fire as his packmates.

Keep your torch on me, bitch.

He took another step forward and inhaled deeply, letting that gorgeous smell fill his nostrils. The other two hesitated, uncertain what to do next. But she didn't know that.

He barked at them, and they took a step forward.

His nose told him she was growing more fearful, and he could see her legs shake. She was tired. Her torch lowered and aimed right at his eyes.

Yes. I'm your target. I am. Not them. Me.

His cousins drew courage from him and took a couple more steps toward her. Soon enough, they would be within jumping distance.

· · · · ·

The wolves were closing in.

She was exhausted and could barely keep standing.

There was no way to defeat them, not even at her peak, let alone in her present state.

Time was running out. She had to make a decision, and she had to make it now. There was no way to save her son.

She would have to leave him behind.

· · · · ·

The inevitable victory and tasty meal were both at hand. He paused to relish the moment. Certain of overcoming their prey, they all moved in the same instant.

She moved at the exact same instant.

As they leapt, she jumped out and sideways. Her sword flashed, and one of his kin screamed and dropped to the ground. He had a massive gash across his side.

She was already running across the clearing, limping slightly on that nasty-smelling leg. His other kin was chasing her, but she was fast and agile, and he wouldn't catch her.

He didn't care about that, or about the stranger he could smell who was watching them, because the cub was lying there, helpless, making small noises. It was lit in an odd way, too, making its soft features more compelling.

His mind filled with desire, he took a step toward the cub. His mouth fell open, saliva dripping. For some reason, he found it difficult to get nearer—*was this how twoleg cubs survived?*—but he was no ordinary wolf. He pushed through.

The cub blew up at him.

• • • • •

Having made her decision, she moved swiftly, slicing with her sword and running toward the edge of the clearing. One wolf fell injured to the ground while the other ran after her. She flung her torch at it to slow it down.

As she escaped, the werewolf took a step toward the baby. It had hungry eyes, but it also seemed . . . desperate. As it came nearer, the small talisman placed on the baby's chest started radiating outward in a bright aura of white and silver.

The great beast yelped as if violently struck by the talisman's aura. It closed its eyes then reopened them slowly. Determination was mixed with hurt, suspicion, and anger. The other wolves reacted even more strongly and limped away from the clearing, whimpering, their tails between their legs.

But the werewolf was made of sterner stuff. It collected its courage and moved with obvious effort further into the aura. It needed only two steps to reach the baby, but each step took many seconds. Clearly in pain, it was shaking its head, grunting with exertion, and snapping at an invisible fire burning its thick coat. Still, it persisted, obsessed with getting to the baby.

Eventually, the werewolf made it.

It stood over the baby and opened its mouth to deliver the killing blow. Then it froze. Its muscles strained as it tried desperately to lower its head and grab the newborn. The massive jaw moved an inch lower, and the werewolf howled in frustration, unable to shake off the mysterious force that was keeping it from the tiny, helpless prey inches in front of its nose.

Then it lifted its enormous paw, the claws gleaming in the strange light emanating from the infant's chest, and reached with it ever so slowly toward the baby's face. The werewolf's body was shaking with the effort. The light of the aura got brighter still.

The tip of the werewolf's claw touched the baby's temple.

The aura emanating from the baby's chest became blinding and then the light . . . inaudibly, psychically . . . screamed.

· · · · ·

He saw the entire thing. There was no way he could help the woman, or the baby, or fend off the wolves. He had seen them hunt before.

It was not a sight he cared to see again.

When she left the baby, he sympathized with her impossible choice. But just as he was turning away to leave the unfolding horror, the light show began, and out of the blinding sphere of light in the middle of the clearing, the werewolf fled, howling and yelping.

Then the light faded, the wolves were gone, and the infant boy was still, somehow, right there in the center of the clearing. The boy started to whimper and would soon begin to cry.

He ran over. The boy's tiny face was bleeding profusely. His big blue eyes looked up questioningly and, he noted with some urgency, hungrily. The poor thing had only just been born; he would need to be fed very soon. He lifted the wriggling infant, missing a dull chain with a small trinket sliding off the boy's naked chest and falling into the low grass below.

Then he wrapped the little boy inside his coat and ran.

AIDAN (FOUR)

"Papa, when do we go hunting?"

Faergus looked at his son sitting cross-legged on the floor. "You know, Aidan, that's an excellent question. You're surely almost ready . . . ," Faergus's voice trailed off as concern crept across his aging face.

"But when will I actually be ready?" Aidan pleaded. His round brown eyes were wide open, and the big scar running down the left side of his face glinted in the candlelight.

"Oh, you gotta let the boy go at it fer real, Faergus," said his mother, who was listening in the shadows. Her soft voice startled them both. "He ain't a wee boy anymore, ya know."

Aidan climbed to his feet. At roughly six feet tall, he towered over his parents.

"See, Papa? Even Mama knows," he said, "it's not fair. All the other kids—"

"Don't talk to me about other kids!" Faergus cut him off. "You're not like them, Aidan. You're . . . special." He turned toward his wife and raised his palms. "Isla, help me, dear."

She did not respond.

Aidan was defiant. "I don't care! If they are old enough to die, then I am old enough to hunt!"

The room descended into an uncomfortable silence. Then Isla spoke again.

"Faergus, I think it's time. He be thirty soon. He can hunt." She took a long inhale, then added with a note of sadness, "And we could use the extra food. Winter is by."

Aidan, his face triumphant, turned back toward his father.

Faergus sighed.

"All right, Aidan. We'll go hunting tomorrow."

Aidan yelped with joy and kissed his father on the forehead, cupping Faergus's silver mane in his hands. Then he wrapped his arms around his mother, lifting her up from the floor.

"Put me down, now, silly boy." She giggled. "Go make yerself useful."

Aidan grabbed the empty bucket. As he ran outside, he started whistling, and his long black hair flew back, revealing his mangled ears.

• • • • •

Aidan loved to shoot.

With careful instruction from his father, he had spent several years making bows, learning how the wood should flex, how the carve could inspire greater tension and power, and how the bend could instill stability. Every time, after weeks of hard work, he would proudly show his creation to Faergus, who would examine it with an expert craftsman's critical eye.

He would always reject them. Initially, Aidan became frustrated, even angry, as his bows became firewood to cook dinner. But eventually, he started to appreciate the flaws that Faergus was seeing. He began to feel the wood, finding the invisible inflection points that would make or break a bow. He read grain patterns with his fingers, and let the wood tell him where the string should go, how taut it had to be, and where the grip would best balance the wishes of the arrow.

His creations improved.

Every bow was still rejected, although they no longer ended up as firewood. Faergus had taught him how to find people at the Shallows docks to buy his bows, netting them much-needed cash or household supplies. With his parents aging fast, it was critical for their survival, but Aidan understood that his father had given him a valuable trade.

Aidan's bows became known, and people from the Upper Shelves would seek them out. Once an adventurer—one of those mysterious figures who risked life and limb looking for fabled artifacts and buried treasure—paid him enough for a bow to replace the roof on their small house. The bow incorporated a clever trick where it could shoot two arrows at once. Aidan quoted the price as a joke, expecting the adventurer to laugh.

The adventurer didn't laugh and bought it on the spot.

Yet his father still didn't think that the bow was good enough. Nor the two dozen that followed. He kept rejecting them, and Aidan kept selling them, although no one ever paid nearly as much as the adventurer had.

Until this one.

It was his two-hundred-and-seventy-third attempt.

It had every feature, all executed to perfection: His mastery of wood that had allowed his bows to be so light and strong; his special grip, which could adjust to trade range for impact; his double-arrow trick, improved so it could be used to hit two targets, up to twenty degrees apart. And his most impressive feat, a slave string that would allow an arrow to curve slightly in flight. An expert marksman could use this feature to hit something—or someone—hidden behind a bush or around a corner. He had designed this feature for years and had finally implemented it.

It was the finest bow he had ever made.

• • • • •

When he presented the bow to his father, he fully expected another rejection. He had resigned himself to being a bowmaker, which wasn't a bad trade. He also felt that this bow was special enough that he could perhaps get another hefty fee for it.

Instead, as Faergus took the bow into his hands, his examination turned into contemplation. He lifted the bow and rested it on his index finger, letting it wobble slightly. His eyes traveled from one end to the other, as he moved his other hand all over, not quite touching the bow but sensing it nonetheless, becoming one with it.

Aidan knew that feeling well.

Then Faergus brought the bow slowly toward him, leaning over and smelling it before letting it drop gently into his lap. He gave out a small, satisfied sigh and crossed his hands over it. Then he looked up at his son, smiled, and nodded.

"It's good," he said, and Aidan's heart almost burst with joy.

• • • • •

People from the Shallows didn't usually venture out of Port Kyber. For one thing, the toll to take even the cheapest route to the surface was prohibitive. That route, a dangerous climb via a rickety rope and wooden staircase that snaked upwards along the edge of the Gash, cost twenty coppers. A trifle for most, but a fortune in the Shallows, where it could feed a family for a week.

Every year, several people died as they fell off the staircase. The city viewed having fewer Shallows residents as reasonable, even desirable; they rarely bothered to fix anything, even as some steps developed dangerous cracks. Crews would only make repairs when a step broke clean through, hurtling its unfortunate occupant hundreds of feet to their death below.

In Kyber's cynical fashion, they charged the toll as you began your ascent, and called it the "Stairway to Heaven."

Still, it was the cheapest option, and his father taught him how to navigate it safely. Eventually, as the income from selling his bows grew, they could afford the next cheapest route, a winding tunnel almost a mile long. You had to carry a torch, which gave you a lungful of smoke as you made your way to the ocean overlooks that served as breaks along the path. It also shut down at night as nocturnal critters flooded the tunnel, but it was still a much safer way out of the Shallows.

Hunting became his respite, and his bow made him extremely deadly.

Aidan's marksmanship was so great that Faergus served as guide instead. This also allowed his father to focus on his search, for something he refused to discuss, saying only that he would show it to Aidan when he found it.

They sold their bounty to the Steadfast Inn, which prided itself on fresh meals. He got to know the inn's owner, Bhaven, and discovered that the Steadfast had a particular interest in exotic meats. He never understood why anyone cared for goblin flesh, but one of these dangerous creatures would fetch an enormous sum. From that point onwards, instead of hiding, Aidan and Faergus sought out every opportunity to nail a goblin. Aidan's skill meant that when he finally killed one, the affair was entirely humdrum; he used the double arrow, and the goblin, more than two hundred feet away, was struck simultaneously in both the heart and the eye.

Not that there were goblins regularly traveling around the Kyber peninsula. Still, for Aidan and his father, coming upon one was cause for celebration. He no longer feared anything; he knew his bow would save them.

So when the werewolf killed Faergus, it came as a complete shock.

• • • • •

It was midday on one of their hunting trips, and they were roasting a pigeon when they heard a howl. Aidan reached for his bow.

Faergus tensed.

"What's wrong, Papa?" Aidan asked.

"That howl, son," Faergus said. "It's not a normal wolf."

"Huh?" Aidan was puzzled.

The wolf howled again; this time, much closer.

Faergus jumped to his feet. "It's a werewolf!" he said urgently. "Go, Aidan. Your bow will be no good here." He drew his sword, the half-silvered blade gleaming in the sunlight, and lowered himself into a battle stance. "Go, I tell you!"

Aidan was confused but did as his father ordered. He didn't know what a werewolf was, and they had never separated during a hunt. But he trusted his father, so he started walking toward the opposite edge of the clearing. Then he heard the sound of bushes splitting apart and turned around.

Walking slowly into the clearing was the largest, most menacing wolf he had ever seen. It must have been four feet tall at the nape, and its head was enormous. But it wasn't that, or the rippling muscles, or the gleaming yellow teeth dripping with saliva—it was the wolf's intelligent eyes, assessing and calculating in a way that no animal should.

It was almost . . . human.

Aidan brought his bow up and notched two arrows. Faergus, squaring off against the wolf, barked over his shoulder, "Run, boy, run! Your arrows can't hurt it!"

He let the arrows loose anyway, and they hit the wolf right where he intended; one in the right eye, the other right under the jawline and into the neck. It was a deadly strike, one that would have dropped an elephant. Instead, he watched as the arrows bounced off harmlessly.

The wolf grinned. Then it lunged toward his father.

"Run!" Faergus shouted. "*Now!*"

• • • • •

The sounds behind him spoke of a fierce contest, but by the time he'd climbed the nearest tree, it was all over. The wolf was hurt, blood marking its thick fur, and it was panting. But it had his father on the ground, immobilized under its massive front paw.

Over the next thirty seconds, Aidan shot his entire quiver in frustration and fear. Every single arrow hit its intended target. Every one of them did the same thing as the first two, bouncing off the creature harmlessly. The wolf glanced in his direction and made a terrible cackling sound.

Is it laughing at me? Even through his mounting despair, Aidan was incredulous.

Then Faergus stirred and shouted.

"Find the talisman!"

The werewolf bit down and tore his father limb from limb.

• • • • •

His mother's grief was harder to bear than his own. She passed a fortnight later. Before she died, she revealed that Faergus wasn't really his father. "We tried our best," she whispered as she lovingly touched his scarred ears, too weak to speak aloud. They had cut his ears to hide his elven blood, to "save him from being picked on."

Angry as this made him, he couldn't quite muster the strength to ask if she had him with someone else, or who it might be.

As for the talisman, she said that Faergus was obsessed with something out there in the wild that he needed to find, and it was connected to Aidan. By that time, she was no longer lucid and didn't speak another word before leaving him an orphan.

It was the eve of what he now knew should have been his Thriceteen.

• • • • •

Aidan continued to make and sell bows, hunt, and sell meat. He also used his notoriety as master artisan to join the new library, set up after the fires, between the inn and the bordello.

He read everything he could find about talismans.

What the talisman looked like, he didn't know, nor why it mattered. But he continued to search and read, and he learned about the power of these rare and mystical items. He realized that if they were connected, then the talisman would make itself known when the time came.

Just like his father had said.

• • • • •

He stood in front of the Steadfast with a new purpose.

Yesterday, when he emerged from the tunnel with a cart full of game, some scamp approached him and delivered a note. It read simply:

"Dear Bow Maker, We wish to extend a business offer which should be of significant benefit to both parties. Please join us midday tomorrow at the Steadfast Inn for a conversation."

Why not?

ASSIGNMENT

"Why, to steal for me, of course." Bradd grinned.

"*Steal* for you?" Lormek was taken aback. "First off, I don't steal. And anyway, why do you need us to do that? Don't you have plenty of, you know, thieves around?" Garrett chuckled.

"Indeed we do, Lormek. Indeed we do," Bradd responded. "But let me explain what we need stolen first. And to do that, I need to ask you about Tradebay."

"Tradebay?" Nyelle asked.

"Yes, Nyelle. Have any of you ever wondered why the ships fly?" Everybody spoke at once.

"See? Told you you'd be interested," Bradd said and laughed. "Well, if you've ever seen how they get the ships up the tube"—at this, Garrett nodded vigorously—"you'd know that the dock officers have a special box they place on the ship that nobody is ever allowed to get near. But there is no question that whatever is in the box gives the ships their ability to fly, at least temporarily.

"Well, without getting into the hows and whys of it, which you're not really authorized to know, it seems like one of the dock officers has decided to smuggle one of those boxes out. The Boxes Guild asked us to intervene discreetly to make sure he or she doesn't succeed."

"But why us?" Nyelle asked, pushing her hair aside so she could see Bradd fully.

"Two reasons. One is that we think that somebody in our own ranks is also involved—in fact, we're certain of it—though we don't know who they are. This means they'd likely hear of any plan to foil them unless we use a task force made of new recruits."

"Garrett isn't new," Sollis objected.

"You're right, he isn't. But if he leaks it out, he's the only one who could have done it, so I'd know. And I think Garrett appreciates that." Bradd looked meaningfully at Garrett, who nodded. "Plus, I don't think he's our mole. He's far too . . . earnest . . . for that sort of thing."

"And the second reason?"

"It's the one I mentioned before. I want to learn more about all of you. Your special abilities should make this job a cinch."

Aidan spoke up. "But why not just go and get the box from wherever it is?" His hand absent-mindedly touched the top, mangled part of his ear.

"We could do that, sure, but then we'd lose the element of surprise and with it our chance of catching the mole," Bradd said.

"Just beat 'em up real good, I'm sure they'll tell you," Nyelle suggested.

"Perhaps. But I suspect that our insider has not been dealing with them directly. Our people can be quite good at hiding, you see."

Aidan nodded.

"Then we have another complication. Whoever is setting this up is being way too obvious about it."

Bradd paused and waited.

"No questions? Really? Nobody?"

He stopped again, but nobody spoke up.

"I'll tell you anyway, smarty-pants. We know that whoever is behind this knows that it is completely forbidden for knowledge of the boxes to leave Kyber—let alone one of the actual boxes or, more importantly, its contents. It is, in fact, one of the few capital offenses in the city."

"Oh, now I see why we need a secret prison," Nyelle murmured, yet everyone heard her clearly. Bradd winked at her.

"Right you are, dear. Anyway, you'd think they would be covert, try to sneak it out without anyone noticing. Instead, it's almost as if we are being led to it. There's a small caravan leaving tomorrow morning toward the capital—a shipment of cargo from one of the large merchant vessels that just docked in the bay. Several carts, drivers, about half a dozen guards, and one merchant. And guess what? We got not one, not two, but three anonymous tips that our missing box is in one of those carts."

"So? What's wrong with that? Didn't you say you had people all over the place?" The golden strand of hair that Sollis had been chewing stuck to her cheek.

Bradd agreed. "Yes, exactly. You can't be smart enough to steal one of these, arrange for it to be smuggled out without raising suspicion, and then have several leaks in your chain. It just doesn't really make any sense.

"So here is what we think is really happening. The whole thing is a decoy. Any boxes in that caravan are not the real thing. The problem is that we have no other leads. I need you all to go after the caravan and see if you can get any clues that would lead us to the real box. And hopefully, the person trying to smuggle it out."

"And how are we to do that, exactly?" Lormek asked. The muscles in his powerful upper arms rippled in indignation.

"I have no idea, to be honest. Maybe a driver will know something, and you can get them to talk. Maybe the decoy box will reveal a clue. It's a low-risk, low-reward play—I don't really expect it to pan out. But as a way to get a sense of the lot of you and how you work together and how valuable you might be to us . . . well, as far as I'm concerned, that's a useful outcome whether you succeed or not.

"Just don't be too noisy about it. We will disavow any knowledge of your group if you make a mess of things. So you gotta be smart and stealthy. Assuming you don't get caught and can prove that the whole thing is a fraud, I'll pay each of you two gold when you return. And while I don't expect it . . . if you actually find a useful lead, then I will make it ten. Each."

Lormek gasped. Garrett giggled.

"Did you say *ten gold*? For each of us?" Lormek's voice was incredulous.

"Yes, indeed. Think your father can do some good with that kind of money?"

"He could build a whole new church with that!"

"So you're in?" Nyelle asked from across the table.

"Hell yeah. You?"

"Yes, why not? Two gold is pretty good for a couple days' work, man." Nyelle grinned.

The rest of the group indicated their assent.

"Well, then . . ." Bradd smiled. "As we like to say on giving an assignment . . . go git!"

13

GARRETT (FIVE)

When Garrett was eight, his parents took him to see Port Kyber from above.

The upper shelves were exclusive. The top one was reserved for guilds and trading houses and was the seat of city government. It stretched from one side of the Gash to the other, inside the volcano, all connected by a continuous railing of volcanic rock. Arranged from the south were government offices, and from the north business ones, and they met in the center opposite the Gash itself.

There was the magnificent council chamber, with its smooth marble floor, glinting with trimmings of silver and gold. It was dominated by a massive oval purpleheart table surrounded by seventeen exquisitely crafted seats for those who comprised the council. Twelve were reserved for the main trading houses. Four were occupied by city officials: the Lieutenant, who oversaw domestic peace, and the collection of fees and tolls; the Grunt, who ensured that the city's complex engineering apparatus ran smoothly, within Kyber and all the way to Stormbridge; the Pope, who made sure that no faith would become dominant and that no wizard could come to rule Kyber via magical means; and the head of trade (known half-jokingly as "the Snake"), who was also Port Kyber's chief diplomat.

In a particularly cynical nod toward the spirit of Kyber, the last seat was reserved for the head of the Thieves' Guild.

Oh, the city would never officially acknowledge the Thieves' Guild. But the Guild was considered an important backstop to all shenanigans. It was everywhere and knew everything. They watched and waited for when the powers of the city would get into an imbroglio that they couldn't solve for themselves without bothering the others.

Then they would get involved.

Having the Guild around to help settle issues quietly was the single most stabilizing factor in Kyber's remarkable ability to grow peacefully over the centuries.

That last seat's occupant was nominated by the other members of the council. In practice, for as long as anyone could remember, the head of the Thieves' Guild had always been elected unanimously. The nominal head of city government, they were known as "Prime."

The chamber had a wide mahogany lectern where important ceremonies would take place. There the parties would take in the magnificent view, unparalleled anywhere else in Corrantha. With the solid marble railing a few feet away, your heart would skip a beat, especially on less windy days when the outrageous folding transparent ceiling would be open to the air.

You would see the volcano's lip extending to your right and left, the offices built into its wall. And in front would be the mind-blowing phenomenon that made Port Kyber possible. From here, it appeared as if someone had employed a clever illusion to mask an entire quadrant of the mountain. But as you saw trawlers and merchant ships come and go, you would realize the truth: a large chunk of the volcano was missing.

That was the Gash.

Straining your eyes, you would notice the Stairway to Heaven winding its way lazily up the side of the Gash, shaking slightly in the wind. You might even see someone scaling it, and rarely, see them fall. Some considered it entertainment.

Directly over the Gash was a thin stone arch, with a small glass dome in the middle. You could glimpse people inside the dome; they would stand there for a few minutes before traveling from left to right. A few of these people would, upon entering the dome, drop down on their knees and vomit into a hole in the floor. Their vomit would disintegrate all the way to the waters below—except for the bits captured midair by the remarkable array of birds flying underneath, having figured this out as a regular and convenient source of nourishment.

The mahogany lectern sported a beautifully carved, tasteful wooden bucket on each of its sides allowing you to discharge your own meal if you became similarly dizzy with the view.

• • • • •

The chamber floor floated over the deep, wide hole that formed the volcano's core.

City records showed that in the decades following the battle of Stormbridge, much of the present arrangement came into being. "Port Kyber's shelf system was created by the hero, our founder, General Kenzer Kelstra," they stated and described Kenzer's legendary victory over the Corranthian army. Local lore told of Kenzer's loyal second-in-command (this part elicited oohs and aahs from the listeners), a high wizard named Zander (or Dalan, or Geldin, or any one of a dozen other names depending on the telling), who enchanted the marble floor of the chamber to allow it to rest gently on the beams without overwhelming them.

In a move that brought in a respectable amount of revenue into city coffers, somebody had the genius idea to build the viewing platform over the Gash. If you could afford the fee, you would be allowed to venture past a heavily guarded gate.

In the room beyond, you would be stripped of anything that could be shot or thrown over a distance. On the walls were posted notices making it clear that to carry a ranged weapon onto the viewing platform was a capital offense, and there could be no mitigating circumstances. Once through the back door and onto the arch, a magical field would detect any violations of this rule. Should that happen, the guards would toss you unceremoniously through a side hatch into the ocean below. Some jokester tried it once, counting on an expensive set of hidden, magically charmed glider wings to fly down safely, only to discover that archers stationed above the chamber were ready to follow through with deadly crossbow shots.

The jokester ended his life predictably: as fish food.

Nobody had attempted it since.

Garrett knew this before his first visit. He also knew why this rule was so strictly enforced; anyone standing on the viewing platform could break the dome's glass and take aim at the council chamber, as the edge of its floor was less than two hundred feet away.

As you started up the arch, you could feel the stairs under your feet rocking slightly, and some people became nauseated. *Stone should never rock that way*, your brain would imply. Garrett's parents told him it was the winds that were constantly buffeting the Gash, and that the arch had plenty of wards against falling. There was no turning back; the trip was strictly one-way. So you would press on and eventually reach the viewing platform.

• • • • •

Looking from inside the dome, the city spilled over the volcano's lip. You might see rising smoke, hinting at industries located on the mountainside. Stretching beyond was a land bridge that extended for miles away from the mountain, defining the Kyber peninsula. On both sides, the peninsula ended in sheer, vertical cliffs. On clear days, you could see a glint many miles away—Stormbridge, the crossing point to Corrantha.

The ocean extending forever to the north and south of the Gash was full of treacherous cliffs and rocks poking out of the water's surface, making it impossible to attempt a landing. This made Port Kyber essential to trade since it presented the shortest safe path from the east into the inner continent. Ships would dock to load and unload their wares, and the peninsula allowed them to be carried in and out of Corrantha in a couple of days, instead of the two weeks it would otherwise take to travel around the endless cliffs.

You could also see directly into the council chamber, which was awe-inspiring for many visitors. For Garrett, though, it was the city below that held the true attraction.

The seven levels were arranged into the volcano, each level having one or more shelves extending into the mountainside and over the water. The levels were roughly two hundred feet vertically apart. At the surface of the water was the Shallows, the lowest district in elevation and reputation. The Outer Shallows were built on floating wooden platforms, with dilapidated buildings sprinkled in a maze of alleys created over centuries of unplanned sprawl. You could see the tunnel openings carved into the mountain, leading to the cavern-laden Inner Shallows and the Deep Shallows beyond them. That was a truly dangerous, uncharted place.

The Shallows Docks stood out amid the chaos. It was a massive wooden platform where a dozen large ships could dock at a time, and where the famous Steadfast Inn and the infamous Classy Lassy were placed on opposite ends. Garrett knew that the owner of both establishments, the old dwarf Bhaven, was begrudgingly respected by the merchant families. Respected because his independent access to information was unparalleled, and he would trade it with them; begrudged because he kept to himself and refused to relocate to the upper shelves, which made him difficult to monitor.

The Shallows was the only district at level seven.

At the sixth level were the subshelves, a safer and more favorable place to live if you could afford it. Each catered to a particular kind of humanoid community and reflected their predilections. Dwarvenrock was very orderly and carved with meticulous care. Elfmantle, the smallest, was far more delicate and had a canopy overgrowing it from branches that somehow grew from that district's side of the mountain. Next to it was the largest, Humanridge, which lacked a theme but was easy to navigate. It was also the most heavily populated. And situated a bit away from the others, separated by the Elevator tube, was Garrett's favorite, Gnomeledge. That district seemed utterly chaotic unless you were a gnome like he was.

Your eyes would scan the rest. The fourth shelf, with craft and shopping districts; the third, dominated by Greenpark with its tree houses and fields with specialty crops, which would otherwise seem natural except for being in the middle of a volcano; the second, occupied by those of means and influence (like his own family); and the top shelf with its council chamber.

But your attention would inevitably be drawn to the fifth level.

It was called Tradebay, and it was the beating heart of Kyber.

• • • • •

Garrett remembered how different Tradebay had seemed from above. He was familiar with the district since his family had an office there. Growing up, he never wondered how the ships got there, seeing as the shelf was some four hundred feet above the waters below, or for that matter, what made the ships fly.

Tradebay stretched more than a thousand feet across the center of the volcano. It was supported by stone arches like the buttresses that held the council chamber, and it had two levels; the top was for people and wares, and the bottom was for offices and craftsmen who could fix the damaged hulls of docked ships.

Such vessels would travel to Tradebay via the Elevator. Located across from the Shallows docks, it was a massive volcanic rock tube jutting fifty feet into the water.

A ship headed for Tradebay would pay a hefty fee, five times as much as at the Shallows. Then three officers of the Boxes Guild would board. Two would carry a large box to the helm and strap it down. The third would kneel down and engage in an elaborate ritual with the box.

Only the Boxes Guild knew the secret of the boxes.

Once the ritual was complete, very slowly at first, the ship would begin to rise out of the water and up the tube. This surreal experience would frighten many who encountered it for the first time. Every so often, a sailor would jump overboard and swim across to the narrow strip of beach to rest and collect their courage.

At the top, the ship would slow down and come to a rest, floating at the mouth of Tradebay. There, awaiting Tradebay officers would connect the ship to strong cables emanating from the top arches. The ship would start moving alongside the wide platform until it reached its assigned dock, where it would be pulled in and go about its business.

People living below Tradebay considered the floating ships above them as routine. Those living above that level couldn't be bothered to think about it at all. But a visitor seeing it for the first time might reasonably conclude that they had lost their mind.

Seeing it from above gave Garrett a new and exciting perspective. He stuck his face to the glass, watching a ship emerge from the Elevator tube. He knew that Tradebay had the most powerful magical wards in the city, stabilizing the air around the platform such that none of the ships would be bothered, allowing it to operate in even the fiercest of storms. He knew of the wide tunnel leading from Tradebay to the surface, allowing for rapid movement of cargo. This was an advantage over the Shallows docks, from where boxes had to be carried by hand via a series of steep stairways up to Tradebay, before being loaded onto carts and wagons. Seeing it from above gave him a powerful sense of how it was all connected.

And, as his father broke his reverie to tell him that their time was up, Garrett decided that he would find out the secret of the flying boxes.

• • • • •

By the time he was fifteen, Garrett was living at the Steadfast Inn.

When he joined the Thieves' Guild at twelve, he never expected that his family would learn of it. But they did, and after a fierce shouting match, his parents presented him with a simple choice: quit the Guild to join the family business or quit the family to preserve its honor.

His decision felt preordained. He had come to appreciate how boring the trading business was. The Guild, on the other hand, offered plenty of excitement. There he had learned how to melt into shadows; how to read body language to avoid trouble or gain an edge; how to steal enough to support himself without being discovered. He gained fresh insights about the extent of the Guild's reach, with its invisible tentacles spread around Kyber and beyond.

As he went through training, Garrett noticed that the primary focus was on obtaining information. He realized that the Thieves' Guild was so named not because they stole—though they did plenty of that—but rather because they took the initiative from everyone else.

It was impossible to operate in Port Kyber without the Guild knowing, which was how they maintained their enormous power in the city's governing hierarchy. That, and they rarely chose to act on that knowledge. The Guild's rules and self-imposed boundaries kept resentments manageable. When they did act, they intervened in a way that defused tension, which the parties involved would later remember and appreciate.

That dynamic prevailed for as long as anyone could remember, and it allowed the Guild to engage uninterrupted in a host of covert activities and keep rivals from rising. It was also a great place for Garrett to conduct his research into the flying boxes.

In the meantime, he ran errands for his handler. He was never told why he was asked to drop an envelope in some place or pick up a shiny rock somewhere else, and he knew better than to pry. The Guild did not gladly suffer anyone spying on it, especially from within its own ranks. So he obeyed his orders, and his income was enough for a room at the inn.

• • • • •

He had recently been tasked with a minor mystery: the Guild had noticed that some of its operations were failing in a way resembling a pattern. The location and timing of these mishaps apparently drew attention from someone; they suggested a skilled independent operator was the cause of the disruptions.

Garrett identified a Shallows fence called Willie Wade, who dealt with the stolen goods. He also discovered the location of Willie's warehouse. Garrett's handler was satisfied and told him to forget about the whole thing.

Of course, he didn't.

Instead, Garrett followed his handler to the warehouse where he confronted Willie and, later, the independent operator. She was an extremely tall and frail young girl with the odd name of Sollis. His handler captured her and proceeded to recruit her to the Guild.

His curiosity aroused, Garrett had decided to follow her for a while. The next day, here she was, at the Steadfast Inn, standing hesitantly in front of the saloon doors.

He snuck inside.

THE
Book OF
Revelations

INSERTION

"You know, if I could lay my hands on those boxes, I could easily tell you which one actually mattered." Aidan sounded contemplative.

Nyelle and Sollis exchanged a glance, then looked out from their hiding spot at the edge of Tradebay.

"If they are all fake, then none of them would be the right one," Nyelle said. "Still, do you mind running it by me again? What is it you can do, exactly? Like, the wood tells you things?"

"It's hard to explain, really. It's like the wood's telling me things. Not in so many words, but it can show me how it feels. Like . . . *it hurts right here*, or *this doesn't feel right*, that sort of thing."

"And what happens, exactly, when you touch it?"

"Well, I mean . . . again, I'm not sure if I fully understand it myself. It's like I can talk back to the wood. I can say things like *put yourself together this way* or *twist around that way*, and it does. Then, when everything feels right, the wood will tell me that too, and that's when I know it's happy again." Aidan seemed embarrassed.

"I wouldn't believe you if I hadn't seen it for myself," Nyelle said.

"I would," Sollis said softly. She inhaled. "It's a little like how I feel the energy that makes things go boom." She smiled slightly. "It's in the air all around us. Some places more than others, but it's there, all the time. And in my head, I speak to it too, in a sense. It's just that I understand so little . . . it feels like there's a lot more I could say if only I knew what to say and how to say it."

Aidan agreed. "Yeah, me too. You know, but with wood."

A few seconds passed in silence as they looked back toward the platform on the docks.

"Which cart did you say it was?" he asked Sollis.

"It's in one of those four." She pointed toward a small caravan that had just finished loading. Each wagon was pulled by two horses, and a small group of guards were standing and talking nearby. "Oh, and look, here's Lormek, right on time." Her face was concentrated. "Shush, both of you. Let me listen."

· · · · ·

Lormek walked toward the caravan guards, while Garrett made himself invisible as he approached from the other side. It wasn't hard to do with the typical midday activity on the platform. His small stature meant most people ignored him anyway, and he had a remarkable capacity to ensure that they continued to do so even while he moved right in front of their noses.

I am nothing but a meaningless drone. A speck of dust. Pay me no heed.

And they usually didn't, at least, if they had no reason to suspect any sort of foul play. Garrett, in turn, was very good at avoiding situations where foul play would be suspected.

As Lormek initiated a conversation with the guards, Garrett

slipped under the last wagon. After a moment to ensure that no one was looking, he silently vaulted into it. There he settled amongst the cargo and waited.

• • • • •

"Man, he's good," Sollis muttered under her breath, as they watched the group in front of the caravan erupt in laughter.

"What is he saying?" Aidan asked.

"Just sold 'em some cockamamie story about the church needing something urgent from the capital. Didn't quite catch the details, but looks like they bought it."

"And you can really hear what they're saying all the way from here?" Aidan sounded incredulous.

"Yeah. Sorta. When there's a lot of noise in between, like here, then I sometimes can't make everything out, but as long as they are speaking in normal tones . . . yeah."

"That's so cool!"

"I suppose that makes sense," Nyelle remarked.

Both of them turned toward her.

"See, if I can throw my voice around, then I suppose it stands to reason that someone else could sort of catch it. Right?"

The question hung in the air.

"You know . . . we should try playing around with it sometime."

"How so?" Sollis asked.

"Well, if I can throw it, and you can catch it, then maybe we can figure out a way to talk to each other somehow, like over a distance."

"Hmm. It's not very helpful. You don't need me to reach out to hear you . . . and I don't need you to toss your words at me; I can pick 'em up myself. But we can't flip."

"Yeah, you're right." Nyelle sighed. "It just feels like we're missing something."

They looked at each other.

"Hold on," Aidan said. "How far can you toss out your hearing, Sollis?"

"Hmm. You know, I'm not entirely sure . . ."

"Try it. You can hear the caravan group—that's like fifty feet away. Can you hear those guys?" Aidan pointed toward a small group standing about twice as far on the other side of the platform, arguing.

Sollis's gaze followed his finger, and she started chewing a strand of her hair.

"Barely. I can make out a few words, but it's only because they are arguing loudly about some manifest," she said after a few seconds. "Problem is, there is so much noise around, it makes it really hard."

Aidan's dark eyes glinted. "Gotcha. So in theory, you could hear them better in different circumstances. Okay. So how about . . ." His eyes were scanning farther away, into Tradebay itself—"There!"

He pointed. A couple hundred yards toward the middle of the massive floating dock, two people were huddled, deep in conversation.

"Yeah, I don't think so." Sollis laughed.

"Try."

"I'm telling you, I can't. It's really far away."

"You can't? As in, you can't make magical shockwaves with your fingers?"

Sollis stared at him for a moment, then sighed and turned back toward the two men. She closed her eyes and tried to project her hearing as far out as she could.

"It's too far!" She opened her eyes.

"You're not trying hard enough. Try again."

"Okay, sheesh. I'll try once more, but when it doesn't work, we're done, you hear?"

Aidan nodded.

She closed her eyes again. Her brow furrowed, and she could sense the myriad of conversations unfolding in front of them, a cacophony of sound that, she knew, could be made louder or quieter in parts. She tried pushing out her hearing harder than she had ever tried in her entire life. She never had a reason to listen in on some-one so far away.

It was giving her a headache. She was ready to give up when sud-denly, she could smell it. The unique, delicious smell that always accompanied her magic materialized unexpectedly. There was nothing better in the whole world, no feeling that even came close. *Interesting.* It had never showed up before when she was listening. Headache or not, she wasn't about to let it go.

And then her hearing leapt ahead! Like a cat madly trying to escape her grasp, her hearing flew this way and that, and then it became more than just sound. She could feel the vortices of wind around the wings of a seagull flying far above, was tantalized by vibrations of people talking on the Shallows docks two shelves below, and yes, momentar-ily, could listen in on the two men in the middle of Tradebay. They were talking about repairs to one of the ships.

Above all, she found the smell and the sense of danger it evoked utterly intoxicating.

The headache turned into a migraine. It started pulsating and then became too much to bear. She had to stop. Inhaling deeply, taking in the last of the wonderful scent, Sollis closed her eyes and rubbed her temples before slowly opening them again.

They were staring at her.

"What?" she asked hesitantly.

Aidan and Nyelle exchanged a glance, and then Aidan spoke softly. "Your eyes . . ."

• • • • •

Lormek took his place next to the merchant sitting in the Corranthian trade barouche. Across from them sat a King's trade representative. Behind them were stacked several boxes instead of the more typical vis-à-vis.

The merchant grinned at him.

"I understand that you're Rajiv the churchman's son?"

Lormek affirmed. "Yeah. Clearly, not his, you know, *actual* son," he added jokingly, gesturing at his obvious dwarven features.

"Right, of course." The merchant chuckled. "Nonetheless, I heard he took in a child to raise as his own. Just didn't expect I'd ever run into you."

"Is that important?"

"No, I suppose it isn't," the merchant said after a moment's thought. "Anyway, nice to meet you. I'm Alferd."

Lormek shook his hand firmly yet carefully, so as not to apply too much pressure on the soft flesh of the well-appointed merchant. He could break Alferd's bones quite easily if he wanted to do so.

"So you know my father?"

"Well, everyone knows about your father. They say he's the one who keeps the Shallows from getting too . . . ," Alferd let his voice trail off.

"Too what?" Lormek maintained his casual tone.

Alferd eyed him for a moment. "Too *shallow*, I suppose. Can't have those poor people all over the place without nobody to take care of them, right? Make the city look bad."

"Right. Yes . . . of course."

"Always figured that's how he kept that church going and the place clean. That's real holy work, it is. And then adopting a Mudder . . . uh, darkskin . . . stroke of genius if you ask me. How can anyone not love him for that? City must be paying him on the side . . . Thieves' Guild probably." Alferd winked, then reached into his jacket and pulled out a thin silver case. "Cigarette? It's Robban."

Summoning a politeness he didn't feel, Lormek shook his head. "No, thank you. I don't smoke."

"Suit yourself." Alferd turned and offered the case to the trade rep, who took out one of the long, delicate, expertly rolled slims and nodded his thanks. Alferd leaned over and lit it for him, then one for himself, before settling back into his seat and blowing out a cloud of smoke. "Really nice, these. I buy a bunch every time I get over to Robbana. This is my last batch, so I definitely need to get some more this time."

He smiled.

"Anyway, gonna be a few days before we get there, you know . . . if you change your mind, just ask. Always happy to share with an adopted son of the city!"

• • • • •

"What about my eyes?" Sollis demanded.

"They are . . . yellow . . . ," Aidan whispered.

"Yeah," Nyelle spoke up. "Remember when you did that shock-wave back at the inn? There was a strange aura?" Aidan's fingers jerked at the memory of the jolt he had taken from it.

"Yeah, like I said last night, it's part of the magic thing I can do."

Nyelle lifted her hand toward Sollis's face. "Well, your eyes have that color now . . . wait, no. It's gone. How strange." She eased back.

"Huh. My eyes get like that after I do one of my tricks. You probably didn't notice it at the inn. But it's never happened before while I was listening in on something . . . I thought I just had really good hearing."

"Interesting! So the hearing thing, it's magic, too?" Aidan asked.

"Apparently so. I didn't know for sure until now."

"So what did you hear?"

"Honestly, it wasn't like that . . . I tried really hard and nothing happened. I was about to give up, and then the whole thing sort of exploded, and I could hear all over the place—down in the Shallows, the birds at the Gash . . . even your guys over there. But it was all jumbled, just a whole bunch of noise all at once. Gave me a serious headache."

They grew silent.

Aidan pointed at the caravan. "Look, they are about to head out. Lormek is in that coach with the merchant and that other guy. I guess Garrett is in there too . . . either of you see him?"

"No, but that doesn't mean anything. After what he showed us yesterday, that's exactly what I'd expected. He said he'd be on the last cart," Nyelle said.

"Yeah. Sneaky bastard, ain't he? Still, I wish we could . . ." Aidan jerked his head back. "Wait! I know!"

They looked at him quizzically.

"Nyelle, can you speak so that if Garrett was in that cart, he could hear you?"

Nyelle cocked her head to the side. "Maybe. I never tried it . . . usually I have to see the person to know how to make the sound specific to them. But that's with strangers. I do know Garrett, so maybe even if I can't see him, as long as I know where he is?"

"Great!" Aidan turned to Sollis. "And can you listen in on the cart? Like the inside of it?"

"Yeah, it isn't that far away, and I definitely can focus on something if I know where it's happening—even if it's behind a wall."

Aidan was getting visibly excited.

"That's so cool! I figured it out. Nyelle, why don't you try to say something to Garrett? Like . . . tell him to confirm for us quietly that he's there. Then Sollis, you can listen in, and if it works out, then you should be able to pick up his answer. We can use him to channel both of your talents!"

The two women glanced at him, at each other, then back at him.

"I'll be damned. That might work . . . definitely worth a shot. You ready?" Nyelle eyed Sollis, who nodded slightly, then sat up and concentrated.

"Okay, here goes . . ." Nyelle took a deep breath, then spoke softly, "You bugger, it's Nyelle here. if you're in there, say so, just keep it under your breath—Sollis can hear you." Her voice faded quicker than it should have, as if an echo was deadened.

"I had to make it go out quick," she whispered apologetically.

A moment passed.

Sollis snorted. They looked at her in surprise.

"Yeah, he's in there all right." Her face relaxed. "Said he and two of his bugger friends are playing keepsies with some bread crumbs. I guess the roaches are keeping him company."

"Ha. Neat trick, that!" Aidan said in satisfaction. "Glad we tried it. All right, we better head out—they still have to clear the toll plaza, which will take them a little while with all this traffic. We can get a couple of miles head start on them."

They trotted up the gentle slope of the main walkway out of Tradebay.

Sometime later, the caravan headed out as well.

NIGHT SHIFT

"Everything okay in there, Garrett?"

Garrett started.

I swear, every time she does this, it makes me jump! Then he whispered, "Yeah, nothing much happening. They are settling in for the night. Once things quiet down, I'm going to slip out and find something to eat."

About thirty seconds passed as Sollis relayed the message to Nyelle and Aidan, resulting in a discussion of their next move.

Nyelle's response finally came. "You'll get used to this way of talking. I'm really glad Aidan figured it out. It's very useful, even if it's weird. Anyway, Lormek says he left some dinner for you by the front of your cart, under a cloth. Looks like you're having rabbit and cheese. He also says the box must be in one of the two middle wagons."

"The cargo ones, yes. So . . . did he figure out anything else?"

"Nothing conclusive, but he thinks the merchant is only partly involved. Like he was asked to help without knowing why and just took the money. The King's trade rep is clueless, but his presence makes things more complicated."

"Gotcha. I'll see if I can get into at least one of those wagons for a look-see without getting caught. Oh, and Sollis, tell the others I didn't want to search the one I'm in either while we were on the road, with the guard sitting right up front. I'm going to give it the once-over later too. It doesn't have any of the trade containers, so I can't imagine it has anything important. I got a good nap on the way instead, so I'll be ready for my night shift."

Garrett chuckled softly as he waited for Nyelle's voice to resonate in his ear.

"Sounds good, Garrett. Good luck—we hope you find something. Lormek will jump in if there's a need, otherwise just do your thing. The three of us are going to get a head start on the caravan again so we'll catch up with you tomorrow evening when you get to Stormbridge. Plan is to slip out with whatever we find before they cross over, and then head back to the city to report. Oh, and Sollis is going to sleep, so if you need something, tell her now."

"No worries, I'm good. Me and the roaches are gonna have a lovely evening together," Garrett said. After a couple of seconds, he added, "Buddy here thinks I'm the bomb because I let him have a crumb earlier. Wait till he gets the leftovers from dinner!" He smiled, imagining Aidan snickering and Nyelle rolling her eyes while Sollis delivered the message.

"Garrett, out."

• • • • •

Under the cover of darkness, or even in low light conditions, Garrett could practically disappear. He could sidle right up to someone standing in front of a fire, warm himself at the flames, and then leave, going completely unnoticed the entire time. He could cross in front of them, and they wouldn't realize it unless they were especially perceptive—and on high alert.

Even then, they would typically suspect a gust of wind—not that a living creature had just passed under their nose. Had he found that sort of thing appealing, Garrett could have become an assassin, although his diminutive stature meant cutting someone's throat would have required a step stool. In truth, even the idea made him queasy.

Garrett never gave it much thought. Somehow, his body blended into the shadows, becoming an extension of the darkness. It came naturally to him, but he knew from his Guild experience that his skill was unusual. He wasn't certain if anybody noticed quite how easy it was for him to hide or sneak around. His instructors, who often marveled at how he aced his tests and gave him ever more absurd challenges, must have suspected something, but nobody ever said anything to him about it.

As night fell and the sounds of camp were dying down, Garrett climbed quietly out of the wagon. As long as he was careful to avoid any traps, the guards would never have any clue that he was there.

The problem wasn't the guards.

· · · · ·

Both wagons were fully covered with a leather tarp wrapped and tied tightly over them. There weren't any flaps he could open easily; the containers were not expected to be examined until they reached Corrantha, and the caravan company wanted to ensure that their contents arrived intact. The wildlife had a way of getting into wagons and had an affinity for the exotic, like bananas, coffee beans, and Robban tobacco. The caravans that made the trip between the capital and Port Kyber were well aware of this danger and had ways to limit potential losses.

His real challenge was to figure out how to get on board.

There was no way to retie the bindings if he loosened them. Securing the carts required at least two people. The guards would immediately notice anything untoward when they did their morning inspections. Tampering would be obvious, the alarm would be raised, and Garrett would be discovered in his little hiding spot.

Still, he had one major advantage.

He was tiny.

So tiny, that maybe he didn't have to be a person.

• • • • •

He first checked the bottom of the wagon, but it was shielded on the inside by a solid sheet of wood. Garrett expected as much. Even if he could have squeezed through the tiny gaps between the bed boards, there was no way he could get inside without cutting through the wood. That would be noisy. And even if he could pull that off quietly, it would only get him to the sturdy bottom of the stacked boxes.

For the umpteenth time, he wished Aidan could be there with him, telling the wood to part ways and make room.

Seeing no other option, he found a corner in the back where the leather tarp was secured and got to work.

A few minutes passed in silence.

"Dammit!" Garrett jerked his hand back while swearing under his breath. Small and nimble as his fingers were, the knots were complicated and hitched tight. One of them had just served him a nice dose of "fuck you" in the form of a painful burn as his finger slipped.

He sucked on it until it stopped bleeding. The guards passed by on their rounds, coming within a few steps, yet completely overlooking him.

It took him another twenty minutes to get two of the knots undone. His injured finger already swelling, Garrett winced as he squeezed his tiny hand through the small gap, grabbed ahold of the leather, and took a deep breath. Then he pulled.

Slowly, the leather gave way. After a minute, the gap grew enough that a large cat could fit through it.

Or a monkey.

Which was exactly what Garrett was hoping to become.

• • • • •

The cart was full. Garrett could barely fit between the tarp and the boxes. However, his ability to hide in shadows didn't mean he could see in darkness. He had to admit that perhaps he hadn't really planned this through very well. As he sat quietly pondering, his eyes adjusted, and the contours of the boxes came into dim view.

Garrett blinked.

He blinked again.

There was a light source inside. A very faint one that wouldn't have shown in daylight, or even near a fire. But in the darkness within the wagon, it made for an unnatural aura. An aura with a strange, yellow-ish-blue color. A color he had only seen twice before; once around one of the boxes that made ships fly and again when Sollis made that shockwave back at the inn.

His heart beat faster.

He calmed his breathing and let his eyes adjust fully. Examining the dimly reflected light, he judged that its source must be near the center of the wagon.

• • • • •

Garrett woke up to the sound of rushing feet and shouts ringing through the camp.

"Come here!"

"Check this out!"

"Someone got into one of the wagons last night!"

He smiled to himself. Then, taking care to stay within the shadows under the cart where he'd slept, he eased his way out the back and toward the guards' impromptu conference. Sucking on his sore finger, he crouched back on his heels, watched, and listened.

"Look at this!" one exclaimed. He held up the corner flap where Garrett had undone a couple of those tricky knots.

Another, who seemed the most senior, bent to examine the knots. Garrett guessed he was the captain. "Were these tied properly? We know there are problems with the wildlife around here." The captain stood up and scanned the group surrounding him. "Who did these knots?"

After a moment, a member of the little troupe stepped cautiously forward. "I did, sir."

Garrett could see his fear, but the guard still managed to keep his gaze level with the captain. Garrett quietly admired him for that.

The captain examined the guard for a few seconds. "It's Veelye, isn't it?"

"Yes, sir. Named after my gramps."

"Well, *Grandpa Veelye*," the captain said the name contemptuously, "care to explain how come your knots are untied this morning?"

"I don't know, sir."

The captain stared at him. Veelye was clearly uncomfortable. "Sir, I was a sailor for fifteen years before I took the job with this company. I'm sure no animal could undo them. I know my knots . . . sir." His voice broke slightly.

Glaring, the captain gestured toward the corner of the cart. "Well, take a look at these . . . because something or someone opened them!"

Veelye bent to inspect the flap. Garrett held his breath.

"Well, sir, it looks like someone undid them last night . . . sir." He stood up.

"I know that, you dolt!" the captain barked. Veelye shrunk visibly.

The captain turned to the rest of the guards. "We need to search the camp immediately! If the intruder's still here, we'll find them. Start with the carts—and you, Veelye, help me undo these so I can see if anything's missing!"

Now that they had decided it wasn't an animal's doing, Garrett realized that his prospects for a peaceful getaway were rapidly deteriorating. With the guards actively seeking invaders, his ability lost much of its potency. They would be able to see him now that it was morning and they were searching. And at this moment, it looked like he had nowhere to go without leaving the relative protection of the wagon under which he was hiding.

These caravan company guards were diligent.

Garrett turned his head frantically, searching for an escape route. Nothing seemed particularly promising.

Right, he decided. *Gonna have to make a break for it*. He prepared himself to roll and run for the nearest decent cover, but he knew he couldn't make it that far without the guards getting several good shots at his back.

They were going to hit him. His stealthy leather tunic was little protection from their arrows.

Just as he was steeling himself for desperate action, and the guards prepared to begin their search, a familiar voice boomed in the background.

Garrett felt relief flood through him.

"What seems to be the trouble, my good officer?" Lormek was making his way toward the guards, a broad grin on his face. "Looks like you're having a spot of bother?"

"Yes. Someone broke into one of the carts last night," the captain responded.

"Did they now? Oh, that's certainly troubling," Lormek said, walking up to the captain. "Can I see it? We have a lot of pilfering going on in the Shallows every day . . . I constantly have to watch out for signs of break-ins. My dad doesn't really mind if people steal food, but the church still needs to keep its funds safe to pay for it, you know."

As he spoke, the guard's carefully checked hostility slowly transformed into slight befuddlement. Garrett had seen it before when they had made their way into Tradebay; he couldn't help but marvel at Lormek's ability to win strangers' trust by—for all Garrett could tell—constantly speaking at them. Plus, he had that damn smile.

The captain gestured again at the flap, and Lormek leaned close to inspect it. He was still talking, an endless stream of meaningless observations and chitchat, and Garrett found himself easing up. It was as if Lormek was really saying, *don't worry, everything will be all right.*

"Aha!" Lormek stood up, looking at the captain, who in turn instinctively stood to attention before checking himself.

"Did you see the blood on the knot?" Lormek asked.

The captain stared at him, blinked, then bent down and looked closely at the knot. He stood up again.

"Truth is I didn't, but so what? All it does is confirm somebody broke in." Then, faced with Lormek's patient, smiling face, the captain added more hesitantly, "Doesn't it?"

"Sure it does, my good man, sure it does! However . . . notice the size of the opening?" Lormek pointed at the corner.

"It's pretty small . . ."

"It is indeed!" Lormek leaned back and slid his hand through the open flap. His powerful arm shot through to just under his elbow but could reach no further. He pulled it back out. "Look, I know I'm not particularly slender, but at the same time, I'm a dwarf, right? I'm not very big."

The captain agreed.

"And yet there's no way I'm getting in through that hole. Anyone else care to try?" Lormek made a sweeping gesture at the guards.

Nobody moved.

"So obviously, it couldn't have been an intruder, per se." Lormek smiled.

A couple of seconds passed.

"Could have been a goblin," Veelye ventured.

Lormek turned to him. "You're right. It could have been . . . but that's why the blood matters. If it were a goblin, then the blood would have been green!" Lormek turned back to the captain. "Look, my dear captain. I think what you're dealing with here is one of those lava monkeys, you know, the extra clever ones that steal stuff all over in Tradebay. Maybe one of them followed us. They are the only animal capable of undoing these fabulous knots . . . and the opening is just the right size for one of them to get inside." Lormek's smile broadened.

The guards were nodding. The captain's shoulders sagged a little. For a second, Garrett thought, he seemed defeated, cheated out of his quarry.

"Here is what I suggest. Let Veelye open a few more of these knots so one of you can check the cargo and see that it's safe. I bet that they were only searching for food or loose trinkets, and if so, the evidence will be clear. And anyway, we really do have to head out again—right, Alferd?" Lormek added in the direction of the merchant, who had sidled up quietly.

Alferd agreed. "You can say that again! We can't afford to miss the crossing window . . . that will mean a whole day's delay," he said as he made a motion of counting coins with his fingers. "Still . . . you'll make sure none of the boxes are missing . . . right, captain? Because trust me, we can't afford for any of them to go missing."

The captain looked at them helplessly. "Okay. We'll need about thirty minutes." Turning to the guards, he continued, "Veelye and Benners, you work the knots. The rest of you, get us ready to move on my command!"

Garrett sighed in relief. As careful as he was last night, it had been extremely tight in there, and he had accidentally nudged a box open on his way out. As luck would have it, it was filled with exotic fruit.

The banana peel he left behind would give the guards all the confirmation they needed.

STORMBRIDGE

They arrived at Stormbridge about an hour before the crossing window closed. Everyone in Kyber referred to it as Passing Tide, because that was when the bridge would reveal itself in all its glory and allow for easy travel.

Lormek gasped when it came into view.

Stormbridge marked the border between Corrantha and the independent city of Port Kyber. It spanned a chasm of six hundred feet over jagged rocks and rushing white water. From this distance, the torrent made a constant growling sound, like that of an angry wolf. Even during Passing Tide, when the waters were at their lowest, they were extremely dangerous. Only a lucky few foolish (or desperate) enough to try and cross below the bridge would make it.

The lands on both sides funneled invitingly into that chasm. Indeed, wading into the riverbed at either end, the first forty feet or so were shallow and stable. You could step off your mount and remove your boots, letting your toes dig into the soft sand as the cool, clear water swirled lazily around your feet. Breathing deeply, you would smell the crisp and salty air and relax. It felt safe and quite pleasant. It could easily dull the senses.

That false sense of security was the chasm's gravest danger.

Anyone deciding to skip the bridge toll and instead cross along the bottom would, without warning, feel the ground give way. The transition was shockingly sudden. Horses and pack animals would stumble, lose their footing, and be quickly swept away by a stream that instantly turned torrential. Riders lucky enough to be thrown off would have to be strong swimmers to merely keep their heads above water. Not that it would save them; both mount and rider would be dashed against the jutting, sharp rocks or smashed painfully by invisible ones lurking underwater. More often than not, it would be both.

Exceptional swimmers could make it to the other bank. They would head to the northernmost point of the sunken shore, then out toward the underwater shelf, feeling carefully for the telltale signs of its imminent arrival. There they would take a firm, final step away from the ledge beneath them and be immediately claimed by the current. As their heads broke above water, gasping for air, their next task was to avoid being slammed or gutted. They would spend the next hour swimming as hard as they could against the powerful stream, aiming to remain in the less hazardous, narrow band underneath the bridge itself. Eventually, if they avoided dying on the rocks, they would reach the other side. There they hastily made it to higher ground before the swiftly rising tide could claim their exhausted bodies.

Other than the lunatics who did this for amusement, no one who had made it through once would ever consider doing it again.

Locals considered the long, gently curving peninsula from Corrantha to Port Kyber—with its white waters gushing at the tip of one end and the sunken volcano at the other—to be a cosmic dirty joke played by some mischievous god. And so, in the spirit of Kyber, the chasm under Stormbridge was known as "the Spasm."

• • • • •

Their caravan joined the back of the queue. About a dozen wagons in all were aiming to cross before the rising tide would make it unsafe to do so until the next day. Those that had already made it through to the other side were being inspected by customs officials from Corrantha City. The aptly named Kyber Stormtroopers—the forty-strong elite guard posted to the Stormbridge border—were directing people and wagons and monitoring all movement.

Reviewing their activity, Lormek found himself appreciating their efficiency. Then his eyes were drawn to Stormbridge itself.

It was anchored up the inclines on each side of the Spasm. A magnificent arch made of volcanic rock further reinforced with huge diamond braces, the bridge was wide enough to allow two wagons abreast, one in each direction, along with a central footpath between them. It was generally assumed that powerful magic was used in the creation of Stormbridge because even the most respected dwarven artisans would be severely challenged working with these materials at such a gargantuan scale.

Seeing it glint in the afternoon sunlight, the diamond ends shining across the black span, Lormek thought it was the most beautiful thing he had ever seen in his life. He was overwhelmed by the sheer impossibility of its existence.

He mused as to why such a remarkable construction was even necessary. Even if Stormbridge were submerged in tidal waters with only its center visible, as it was most of the day, he wondered why it couldn't have been made of wood, like a traditional bridge.

• • • • •

"Whoa there!" the Stormtrooper signaled the driver. Lormek noted how the Stormtrooper's bored look was belied by his sharp, inquisitive eyes. *Wouldn't wanna mess with this one*, he thought.

"Name of company?"

The cart ground to a halt.

• • • • •

Indeed, to understand the nature of Stormbridge, you'd have to risk your life in one of the legendary squalls that pummeled the area. They were called "stone storms" and were a death sentence to anyone caught inside of one.

Stone storms earned their name by lifting up the massive rocks strewn along the Spasm and sending them hurtling through the air. The largest was over the size of a wagon, and they would tumble majestically as they flew, before crashing angrily onto the bridge. The booming collisions would be followed by a low rumble that spread away from the bridge's center.

The largest of these explosions were accompanied by the ground shaking.

Stone storms were so fierce that they would instantly pick up and rip apart anything not moored to the ground. A loaded wagon might resist for a moment before flying into the air, disintegrating slowly into component parts while the agonized sound of breaking wood dissolved in the furious winds. Animals hitched to it were ripped apart by invisible forces tearing at them, their doomed braying lost in the cacophony. People caught in a stone storm could only survive by hugging the ground with all their might, praying that the fearsome tempest would not lift them away.

The massive rocks thrown through the Spasm by each stone storm would effectively rearrange it, even as Stormbridge shielded the area directly underneath from most of the chaos. Stormbridge itself, though, had lasted through centuries of this unrelenting abuse. It provided a stable, quick, and safe three-day trade route between Corrantha City and Port Kyber, and through the latter's famous port, to the eastern continent beyond. This would shave at least two weeks off the trip and permitted trade in perishables that would otherwise spoil.

Control of the port was so lucrative that a war—the Battle of Stormbridge—was fought over it. Whoever controlled Stormbridge controlled Port Kyber itself and would become very wealthy indeed.

• • • • •

The driver was about to get moving again when Lormek stood up.

Alferd, who was smoking, looked up at him in surprise.

"What are you doing there, bud? Sit down. We're about to make the crossing."

Lormek lowered his head. "I know. But I'm not feeling so well." Then, turning toward the driver, he added, "Please hold for a moment, all right? I'm going to get off."

Alferd cocked his head quizzically.

Lormek feigned an uncomfortable smile in the merchant's direction. "I . . . maybe . . . I ate something I shouldn't have at lunch," he said weakly. "One of those roots was really bitter . . . my stomach can be sensitive."

He could see Alferd and the King's trade rep exchanging a look. "You know, it's not so bad once you make the crossing for the first time," Alferd offered.

Lormek grimaced.

"No, really, it's just my stomach . . . I . . . gotta, uh, go before it gets really unpleasant in here." He started climbing off the wagon.

"What's the holdup?" shouted the driver of the next wagon.

"We'll only be a moment—church boy here has a touch of bridge fever!" Alferd shouted back, then turned to Lormek as the latter jumped down to the ground. "You sure, kid? Didn't you say you had to pick up some important papers? We're late, so I don't think we can wait for you."

Lormek glanced up at him. "Yeah, but . . . I'm sure it will be all right. My dad will figure it out." He grimaced again. "Look, I really, really have to go. It was lovely meeting you!" he said before turning around and heading toward the woods that grew on both sides of the path.

Alferd sat back in his chair. "Good kid. Glad we have his dad to take care of the poors."

The trade rep indicated his agreement. "We can go now!"

The driver picked up the reins, and the small caravan started forward.

· · · · ·

"Stomach trouble, huh? Poor baby," Sollis said, offering him a bunch of leaves as she pointed deeper into the foliage. Her usually deadpan expression betrayed her slight amusement.

Nyelle and Aidan both chuckled.

"All right, all right. It worked, didn't it? They bought it," Lormek responded, brushing Sollis's hand away gently. As his fingers touched hers, he felt a pleasant tingle, and his cheeks warmed. "So, uh . . . where's Garrett?"

"What do you mean? Isn't he right behind you?"

"Not that I'm aware of . . . my job was to cause enough of a distraction so he could slip out. I assumed he was already with you."

A moment passed in tense silence.

"He's probably just doing his hiding tricks, and in a moment will try to scare all of us." Nyelle raised her voice, "Come on, Garrett, show yourself, okay? We don't have time for this. We gotta head back to Kyber."

Nothing happened.

"I don't think he's hiding," Aidan said. They turned in surprise, then followed his gaze.

In the distance, as the last wagon made the final approach to the bridge, they could see Garrett hanging awkwardly out the back, looking frantically in every direction.

At that very moment, one of the Stormtroopers saw him too.

· · · · ·

"Giddy up!"

The shout, accompanied by a sudden jolt, woke Garrett up. For a moment, he felt disoriented; the comfortable spot in which he was napping felt nothing like his room at the Steadfast Inn. For one thing, his bed was moving.

Downhill. At a steep angle.

There was only one place this side of Stormbridge where this would be true—on the final approach. Kicking himself, Garrett considered that it would be very bad news if this were true.

He peeked outside to confirm that they were about to cross the bridge. Once they were on the other side, he would surely be found in the subsequent border inspection.

He had to leave before they got onto it!

Moving quickly, he first felt to make sure he still had the small, strange metal object he had acquired the previous night. Then, checking that none of the guards were looking in his direction, he hoisted himself over the sideboard. The wagon was leveling off, and he could hear the horses' hooves change as they stepped onto the volcanic rock of Stormbridge.

He hung off the wagon for a moment, searching for a discreet escape route.

It was not to be.

"Hey! You there, stop!"

One of the guards had spotted him and was running over, his shouts alerting three others in the vicinity. The wagon slowed as the driver drew the reins. All four guards were rushing toward him, nocking their bows as they closed in. There was only one direction he could go.

Swearing in every language he knew, he dropped to his feet and ran right into the Spasm, ducking as two arrows flew over his head.

He knew it wouldn't take long before he was a sitting duck—if he didn't drown first.

• • • • •

"That's really not good," Nyelle said somberly, as they watched Garrett run down toward the rising waters. "Nobody survives that."

As if to confirm her statement, the pursuing Stormtroopers stopped at the edge of the water. Then one of them shouted to Garrett, who was already almost waist-deep.

Lormek turned to Sollis, whose face was angled toward the unfolding scene. "What are they saying?"

"He just told Garrett to surrender or he will die."

"That's fair. Did Garrett respond?"

"Yeah. He said he was thinking about it."

"So, what now?"

Aidan was seized by a sense of urgency. "Tell him to surrender," he advised Nyelle.

"What? If they catch him, he'll blow our cover!"

"He won't get caught. Trust me. I'll fix it. Just tell him to surrender . . . and tell him to be ready because he won't actually have to go with them."

Nyelle looked at him quizzically, then shrugged her shoulders and relayed the message.

• • • • •

Seriously? Garrett thought as Nyelle's voice whispered in his ear. Not that he had time to think, as the rushing waters threatened to drown him. His toes curled, holding to the sand, but he was already swaying with the current. In a few minutes, it would sweep him away. He glanced behind him at the many pointed, rocky ends jutting out of the surface.

"Just so you know, Sollis, I won't last an hour under interrogation," he muttered as he waded toward the shore. He held his arms wide, palms up. A swell splashed his face, and a briny smell filled his nostrils. He licked his lips, tasting the salt. Two guards stood there waiting, their arms held ready to pull him up. The other two were heading up the hill, one of them taking a seat next to the driver of the stalled wagon and the other joining them on foot. A couple of seconds later, the wagon started moving again and lumbered onto the bridge.

Garrett reached the shore.

The two guards grabbed him and fished him out. *Like a cork out of a bottle*, he thought as he dejectedly accepted their help. One of them quickly turned him around, while the other tied his hands behind his back. Their efficient, coordinated movements spoke of their excellent training. He knew they were the best that Kyber had to offer and, for a moment, forgot his predicament as he couldn't help but be impressed with how well they did their jobs.

The guards marched him away from the swirling waters, one each to a side.

His thoughts raced, wondering what the hell the others were thinking, what the Kyber prison was really like, and whether he might be able to get in touch with his family.

It happened quickly.

The guard on his left froze, then toppled forward, an arrow sticking clean through his neck.

Garrett didn't hesitate.

By the time the other guard noticed something was amiss, he had been shoved off his feet, and Garrett was already midway up the incline. As the guard brought his whistle to his lips, he watched incredulously while the gnome melted into the scenery and disappeared.

• • • • •

Aidan lowered his bow and turned to the others. "Time to go!" he said urgently.

Nobody moved.

"What?" he exclaimed.

"Your plan was . . . ," Lormek started, then closed his mouth. His voice was shaking.

"You killed a fucking bridge guard!" Nyelle blurted.

Aidan turned back to her. "Well, yeah . . . I mean, what else did you think I was going to do?" He shrugged, then added, "Did you have another plan? At least I gave him a chance."

Nobody said a thing.

"In that case, we need to scram. No one will think to search this far away, but eventually the search will expand, and we better be long gone by then."

As Aidan finished, the sound of whistles and horns started echoing across the Spasm.

They looked at each other, turned on their heels, and ran.

DREAMS AND THINGS

"We better stop here and wait for him." Aidan's voice was strained.

"Thank god." Nyelle plopped down unceremoniously on the ground. "It feels like we've been running through the woods forever!"

Aidan stood bent with his hands on his knees, catching his breath. A moment later, Sollis arrived, her long strides making her seem as if she was floating through the dense brush. As she got nearer, her bloody shins and bloated ankles told a different story.

"I think I managed to get scratched by every kind of thorn in existence," she blurted.

"Yeah, that doesn't look good. Looks like you picked up some poison ivy, at least. And is that a bite mark?" Nyelle was pointing at Sollis's left ankle.

Amongst all the scratches, two holes seemed distinctly like a bite.

"Damn. I for sure thought I managed to avoid it," Sollis murmured.

"Avoid what?"

"The arphyd." Her ankle was visibly swollen. She wobbled on her feet. "I don't feel so good," she said before Aidan grabbed her and gently let her to the ground.

"Where's Lormek?" he asked.

"He's short. Can't move as fast . . . told me not to wait."

Sollis's ankle was now twice its normal size and turning a shade of green. She winced and groaned in pain. "My head . . . it hurts. A lot." Holding her palms up to her face, she muttered in a somewhat bewildered tone, "I can't see my hands." Then she closed her eyes, and her breathing turned shallow.

"Arphyd poison is bad news." Nyelle glanced at Aidan. "She's not gonna stay lucid. How are we going to carry her into the city in this condition?"

"I have no idea. This is going from bad to worse. Bradd was clear about it—we fuck it up, he'll have nothing to do with us." He sat down and wiped his brow. "With them searching for the killer, I don't know how safe it is for us to go through the Tradebay tunnel. We can get in through the Shallows route, but not if we carry her along. It's not an easy path."

"Not to mention that soon enough she will begin to hallucinate. Who knows what she might imagine in that cramped tunnel? All we need is for her to trigger one of her shockwaves because she's seeing things—she'll bury us alive."

They looked at each other silently for a few moments, then both raised their heads at the sound of someone else arriving. Lormek burst out of the bush, his face red with exertion. Once he saw them, he stopped and caught his breath.

"Oh, there you are. Hey guys, what's up?"

• • • • •

Lormek's hands projected an ethereal aura over Sollis's ankle. Faint green streaks seemed to be pulled out of the wound. Then the aura slowly dissipated, and he lifted his hands to reveal that her ankle appeared normal. The vicious bruises and crisscrossing scrapes on her lower shins were fading.

"She'll be back in a minute or two. I do decent work, but nowhere near as good as my dad. When he does this, you're back in business in seconds," he said apologetically.

They stared at him in wonder.

"Are you kidding me?" Aidan blurted. "It's incredible! I guess Bradd wasn't lying when he said he didn't know what you can do, because let me tell you, buddy, I now feel a heck of a lot safer with you around. I never realized anyone could do healing stuff in the field. I always thought it required a church and an altar."

"I suppose you're right . . . Healers usually follow Freyg, and she works through her shrines. It's a little complicated. But I get my healing from Thor, who is more of a field general. So I can do stuff like this anywhere, but my power's limited."

"Well, I sure as hell prefer having you around than someone who needs to build a fucking shrine every time they need to heal anyone."

Nyelle confirmed. "We for sure thought we were screwed. No way we could carry her into the city in her condition."

"What condition?" they heard Sollis say. Their heads turned toward her in unison as she sat up. "Is everybody all right?"

They started laughing. After a second, a somewhat confused Sollis joined them. And so it was that none of them took note when Garrett, who wasn't trying to hide at all, finally arrived. At least not until, with his hands still tied behind his back, he planted himself right in the middle of the group and in a pained voice demanded: "What's so funny?"

And with that, he brought down the house.

• • • • •

"You all right, Aidan?" Nyelle tossed the bone she had just finished gnawing on back into the fire and took a swig from her waterskin.

"Yeah . . . don't worry about it. It's . . . ," Aidan's voice trailed off as he stared at the flames. His face was somber.

"It's what?"

Aidan didn't respond.

"Come on, man . . . we all watched you murder a Stormtrooper to save Garrett's life. If you can't trust us, you might as well trust nobody. We're in this together now, whether we like it or not."

Aidan sighed. "I suppose you're right." He readied himself. "This hidden clearing . . . the reason I knew it was here . . ." He sighed heavily again, then raised his eyes. "Well, you see . . . it's where my father died."

Nyelle gasped, her hand rising to cover her mouth.

"Wait. Like, right here?" Garrett asked.

Aidan lowered his chin, then glanced up. "Yes, right here. In fact, we were sitting and eating just like we are doing right now when he attacked."

"Who attacked?"

"The werewolf."

A moment of stunned silence followed. Then Sollis spoke. "A werewolf? Here?"

"Yes. I watched him . . ." Aidan's eyes filled with tears. "I watched him tear my dad apart. There was nothing I could do."

"But . . . how did you survive?"

"My dad told me to run away and hide the moment he saw the wolf. I was sitting in that tree right there." Aidan pointed toward a massive oak at the edge of the clearing.

"Sure it wasn't a direwolf?"

"Yeah, I'm sure. I hit it with all my arrows. None of them pricked it. My dad had a silvered sword and managed to slash it, but the wolf was too big."

Sollis lowered her head toward him. "And the werewolf didn't follow you?"

"No, he didn't. I'm not sure why."

"Lucky, that."

Aidan agreed.

Lormek cleared his throat. "So, uh . . . sorry to be an idiot, but . . . what's a werewolf?"

· · · · ·

"Holy Thor, I'm not sure how I feel about that," Lormek said a few minutes later. "And you say they become human for three days each month?"

"Yeah, I think when the moons align," Garrett responded.

"That's crazy." Lormek shook his head.

"Yup. Thing is, there have been persistent rumors of them around these parts, but I always thought they were never brave or foolish enough to cross over from Corrantha. I remember there was a story one time at dinner of some random dude in the Shallows being eaten by one. Supposedly that made it hard for the Steadfast to get certain kinds of meat for a while . . . I was just a kid. Anyways, my dad said there's no way for the werewolves to make it through . . ."

Garrett stopped mid-sentence at the sudden gasps around him. Then the realization dawned on him. "Oh, shit," he checked himself, seeing Aidan's tearful face. "I'm so sorry."

After a moment, Aidan shook his head slowly. "No, it's all right. My dad was just some random guy in the Shallows for those in the Uppers. And we did a lot of hunting for the inn, it was good income. So I suppose that makes sense, from their perspective." His voice turned to a barely audible whisper. "I just . . . I just wish he was still here."

Nyelle moved over to Aidan and gave him a hug. He placed his head silently on her shoulder and closed his eyes.

A few more moments passed in silence, and then Garrett spoke up again, his childlike voice contrasting with the tense emotions around the campfire.

"So . . . not to mess with the mood or anything, but . . . wanna see what I found?"

• • • • •

They gathered as he lay down a cloth. Then he reached into his jacket and pulled out a strange object, which he rested in the middle of the fabric. It was the shape of a perfect hexagon, chunky and flat, about the size of a large grape, and set with a round hole in the middle.

"Weird, huh? I have no idea what it's for."

"What's it made of?" Lormek asked.

"Some sort of metal, but I'd never seen this kind of metal before in my life. Here, check it out." Garrett handed the object to Lormek, who took it gingerly and weighed it in his palm. He brought it up to his nose and then tried to bite it.

"Tough. And heavy. Smells like nothing, but tastes cold. Also, what an odd shape. Why the six sides?"

"Yeah," Garrett affirmed. "Awkward. I certainly felt it rubbing my hip as I was running away from the guards, I can tell you that." He massaged his side. "It's definitely not bronze or silver or even iron."

Lormek turned it over. "It almost looks like a tiny wheel, but only the center hole is round, which makes no sense. It can't roll." He felt with the tip of his finger through the circular opening in the middle. "Did you notice the grooves on the inside? I can feel them."

"Yeah. It's like a series of holes on top of each other. Very weird."

"Maybe it's for carpentry? I suppose you could use it to guide a big nail through . . . the edges would make it easy to grab with your fingers as you hammer. With all the work on my dad's church, I know construction, but I've never seen anything so . . . perfect. Even if we knew the metal, the detail is remarkable." Lormek handed the object back to Garrett, who shook his head.

"It's okay, you're welcome to carry it now." He winced. "I ended up sleeping on it for a few hours, and I think I have a permanent scar now. Could it be some sort of magic?"

"I doubt it," Sollis said. "I'm not a wizard or anything, but I know that magic can't create entirely new things out of nothing. It has to work with what's around us."

Lormek, who had been examining the object closely, said, "Did you see the markings?"

"Huh? What markings?"

"Look, right here." Lormek was pointing at one of the flat sides above the hole.

Garrett leaned in. "I hadn't noticed those. I wonder what they are."

"Seems intentional. Precise. Maybe some kind of runes? Do any of you recognize the script?"

They passed the object around, shaking their heads in turn.

"So . . . where did you find this, exactly?" Nyelle asked as she held it between her fingers.

"Oh, right. Well, I got into one of those wagons—boy, they sure make it hard—and it was, like, a real tight squeeze in there. I could barely move. Anyway, it was also, like, totally dark because the leather cover blocked the moonlight. So I couldn't see a thing, you know?"

Nyelle waited patiently.

"Yeah, except I could. Like, as soon as my eyes adjusted. That was when I knew I found something."

"What do you mean?"

"There was a light in there. Super faint, but in that darkness, it made like a torch. So I kinda noodled around the top where there was a little bit of room till I made it past the outer boxes, right?" Garrett satisfied himself that he had their attention.

"Then I see there's about a foot of space around one box, right in the middle of the wagon. It isn't stacked like the rest of them either. Just sitting there on its own. And—get this—it looks just like a box from the docks!"

"Really? They actually had the box? Bradd said it was a fool's errand."

"Oh, it was. That much was obvious; the box was painted to be like one of those other ones, but it wasn't actually one."

"How do you know that?"

"Well . . . see, uh, it's been a bit of a thing for me to find out about these boxes." Garrett chuckled nervously. "I'd gotten close enough to a couple of them before to see that they had certain things in common . . . this box didn't have none of that." Garrett stopped suddenly and reached out to take the object back. He turned it over in his hand.

"*That's* where I'd seen this before!"

"Seen what before?"

"The metal! The real boxes have these weird corner braces, and the lock fasteners too . . . I'd always wondered what they were made of. It's the same material as whatever this is."

"Huh. Interesting. Okay, go on then," Nyelle urged Garrett.

"Right. Well, the thing was, the box was showing off this aura, and it was where the light was coming from. Now, I figured a real box with whatever's inside one of them might do that, but this wasn't a real box, so how could it shine like that? So I went down and inspected it. Dude . . ." He turned to Aidan. "I wish you were there. Woulda been so easy for you to just tell the box to open."

Aidan smiled.

"So anyway, finally I got it open, but there was nothing in it, just straw. But the light moved!" Garrett paused. "See, when I opened the top to peek inside, the light changed. So I closed it and opened it again, and then I realized that it was the paint that was giving off the light. When I was opening and closing the lid, the light moved with it too."

"Phosphorus ink?" Sollis asked.

"That's what I thought, but here's the thing—the color was all wrong. You know that blast you made back at the inn? It had that strange color?"

Sollis agreed. "Of course, I know it well . . . kinda yellowish-blue. The color of magic."

"Exactly."

"Did it smell funny?"

"Huh? How the hell should I know? I didn't sniff the box." Garrett laughed.

"What's magic paint? Why? And who of all things would paint a decoy box with it?" Nyelle murmured.

"Weird, huh?"

"Very weird."

"Anyway, before I left, I decided to feel around the box real good, just to make sure, and that's when I found this thing tucked away, hidden in a corner. It was stuck in a way that most people wouldn't notice, but I have really small fingers, so I felt it right away. I pried at it for a few moments, and it came off in my hand.

"Then I made my way out. Mistakenly popped open one of the fruit boxes when my pants caught on a corner, so I got myself some dessert for my trouble. Oh, and . . . great idea about the monkey, Lormek," Garrett added as he finished his story. "Seriously."

Lormek nodded. "There's more to this than meets the eye. But unless anyone else has anything to say, I'd like to grab some shuteye. Been a rough day."

· · · · ·

"Get up. Quickly."

Nyelle opened her eyes. It was still the dead of night, and Aidan's face was right next to hers, his finger to his lips. "Shhh . . . look," he whispered.

She sat up quickly and followed his gaze. Lormek's sleeping form was surrounded by a yellowish-blue magical aura. "He's been like this for a little while," Aidan added. "I was keeping watch, and it just happened."

"Should we wake him?" she whispered back.

"I'm not sure . . . I thought about it, but I'm a little afraid of trying to touch him in this state. What if the aura burns us or something? Remember back at the inn?"

Nyelle nodded.

They continued to watch in silence.

The aura moved toward Sollis.

INTERLUDE: LORMEK'S DREAM

Pondering the day's events as he settles down for some much-needed rest, Lormek listens to his heart beating its slow, sure rhythm. A quick prayer to Thor melts into darkness, calming him and providing him with reassurance as he drifts away.

Sometime later, he wakes up, opening his eyes with a start. For a moment, he wonders if he has gone blind because it is pitch-dark, but soon Lormek realizes that a faint glow is coming from his left. It is pale yellowish-blue and has an odd humanoid shape to it. As he stares at it, he realizes that the glow is surrounding Sollis.

He is excited—and nervous.

Lormek gets up and creeps over to inspect her sleeping form. Even surrounded by the glow, she seems to be sleeping peacefully. As he stands there, mesmerized by her features, he finds himself compelled to touch her. He tries to brush the thought from his mind, to turn and go back to sleep.

He can't. The compulsion is too strong.

His hand reaches out slowly, involuntarily toward her.

Her eyes pop open wide, staring right into his very soul. And yet, she stays frozen as Lormek's hand keeps moving inexorably toward her. He exerts every ounce of willpower he has to stop, but it is not enough; his hand has a mind of its own. She looks at him even more intently as his fingers tremble ever closer to her chest until he touches her breast. Then, in a flash, she disappears.

Lormek screams.

And then he wakes up. Everything is quiet. It's still the middle of the night. There is no glow anywhere.

STAIRWAY TO HEAVEN

"Okay, everyone, we wanna get there as soon as the tunnel opens—the earlier we go, the easier it is to get through to the second overlook without bumping into anyone," Aidan urged the group.

"Is the tunnel that crowded?" Lormek asked.

"It can be. But it does lead to the Shallows, so . . . you know."

"Yeah." Lormek grinned. "Not exactly the destination of choice, is it? Take it from a Mudder who knows," he added, an edge creeping into his voice.

Aidan and Nyelle exchanged a quick glance.

"Right," Aidan spoke. "So we better get a move on."

"But there's another way in, isn't there?" Garrett piped in.

"Well, sure, but we agreed it wouldn't be safe to go in through the front door."

"That's not what I was saying."

Aidan stared at Garrett.

"Come on, you know what I mean. The staircase," Garrett added in a slightly shriller tone as he struggled to contain his enthusiasm.

Aidan sat back and let out a sigh. "That thing is a death trap. Trust me, I've gone up and down it a few times with my dad. We almost fell off it more than once."

"But you made it through every time, didn't you?"

"I suppose so," Aidan reluctantly allowed.

"Excuse me, but what are we talking about?" Nyelle asked.

"The Stairway," Sollis said quietly, paused, then added, "to Heaven."

"The Stairway to Heaven? That's a funny name."

"Yeah. It's a rope and wooden staircase that makes for a steep climb around the edge of the Gash. If you're careful, you can get in and out of the Shallows that way. I used it quite a bit when I was training with my magic, which I did a lot outside the slopes. It doesn't cost much to make the climb. Not many people use it, which suited me just fine."

"That sounds perfect. What's the catch?"

"They don't maintain it very well . . . easy to fall off it, or even through it if a step breaks under you, which they do sometimes. Because it's right at the Gash, it's windy, and they rarely replace the anchors. Sometimes you get swooped by hawks and eagles if they get hungry waiting for someone to throw up on the viewing platform. If enough of them come at you at once, you might lose your balance and fall over. I'd seen it happen once," Sollis concluded.

Garrett agreed. "Exactly! And that's why they call it that! It's like, you might die, but at least you'll have a nice view!" He chuckled. "You can see it happening from the floor of the council . . . some people sit in audience at government meetings just so they can watch and make bets on whether someone will fall off that day."

"Of course they do," Lormek said with a frozen smile. "He's right though. I'd been to the bottom before—it's at the far edge of the beach. The guard at the tollbooth always seemed so sad and bored, but they never talked to me no matter how hard I tried. I think it's a kind of punishment to be posted there. Still, it sounds like it's the least conspicuous way to get in and out of town. What do you think, Aidan?"

Aidan sighed. "I suppose so. Okay, let's do that, but everybody, please be very careful."

· · · · ·

"Here it is."

They stood in a lightly wooded area at the end of the Kyber peninsula, near where the volcano rose. The cliff's edge was marked by twisted trees that clung to it at impossible angles over the sheer drop. Peering over cautiously, Garrett couldn't even see the bottom; a layer of low-hanging clouds hugged the mountainside midway down. The smell of ripening berries and citrus fruit growing on branches stretching over the ocean wafted into his nose.

Aidan pointed toward two stakes by the cliff's edge. The ropes extending away and down the mountainside from them had seen better days. The gap between them was just wide enough to fit two people if they faced each other.

"Cool!" Garrett exclaimed.

Nyelle stared at him, then gulped. "That looks . . . terrifying."

"Just follow my lead," Aidan said. "I've done this several times when I was younger, and I'm better at talking to the wood now. The stairs won't fail me. We'll go slowly. Copy my movements, and we'll do fine. Oh, and keep close to the mountain at all times. That way the wind won't catch you easily, and you can keep more or less stable. The less you move, the better, trust me."

"Lead the way, chief," said Sollis. "I've done this too, and though I don't have your powers, I'm tall enough to grab the anchors to stop the swaying. Garrett, you stay behind me. You're the lightest, so whatever you do will affect us the least."

Garrett nodded as Aidan turned toward the gap. He stopped for a moment, looked down, and took a deep breath. Then he seemed to sink below ground as he took the first stair.

Nyelle, who was next, could feel her mouth go dry. Her leg shook involuntarily as she followed, and she ended up placing her foot down more firmly than she intended. The stair wobbled.

"Watch it!" Aidan said behind his back. Nyelle exhaled slowly to calm herself. As she took another step down, she could feel Lormek grab ahold of the rope behind her.

• • • • •

The stairs were unevenly spaced and rocked with the climbers' weight. They hung off of two guide ropes that also served as handrails. The inside guide rope was anchored to the side of the volcano every few feet. The outer guide rope was in turn anchored to overhanging horizontal stakes above the stairway. Sollis had to duck her head slightly every time they moved past one of those, but she also found them convenient to hold on to.

The smell of sea salt permeated everything, heightening their senses. They could feel every fiber of the ropes and sense every imperfection of the volcano's smooth outer wall as they brushed against it. As they reached the edge of the Gash before the staircase turned back on itself, they couldn't help but admire the city from this vantage point. They could see the council chamber extending from the far end of the volcano and over the shelves, and the circular row of offices surrounding it on both ends. They could see the flocks of birds circling endlessly below the viewing platform and hear their calls, a wild musical score that spoke of anticipation and hunger. They could see Tradebay and the ships coming up and down the Elevator, and at the very bottom, the outer Shallows and the Docks.

It was home.

It had been slow going for about a half hour, and they were not even close to midway when Aidan stopped and raised his hand in warning.

"What's going on, Aidan?"

"This stair . . . it's going to break clean through if anyone steps on it." Aidan pointed at what appeared to be a groove in the center of the next step. "Hold on, let me talk to it. It's a pretty serious injury but I can show it how to heal itself. Stay still please, I don't want to fall off." Pressing himself against the volcano, he stretched down carefully until his hand made contact. They watched him quietly as they leaned against the mountainside and away from the constant gusts of wind.

Garrett, who was growing impatient in the back, spoke up. "What's he doing?"

"He's telling a stair how to mend itself," Sollis murmured behind her shoulder.

"Really? Just like that? Wait, I wanna see it happen!"

"No, don't move!"

But it was too late. Garrett's nimble movements carried him around Sollis on the outer edge. "It's no problem, I'm very light," he exclaimed as his tiny figure leapt and danced on the small, precarious foothold, sending several stairs wobbling.

"Garrett, stop!" Nyelle's voice was urgent as Garrett descended toward her. Several large birds were flying toward the little group, attracted by the noise.

"Don't worry about it." He stepped onto the same stair she was standing on. "You won't feel me coming around you . . . I'll just pop over here . . . whoops!"

The exclamation crossed his lips as an eagle dove straight at him, sideswiping him at speed. He lost his footing and grabbed on to the outer rope in an attempt to catch himself.

"Goddammit!" Aidan exclaimed.

He was crouched down and positioned precariously, and he fell forward onto the stair he was working on. The sudden movement sent violent shudders up and down the staircase. They heard wood cracking below, then heard it again from above.

"Oh, shit!" Sollis shouted from above

It happened quickly. She felt the overhead anchor she'd been holding weaken and break. The wood snapped in her hands, and she was tossed to the side, toward the empty air. Her height working against her, she toppled over the now slack outer guide rope. She made a last, flailing attempt to grab on to something, anything, but couldn't.

Sollis fell.

They all watched in horror as her tumbling figure made its way down along the mountainside before she pierced the low-hanging clouds and disappeared.

• • • • •

"You . . . fucking . . . idiot!" Nyelle was livid.

Garrett's face, perhaps for the first time in his life, looked stricken. His eyes were full of tears.

"You killed her! You killed Sollis!" Nyelle's cheeks were flushed.

Garrett sank to his knees in shock. "I didn't mean to! I just wanted to see Aidan fix the wood! I'm sorry!"

"Oh, you didn't mean to . . . that's okay then. I'm sure Sollis would forgive you since you didn't kill her intentionally. No, wait, you know what? I just thought of something. She wouldn't be able to forgive you because she's still fucking dead!"

Lormek, who had been quiet as the scene unfolded, spoke up, straining with effort to control his emotions. "When we get to the bottom, if we can recover her body, let's take it to the church. My dad can't raise the dead, but at least he can make her look okay. For a funeral or . . . or something," his voice broke.

"Any chance she's still alive?" Garrett pleaded.

"No way. It's a very long way to the bottom—and while there's the beach down there, it's likely she fell onto the rocks. We're almost at low tide . . . these rocks break ships with little trouble. Best we can hope for is that the tide doesn't wash her away by the time we get down—we'll never find her body then."

"We have another problem," said Aidan. They turned toward him. His face was pale, and he was pointing at the stair he had been trying to mend. It was broken, its two halves dangling from the ropes. "When I fell forward, my weight went right through the crack. I managed to grab the ropes, so I didn't tumble down like Sollis did."

"Gawds. We almost lost you too?" Nyelle struggled to maintain her composure. "Can you fix it? I just can't imagine trying to jump it with the stairs swaying like this."

"Yes, but it will take me a little while. Even then, you'll have to be very, very careful as you step on it—it's much harder for the wood to rejoin once it's fully broken. That kind of wound leaves a scar that lasts forever."

Everyone took refuge in their thoughts as Aidan worked, and Garrett's quiet sobs were carried away by the wind.

· · · · ·

A couple of hours later, a despondent group of four made their way down the final stretch of stairway, this part built into the cliff. Their shoulders were hunched, their moods tragic. They nodded gravely to the lonely guard who eyed them with boredom before pointing at the sign proclaiming:

WELCOME TO PORT KYBER! ENJOY YOUR STAY.

ENTRY IS FREE. DEPARTURE 20C/PP

Then he let them through the small gate.

Lormek stopped and turned around. "All right. The tide is rising, but we should have time to search. If her body ended up anywhere near the beach, we should find her."

"I'm sorry guys. I really am." Garrett raised his face, covered in dried tears, to face the group. "She didn't deserve to die just because I was curious."

Nyelle agreed severely. "You're right, she didn't. I have no idea what we're going to do with you, but you need to grow up." She turned to the rest. "Let's spread out and search. Once we report to Bradd, I think I'm done with all this. Money's good, but being alive is better." To herself, she added quietly, "Especially as little as I have left of it."

"You're certainly right about that last bit."

Four heads turned around in surprise. Sollis strolled casually up the beach, a wry smile on her face. Her hand was trying in vain to contain her long hair swirling in the wind. It gave her an even wilder look than usual. "I lost my hat on my way down," she added apologetically.

Lormek was the first to recover. "What . . . you're alive? How?"

"Turns out that stress brings out the best in me." Sollis's smile turned into a wide grin.

Garrett, who'd been gaping at Sollis in stunned silence, sprang to life. He ran to her and hugged her tightly. "Oh, I'm so happy!" He buried his face in her midriff. The sight of the young gnome latching on to the wildmage twice his height was so ridiculous that the tension dissipated all at once, and everybody burst out in laughter, even the jaded guard.

"Well, you better tell us what happened and how you're still alive, but let's do it at the inn," Aidan said and started walking briskly toward the cave entrance to the beach. "Don't know about any of you, but I suddenly rediscovered my appetite!"

• • • • •

The room at the inn had a couple of bunk beds, and Stinky set a table and five chairs in the middle. One of the serving wenches had followed him with pitchers of water and ale and platters of bread, cheese, and jerky. The plates were mostly empty by now.

"Okay, Sollis, so tell us how the hell you are still alive," Aidan prompted.

"Right . . ." Sollis hesitated for a moment. "Remember the story about how I discovered magic in the first place? The kid who tried to beat me up?" She took a deep breath. "I've been trying ever since to make something like that happen again, but it's never quite worked."

"I thought you figured out a couple of new magics?"

"Yes, I did—like the cold fire dart I told you about. But I did that through experimentation. I taught myself, basically. Once I knew I had magical affinity, I researched whatever I could about it and then inferred a lot through trial and error. I suppose wizards are shown how to do it, but . . . you know." She rubbed two imaginary coins between her fingers.

"Sure. The only wizarding school I ever heard of is in Corrantha City."

"Yes," Lormek said. "Alferd talked about it in the caravan. It's apparently impossible to find the school without an explicit invitation, and you don't get one unless they want you to. Nobody ever gets invited unless they are really wealthy—like lords—and they have to pay a fortune to be tested to see if they can stay. He said very few are accepted, and then nobody hears from them for like a couple of decades before they come back and join the Magic Corps."

"What's the Magic Corps?" Garrett asked.

"Alferd described it as a sort of special force that serves at the pleasure of the King. They do amazing things with magic—he said they built Stormbridge—but their primary purpose is to protect the realm from invaders. The current King apparently keeps them at arm's length. Alferd got a little vague at that point." Lormek leaned back into his chair.

Everyone's heads spun with wizards and mysterious invaders until Sollis spoke again. "Cool. Well, I think what I did was probably how real wizards train, only badly. In teaching myself, I didn't have a list of effects I could learn and build on, so I had to come up with everything on my own. Lots of 'can I do this?' and 'what happens if I try that?' That's how I figured out that magic can't create something out of nothing—I kept trying to conjure a bunch of gold." Sollis chuckled. "Well, it doesn't work that way. I can reshape things around me—like take the current in the air and make it focus and explode in a certain direction, which becomes a shockwave. That sort of thing."

"Gotcha. So what happened when you fell?" asked Garrett.

"Ah, yes. You probably saw me enter the cloud—I really freaked out, because it went all dark and cold and I knew I was going to die. Came right out the bottom, and then without thinking I moved my fingers in a way I never tried before, and the air rushing past me reversed course and pushed underneath me instead, creating an air bubble. I was maybe twenty feet above the ground at that point. Just came down gently from there."

"That's so cool! So you can fly now?" Garrett couldn't hide his excitement.

"No, not fly. But I think I can fall from any height pretty much and just float down to the ground. It was completely instinctive. I had no idea this magic existed; it simply happened. Just like that first time with the bully. It seems like in the right conditions, I'm primed to come up with new magic on the spot."

"That is a very useful piece of knowledge. My suggestion is we keep it to ourselves." Nyelle turned to Garrett. "That means you, too—*especially* you—do you hear? Don't tell Bradd about this. It can save our asses someday, and I don't trust him."

"Oh, of course not! No way I'm telling him . . . it's the coolest secret ever, and it's just ours! Cross my heart and hope to die!"

Afterward, they examined the mysterious hexagon from the caravan, but could not settle on any conclusions about it, and eventually left it resting at the center of the table. Which is why they all missed the moment when it started glowing faintly as they were asleep.

INTERLUDE: SOLLIS DREAMS

Did I fall asleep? Did I die?

Sollis is awake, but she isn't sure whether in her head, in the real world, or in the afterlife.

Where am I?

Not the real world, unless she was awoken in the eye of a storm. Wherever she is, it is absolute bedlam.

The wind blows ferociously around her, so gusty that a step in any direction would be suicide. Lights and colors dance madly within the columns of air, making her head spin and her eyes water. She can feel a migraine coming, but she isn't able to shut her eyes.

This is crazy! And where are the others?

Wait. What did she just see? For the briefest of moments, it seemed like the lights and colors took shape. People? Sollis has a strange sense that two of them are very important to her, but she has no idea who they are. She shakes her head. Maybe it is a trick of the mind.

Now there are flashes of magic color inside too, and she yearns to touch them. She reaches out her hand, then pulls it away from the swirling wind, fearful of what might happen. But the color keeps calling to her, and she reaches out her hand again, her fingers shaking as she tries to push through the maelstrom. For a moment, there is a sense of exhilaration, but then her entire body is ripped apart as she is pulled into the vortex, and is consumed by the blinding magical light. It feels like . . .

Home.

• • • • •

Sollis woke with a start, her brow covered in cold sweat. After a second, she realized that Lormek was holding her hand, offering her a cup of water. He had a worried look, but his expression made her uncomfortable. She jerked her hand and scanned the room. It was morning. The others were gone.

"What's going on?" she demanded.

"It looks like you had a terrible nightmare . . . We all woke up to you moaning and turning, but we couldn't wake you up. I volunteered to stay here to watch you. The rest went down to grab breakfast. Are you okay?"

"Yes, I'm fine! Now move and let me get ready. We're going to go meet Bradd, right?"

Lormek hesitated, then stood up to leave. Before he closed the door, he shot her one last look of concern which lasted a fraction too long.

It made her skin crawl.

A GROWING
LIST OF CHARGES

"All right, folks. Whatcha got?" Bradd unfolded his arms and leaned forward. Nyelle found his cheeriness unsettling.

Bradd's tone gave Aidan pause. He sought inspiration around the table but found none. He cleared his throat. "Well . . . we followed and infiltrated the caravan."

"And?"

"It was a decoy like you said."

"That's an astute observation. Care to share how you reached that conclusion?"

Aidan hesitated.

"Go on. I need the details before I pay you."

"Right. Okay. So Garrett managed to get into one of the carts and found the fake box."

"Oh?" Bradd turned to Garrett. "And how did you judge it to be fake?"

"It was painted with magic!" Garrett replied.

"Magic paint?"

"Yeah. It glowed in the dark."

"You mean it was covered with glowing ink?"

"No, Bradd. It was a magical aura . . . like the magic of the real boxes. Same color, but this time, it came from the paint rather than whatever's in the box."

Bradd sat back in his chair. "Interesting."

"Yeah. No idea why anyone would go to the trouble of doing it but . . . they did."

"Did you find anything else? Also, I heard reports that a Stormtrooper was killed mysteriously by an arrow that materialized from thin air when they were trying to arrest a caravan stowaway . . . which happened to be a gnome . . . know anything about that?"

The group exchanged a quick glance, and then Aidan shook his head. "No, we didn't, and no, we don't," he responded in a measured tone, holding Bradd's gaze.

"I choose to believe you." Bradd grinned. He closed his eyes for a few seconds, then opened them. "It fits."

"Fits what?" Nyelle asked.

"My theory of who was behind all this . . . Listen, you guys. You did a good job, so I'm going to give you a choice."

"A choice?"

"Yes. You can either get paid the two gold each that I promised you, and we can part ways. Or you could still earn the full reward if you take on another mission for me."

There was silence as everybody stared first at Bradd and then each other. Finally, Lormek spoke. "What do you want us to do?"

• • • • •

"Just look at this place," Lormek murmured. It was almost dusk. They were sitting in a small park, neatly situated within a cluster of tidy buildings. Lormek's face was hidden by the folds of his cloak. Sollis had acquired a new yellow Bretonne hat, and Aidan's scar was masked by a face covering. "It's like a totally different world."

"It is. I grew up over there." Garrett pointed alongside the curving inner wall of the volcano. "And the Shallows might as well be a thousand miles away, rather than just a thousand feet below."

"Everything is so . . . clean," Nyelle whispered in awe. "Which one is it again?"

Garrett gestured toward one of the narrow three-story buildings across from them. People were streaming out, heading in different directions. "That's the one. My father also has an office there . . . I know the building well."

"And you're sure you can get us in?"

"Oh, yeah. This was where I spent many of my days when I was a kid. Things don't change much here. Let's just wait a little bit longer to make sure the laggards have left," Garrett responded without shifting his gaze away from the building. He thought back to his childhood and smiled privately with perspective gained after a couple of years in the Shallows.

"There!" He awoke from his reverie and pointed at a diminutive figure emerging out of the building. "That's the Snake. He always leaves last." The short man stopped to scan the area. His eyes shifted over the park, locking momentarily on their little group. Then he left, his confident stride purposeful and measured.

"Damn, it's like he can see right into my soul," Lormek murmured.

"Yeah, I felt it too," Nyelle whispered nervously.

The others nodded, and Garrett said, "The Snake—all the Snakes, really—are like that. They have to be, I suppose. Anyway, the coast is clear—follow me, I'll take us in through a back door."

• • • • •

"Bradd said it was on the second floor, right?" Nyelle kept her voice low.

"Right. We just need to find it. As a kid, I wasn't paying too much attention to who was where, and many of these offices change hands frequently to match internal appointments and power dynamics in the guilds and merchant houses."

"And we're looking for a title, right? Not a name?"

"Yes, they never put the names on any of these. If you need to search for someone by name, then you shouldn't be here. Anyway, it's the first aide to the Pope. Popeaide." Garrett chuckled. "So look for the papal icon and the numeral 1 next to it, that would designate the correct office."

"I think I see it." Sollis gestured toward a door at the end of the hallway.

"Looks like it." Garrett examined it and confirmed. "Okay, listen. This is where it can get a bit tricky. My father always said that we had to be out of here before sundown or we'd have to stay until morning. I don't know why, but I'm assuming wards come alive at night or something. We gotta be careful."

As if to reinforce his words, as the last rays of sunlight faded and the hallway fell into darkness, the surrounding doors made a series of clicking noises. "Shit!" Lormek exclaimed. "I just tried the door back to the stairway . . . it's locked."

"How the hell does a door lock itself?" asked Aidan. "No, don't answer that. Sollis, is that something you can undo?"

"Not sure. I could try. I've played around with physical manipulation enough that I can knock open simple locks, but I suspect these doors have complex mechanisms."

"Don't try," said Garrett. "They have alarms, so if you screw it up, the place will go nuts. Listen, I can pick at least some locks without triggering anything, but there's no point in turning back before we even try to go forward. Sollis, can you get us a bit of magic light?"

A point of illumination appeared. In the total darkness, the otherwise dim light source shone brightly and lit almost the entire corridor. Glancing up, they saw that it was situated on the brim of Sollis's new hat. "Seemed logical," she said and grinned.

"That's so cool! All right, let's have a look . . ." Garrett tiptoed carefully across the hallway, moving this way and that. About a third of the way through, he abruptly stopped and crouched down. "Just as I thought." He gestured a few inches off the floor. "Tripwire—released when the doors locked."

He examined the wall closely.

"Damn, this is excellent craftsmanship—you can't even see the mounting slots. Totally concealed in the design." He turned back to his appreciative audience. "Why don't you all move toward me? When you get here, you can step over the wire, but I need the light closer so I can check the rest of the corridor."

They successfully negotiated the tripwire and its identical counterpart farther down the hallway, as well as the pressure plate set right in the middle. Garrett was only saved by being so light that a brief misstep did not fully trigger the plate. Then they found themselves before the Popeaide's door.

After examining it closely, Garrett looked up. "Huh. I don't even think it's locked! Should I open it?"

They all exchanged glances, but nobody spoke. After a few seconds, Garrett shrugged and tried the handle.

• • • • •

Even in the dim light, they could see the office was tastefully arranged. It had a big mahogany desk and heavy, velvet-covered chair at the far end by the window, a big file drawer and a couple of bookshelves, and a round table to one side with several plush chairs around it. Nyelle took off her boots and let her toes sink into the thick carpet. "Damn, that feels nice," she said, letting out a small sigh.

"Yeah, the furniture is exquisite . . . really well made," Aidan murmured as his hand caressed the top of the side table. "Very little pain in it."

"So that's how they live up here, is it?" Lormek whispered, his voice sounding strained. "I wonder how many churches my dad could build for the cost of one of these chairs."

Nyelle touched his arm.

"Sorry, just got caught in the moment . . . like that stupid merchant with his stupid cigarettes—each one of those could feed an entire family for a few days in the Shallows."

"That's just an office," Garrett said cheerfully. "You should see some of the houses, dude!" He moved around the office desk and tried to pull open a drawer. "Locked. Should I try to pick it?"

"Before you do that, let's check the bookshelves. Bradd said what we're searching for might be hidden in plain sight. Plus, it's been too easy so far . . . I'm a little suspicious," Nyelle cautioned.

"Sure." Garrett glanced around. "I miss having books around . . . growing up we had our own little library, and all my friends had them too. Looks like this guy's writing one actually." He climbed up on the big office chair and turned over a sheaf of notes that was lying on the table. "Ah, there's the title page. Let's see . . . *Inferior Critters: Stink Rats, Mudders, and the Chain That Binds Them* . . . shit." He raised his eyes to Lormek. "I'm sorry."

Lormek's face betrayed little emotion. "The deepest hatred is the quietest," he said softly. "At least in the Shallows, they call me names openly."

Nyelle squeezed his arm, and Aidan placed a hand on his shoulder. "Don't worry, you lil' Mudder . . . we'll bring this fucker down." Aidan's eyes glinted.

Lormek smiled back at him.

"Aha!" Sollis, who had been quiet until that moment, suddenly exclaimed. Her eyes were strangely lit, and she was clearly oblivious to the emotions in the room. "I finally got it!"

"Got . . . what?" asked Nyelle with a hint of exasperation.

"I've been working up this effect to see magical auras around me—I figured if I could alter the environment using magical energy, then maybe I can also make concentrations of magical energy stand out. Thing is, it's been difficult to develop because I never had a lot to experiment with. But I've got it now."

"So you can see magic stuff?" Garrett asked as he leaned back into the chair.

"Kind of. It's limited, but I can see a small ward on the file cabinet . . . and also that something magical is inside a book right there." Sollis pointed toward a lower shelf on one of the bookcases. Nyelle bent to open it. "No, no, that one . . . right . . . once again . . . yup, that's it!"

Nyelle opened the book and began flipping through it. "Oh!" A loose piece of paper fell out. She unfolded it on the desk. "Sollis, can you come closer? I need the light."

They leaned over to examine the paper. It had a drawing and was covered in symbols and notations in a script none of them recognized. A few markings with question marks were added in pencil, which made little sense.

"Someone wrote 'manual?' at the top. Maybe it's some sort of magic book? Sollis, are you sure this was the magical thing you saw?" Nyelle asked.

"Well, not quite sure—it could have been the book itself. But I suspect it is—the book appears rather ordinary. I have no idea how a piece of paper can be magical though."

Garrett had been scrutinizing the paper. "I bet you it's this right here." He turned it over to them and pointed at the bottom right corner. Someone had spilled some ink, covering a paragraph of the strange script. "Sollis, can you turn off your light for a moment?"

"Sure." She moved her fingers, and the room fell into darkness. They could hear Garrett hop off the chair, and a second later, a tiny sliver of moonlight came through the window as he pulled aside the curtain.

A few moments passed as their eyes adjusted.

"There! Do you see it?" Garrett exclaimed. The page emitted a faint aura. "See? It's magic paint! Just like the box in the wagon!"

"It certainly seems to be the proof we need. We'll take the page with us—we can examine it before we give it to Bradd. Lormek, you okay?" Nyelle turned her head toward Lormek, who had moved to stand in front of the other bookshelf.

"I know this woman . . ." He reached his hand and pulled something off the shelf.

The sound of a wire snapping resounded through the darkened room.

• • • • •

"Uh oh," said Garrett. "I think we triggered an alarm!"

As if to echo his sentiment, they could hear the faint sound of footsteps.

"Doesn't sound like we have too long before they get here! Can we get out through that window?" Aidan asked.

"Let me check." Garrett climbed up the chair to try the window. "It's locked! Hold on." Pulling something out of his pocket, he started fiddling with the lock. They all waited, their heartbeats sounding heavy in the darkness.

"I think they just got to the hallway," whispered Sollis, who had been listening intently. "We don't have much time left."

"Got it!" Garrett opened the window and peered outside. "Who wants to go first?"

• • • • •

Sollis came last, diving theatrically out of the window before floating gently to the ground. A door slammed above. As they retreated into a narrow alley, Aidan looked back to see a head peering out the window, scanning the courtyard.

Nyelle plumped heavily against a wall and winced in pain. "I hurt my ankle," she grunted. "It hurts a lot. I don't think I can walk on it." Lormek bent to her, put his hands on her ankle, and uttered a short prayer. A white aura enveloped her entire lower leg. After a minute, he shook his head. "You sprained it all right—I took care of that. But you broke your heel, and I can't mend broken bones . . . we should go see my dad."

"First we have to clear out of this area, and quickly," Garrett said.

"They will be searching for us, and while I can explain my own presence, it's going to be much harder for the rest of you . . . especially you, Lormek," he added apologetically.

"I saw enough in that office." Lormek shook his head. "Bigger problem is, Nyelle can't walk, and she won't be easy to carry."

The sounds of running guards were getting closer.

"I'll be okay." Nyelle stood up and took a step forward. She stumbled, grabbing on to Aidan. She groaned.

Lormek guided her hand down on his shoulder as she balanced awkwardly between them. "Aidan and I can support you."

Garrett nodded. "All right. We gotta go. Now! Follow me!"

As they went, Sollis listened remotely, occasionally signaling a stop to let a patrol by. Nyelle projected phantom noises away from them to distract any guards that came too close. After weaving in and out of an endless maze of narrow alleyways, Garrett held up his hand.

They stopped.

"Looks like they have the main shelf entrances and exits covered."

"Didn't you say your family's house is around here? Can we go there?" Aidan asked.

Garrett grimaced. "That would be worse than getting caught. My parents made their feelings clear when I left. They would turn us in and recommend that they make an example out of us. We'd get tossed into the secret prison—if we're lucky and they don't execute us for stealing from them. That guy we just robbed? He would be one of the key people making the decision at the tribunal . . . and let's not forget the murder charge they still need to pin on someone."

"So what now? We can't just stay here . . . even if they don't find us tonight, we'll get caught easily in the daytime."

Garrett spread his hands. "I don't know."

Everyone peered around corners, hoping to locate another escape route.

"Stop staring at me like that, you're creeping me out!" Sollis said suddenly.

"What's going on? And we should keep quiet! While they've stopped searching until the morning, there are still patrols about." Garrett's voice sounded unusually grave.

"He keeps looking at me like he wants to eat me, or . . . or . . . I don't know, but it's freaking me out," Sollis responded in a low voice.

"Who is looking at you like that?" asked Aidan.

"He is!" Sollis pointed at Lormek.

Aidan turned to Lormek. "What's this about, buddy?"

Lormek lowered his eyes. "I just had a thought," he murmured. "I'm sorry."

They could practically hear Sollis's eyes rolling in her head as she whispered, "Yeah, I'm sure you did!"

Aidan and Nyelle exchanged a meaningful glance. "What kind of thought?" he pressed.

Lormek didn't respond.

"Come on man, we can't have this sort of thing going on."

"Well . . ." Lormek cleared his throat. "I thought that . . . maybe if we all, you know, stay really close to each other . . . like really, really close . . . then maybe she can float all of us down to a lower shelf?"

Everyone stared at Lormek as Sollis glared. "I'm really sorry, Sollis, I didn't mean to make you uncomfortable," he whispered in a plaintive tone.

"What? No, wait. That might actually work." Aidan turned to Sollis. "Do you think it might work?"

Sollis sounded defensive as she swiveled her head toward him. "I have no clue. I just barely learned how the effect works. But like with everything else, it's a matter of energy—jumping out the window required very little effort. Cushioning a drop between shelves will require a lot more . . . and then if we add the rest of you . . . maybe I can?"

"Let's at least check our options. Garrett, can you lead us to the edge of the shelf, someplace where the guards won't easily see us?"

"Can a ship fly in Tradebay? Duh, of course I can."

• • • • •

With Garrett as guide, they found themselves standing in a gutter that ended abruptly at a locked wooden grate. Garrett pointed at it. "It's used to funnel rainwater down. Open the grate, and you can jump down to your death. It doesn't happen often, but you wouldn't be the first."

"So . . . you wanna open it?" asked Aidan.

"Actually, it's better if you do it . . . they try to stop people from jumping. The locks are excellent, and trapped too, so if you pick one and fail, it will sound an alarm, and we'll be right at square one, except with nowhere to hide."

"So what can I do?"

"Talk to the wood, man!"

After a moment's thought, Aidan reached out to the grate. Several minutes passed, and then he pulled his hand back. Garrett stared at him. "Everything okay?"

"Yup. Check it out now." Aidan grinned.

Garrett pulled on the grate. It swung open easily, the lock still hanging on the frame behind, untouched. "Cool!" he said, then lay down to peer over the ledge.

"What does it look like?" Nyelle asked.

"A long way down. Looks like our best bet is to aim for Tradebay—the top platform isn't very active this time of the night, and once we land, there's tons of ways to get down to the Shallows." Garrett checked over his shoulder. "It's a few hundred feet. So . . . are we actually doing this?"

"You can probably stay behind and come down the regular way," Aidan said to Garrett.

"What, and miss this? No way!"

They scanned each other, then stared at Sollis, who shrugged and raised her palms. "Won't know until I try."

"Anybody wanna pull out?" Aidan asked. "No? All right. Let's tie ourselves together. Who has the rope?"

• • • • •

A ragtag group of five materialized off the edge of a shelf high up in the middle of the volcano. They fell, their trajectory taking them toward a dark segment of the massive floating dock below. Their fall began to slow. As they decelerated, a couple of small boxes on the dock underneath seemed to move by themselves, pushed aside by an expanding air bubble.

The tallest in the group was holding her hands up in the air, her fingers tracing mysterious symbols, which glowed faintly in a yellowish-blue color before fading away. Her eyes were lit brightly with the same color. Her long hair, shining silver in the moonlight, flew wildly in every direction. Then, only a couple of feet above the ground, her hands froze, her eyes closed, and she said, "It smells nice . . . I think I'll take a nap now."

Gravity took over, and the group crashed onto the platform. One of the women yelped in pain as they hit the floor.

A few seconds later, a wide-brimmed yellow hat floated down and settled beside them.

REVELATIONS
TWO-ONE

"Any changes?" Nyelle asked.

"Nope. Still the same." Aidan sighed, turning from the bed where Sollis was lying. "It's amazing that she was able to do that . . . saved all our asses. I can't imagine what they would have done to us if we got caught."

"No kidding!" Garrett's feet were dangling off the top bunk. "Plus, it was so cool, wasn't it? The way the air moved? I never thought I'd fly, I'll tell you that."

Lormek was downcast. "Yeah, well . . . if it means she dies, I'm not sure it was worth it."

Aidan eyed Nyelle, who signaled back. "Hey, Garrett, looks like the sun is coming up. I know it's early, but do you mind checking if you can arrange some breakfast?"

"Sure thing!" Garrett jumped down, landing on all fours.

Waiting until Garrett left the room, Aidan cleared his throat. "Lormek. We need to talk."

Lormek raised his head in surprise. "Talk? About what?"

Aidan exchanged another glance with Nyelle. Following his gaze, Lormek demanded, "What's going on?"

"Well . . . ," Aidan started uncomfortably, then glanced helplessly at Nyelle.

"We need to talk about you and Sollis," she said.

"Me and Sollis? How so?"

"That's what we want to know."

"What do you mean? Know what? There's nothing going on between us."

"For one thing, she said that you were looking at her funny."

"I was just making a suggestion."

"Yes, that's what you said, but clearly not how she felt. And she indicated it's been happening long before then."

"Well, that's unfair, isn't it? Maybe she's wrong? And I apologized immediately."

"Yes, you did. In fact, you said you didn't mean to make her uncomfortable . . . but it was the way you said it . . . why would you say it like that?"

Lormek didn't answer.

"Nyelle, we need to tell him," Aidan said in a low voice.

"Tell me what?"

"What we saw," Nyelle responded.

"What you . . . saw?"

"Yes. Back when we made camp after the bridge. Aidan was standing watch when it happened, and he woke me up."

Lormek's eyes darted back and forth between the other two.

"You were sleeping, but Lormek, you had this aura that came off you. It looked like you, only sort of ethereal. Then it moved over to Sollis and . . . well, I'm not sure how to describe it, but you—or the ethereal you—touched her chest and then . . . well . . . entered her," Nyelle concluded and glanced back at Aidan.

"Huh?" Lormek sounded genuinely surprised.

Aidan answered, "Yes. Like . . . your hand reached out to her breasts and then your whole body sort of dissipated into hers as she was sleeping. It was strange . . . creepy, honestly."

"Why didn't you wake me up?"

"Because the aura was magical, and I was afraid it would burn. Now, do you care to explain what you did to her and why?"

A long moment passed, the only sound being the regular breathing coming from the bed. Then Lormek sighed. "I might as well tell you."

"Tell us what?" Nyelle snapped.

"It's not like that. I'm not sure how to explain it, actually."

"Try."

"Well . . . ever since we met outside the inn, and especially after she fell from the Stairway, I've been feeling this weird compulsion . . ."

"Uh-huh."

"No, you don't understand. It's not that kind of compulsion—like, I don't want to . . . fuck her or anything. It's not like that."

"It isn't?" Nyelle sounded skeptical.

"No. It's different . . . like she's a part of me. Like . . . say you lost a limb in a fight or something, right? And then you think you still have it? You know what I mean?"

"A ghost limb, yes," Aidan said. "My dad told me about it when he was teaching me how to hunt, in case it happened to me."

"Right. Well, it's gonna sound crazy, but it's like that. Like she has one of my limbs, and . . . and . . . I have this insane desire to have it back," Lormek concluded in a pained voice.

Aidan sat next to Lormek. "But you have all your limbs, don't you?"

"Of course, yes! That's why this is so confusing . . . I can't make sense of it. But the feeling is so strong . . . I do my best to contain it, but sometimes it just comes out, and I can't stop myself from staring . . ." Lormek's voice quivered.

Aidan put his hands across Lormek's shoulders.

"Taking it at face value for the moment, is it possible that this . . . compulsion . . . could it present itself magically this way?" Nyelle wondered. "I've never heard of anything like it. What does it mean? Why would you think that Sollis had one of your limbs? And which one could it possibly be?"

"I don't know!" Lormek cried and buried his face in his hands.

At that very moment, the door opened. Garrett burst into the room, carrying a big tray of food, and announced, "Who's your daddy?"

INTERLUDE: SOLLIS DREAMS AGAIN

Sollis is sitting in the middle of a room with walls the color of magic. It's not a large room, although it has six walls instead of the customary four. She sits alone on the floor, and a puzzle is lying in front of her.

"How long have I been working on this?" she wonders aloud.

Hours? Days? Maybe decades. It's a special puzzle; right now it shows her face, but she vaguely remembers that there were instructions, and that by inserting the last piece, the image will be transformed into something else. A hugely, massively important clue—to something.

Have I been here before?

She knows, somehow, that her fate hangs in the balance. Maybe the fate of the world too. All she has to do is interpret that final clue.

Sollis is holding the last piece in her hand. She smiles.

The excitement of finally finishing the puzzle that has troubled her for so long makes her vision blur, and she worries that she will not recognize the picture revealed. Rubbing her eyes, she reassures herself that placing the last piece will surely clear up her vision.

It is time.

Her fingers shake slightly, making it difficult to insert the last piece. Eventually, she manages to place it right in the center of the puzzle. Her vision clears and then, just as she knew it would, the image shifts. Three new shapes replace the image of her face. Three people.

She's one of them.

But before she can examine the newly revealed portraits, a sudden gust of wind blows up through cracks in the floor and scrambles the puzzle into a million little pieces.

She realizes that she will have to do it all over again.

• • • • •

They were finishing up their meal when, with no warning, Sollis sat up straight in her bed with a terrifying scream, cut short by a yelp of pain as her forehead banged into the bunk above.

Jumping from his chair, Aidan rushed over and held her hand. "Are you all right?"

Sollis sat on the side of the bed. "I had a nightmare." She rubbed her head. Lormek handed her a glass of water awkwardly. She seemed confused, then took it and sighed. Her eyes scanned the room. "Why didn't you guys wake me up?" she croaked.

"We tried! We were worried you might not wake up at all," Aidan answered.

"I was unconscious?"

Aidan dipped his head. "How are you feeling now?"

Sollis turned to him. "A little groggy, and I have a nasty migraine, but okay otherwise. What happened? All I can remember is trying as hard as I could to slow our fall—it was by far the biggest magic I'd ever done—and then it all went black."

"You got us down safely all right!" Garrett exclaimed. "Crashed down the last few feet but it was the coolest thing I'd ever done! Oh, and Nyelle hurt her foot again when we landed." He gestured at the wooden crutch leaning against Nyelle's chair.

Nyelle stared at him. "'Hurt her foot' when *someone* decided to shift positions at the last second to avoid hurting himself, you mean."

"Well . . . yeah," Garrett admitted sheepishly. "Aidan made her the crutch with his woodvoice," he added by way of explanation.

Sollis drained her cup and stood up slowly. "I'll be all right. It just takes time to recover my magical capacity. Based on past experience . . . every time I push this hard without killing myself, I can do a little more the next time. I get more in tune with the energy . . . like the magic itself trusts me more, recognizes my body as a more reliable vessel."

Nyelle seemed frustrated. "I have something similar with shaping sounds, but after a while, I hit a point where I could no longer push."

"Yeah, maybe I'll hit a limit too. Who knows? From what I know, properly trained wizards also have limits, but they are a lot more effective in using what they have. I just go until I can't anymore." Sollis smiled. "Anyway, what's the plan?"

"We were going to go over that piece of paper we recovered before handing it over to Bradd," Lormek said.

"All right then." Sollis walked over to the table. "Deal me in."

· · · · ·

They examined the page.

"I've never seen anything written so . . . regularly," remarked Nyelle. "It's absolutely fascinating. Other than the words in pencil, which I think were added later, there are no variations in the gaps between symbols or words, no changes in ink pressure, no differences in similar letters across the page . . . assuming the symbols are letters, of course."

"They have to be," Lormek said. "Yeah, it's really odd."

"Maybe they weren't written?" Sollis suggested.

"What do you mean?" Nyelle asked.

"Well, back in that office you asked if I thought it was from a wizarding book, and I'm pretty sure it isn't. But it might have been made with magic."

"You mean the page was written magically? Why would anyone do that?"

"Exactly. And I don't know, but it's certainly possible . . . now that I've seen it, I could try and recreate the effect—say, to copy a book onto a blank one without having to actually write it by hand. It wouldn't even require a lot of energy, just a lot of concentration."

"That's a cool idea, but wouldn't it be a waste of time for a wizard to sit there while a book copied itself?" Garrett wondered.

"I should think so. Look, I'm not saying it's reasonable, only that it's possible," Sollis answered. "And it might prevent mistakes in tran-scribing, if you do it right."

Lormek, who had been peering at the page closely, raised his head. "Who's got that metal hexagon?"

Aidan laid it on the table next to the page. Lormek picked it up, examined it closely, and put it back down.

"There! See those symbols?" Lormek pointed at the drawing in the center. "Compare them to the tiny runes on the side of that thing—they're exactly the same!"

They took turns examining the page and the item. Aidan was last. As he examined the two, he grinned, and to everyone's shock, started folding the paper.

"What are you doing?" Nyelle tried to grab it out of his hands.

"Just give me a moment . . . I think I figured out something . . . there!" Aidan held out the page, folded neatly so only the drawing was visible. "Just imagine a real object like in the drawing—doesn't it look like a fat, flat nail?"

A couple of seconds passed, then Nyelle said hesitantly, "Yes, I think so. It doesn't seem like any nail I'd ever seen—it has grooves, and without a sharp end, how would you hammer it into wood?"

"You're right, it doesn't look like a nail because it isn't, I think." Aidan held the metal bit next to the flat paper tip. "Look at it now. You see? Say you wanted to join two boards, but you also wanted to be able to take them apart later. You would put this weird . . . screw . . . in on one end, and then you would use this item on the other end to secure it. And if you needed to take things apart, it would be easy—just unscrew the two pieces and they come apart." He turned to Lormek. "You said you know construction. What do you think?"

"I think you're right . . . lots of applications for something like this."

"Whoa. That's . . . genius. And now I understand the matching grooves on the inside of the hole piece . . . otherwise the screw won't tighten," Nyelle mused. "I can't imagine any smith skilled enough to create this with such precision, though, especially on the inside of the . . . shall we call it a tightener? Since we think it's used to tighten the weird screw?"

Lormek agreed. "Yeah, tightener is a good name for it. And the screw that isn't really a screw . . . how about a driver? Because you drive it through a hole."

"Right. Driver and tightener. So I totally see how this could be really cool for building stuff, but . . . how would you make sure they fit one another?"

"Magic, perhaps?" Lormek turned to Sollis, who shrugged. "I suppose you could, but I still have no idea what it's made of, and you can't make something out of nothing with magic—so the metal they used is something we've never heard of."

"I know what the runes mean!" Garrett shouted with sudden excitement. "It's for sizing! It has to be! Say you were making these drivers and tighteners to build things, you'd need them in all different sizes, right? You'd need to sort them out so you don't waste tons of time matching them. The runes must represent sizes! As long as the driver and tightener had the same runes on them, you would know they matched! That also means they are numbers, right?"

Everyone stared at Garrett in surprise. Then Aidan spoke. "You know, Garrett, that actually makes a lot of sense. And I like this idea . . . it means you could combine wooden parts in a way that wasn't so violent." He scanned the group. "Look, you guys. We need to report to Bradd and give him this drawing, but I say after we collect our reward, let's book a trip to Corrantha City. I'm sure we can find someone there who could shed more light on this. Plus, I wouldn't mind staying out of town for a bit." He smiled uneasily. "At least until they give up searching for whoever killed the Stormtrooper, you know?"

Garrett started a little dance. "First, we fly, then we're going to Corrantha City! How cool is that?"

CORRANTHA CITY

"What are you looking at?"

They had just crossed Stormbridge, part of a large twelve-wagon caravan, a rarity even on this busy route. Their group was one of several making the journey, and they kept their own small fire within the camp perimeter. The guard captain had just informed them that they would arrive in Corrantha City around midday the next day.

"It's that portrait I got off the shelf at the Popeaide's office," Lormek responded softly to Garrett. Everyone else had already lain down to sleep.

"Right! Damn, in all the excitement, I forgot all about that. Can I see?"

"Sure."

Garrett leaned over and took the small piece of paper.

"I removed the frame. Been carrying the picture with me since then."

"It looks very realistic. I wonder who made it . . . must be really good." Garrett stared at the picture. "I never even knew you could paint like this . . . can I touch it?"

"Yes, sure. I tried it too. Doesn't feel like ink." Lormek handed him the picture. Garrett brushed his finger over it. "Crazy, right?"

"Yeah . . . it's totally flat—nothing to suggest it's a painting, but I've never seen a drawing with this kind of color and detail where the result is so . . . normal . . . without any flourishes. And it's so small! Hell of an artist to have such discipline. I imagine it would take ages to make. It doesn't quite look like a drawing, does it?"

"Right. I'm not sure how it was created, either. It almost appears like it was made in an instant rather than worked on for a long time. Just look at their facial expressions. I figured if any of us would have seen something like this before, it would be you."

"True. And I haven't . . . must have cost a fortune. You know, I think that guy is the Popeaide." Garrett pointed at the picture. "Wait a second . . . I remember now. Didn't you say you knew this woman? Isn't that why you took it in the first place?"

Lormek sighed. "Yes, indeed. I do know her. It was just so shocking to find her there . . . in that place."

"Who is she?"

"Some lady I saved after a really big storm. She was lost in the tunnels."

"Oh, yeah. Growing up, when a big one hit, I remember my parents saying how more people die in the tunnels than out in the storm. They thought of it as part of the economy . . . kept the deep cave monsters fed." Garrett chuckled.

Lormek stared at Garrett for a second. "Well, that was a big one all right. In fact, it was the storm when I got my powers from Thor."

"Really? How cool!"

"Anyway, I was heading back from the beach, and there was the usual chaos. I took a route that most people don't know about, and there she was, about to . . . how did you put it? Play her role in the economy. I took her to the church, and she left the next morning. A few moons later, she sent me the invitation to meet with Bradd. I never even knew her name." Lormek sighed again.

"Wait, she's the one who invited you? How do you know?"

"Had to be her. After that office, I don't think I care anymore."

"She must have something to do with the Guild."

Lormek raised his head, surprised. "You're right! I hadn't thought of that. I wonder if Bradd would know who she was."

"Sounds like he might . . . damn, I can't get over how real it is." Garrett handed the picture back. "All right, I'm turning in." He lay down. "Good night."

"Good night. I'll stay up a bit."

"Okay. Oh, and Lormek . . ." Garrett hesitated. "Thank you for being my friend."

• • • • •

The continent of Corrantha was the biggest landmass in the world. It spanned the globe almost all the way between the poles. Its millions of inhabitants congregated away from the oppressively hot equator, a vast desert that would take weeks and tremendous preparation to cross. South of that desert, even after the temperatures became bearable, the lands were mostly rocky and nearly impossible to cultivate, and so most gentle peoples lived in the northern half.

Corrantha City was the continent's beating heart.

It was positioned a day's ride from the coast, a thousand miles from the North Pole. It was the most beautiful part of Corrantha, with fertile lands and gentle hills, the bread basket of the world. Seen from a great height, the city would look like the center of a web, with trade routes snaking toward other population centers on the continent, and a loosely defined border another thousand miles away to the south, nearer the equator. That border separated the Corranthian gentle peoples—mostly humans, but also elves, dwarves, and gnomes—from the hardy races, primarily orcs and goblins. The gentle and the hardy fought continuously and rarely mixed, and most assumed this had always been the case.

Its ideal location made Corrantha City extremely important. Its ruler was considered to be the King of Corrantha, or at least the important part north of the border. The King—traditionally human—would serve between twenty and thirty years at a time. The city's political system was complicated but ensured that transitions occurred peacefully.

The current King, however, defied tradition. Emmeka was a fierce dwarven woman who, prior to rising up the ranks of government, was an adventurer. Legends of her forays—in the most fantastical of tellings, to worlds beyond this one—were common in the drinking halls of Corrantha City. When she showed up at the city gates some hundred and twenty years ago, she rode a wagon chock-full of gold and jewels and rare artifacts. She spent her wealth freely, impressing many, while she created a merchant company—the Rocky Road—which in only a matter of decades became the leading trading company in Corrantha, and involved herself deeply in city affairs. Her fierceness served her well in complex negotiations, and whispers abounded that, in private, she knew how to temper it to deal with delicate situations. She was strong, skillful, smart, and perhaps most importantly, proved herself to be reliable and trustworthy.

And so, sixty years ago, in a move that sent shock waves throughout the continent, she became the first dwarf ever to be chosen as Corrantha's new King.

• • • • •

"Wow," Aidan said in wonder.

"Takes your breath away, doesn't it?" Garrett said. "I've been here a couple of times, but I was too young to remember much detail. Though even then it left a big impression."

"I wonder what that's about? They're everywhere."

Nyelle was pointing at a sign that read:

SECURE YOUR FUTURE! JOIN A ROCKY ROAD TRADE MISSION. GUARANTEED FOOD AND PAY!

"No clue. My parents talked about local politics when I was growing up . . . plus to be fair, I wasn't paying a whole lot of attention. It was really boring."

They rode along the main street leading from the eastern gates toward the city center. All around them were buildings, as high as four stories tall, and businesses of all kinds. There were people everywhere, a constant stream of conversations and dealings, greetings and arguments.

"Everyone is dressed so nicely," Lormek murmured.

"No kidding. I'm actually feeling self-conscious." Sollis pulled her hat lower on her head. "Like when I had to hide my ears as a kid."

"And to think we were so pleased with ourselves when we bought new outfits for this trip." Nyelle laughed. "I betcha some of these would cost in gold. And the smells . . ." She sniffed loudly. "Damn, I'm getting hungry."

The wagons drew to a halt in a large square. One of the guards turned toward them. "End of the road, folks. Time to disembark. Give the city guards your entry tokens as you head out of the square, and try not to spend everything you have on the first night." He laughed. "You can find cheaper places to stay closer to the walls. We hope you had a pleasant trip."

Pointing at the badge sewn onto his shirt, he added, "Come back here any day at midday to book another journey with one of us."

· · · · ·

They were walking slowly down the street, staying close together.

"Wow, that was incredible." Aidan smacked his lips. "I thought I'd had any kind of meat imaginable, but I've never had anything like that. And those fruit slices they gave us . . . was it called avocado? So good!"

"You can say that again," Nyelle agreed. "I never knew there were places like this—what did they call it?"

"A restaurant," Garrett answered. "Kyber doesn't have any because it's too small, but all the larger trading cities in the mainland have them."

"Well, I like it. Ordering off a menu? How cool was that?"

"Yeah. It was pretty neat, wasn't it?"

"At those prices, it better be," Lormek mumbled. "If all the food here is like that, I'm nervous to find out what a room is going to cost. We could easily run out of money in a fortnight." He shook his head. "I never would have imagined spending a gold in an entire year before, but they had a bottle of wine that cost that much!"

They turned into another street, heading in the general direction of the city walls.

"Oy there! Where are you from?"

From their left, two well-appointed, dark-skinned dwarves were approaching them with a cheerful expression on their faces. They headed toward Lormek, who stood still, his eyes downcast.

"I'm Brontor, of Highhill, and this is Grinta, of Smallstream." The dwarf smiled, extending his hand in greeting. "And you are?"

Confused, Lormek extended his hand carefully. "I'm Lormek, of . . . uh . . . Kyber."

"Kyber? What a strange name." Brontor glanced at Grinta. "Have you heard of it?" She shook her head, and he turned back toward Lormek. "Where is it? Must be in the south. Next to one of the volcanoes? I thought it was mostly gnomes down there."

Lormek's confusion deepened, and he looked helplessly at the others.

Aidan spoke up. "No, Port Kyber, as in the Kyber peninsula. You know, past Stormbridge?"

"Stormbridge . . . Stormbridge. I'm not sure . . . wait, you mean the port city up north? The place where the ships fly?"

Aidan confirmed with a nod.

"I'll be damned, I didn't even know they had clans up there. Grinta, did you know they had a clan up there?"

"No. I didn't think so either. Isn't it all inside a mountain or something?" She examined Lormek. "But you can't possibly be from around here—you have to be from Decentea." Grinta smiled reassuringly. "So where are you from originally?"

Appearing increasingly uncomfortable, Lormek shook his head. "Port Kyber, like I said. Where is Decentea?"

The two dwarves stared at him in astonishment, then roared in laughter. Brontor clapped his hands. "Good one! You must be a Tallclanner! I gotta hear more." He paused. "Tell you what, folks. Looks like you're in a bit of a rough patch . . . so why don't you come on over, drinks will be our treat!" He started trotting toward a three-story inn across the street. Grinta beamed and gestured for them to follow.

Shrugging, the little group went into the inn.

• • • • •

"Nice ale they serve here." Aidan wiped his mouth. He tried to relax into his seat cushion. Its softness made him uneasy. He scanned the room, his senses overwhelmed by the coldness of wood cut in such uniform manner. "Nice place," he repeated as if reassuring himself.

"It's all right," Brontor replied. "Not fancy, but we like staying here."

"So who are you again?"

Brontor smiled. "We're here on a trade mission. Spent a month in Robbana, then came up here. Our clans are finally starting to trust the Promise."

"The what?"

"The Promise? From Emmeka? The Emmeka Promise?"

"Who?"

Brontor turned to Grinta and raised his palms helplessly. She enunciated carefully and slowly as if speaking to a child, "King Emmeka of Corrantha. The ruler of the continent?"

Aidan blushed. "I'm sorry, I really don't know."

"Where did you say you were from again?" Grinta asked. "Okay. Corrantha City is the seat of the King . . . you know that at least?"

Aidan dipped his head slightly.

"For some reason, several decades ago when the old King retired, they put a dwarf on the throne. Well, it's really just a seat at the head of a long table, but anyway. Never happened before. Shocked everyone to the core, but I will say, it seems like it's been working out well for everyone." She grinned and winked.

"One of the things she did was promise to strengthen ties with Decentea through trade and security. It's something every King says, but she proclaimed it as law and has been doing it for real. Helps that she has our lifespan . . . anyway, her name is Emmeka, and she's a Decentean like us," she concluded.

"How do you know that she's Decentean?"

"Her skin color, silly." Grinta laughed. "All darkskins come from Decentea. He's Decentean too." She pointed at Lormek.

"Huh?" Lormek's face betrayed his surprise. "No way. I'm from Kyber, I told you."

"You think you were born in Corrantha?" It was Grinta's turn to sound surprised.

"Where else would I be from?"

"That's ridiculous. Did you see the people on the street? And just look around you"—she spread her hands at the other patrons—"the locals are all fair-skinned. All the darkskins come from Decentea. We're the descendants of the sun, right? Decentea?"

Lormek stayed silent.

"Look, who were your parents?"

"Uh . . . well, my dad runs a church back home, and my mom's dead."

"You have a church of Thor in, umm, Kyber?" Grinta stared at the holy symbol on his chest.

"No, a church of Freyg." Lormek twitched uncomfortably. "I just . . . ended up this way."

"Well, that wouldn't shock me at all." At that, she grinned and pulled out from her pocket a small symbol of Thor on a silver chain. "He's pretty popular back home, right, Brontor?" Brontor agreed. "But finding a Decentean family out here . . . that's really unusual."

Lormek took a deep breath. "Well . . . my dad . . . he's, uh, human."

Grinta raised her eyebrow.

"He, uh, adopted me when I was a kid."

"Mhm. And your mom?"

"I never . . ." Lormek paused. "I never had a mother."

"Well, that's downright silly. Of course you had a mother, and your parents were Decentean . . . did your father tell you where he got you from?"

"We never really talked about it, no." Lormek sounded increasingly miserable.

"Well, do you remember anything from your childhood? Before you were adopted? Any places? Even a fragment of memory will help. We can probably figure it out."

Lormek's eyes were rooted to the tabletop, and he was trembling. "I . . . well . . . no, I don't. I don't remember anything at all."

"Huh. Well, looking at you, I'd say you were from the north." Grinta turned to Brontor. "What do you think?"

"Gotta be." Brontor raised his arms. "Lowlanders like us are fairer, and your build is stockier. Thing is, the northern clans don't get out much—Emmeka has been trying to pull them into the trade network for a while now. It's a big part of the Promise. I wonder how you ended up out here."

Lormek said nothing.

"Well, that's fun! I wonder what else we're going to find out!" Garrett stood up on his chair and started waving his empty glass. "Hullo there! Can I have a refill?"

• • • • •

"That sure was a stroke of luck, wasn't it?" Nyelle took off her boots as soon as they got into their small room. "Oh, that feels good." She sighed in satisfaction as she wriggled her toes.

"You can say that again. Seems like we have a lot to learn." Aidan plunked down on a cot. "Three weeks for an interview to make a petition for an audience with a scribe? We never could have waited that long."

"Not without finding a source of income," Lormek said. "And this is a cheap place!"

"Yes. But I think, between me and Garrett, we could have figured it out." Sollis smiled at the gnome, who beamed up at her. "There are so many business conversations going on here all at once."

"I'm sure I could scare up a hat full of silver playing downstairs." Nyelle lay down on one of the two beds. "Still, sounds like it would have taken a long time to make any progress, so thank the gods for those two agreeing to help introduce us." She turned on her elbow to address Lormek, who was staring out the window. "You okay, buddy? We're relying on you tomorrow."

Lormek turned around to her. "Yeah, I'll be all right. Just a bit of a shock to the system . . . you understand."

"Sure I do. But it does explain a lot, doesn't it?"

"It makes sense, yes. Thing is . . . I never admitted this to anyone in my entire life before . . ." Lormek took a deep breath. "I really don't remember anything before my father took me in. I wasn't just being cautious."

"Nothing?"

"Nothing at all. Not a single moment. Not even fuzzy. A complete and total blank." Lormek moved over and sat down at the edge of the bed. "So . . . if they're right and I came from . . . Decentea . . . then who are my parents? Which clan did I come from? And . . . why did they desert me? They said the northern clans are insular and very loyal, so why would they leave me like that? How bad must I have been as a child? I have never felt as worthless as I do right now," he ended, his voice breaking.

Nyelle touched Lormek's back. "Don't say that, Lormek. I'm sure there was a good reason, and it wasn't because you're worthless. You certainly matter to us, right guys?"

They murmured their assent, except for Sollis, who stayed silent as she considered the question. Then, as everybody started moving about in preparation for sleep, she nodded slightly, but nobody seemed to notice.

NUT AND BOLTS

"Yes?" The clerk, a middle-aged human with a neatly trimmed beard and bushy eyebrows, raised his eyes from his paperwork.

"Oh, uh . . . hi. I'm Lormek. From Port Kyber." Lormek tentatively stepped into the small office. "The guards told me to speak with you."

"Then speak."

"Uh . . . I came here to get an audience."

"Lots of people want audiences. Is this your first interview? I haven't seen a Lormek mentioned anywhere." The clerk examined an appointment book. "No Lormek. How did you even get in here?" His palm hovered above a bell on his desk.

"Right." Lormek cleared his throat, then squared his shoulders. "Brontor from the lowland delegation sent me here. I guess they haven't had a chance to update the list."

The clerk pulled his hand into his lap. "Yes, I know Brontor." He scanned Lormek up and down for a moment. "Are you from his tribe?"

Lormek found the clerk's look extremely disconcerting. "No, uh . . . I'm from Port Kyber."

"Right, you did say that . . ." The clerk leaned back in his chair. "You just look so much like the rest of 'em from over there . . . got me confused. Then again, lots of you around these days, isn't it so? Bound to be some in all kinds of places."

Lormek felt his face flushing.

"So what does a Decentean dwarf from Kyber come to me for? I don't handle trade stuff. Surely Brontor told you that."

Lormek swallowed. "Yes, he did. Umm . . . I'm seeking an audience with a scribe."

"A scribe?"

"Yes. We . . . that is, I have something that nobody knows anything about. Something I found. I thought that maybe your scribes would be able to help figure out what it is."

The clerk raised his eyebrow. "Oh? And you traveled all the way out here? It's not a cheap outing . . . it must be very important to you."

Lormek's body stiffened.

"Well, our scribes are pretty busy, as you can imagine." The clerk leaned over to pull out a notebook and opened it. "Let's see . . . I can probably set you up for something in, say, six weeks?" He glanced up, watching Lormek's reaction.

Lormek shuffled his feet. "We . . . er, I don't have that kind of time, sir. I was wondering if I could see someone more urgently."

The clerk closed the notebook and leaned forward. "Lots of people say their business is urgent, but you seem both sincere and uncomfortable. Your clothes tell me you spent what must have been, for you, an enormous sum to get here. And you keep referring to yourself in the plural. So, Lormeks of Kyber . . . what is so urgent?"

Lormek closed his eyes and took a deep breath. Exhaling slowly, he reached into an inner pocket and brought out the tightener. He put it on the desk and smiled uneasily.

The clerk picked it up, turning it this way and that as he examined it. "Interesting. Never seen anything like it before. What is it for? What's it made of? And who's we?"

"No idea. That's why I seek an audience," Lormek answered more confidently. "And you're right, I'm not here by myself. My group would all love to attend an audience if we could, but I'm the one making the petition."

"Indeed." The clerk laid the tightener down on the table and gestured for Lormek to retrieve it. "You don't want a scribe; you want an adept, someone who might know the purpose of this. And in that case, you're in luck because very few people seek an audience with adepts. Let me see . . ." He grabbed another notebook and flipped through it. "Yes, I can set you up with someone this afternoon. Would that work?"

Lormek nodded, relieved.

"All right then." The clerk scribbled something on a piece of paper and folded it into a small envelope, to which he applied the royal seal. "Ask at the front gate for directions to the Royal College and go there midafternoon. Give this to the guards there."

The clerk rose from his seat to hand the envelope to Lormek, then ushered him out of the room. Just as Lormek was leaving, the clerk spoke again, chuckling. "Oh, and Lormek . . . tell your father Frent sends his regards, will you? And you can bring one of your friends later if you like . . . maybe the elf girl?" As Lormek froze, Frent laughed and closed the door behind him.

• • • • •

"So he actually knew you?" Nyelle asked.

She and Lormek were approaching the Royal College. They walked down a wide path, surrounded on both sides by evenly spaced trees and well-manicured flower beds. Lormek found the effect to be calming, even inspiring.

He drew in air deeply. "Yeah, but he didn't let me know until the moment I left."

"Any idea how?"

"None. My dad has plenty of visitors, of course, but they are usually from the higher shelves. I think I'd have remembered somebody like him." Lormek hesitated. "Still, ever since I left, I can't shake the feeling I do know him—something about the way he laughed."

"One more mystery to add to the pile then."

They reached the college gate. A richly appointed sentry stepped out and greeted them in a formal tone: "State your business."

"Right. We have an appointment with an adept." Lormek handed over the envelope. The guard gestured toward a bench just inside the gate as he walked back into his booth. They sat down, admiring the huge courtyard and the massive building looming behind it. You could count three stories of its unusually tall windows, but it might well have been six, and its watchtowers extended even higher. *Tall enough to reach another shelf,* Nyelle thought, *at least!* The top of each tower had a large round chamber surrounded by a narrow walk, and people were leaning against the parapets in conversation, smoking.

A few moments later, a gnome wearing a blue robe emerged from the building and walked briskly toward them, gesturing for them to stay seated. "Makes it easier to have a conversation at eye level." She winked, her blue hair and childlike face making the statement seem whimsical.

"Not with me, it isn't." Lormek laughed. He jumped down from the bench and bowed slightly. "I'm Lormek and this is Nyelle."

"Charmed. I'm Xephyna. Frent mentioned last night that you might be coming by. Wanna go into my study and show me what you have?" The gnome turned around and started to walk back.

"Wait, did you say last night?" Nyelle asked, but Xephyna was already halfway to the building and didn't answer.

· · · · ·

"I don't get many visitors," Xephyna said apologetically as she cleared up a corner of the extremely low table that filled the center of the room, moving books, papers, and various items into boxes and onto chairs. The table did not have any legs but was suspended from chains set into the ceiling. Xephyna pushed a lever mounted into the wall. With a series of clicking noises, the table slowly rose. She pulled back on the lever, and the table halted a couple of feet higher. Xephyna dragged a low bench to the newly raised surface, climbed on it, and smiled expectantly.

Lormek placed down the tightener and stepped back. Xephyna bent over to examine it closely with a magnifying glass she grabbed from a nearby pile.

"Ooohhhh . . . now that is unusual."

"Yes," Lormek said. "We think we know what it's used for."

Xephyna was examining the runes closely. "And what would that be?"

Lormek exchanged a glance with Nyelle. "Construction."

"Mhm," Xephyna murmured. She laid the tightener back down and looked at him.

"We . . . uh . . . we found a drawing of something that might fit inside of it, and we think they are used to fasten two pieces of wood without having to nail them together. We call them driver and tightener."

"Can I see the drawing?"

"No, we had to turn it over to . . . er . . . to our boss."

Xephyna cocked her head. "Fascinating." She jumped off the bench and went over to a set of drawers. Opening one of them, she pulled something out, then hopped back on the bench and set down a grooved metal object.

Nyelle gasped. "It looks just like the drawing!"

Xephyna picked up both pieces and twisted one into the other with a bit of effort. They fit. "They are called nuts and bolts. The piece you brought is a nut."

She beamed at them.

"It's a really new technology. Your observation is correct; they are used to adjoin wood and other materials so they can be separated later without having to break them. We are still testing them out. However . . ." She gestured for Lormek, who had been staring at the pieces, to pick them up. He twisted them free and then put them back together before handing them to Nyelle who copied his actions with a face full of wonder.

"The bolt is made of iron," Xephyna continued. "Your piece, though . . . it's made of something else entirely." She held out her hand, and Lormek handed her the bits. She took them apart and held up the bolt.

"This one is really well made—I crafted it myself, and it's our best so far, but it still isn't anywhere near as perfect as this nut. That's why they don't fit seamlessly—I wish I could create grooves like this, but I can't. *No one* can."

"Maybe it's magic?" Nyelle asked.

"Maybe. I doubt it. A wizard would have to spend a fair bit of time to figure out how to make something like this, and it's not the kind of thing they normally do—not to mention that nuts and bolts are a new invention. Only a few of us here at the college even know about them. At least, that's what I thought. And that material . . . you said you come from Port Kyber, right? Where did you find this?"

"It's a long story. Do you know what the runes say? We thought it might be an indication of size, so you can tell which, uh, bolt"— Lormek felt the new word with his tongue—"fits with which nut. But we've never seen this language before."

"That's likely correct," Xephyna agreed. "I know that language, but let me ask you something first—the drawing you had—did it have some of those runes too? Could you read anything on it at all?"

"Yes to both," Nyelle answered.

Xephyna looked at Nyelle patiently.

"It had some of these runes next to the drawing of the bolt in the center, and someone had written the word 'manual' at the top." Nyelle thought for a second. "But it was added on in pencil—the page itself was written in a very fine script, extremely regular, like no book any of us had ever seen. No deviations at all. Every letter appeared identical to any similar letter. That's why we thought it might be magical—like a page from a wizarding manual or something."

"Logical conclusion . . . especially if you've never seen a wizarding book before." Xephyna chuckled. "But no. The word 'manual' refers to it being an instruction book—around here, adepts create these to allow us to understand each other's work. It sounds like your page was from a book like that, but not one of ours. Hold on a sec . . ."

She jumped off the bench to retrieve a scroll case. She pulled a couple of scrolls from it and unrolled them on the table, pointing. "Like this?"

Nyelle and Lormek leaned over, then stood up and nodded their heads.

"Interesting . . . very interesting," Xephyna said.

"From all I can tell, it's the same script. What is it then? Do they speak it in . . . uh . . . Decentea? Is that where it's from?" Nyelle asked.

Xephyna shook her head. "Oh no. We're a lot more . . . civilized than they are over in Decentea. No. The runes are numbers, and the script itself is written in a language that is from another world entirely."

Nyelle's voice betrayed her amazement. "Another . . . world?"

"Yes." Xephyna nodded vigorously. "We don't know much about it, but for well over a century, we've collected a small assortment of bits and pieces that must have come from it. The nut you brought is made from a metal which we believe is called 'steel.' We have a couple of other steel pieces under guard in the royal treasury."

She picked up the nut again, twisting it in her palm reflectively. "The material is much stronger than anything we know how to make. We think it's still primarily made of iron, but we have no idea how to turn iron into this. Its load-bearing capabilities are so much better than anything we know of—even the huge jade and diamond rein-forcements in Stormbridge."

Xephyna stopped, considering something, then spoke up again. "Most of these pieces have been smuggled out of Port Kyber."

Nyelle and Lormek looked at her in confusion.

Xephyna's tone betrayed her surprise. "You've never considered all the strange things about Kyber?"

Lormek shuffled his feet. "Well, uh . . . not really?"

Nyelle piped in. "I suppose the flying ships are weird?"

"Just the ships? What about the shelf system? What do you think is holding it all up? And the volcano—you realize it's active, right?"

Lormek stared at her. "I thought it was, you know, magic?"

Xephyna laughed. "That would be some magic. Sure, you can place wards on stone to make it stronger, although those shelves would require a lot of wizards and a ton of magic. Even then, no magic anybody knows of can save you from melting in the middle of an erupting volcano . . . you do know that it's erupted at least three times in as many centuries, right?"

They shook their heads.

"Surely you must. The lowest shelf—the Shallows, right?"

They nodded.

"It has been taken by flame every single time. The last one wasn't more than twenty years ago. The two of you must have been alive then."

"You mean the big fire? I lost my mom in that one," Nyelle whispered, her eyes glistening. "But I always thought the volcano didn't actually erupt."

"Yes," Lormek said. "Everybody knows the mountain was just releasing some steam . . . my dad says we should be grateful for it because an actual eruption would wipe everything out."

Xephyna was amused. "Oh, it erupted all right. Or it should have, anyway. The lava went out into the ocean instead and created a whole fresh supply of those crazy rocks, you know, the ones floating around and flying in the stone storms. We felt the tremor all the way out here in the capital. We don't know why it happens this way. I was around for the previous one too. Stormbridge is the only reason the peninsula stays attached to the continent . . . it gets pretty violent out there—especially at the chasm—when the volcano erupts."

Nyelle and Lormek looked at her helplessly.

"All right, you two. I'm not going to press you anymore about how you got hold of the nut, but I'm going to keep it—if you want to see it, you can always come visit me, but it's no use to you, and it's definitely of use to my research. Don't worry, you will be amply rewarded—take this." Xephyna handed them an official-looking slip of heavy parchment. "The treasury office near the town center will give you a hundred gold for it."

Nyelle gasped. "One hundred . . . gold?"

"Yes. I know it's not very much, but it's the most I'm authorized to pay for rare finds like this one. Is it enough?"

They nodded, dumbfounded.

"Super!" Xephyna picked up the nut and jumped off the bench. "Now if you'll excuse me, I have a lot of work to do. Can you see yourselves out?"

They turned to leave, but then Nyelle stopped. "Wait. What about the runes? You never told us what language they were."

"Oh, right." Xephyna turned her head and grinned. "We believe it's called English."

GONE GHOST

Nyelle and Lormek walked in stunned silence.

Lormek kept thinking back to his upbringing. Brontor and Grinta were right—he was born somewhere in Decentea. The evidence was all around him. But why couldn't he recall anything from his childhood there? Was he truly so young that it was beyond his memories? What happened to his birth family? He had absorbed enough the previous day to know that Decentean dwarves did not easily give up on their kin. Did his whole family die? How did he end up in Kyber? Grinta had explained that the Tallclans of the north never sailed, believing that large bodies of water were divine warnings that should be heeded closely. Frustratingly, something else was nagging at him. He felt it was important, yet no matter how hard he tried, he could not figure out what it was. Worse, every time he tried to concentrate and bring it forward, his discomfort grew, and he ultimately found himself thinking about Sollis. She was becoming an obsession; it made him uneasy. He couldn't wait to speak to his father about it.

To Nyelle's efficient mind, there were too many coincidences in the stories they'd been told. She thought back to their introduction to Bradd and his story about recruiting them for their special gifts. She wasn't sure if she believed him anymore. For one, Bradd didn't seem particularly interested in the page they gave him, the one with the magic paint. It spoke of the conspiracy and the Popeaide's involvement, and for all she could tell, it was their combination of unique skills that had allowed them to pull off the heist. Yet Bradd shrugged it off, and when they told him they were traveling to Corrantha City, he seemed relieved. Also, somehow, people in the city were clearly expecting them to arrive. Didn't Xephyna mention she was told they were coming last night? But Lormek only visited the clerk this morning. The adept's comments about the nut being from another world and the strangeness of Kyber stuck with Nyelle too, as did the memory of Lormek's disembodied figure accosting Sollis. Something was off, and she was determined to find out what it was.

The bored sentry who exchanged the parchment for two small bars of gold embossed with Emmeka's profile—the preferred form of payment, apparently, for that amount—didn't even look up at them. As soon as he paid her, he hung a CLOSED sign in the window.

Nyelle held the gold bars in her hand in disbelief. The amount of wealth they represented was so vast that she could scarcely imagine it. She reminded herself that it was not unusual in this place and closed her eyes for a moment before turning to Lormek.

He was standing there, shaking slightly, his face drained of color. "Lormek?"

His eyes rolled into the back of his head, and he tumbled to the ground.

• • • • •

"Here . . . drink this." Nyelle offered Lormek a steaming cup.

Shaking, he raised it to his lips and took a sip. "What is this?" He made a face.

"An herbal tea my mom taught me how to make. I collected the herbs on our way here, so it's fresh. It will settle your stomach. Now tell me—what's wrong?"

They were sitting at a corner table in the inn where they had met Brontor and Grinta. The bar was starting to fill up as patrons slowly came in at the end of their day's business. Lormek took another sip and winced. "I hope you're right . . . it tastes awful!"

Nyelle pushed a plate with buttered bread toward him. "Eat something. Are you sick? You are very pale."

Lormek shook his head. "Not sick, no, or at least I don't think so."

"So what happened to you? You pretty much fainted outside the office with no warning."

Lormek took a bite of bread and chewed slowly. "It's hard to explain," he said finally.

"Everything is hard to explain with you. We've been through enough together that I've come to expect it."

"All right. But promise you won't get mad."

Nyelle raised her eyebrow.

"It's about . . . well, it's about Sollis. I felt like . . ." He paused and took a deep breath. "I felt like she was gone."

"Gone?"

"Yes. You know how I told you about her being like a . . . ghost limb?"

Nyelle cautiously tilted her head.

"Well, it felt like I lost her. It. The limb. Like . . . whatever piece of me she represents disappeared."

Nyelle sat back and stared at him. "Are you telling me that you can sense her from a distance?" she asked, measuring her words.

Lormek lowered his eyes. "Yes," he mumbled. "I think I can."

"Wow. Things just got a whole lot creepier," Nyelle murmured. "Anything else?"

"No. But . . . Nyelle, she still feels gone," Lormek said weakly.

"Wait, what? They are all back in our room waiting for us . . . or are you saying she's not?"

It was Lormek's turn to nod.

"Well, then we have to go and find out immediately!" Nyelle placed a couple of coins on the table and strode outside, while Lormek took a last sip of her tea.

"Tastes just awful," he muttered, then shoved a piece of bread in his mouth and followed in her footsteps.

• • • • •

Nyelle and Lormek were stopped short by the proprietor, a short and stocky human only a few inches taller than Lormek. "You better be leaving now."

"We would like to go to our room, please," Nyelle said, then added, "We did pay for three nights in advance."

"That won't begin to cover the restoration costs," the proprietor growled as he signaled to the two bouncers who were overlooking the main bar area. They approached warily, their hands resting on the hilts of their shortswords.

"Restoration costs?"

"That friend of yours . . . the tall one. Almost burned down the whole building. If I'd known she was a wizard, I wouldn't have let you in at all. Too many accidents when wizards get tipsy." The proprietor eyed Nyelle. "So you better leave. There's nothing left here for you."

Nyelle glanced at Lormek in surprise, then turned back to the proprietor.

"What about our friends then?"

"Gone. Taken. The guards that took them came prepared, but I think one of them died in the explosion."

"Guards? Explosion?" Nyelle was incredulous.

"Yeah. Not local either, though the arrest seal was issued here. Said they were from Kyber."

Nyelle exchanged another look with Lormek, then reached into her bag.

The bouncers backed into fighting stances, half-drawing their swords.

Nyelle smiled at them, keeping her posture relaxed. "We'd really like to see the room if we can. Maybe we can find a clue we can use to find our friends. What's the total damage?"

"I'd estimate twelve gold to fix everything up." The proprietor scanned her up and down. "Unless you just sold a crate of Robban cigarettes, I can't imagine you'll cover it."

Nyelle pulled out a gold bar. "Can you make change?"

• • • • •

"Holy . . . shit," Nyelle muttered.

Their room appeared like a piece of meat that had only been cooked on one side. The floor, walls, and ceiling next to the door were darkened as if charred over an open flame. The other half of the room was untouched. The scorch marks ended abruptly at an invisible line separating the two halves, and debris from the shattered bunks spoke of a struggle.

Lormek moved his hands carefully over the wall. "They aren't quite burned. Sollis must have used one of her shockwaves." He rubbed hard on a spot. "Yes, it wipes off."

"Didn't the owner say somebody died?"

"He did, but I'm not sure how much he actually knew. She told us she can knock people back pretty good with those shockwaves, but it shouldn't kill them outright."

"Unless they get smashed against something." Nyelle knelt by the wall, examining what was left of the beds. "Look at this. These beds were broken by something shoved into them with a lot of force . . . or someone."

Lormek walked over and knelt next to Nyelle. He picked up a large splinter and turned it slowly in his hand. "Damn. It's covered in blood. So what do you think happened afterward?"

Nyelle stood up. "You said you felt like she was suddenly gone, right? How much gone? Like dead, or something else?"

Lormek thought for a moment. "No, or at least I don't think so . . . more like cut off. From me. Cut off from me." He inhaled, feeling his cheeks getting warm.

"Cut off. Huh. I wonder . . ."

"What?"

"I wonder if they had some way to muzzle her. Like her magic. Didn't the owner say they came prepared? What did he mean by that?"

Lormek stared at her. "I thought he just meant they were ready for a struggle or something. You think it was something else?"

"What if they came in with full knowledge of her powers? And had some way to stop her magic?"

"Couldn't they just tie her up?"

"I'm starting to think that maybe she is a lot more dangerous than any of us realized . . . I mean, just look at this room!" Nyelle gestured around. "If they knew about her, they would bring something to counter her. I know I would."

Lormek spoke softly. "Just like Frent."

"Excuse me?"

"Like Frent. You know, the clerk. At the palace. He knew me, remember? He knew all of us. Seems like all sorts of people know about us."

Nyelle sighed deeply. "Just when I thought the day couldn't get any weirder."

• • • • •

Their investigation complete, they took leave of the inn and its suddenly deferential proprietor. The city shone with the setting sun, painting everything with a reddish glow. "So what do we do now?" Nyelle wondered aloud, as she found herself absentmindedly listening to the faint echoes of their steps. They could hear bits of conversation coming from the buildings around them, as people set-tled in for the evening.

"We need to figure out where they've been taken." Lormek felt weighed down with a deep loss he didn't understand. It was like he was slowly losing his mind, his thoughts constantly distracted by images of Sollis. He cleared his throat. "I guess we could go back to the royal grounds and see if Frent will see us again."

"Not a bad idea." Nyelle sounded distracted.

They heard a loud crack from their left. They both stopped, and Lormek pulled out his dagger, but there was nothing there.

Nyelle chuckled. "I had no idea I could do that."

"Do what?"

"You know how I can shape the sound of my voice or an instru-ment I'm playing?"

Lormek confirmed.

"Well, turns out I can do it with any sound around us . . . that crack was your footstep, amplified and then thrown against that build-ing." She pointed. "I wasn't really doing it intentionally, but my mind has been obsessing over the echoes. Here, check this out."

Nyelle closed her eyes for a few seconds. When she opened them, he heard a child asking his mother for dinner—in the empty air right in front of him.

Lormek jumped.

"See?" Nyelle smiled. "That happened there"—she pointed at the two-story building where the crack had come from—"and I was able to hear the sound, catch it before it died, bring it here, and make it louder."

Lormek looked at her. "Does it mean you can also hear things magically?"

Nyelle shook her head. "No, I don't think so, I just always had good hearing. But this is an interesting thing to learn . . . I never real-ized this was possible with all sounds, not just mine."

"I wonder what else you can do."

"Me too . . . judging by the last few weeks, I have a feeling we'll find out soon enough. Anyway, let's stay at the place we met Brontor and Grinta and see if we can get an urgent audience tomorrow."

INTERLUDE: ANOTHER DREAM FOR LORMEK

What happened to them?

Lormek closes his eyes and tries to focus his mind on prayer, but for the first time in his life, he can't find solace in Thor. His mind keeps slamming against the void, the emptiness that fills him now. It is so vast that, for the first time in his life, it has displaced his shame.

What happened to her?

Now, all he feels is desire.

Nyelle's rhythmic, shallow respiration comes from above. He admires her ability to stay calm through everything that's happened and, as he floats up near the ceiling, smiles in appreciation at her sleeping form.

Oh! There she is!

His eyes shift to Sollis who is suddenly there, hovering next to his motionless body lying in the lower bunk. Relief washes over him. He opens his mouth to greet her, but she can't hear him. Instead, she gazes down at his sleeping body, and he finds himself unable to move from his vantage point above.

It makes him uncomfortable.

Without warning, her eyes shoot two thin rays of magic color at him—the other him, the one on the bed—and it engulfs him. A moment later, he stares in horror at his own corpse, the rotting flesh slowly melting off its bones. It happens slowly at first, then faster and faster until only a gleaming skeleton remains, grinning hideously. And then the skeleton collapses, and the bones turn into dust.

Sollis raises her head to him, smiles, and vanishes.

• • • • •

They were getting ready to leave when a knock sounded on the door. Lormek pulled out his dagger while Nyelle opened the window and stood by it, ready to jump and run.

"Who is it?"

"It's Grinta . . . open up, you guys, it's important!" came the response in a familiar voice.

"Grinta?" Lormek ushered her in. "What are you doing here?"

She glanced at him, then at Nyelle. "Close the window, will you? It's a bit chilly." Grinta sat down. "We guessed you might stay here. Brontor already left, but I stayed behind so I could tell you in person—leave. Go back to Kyber."

"What? Why?"

"You're not safe here." Grinta glanced around. "Where are the others?"

Lormek sat down. "They disappeared yesterday . . . we think they may have been arrested."

Grinta agreed. "That would make sense."

"It would?"

"Yes. Listen, did you ever get your interview scheduled?"

"We did, yes. Thank you very much for setting it up for us." Lormek smiled.

"Huh? You already had it?"

"Yes, we did . . . yesterday, in the afternoon. We thought you made it happen, like you told us."

Grinta stared at him. "We did . . . yesterday . . . during our first break in trade talks, like we told you we would." She stared at Lormek. "You were supposed to go in yesterday around lunch to confirm your appointment for *today*."

"Yes, that's what we thought too, but then I went over, and they just let me in . . . ," Lormek's voice trailed off.

Grinta raised her bushy eyebrows. "I mean, the royal court has been far friendlier toward us since Emmeka, but . . . that's practically unheard of. Who was the clerk you saw?"

"He said his name was Frent."

Grinta sat bolt upright. "You saw *Frent*?!"

TALISMAN

"Okay, you two. That's as far as I go."

The sun was setting, glowing red at its zenith. Kuuri, the little moon, was already climbing, giving off an eerie shade of blue, and the crescent of Anni, the big moon, was starting to show behind it. Nyelle and Lormek rose from the wagon and stepped down to the road. The farmer smiled at them and pointed. "Keep heading that way. If you walk through the night, you should be at Stormbridge by crossing time tomorrow. Just be careful till you get there. They say it's safer on the other side." Lormek smiled at the farmer, who tipped his hat before starting his cart again, heading southward toward the coast.

"I'm not used to being treated so . . . normally." Lormek blushed happily.

"I hear ya. One of your kind on the throne . . . And what a turn of events! Frent being the King's own Pope, then pretending to be a clerk just so he could meet with you . . ." Nyelle shook her head. "We've been going over it for hours, but I'm still utterly baffled by it all."

"Tell me about it." Lormek sighed. "So . . . do you think the Kyber watch is searching for us as well? I mean, I'm glad we could hitch a ride with that fella and avoid the caravans, but I'm wondering how cautious we need to be."

"Honestly, I don't think so, but like we agreed, better safe than sorry. Which means . . . shall we get off the road?"

"Yes," Lormek said. "We probably should. Gonna be a long night."

• • • • •

They only stopped a couple of times for a short rest and generally stuck to fields still in view of the main road. As night fell, they made wide berths around caravan company camps, and now, as dawn broke, they made a similar detour to avoid the camps of caravans heading the other direction, into Corrantha City.

They were going around a large hill in a lightly wooded area away from the tended fields and farms. Entering a large clearing, Nyelle stopped. "We should take another break. My legs are killing me." She yawned.

"Don't do that!" Lormek laughed and promptly proceeded to yawn as well. "Good idea. Plus, all this walking made me hungry."

They sat down on a small mound of dirt. "Don't let me lie down or I swear I'll fall asleep on the spot," Nyelle grunted as she took a swig from her waterskin.

"I don't think you will." Lormek's tone was unexpectedly grave. Nyelle raised her head in surprise, then followed his gaze as he stood up, drawing his dagger.

Entering the clearing was the largest wolf she had ever seen. It was taller than Lormek. Its eyes were strangely intelligent, assessing their movements patiently. Big as it was, its head was almost comically large, and she caught herself chuckling before the cold realization hit her.

They were going to die here.

The wolf moved slowly, deliberately toward them at a bit of an angle. She could swear that the wolf did it on purpose, readying itself to cut off any possible retreat. Then it opened its mouth, its huge fangs gleaming in the rapidly fading moonlight. It flicked its tail once, twice, seemingly in anticipation.

Nyelle was struck by the notion that the wolf was grinning. She unthinkingly grasped her lute, taking comfort in its familiar shape. One of the strings hummed softly as it brushed against her fingers.

The wolf moved closer, monitoring their movements.

Lormek threw his dagger at it. He threw it hard, and the dagger hit squarely in the neck below the creature's ear. Lormek's powerful muscles ensured that it was a devastating, deadly blow, and it would have surely killed the wolf outright—were it a normal wolf.

Instead, they watched in horror as the dagger rebounded harmlessly. The loathsome creature shook its head slightly, and, in the most terrifying manner that Nyelle could imagine, it proceeded to wink at them.

"It has to be a werewolf," Lormek murmured. "Just like Aidan said. I would never have believed it if I hadn't seen it." He paused and turned to Nyelle. "There's nothing we can do. I just want to let you know that I really loved the time we spent together. You are . . . my friend." Then he turned back, sank to his knees, and held the symbol of Thor tightly to his chest, praying in a language she'd never heard before.

The werewolf was taking its time, clearly enjoying the moment.

It took another couple of steps toward them. It was not even twenty feet away now, and she knew that it could cover the distance in a single leap. But it just stood there, twitching its tail.

"It's playing with us," Nyelle whispered in awe, then repeated it much more loudly as if she couldn't believe her own words. "It's playing with us!"

Lormek's prayer became louder. He spoke a series of strange words rapidly and in a rising crescendo. Both she and the wolf stared at him in puzzlement. Then, without warning, lightning shot through the clear sky and struck the huge beast.

Its agonized scream would visit Nyelle's nightmares for years.

The werewolf was thrown back to the edge of the clearing, its fur igniting instantly. Its howls of pain and rage made it clear—this was no longer a game. It rolled on the ground to put out the fire.

"Let's go!" Nyelle screamed, and bolted, but then stopped cold; Lormek was lying motionless on the ground, his hands still clasping his holy symbol tightly.

Her mind in a whirl, Nyelle knelt next to him, crying and shaking him violently. "Don't you die on me, you idiot! You saved my life! You can't die, d'you hear? I . . ." Her vision blurred as tears streamed down her cheeks, and she tried to lift and pull him away, but he was far too heavy. She stood up, trembling and choking on her tears. "How was I supposed to know?" she whispered before turning to run.

The wolf had recovered and was standing right next to her, smoke rising from its body, its fur mostly gone. It opened its mouth with a deep, angry growl.

Game over, she thought.

Reflexively, she grabbed her lute.

She saw what happened next as if she were watching the scene unfolding in front of her from above.

Terrified and half-blinded with tears, Nyelle's fingers moved of their own accord, strumming the lute with urgency. The tune wasn't pleasant; indeed, it was angry, hurtful, a song of blood and battle. As she played, the sound became one that no string instrument could produce—a ferocious, demented, malevolent note. A note of rage. It matched the growl of the werewolf, only a thousand times harsher and more violent.

The wolf leapt.

She sensed the invisible fist expanding from her lute, tearing through the air. Nyelle remembered later that it was eerily quiet as the sound shaped itself into physical form. The fist shattered against the wolf, striking it head-on, and the beast flew back, landing heavily on its charred back. The injured wolf bounced once and yelped in agony before slowly rising to its feet. It scratched at the ground and growled. Nyelle collapsed to her knees, more exhausted than she imagined possible. The lute fell slowly to her side; her head fell to her chest.

Using all her willpower, grunting with the effort, she lifted her head slowly.

Right in front of the werewolf, where its impact had left a small furrow, a white light began to shine. It brightened rapidly. Nyelle squinted, and through the light, she saw the wolf's eyes widen in fear and, she could swear, recognition. Then the light became blinding, and she could no longer see at all.

"Well, then," she heard herself say before she fell over on Lormek.

• • • • •

When they woke up, the clearing was quiet, and the sun shone over the horizon.

"What happened?" Lormek asked. "Aren't we dead?"

"No." Nyelle shook her head and grimaced. "Ow. My head hurts."

"All I remember is praying to Thor really hard . . . then blacking out."

Nyelle stood up awkwardly, her head swimming. "Thor for sure answered your prayer . . . a lightning bolt appeared out of nowhere and struck the werewolf!" She brushed herself off.

"Whoa. Really? I had no idea that would happen. Did the wolf die?" He rose and scanned the clearing.

Nyelle shook her head slowly and winced. "Damn . . . gonna need to keep my face on straight for a while," she muttered. "No, it didn't. These things are tough, aren't they? Anyway"—keeping her head up, she reached down carefully to pick up her lute—"it jumped me."

"It jumped you?" Lormek was incredulous. He stepped in front of her, and she couldn't help but be struck by the genuine concern on his face. "But you're still here. What happened?"

"I . . . I played. A tune. It was ugly. Nasty. Mean. I don't know what it was, but . . . in a way, it worked like the thing I did on the street back in the city . . . but much more powerful. Like . . . like I threw the sound at it." Nyelle sighed.

"You threw the sound at it? And it got hurt?"

"Yeah. It flew back over there." Nyelle pointed toward where the wolf had crashed to the ground. "But I didn't manage to kill it either. So then it got up again and . . ."

"And what?"

"Some strange light came from the ground and scared it away. Then I blacked out."

Lormek walked over and bent down. After a minute of searching in the dirt, he picked something off the ground. He turned it around in his palms. "Gotta be this."

Nyelle walked over. "What is it?"

Lormek showed her a small, plain-looking silver trinket on a chain. It had three tiny heads of a rat, a wolf, and a bear. "What a strange thing," she said. "I wonder if it's one of those rare items that Aidan told us about."

"You mean a talisman?! That would definitely explain it . . . they are pretty magical, aren't they?"

Nyelle nodded and he continued. "We should give it to him when we find him . . . he'll know. He was pretty obsessed with them."

"So how are you feeling then?"

"A little woozy, but otherwise all right. How about you? Can you keep going?"

• • • • •

Jogging most of the way, they reached the bridge right at closing, and with the help of a gold coin, they convinced the Stormtrooper to let them through. They still had to hurry, as the waters were rising fast, already lapping at the ends of Stormbridge's arch.

Walking away afterward, Lormek spoke. "You know, I was half wondering if they were going to arrest us."

"Why?"

"Well, the watch came after the other three, right? And we were working together."

Nyelle paused. "I suppose that's fair, but . . . I've been thinking about it. Garrett was a stowaway and an escaped prisoner. Aidan actually killed one of the Stormtroopers. And Sollis . . . we saw the room . . . even if she wasn't going to be taken in, the explosion she triggered would have led to her arrest. Unless they knew about the office break-in, you and I have done nothing wrong."

"True. Still, seeing as how they knew us back at the palace . . . Nyelle, what happened to our friends? What do we do when we get back? There are so many questions." He sighed heavily.

Nyelle squeezed his shoulder. "That's for sure. Too many!" Then she stopped. "I can't really think about this anymore; I'm totally spent. Why don't we camp for the night?"

"Good idea. I doubt we'll see werewolves on this side of Stormbridge." Lormek smiled and pointed at an area slightly off the path. "Why don't you set up over there? I'll go fetch firewood and some fresh dinner."

As he turned to leave, Nyelle spoke up.

"Hey, 'Mek?" She hesitated. "I'm really glad you're alive."

CHURCH OF TRANQUILITY

They got back to Kyber the following evening, going directly to Tradebay. Even at this hour, the large parking area marking the edge of the floating docks was busy. They made their way to one of the many small offices on the lower platform. A sign indicated it was the headquarters of the Lavaflow Merchant Company.

It belonged to Garrett's family.

The office was quiet, but the door was slightly ajar and light shone through.

They stepped inside.

A young gnome was sitting at a desk, poring over a ledger. As they entered, she said without raising her head, "It's too late, come back tomorrow."

Lormek cleared his throat. "We're here about Garrett." He sounded far more confident than he felt.

The gnome raised her head and examined them. "Garrett?" She narrowed her eyes. She looked like a teenager.

They smiled encouragingly.

A few seconds passed. "You've got the wrong place." She lowered her head back to her work.

Lormek, in a tone so gentle and empathetic that Nyelle could sense its healing power, asked, "Ma'am, your hand is shaking all of a sudden. We're his friends, and we want to find him . . . please, can you help us?"

The gnome didn't respond, but her shoulders started rocking. They waited. After a moment, she raised her head toward them, tears coming down her cheeks, and with her voice breaking, she exclaimed, "They're going to execute my brother!"

• • • • •

Her name was Halleena. Sobbing as she spoke, she explained that her family had learned of Garrett's arrest, subsequent tribunal, and death sentence for being involved in some horrible plot, on that very morning. Even though Garrett was estranged from the family, her parents had tried to appeal the verdict. She told them that Garrett was her older brother, and she missed him dearly after he was tossed out of their home.

Was her parents' appeal likely to succeed? they inquired, but Halleena didn't know. They inquired about Sollis and Aidan, but Halleena knew nothing about them. "Garrett would never murder anyone!" she insisted several times.

They sat with her for a little while, recalling Garrett's quirky sense of humor and how he could always lift the mood and make light of difficult moments. Eventually, she calmed down after Lormek held her, his embrace calming and his voice soothing. Just before they left, she looked up at him, her face filled with wonder. "Are you really his friend?" she asked. When he nodded his assent, she said in a small, childlike voice, "I'm glad."

It was such a tender moment that Nyelle's eyes got blurry.

• • • • •

They decided to make their way to the Steadfast Inn and search for Bradd in the morning.

As they walked into the common room, they were struck by how full and lively it was. Sailors, visiting merchants, and locals exchanging tall tales, making deals, issuing threats. A bard was on stage and Nyelle listened. The bard was skilled, but lacking in confidence, and kept making small mistakes. Worse, she evidently recognized her mistakes, and they frustrated her, which further hurt her performance.

With newfound recognition of her own expanded abilities, Nyelle made the performer's melodies just a bit more dramatic and enchanting, the delivery more meaningful. The bar audience, most of whom were ignoring the music, grew quiet as the enlivened song caught their attention. The bard noticed it too, and Nyelle could see the surprise and delight in her eyes. After a moment she seized on it, feeding on the energy in the room, and her confidence grew. Her performance began to genuinely improve, and in a little while, Nyelle stopped manipulating the sounds and just enjoyed the show. Many more coins were making their way into the bard's hat. *Much better*, she thought and smiled. *She will eat well tonight.*

She also noted to herself with satisfaction that she could now manipulate sound for an entire crowd.

Lormek nudged her elbow. "Enjoying the show?"

Nyelle bobbed her head.

"Did you have anything to do with the song getting better?"

Nyelle winked at him and grinned. "A girl can't spill all her secrets."

"Ha. Well, I have bad news—Treena said the inn is full, no room."

"So what are we going to do?"

"I figured we could go to the church, if you're okay with that." Lormek hesitated. "Plus, I'd love to ask my dad about what Grinta said." He glanced up at her. "He's a good guy. You'll like him, I promise."

"From all I've heard, he sounds like a bloody saint!" Nyelle laughed. "Lead the way, Lormek. I'm honestly curious to meet him."

· · · · ·

Rajiv was in the middle of feeding some thirty homeless. His face lit up when he saw them, but he didn't stop serving until everyone in line had a bowl of soup and a chunk of bread.

Then he turned to them and hugged Lormek deeply and affectionately. Watching from the side, the warm embrace stirred a deep sense of belonging in Nyelle. She didn't have to wait long to satisfy it; after he was done with his son, he offered her his arms, and she found herself assenting sheepishly.

His hug was transcendental. She was instantly comforted, feeling safer and more loved than ever before in her life. She was a little sad when it ended, but then she saw his grin, and it made her happy. She looked at Lormek again, with a new appreciation for his unusual nature. *No wonder he can touch people the way he does*, she thought. *What a blessing to grow up this way.*

Lormek gave his father his own share of their gold and told the tale of their adventures over dinner. Nyelle noticed that he kept the details of the robbery and their meeting with Xephyna vague. Rajiv was focused and present, only rarely asking for minor clarifications. After Lormek concluded, he sat back in his chair.

"Quite a story there, son," he said. He turned to Nyelle. "What about you, young lady? Anything you'd like to add?"

She felt like she would do anything to please him, tell him anything he wanted to know. But her mind was blank, so she just shook her head instead.

Lormek said, "So Dad . . . uh . . . we never talked about this before, but . . . can you tell me where I'm from?"

Rajiv smiled. "Decentea, apparently." He chuckled. "Honestly, son, does it really matter? I found you here, in Kyber."

"Yes, Dad. It does matter. It matters to me now. I need to know."

Rajiv poured himself a bit more ale from the pitcher. "Well, son . . . the truth is, I found you on the little strip of coast by the Gash. There was a big storm, and you know how I sometimes like to go looking for survivors afterward."

Lormek confirmed and glanced at Nyelle. "We've gone together a few times. That's how I came to like the smell of the storm." His hand rose to touch the symbol of Thor on his chest.

Rajiv took a sip. "Indeed," he said. "So after a storm, I went there, and there you were, lying on the beach. A small unconscious child. Certainly not a sight I would have expected to see, especially considering how dwarves are notorious for hating boats." He took a deep breath. "I took it as a sign from Freyg. A test, of sorts. She's rather fond of dwarves, you know. I figured perhaps she wanted to see if I was up to the task. I believed it all the way until . . ."

"Until what?" Nyelle heard herself asking eagerly.

"Until Thor adopted him from me," Rajiv answered and took another sip. There was a slight edge of pain in his voice.

Lormek grabbed his father's hand. "You know I love Freyg, Daddy. Who knows the ways of the gods? Maybe they agreed on it together," he said.

Rajiv laughed. "That's a lot of planning for two gods to do over one little dwarf, don't you think? Anyway, what does it matter? You're my son, and I think you're perfect. So . . . what are you going to do about your missing friends?"

They shrugged. "We have no idea," Lormek said.

"Didn't you say you were working for the Guild now? Surely they could help?"

"Not exactly working for them." Lormek seemed embarrassed.

"No?" Rajiv gestured at the small pile of gold coins on the table. "Tell me again where these came from?"

Lormek blushed and lowered his eyes uncomfortably.

"It's all right, son. You have to find your own way, and in all fairness, your tales of the big city intrigue me."

"Speaking of which . . . how do you know Frent? And more importantly, how does he know 'Mek?" Nyelle piped in.

Rajiv stared at her. "Right, yes. I haven't seen him in a long while. We used to be pretty good friends before he moved to the city. He actually helped me and my Gilda set up the church back in the day. Good man, kind, very devout."

He turned back to Lormek. "Anyway, the year I found you was his last one here—he actually spent some time minding you, son. I'm a little surprised you don't remember him, but in truth, you were deeply traumatized, and it took a while for you to recover—you often behaved like a toddler in the first few months after I brought you home."

Lormek sat up suddenly. "Wait! Frent's Uncle Bee? He looked so different!"

Rajiv laughed. "His name is actually Bernelius Frentenga."

Nyelle raised her eyebrows at the unusual moniker.

"He's heir to the Frentrunner fortune, an important trading company with a seat at the big table. I guess he changed his appearance and is using a nickname. His younger brother Albergino was recently promoted too. He's now first aide to our Pope here in Kyber."

Nyelle and Lormek exchanged a furtive glance.

"What's going on?" Rajiv asked.

"Uh . . . ," Lormek started. "Oh boy," he muttered. "Dad? Will you promise you won't get mad at me?"

Rajiv crossed his hands on the table. "Go on, son," he said in a firm but kind voice.

"Remember the office I told you about? The one where Bradd told us to go look for information? It was the Popeaide's office." Lormek's face was turning increasingly miserable.

Nyelle watched as Rajiv absorbed this bit of news, wondering what would happen next. To her amazement, he started laughing. She glanced at Lormek, who was so startled that she couldn't help but giggle.

"Of all the people in the world . . . my sweet, generous, loving, clueless son goes and robs the one person in this town who's in charge of helping me run this place!" Rajiv raised his glass before draining it. "By Her grace and wisdom, I sure do hope that he never finds out!"

· · · · ·

A few minutes later, as they were getting ready to retire, Lormek spoke up again. "Dad . . . can I show you something?"

"Sure, son. Is it another surprise? I swear, I haven't had such a fun evening in a very long time!" Rajiv responded, grinning.

Lormek pulled a folded piece of paper from inside his tunic. "Dad, do you remember the elven woman we helped last year?"

Rajiv thought for a moment. "I think so. You picked her up on your way back from the beach when you got your calling, right?"

"Yes, her. When we were getting evidence out of the Popeaide's office, I also got this . . . well, I don't know what it is exactly. It's like a painting but doesn't feel like one. It looks extremely real." He handed the picture to his father, who unfolded it. "I think it's her, right? And is that Frent's brother with her? I think it's some sort of family portrait."

Rajiv examined the picture. "Yes, while I haven't met him yet in person, I do believe that's Albergino Frentenga. And this sure does appear to be the lady we hosted. She's probably his wife. Didn't you say earlier that she invited you to the meeting with the Guild?" He handed the paper back to Lormek.

"Can I see?" Nyelle asked. Lormek passed the paper to her, and she unfolded it.

She gasped.

"What's wrong?" Rajiv and Lormek asked in unison.

Nyelle's face was drained of color, and her eyes were full of tears. She opened her mouth, closed it, and swallowed hard. She opened it again, but no words came out. Rajiv leaned forward across the table and held her shaking hand, which seemed to reassure her. She inhaled slowly. "That's my mom," she whispered, almost inaudibly.

Lormek stared in shock. "Your mother is married to Popeaide? Didn't she die in the fire?!"

REVELATIONS
THREE-TWO

I t took several minutes for Nyelle to tell her story. "So that's what happened," she finished. "I never found my mom after that. So many people died that night—do you remember?" Rajiv nodded. "If she lived, there's no way she wouldn't have found me . . ." Her voice broke again. She felt Rajiv squeezing her hand. "Or at least that's what I thought." She smiled ruefully.

"When my boy here found her in the tunnels a few months ago, she was searching for something. Perhaps she was still searching for you?"

"Did she tell you anything?" Nyelle's eyes darted back and forth between father and son.

"No, she spoke very little." Rajiv shook his head. "But after she recovered, she seemed very intent. It was clear that she was trying to find something or someone. Uppers don't come here unless they have a good reason. Anyway, now that you know, you should be able to find her and ask her yourself."

Nyelle shook her head slowly, her lip trembling. "I'm not sure I want to now."

Rajiv smiled. "I understand. Why don't you sleep on it? See how you feel in the morning." He turned to Lormek. "Son, why don't you go and set up an extra bunk? I'll show your friend around the church."

Lormek consented and left the room.

"So . . . does he know?" Rajiv murmured.

"Know what?"

"How you feel about him."

Nyelle could feel her face turning hot. "Uh . . . I . . . what do you mean?" she stammered.

"Funny thing about humans . . . we can be pretty observant. We get more out of our short lives that way." Rajiv winked. Running his fingers through his white hair, he said, "I've been around for a bit, you know. That wasn't hard to figure out."

Nyelle stared at him in wonder.

I wish he was my dad.

"It's all right. But you have to understand—he's very young. Practically still a child. I don't think he fully grasps that I'm not too much longer for this world either. He is dwarven, after all, even if I raised him as my own." He sighed softly. "I sometimes think he assumes I'll live as long as he will . . . in truth, he will be orphaned again, and fairly soon."

"Are you sick?" she asked uncomfortably.

"Oh no, child, not at all." He laughed. "Except with the disease of aging, which we cannot avoid . . ." He stopped and examined her face. "Wait. Why did you react that way?"

"Umm . . ." Nyelle was caught by surprise. "I . . . never told this to anyone . . ." She covered her mouth with her hand. Somehow, in Rajiv's presence, she found it impossible to hold back her terrible secret. The one she'd kept from everyone else in her life.

"Do you wish to tell me?"

She inhaled deeply and let herself feel the warmth of his hand. "I suppose so." She paused and swallowed. "I'm going to die soon too. I'm aging too fast," she blurted out.

"How old are you?" Rajiv asked.

"One hundred and nine."

"Still but a child," he murmured. "But you look older than that, for an elf."

She nodded helplessly. He leaned forward and examined her.

"Perhaps you are not elven?"

Nyelle felt herself jerk with the shock of sudden recognition. He held her hand tightly, and after a moment, she felt the tension slip away.

"Would you like me to find out for sure?" he asked. "I am a diviner. Freyg has given me the ability to see things for what they truly are."

She agreed weakly.

Rajiv raised his hands and let them hover over her shoulders. His lips started moving, and she realized he was praying. In her peripheral vision, she caught a glimpse of a faint golden aura and, glancing downward, saw that it covered his arms. She lost her sense of time as serenity overcame her, and her body relaxed in submission.

"Just as I thought," she heard him say sometime later. Opening her eyes slowly, she saw him sitting upright in his chair. "You are indeed only part elven, part human, and you are therefore aging normally. Indeed, I should say that you appear extremely healthy for your age; you might even live as long as some dwarves."

Nyelle couldn't find her tongue and simply dipped her head.

"The woman in the portrait—your mother—you say she was fully elven?"

"Yes," she replied softly. "No doubt about it."

"Then there is the mystery of who your father was. From our conversation, am I to understand that you never knew him?"

Nyelle shook her head. She was dumbfounded. She scrambled to make sense of her emotions, and her mind worked furiously to reframe the context of her life.

"Did your mother ever tell you anything about him?" Rajiv sat back in his chair, folding his hands in his lap.

This simple question, and Rajiv's gentle manner, brought her back to the present. She thought about it, trying to reach as far back into her childhood as she could. "Not much," she said. "She told me he was a visiting wild elf, someone she fell madly in love with, and he left before she even knew she was carrying me. Now that we're talking about it, I get how silly it sounds because that's not how elves are, but Mom was . . . different. I realize now that she never told me much about him at all. It just didn't really seem to matter, and Yorros—he was my adoptive father—was so nice." She raised her face toward him. "I tried to find my real father—spent a few years but discovered no clues."

Rajiv smiled reassuringly. "I knew Yorros. He was a good man. And it seems to me like you were looking for the wrong person!"

INTERLUDE: LORMEK REMEMBERS

Lormek drifts off to sleep in his old bed, finding the sound of Nyelle's quiet breathing from across the room to be comforting. *It's good to be home.* His mind begins to wander.

He finds himself at the shore. It's a beautiful day, and the beach is quiet. He breathes in deeply and realizes why he is the only one there. A storm is brewing. A big one. It's building quickly.

He loves a good storm.

Lormek stands there, letting the rain pelt him, spreading his arms, laughing loudly like he has done so many times before. But something is different this time.

He is suddenly filled with doubt as the sky darkens and becomes more violent than any he has ever experienced. Suddenly fearful, he tries to run, but his feet seem rooted in the sand. *Thor?* he beseeches weakly, but in his heart, he knows that no god can save him from this. Not even his god.

He looks down and sees his feet buried several inches in the sand, slowly and inexorably sinking further. He can't move. The storm overtakes him. Water pools around him, covering his eyes, filling his mouth and nose, and he cannot see, cannot hear, and cannot breathe anymore.

The last thing he remembers before sitting up in a cold sweat is the feeling of being buried alive under a rising mound of rocks and sand as the storm rages angrily overhead.

And in the storm, he sees the face of Sollis.

• • • • •

After helping Rajiv with his early morning routine, Nyelle and Lormek made their way to the inn. The start-of-day crowd, made of officers from docked merchant ships and fishermen, was already mostly gone.

The brute was at his usual post. He stood up and blocked the path through the back door. "No entry!" he said firmly.

Lormek grinned at him. "Heya, Stinky. We wanna go see Bradd."

"No entry!" Stinky repeated. Then, lowering his voice, he added, "Sorry, guys. Treena said no one through."

Lormek and Nyelle looked at each other in surprise. "Okay, Stinky," Lormek responded. "We understand. We'll come back later." They turned on their heels and went outside.

"What was that all about?" Nyelle wondered.

Lormek shook his head. "No idea. No point in arguing with him, he won't budge."

Nyelle grunted. "So what now? If we can't see Bradd, where can we go? I want to find out more about my mom! And search for our friends too, of course." She smiled uncomfortably.

"How about the library?" Lormek suggested. "Now that you

know your mom is alive, and connected to the Frentenga family, maybe you can find a lead there? They won't let us anywhere near the upper shelves without Garrett or a letter from Bradd."

"I suppose it's worth a shot," Nyelle responded. "I grew up in the old library at our house, and this new one is set up the same, so I know my way around it . . . but I read mostly about music and the bard Zacharias. I didn't bother too much with anything else . . . anyway, at least it will be something to do."

The guard at the library recognized Lormek and moved aside. Then he noticed Nyelle and his face lit up. "You're his daughter!" he exclaimed and pointed at a freshly installed sign behind him:

YORROS LIBRARY

IN MEMORY OF A GREAT MAN

HE TAUGHT US TO READ

Nyelle grinned. "Yeah, it's me. How did you know?"

The guard stepped in after them and pointed to the wall. Nyelle gasped. A family portrait hung there, showing a man, her mother, and a younger version of herself. Underneath it, a plaque read:

YORROS AND WIFE

PERISHED IN THE FIRE

AND DAUGHTER

"Just got put in last week, together with the sign outside," the guard said. "Looks like somebody important up on Two"—he pointed upward with a meaningful face—"decided to care about this place all of a sudden . . . they also sent in a bunch of new stuff."

The guard gestured toward a side room, where they could see two wheeled carts heavily laden with books. "Hasn't been sorted yet," he said apologetically.

"Wow," Lormek said. "That's really great . . . I gotta tell my dad!"

"Your father's Rajiv, ain't he?" the guard asked.

"Yes, I'm his son."

"He was here when it all came. I think he had something to do with it . . ." The guard seemed embarrassed. "I kinda overheard them say that the Popeaide sent this stuff down."

"Can we check it out?" Nyelle asked.

"Of course! Do as you will." The guard bowed to Nyelle and went back outside.

Lormek and Nyelle looked at each other. "I didn't expect this," she said finally. "This portrait . . . I remember sitting for it. I had no idea that it survived the fires."

"Ha. Well, I think we deserve a bit of good news, don't you? Do you need a moment?"

Nyelle shook her head.

"Then I say let's check those piles . . . if they came from Upshelf, who knows what we might find!"

· · · · ·

A couple of hours later, they sat in the middle of the room, surrounded by piles of dusty tomes. "So much useless stuff!" Nyelle sighed. "I guess this was less of an educational endeavor and more of a house cleaning for someone."

"Yeah," Lormek said. "I mean, it might be fascinating if you cared about council business three hundred years ago . . ." He placed a book carefully on one of the piles. "That one goes on and on about one of the caravan companies—which goods they were going to ship for which merchants." He stretched his arms and yawned.

"I gotta take a break." Nyelle stood up. As she did so, she bumped into one of the piles, and books scattered all over the floor. "Oops!" She laughed, then turned to Lormek.

He was holding a small, mostly burnt, thin notebook. Getting up slowly, he looked at her, his face full of care and kindness. She felt goosebumps as he handed it to her. "This fell out when the books toppled. Check it out," he said.

The letters "JOURN" could still be made out across the top. Toward the bottom, somebody had scribbled a name.

It was "YORROS."

Yorros's Journal

Oh, my darling wife! Oh, my beautiful daughter! For fifty years I could not find the courage to tell you the truth, and now, in the anger of the moment, I have lost you forever.

What have I done?

I can only pray that your souls find peace in heaven, while mine rots in hell.

Enrielle, my love, my heart, my soul! When I saw you, I immediately knew; and when I saw your daughter—our daughter—it became a certainty. While you had forgotten the long-ago night in the storm when we first made love, the bond of a father with his firstborn—his only-born!—cannot be denied. But I could not explain this to you, for you were elven and proud, and I was a bastard and a coward. I told myself that if you knew it was I who sired the child, you would surely have left, for that was your nature.

In trepidation, I approached you, offering to adopt her to help convince you of my good intentions. As if she were not mine.

When you accepted my proposal, it was the happiest moment of my life, and the decades that followed were happier still.

Seeing her grow up was my greatest joy, even as I held back seeing her search for a father she thought she never knew. When she started worrying about aging too fast, wondering if she suffered from some strange ailment, it was the hardest battle I ever fought to not speak plainly and explain that, with her father's partly human lineage, she must also have human blood.

And I wanted to scream at her: Nyelle, my daughter, you are not short-lived. You are a bastard, a half-elf, like me!

As you went to slake your thirst for adventure, even though you always kept the details of your travels from me, I knew that you would come back to me. This gave me reason to live like naught else. Raising our daughter while you were gone, I tried to be strict as you instructed. Alas, I could not avoid spoiling her, even knowing that you would rightly be upset with me upon your return. Did you ever find what you were looking for, my love? Did you find the talisman from the war?

Then, as I'd always feared, the moment came when you grew tired of me. Seeing the signs of my age, the vitality of your six hundred years making a mockery of my pitiful hundred-odd. Still, I could not bear to tell you the truth, and in my embarrassment, I screamed at you to leave. When I heard the door slam, I became possessed with terror and shame. It took but an hour to gather my courage to call you back, but by then it was too late. The terrors had begun.

I spent day and night seeking you, Enrielle, my love. You and our precious daughter. But with such devastation as was wrought that night, with so many dead, mounds of bodies and skulls and humanoid ashes, the conclusion was inevitable. You passed away, never knowing the truth. My only daughter died thinking she was sick, and that she never knew her father, when in truth, he was beside her, raising her, for most of her life.

As I sit here, together with the rest of the refugees, and I write this, my heart is broken, and my hand is shaking. I cannot comprehend a life without you or my precious baby girl. That you died in anger because of my lies is unforgivable. But I shall repent later. I will toss myself from the overlook and into the waters below, the only fitting penance for my crime of deception.

• • • • •

After finding Yorros's journal, they fled the dusty tomes for the bar at the Steadfast Inn.

"So your adoptive father was your *actual* father?" Lormek asked in disbelief.

Nyelle set down her wine glass carefully. "Sure as I can be . . . it all fits," she said. "To think that I lived all these years under a cloud . . . Lormek, I was so worried about my illness that in my head, I was already dead!"

"Sounds painful," Lormek said.

Nyelle sighed. "Truth is, it shouldn't have mattered . . . I think, after that horrible night, that it became a bit of an obsession. Like, I lost everything already, you know? What did I have left? And I knew I had this mysterious disease killing me from the inside. It all made a weird kind of sense. I want to live better now!" She grinned at him, then leaned forward and put her hand on his. "You know, Lormek . . . it's okay if you'd like to kiss me. You're old enough."

Lormek was left open-mouthed. The warmth of her hand felt good, but his mind was in a whirl. He felt as if an invisible tentacle was suddenly clawing at his guts, trying to pull them out. Images flooded his vision, first of him in the fighting pits, then as a rotting skeleton under a mound of dirt, then of Sollis looking at him from above. He felt himself dry-heaving.

His hand jerked away, and he opened his eyes. Nyelle was staring at him in horror.

"I . . . I'm sorry . . . ," he mumbled. "I . . . it's not you . . . I like you . . . ," he said and shuddered, his mouth full of the taste of mud and his skin crawling with a million ants.

She jumped up tearfully and ran outside.

Lormek lowered his head in shame. *Just what this Mudder deserves. At least it's all over.*

PRISON RAT

"Psst."

Garrett opened his eyes. The dim light from the hall-way outside glinted off the iron bars driven deeply into the volcanic rock, set with a hinged iron door. He was in what appeared to be a natural cave, seemingly deep underground.

"Psst."

He was lying on a cot. As he sat up, Garrett's hand nudged a small bowl, and he felt a splash of water. He saw a second bowl with a chunk of bread and an apple.

"*Psst!*"

The voice was coming from the back of the cave. "Who is it?" he asked.

"Come over here," the voice said.

He walked over slowly. "I can't see you."

"To your right. Look closer!"

He turned his head. Finally, he saw the outline of a brobdingnagian rat sitting in the shadow. He rubbed his eyes and squinted, but the rat was still there, staring at him patiently.

"What the hell . . . ?" Garrett whispered.

The rat said, "Yes, it's me," then let its tongue hang out.

"How am I talking to you? Wait, I can speak to animals?"

"What? No, silly. Even if you somehow could, animals aren't intelligent enough to hold a conversation. It's more like I'm talking to you," the rat said. "See, when I'm not a rat, I'm a gnome, like you . . . I'm a bit, uh, plump for my species in either form," he added apologetically.

"When you're . . . not a rat?"

"Yes. Name's Karrott, by the way."

"Uh . . . Garrett. Where am I?"

"The Shallows prison. Welcome."

• • • • •

Karrott turned out to be especially charming—for a rat. He explained that he became one as an adult following an encounter with a dire rat in the deep caves of the Inner Shallows. He barely survived it, but not without being bitten. "I always thought it had to be an actual werecreature that bit you, but it turns out that it's the dire ones that carry the disease. Once you change form, the disease dies, because it's no longer needed," he explained.

"What were you doing there?" Garrett asked.

"Research. Trying to understand the mechanism of were-ing, since werecreatures are never born that way. Turns out that exposure to the bite of a direrat, direwolf, or direbear can infect with the disease. It happens rarely—the bite is toxic, and the victim usually dies quickly and becomes a meal, like I should have. But if they survive, then the transformation can occur. That's also why most werecreatures are impossible to talk to—the were-ing increases their intelligence, but they still start off as animals."

"What are you doing here?"

"I found this place when I was wandering around after my initial transformation. It's pretty well hidden, but rats can fit through all sorts of holes." Karrott let his tongue out again, in a gesture Garrett realized was a smile.

"Wait. Didn't you say you were a researcher? Don't you want to tell people about your discovery?"

"I thought so too at first," Karrott admitted. "But when everyone just tries to kill you on sight . . . it's even worse if you say something to them."

"Couldn't you wait for when you were gnome again?"

"Yes, I could. But by then I was captivated by this place, and all the stuff even deeper below, and found that being a rat was pretty useful for my research. Honestly, the threedays when I am, well, old-me . . . they are the worst. Speaking of which, mind if I grab some of that food off your bowl? I need to store it for my next gnome phase, which is coming up pretty soon."

"Help yourself," Garrett responded. "I'm not hungry."

Karrott came into full view. He was very large and solid, but what made him stand apart were his intelligent humanoid eyes and tiny opposable-thumb hands. He grabbed the bread and quickly disappeared into a crevice, reemerging a moment later.

"Excellent," Karrott said. "I'll deal with the apple afterward. Now, you're the first gnome I've ever run across in the prison. Why are you here?"

• • • • •

Last thing Garrett could recall was being taken in front of the Kyber tribunal, where the three of them—he, Aidan, and Sollis— were summarily sentenced to death for their crimes. The serious ones were murder, robbery of a designated city official, and access to restricted knowledge. The latter was clearly in reference to the flying boxes. While the murder and robbery could, on their own, be handled through a sponsor, the last charge was too severe for quiet intervention. They didn't have a sponsor, anyway; the Thieves' Guild did not acknowledge the existence of anyone in their organization by the name of Bradd.

For unauthorized access, the Boxes Guild demanded that they be put to death.

"We were given something to drink, and all three of us passed out. Then I woke up here," Garrett finished.

"I can go look for the other two if you like," Karrott said. "Prisoners don't usually last long here, so there aren't many cells. Can you tell me their names?"

"Aidan and Sollis. You'll recognize Sollis easily because she's really tall and has an anti-magic collar on her." Garrett grimaced. "How long do you think we have?"

"A few days to a couple of weeks at most. The executions don't seem to be on a schedule. Somebody comes in once a day to replace the water and food bowls, and then at some point, I guess they spike the water and grab you while you're out. At least they kill you in your sleep." Karrott bared his ragged incisors in an unnerving attempt at a grin. "I'm being serious. Why are you laughing?"

"Never seen a rat grinning before." Garrett giggled.

"Oh . . . right. I forgot myself for a moment. It's been a while since I spoke to another gnome. So your friend is a wizard?"

"Kinda. More like a talented magical funnel . . . she's good at it but doesn't know what she's doing most of the time. I'd love to know if they're here. Thanks, bud!"

"Fair trade for the food. And anyway, now I'm curious. It's not like wizards are everywhere . . . to find one down here is a treat. Might be useful to my research." Karrott squeezed through the bars and disappeared down the hallway.

• • • • •

"They're here all right," he said when he came back. "The wizard can't talk because of the collar, and her wrists have restraints that restrict finger movement. But she understood me, and I think she was angry."

"How do you know?" Garrett demanded.

"Even with limited mobility, the signaling she used was clear enough. Her eyes also changed color briefly. Do all wizards do that?"

"She's a wildmage, not a wizard, and I have no idea. I think everything about her is unique. What about Aidan?"

"Different story. He didn't talk much. Seemed depressed. Said he was the only one that should be put to death, it wasn't fair to you and the girl. I guess he killed somebody? Anyway, he'll get his wish soon enough." Karrott sat back on his haunches. "He gave me his food too."

Garrett thought for a moment. "You said you found this place when you were in the Inner Shallows. But you had to get in here, right? How?"

"The prison doesn't have a door to the Inner Shallows."

"It doesn't? So how do they come in and out?"

"Oh, right. There's a sort of tube that goes up through the rock and then the water. Looks like it ends up at the bottom of the docks. I once climbed up partially to check it out but didn't want to risk my life by going through the water part," Karrott explained.

"So what do you do when you turn . . . gnome?"

"Oh, there are many natural pathways to get in and out if you're small enough. I don't just stay in the prison, and I make sure to get out while I'm still a rat. There's so much to learn everywhere . . ."

"Okay, so . . . do you think there's a way for us to get out of here before they, you know . . ." Garrett hesitated for a moment. "Before they kill us?"

Karrott cocked his head. "Aren't you criminals?"

"Yes, I suppose we are. But it's not really our fault. We were misled and, I think, played with by people with bigger agendas. Once we were caught, it was convenient to get rid of us." Garrett sighed. "I guess that doesn't make much sense."

Karrott stretched himself up to his full height. He stared at Garrett first with one eye, then the other. "I never really understood all these rules anyway," he admitted. "You can't squeeze through the bars—you're not small enough. Still, there is one way for you to go see your friends . . . but you're not gonna like it."

"Oh?" Garrett leaned forward. "What is it?"

Karrott dropped on all fours and scurried over to a wooden plate on the floor. "You may fit in here."

Garrett lifted the plate, then immediately retched, dropping it. "Eww!"

"Yeah." Karrott bobbed his head. "That's why they have the plate—it blocks the smell."

Holding his nose, Garrett lifted the plate again and peered inside. "It doesn't actually look that bad," he said after a moment. The hole opened to a small tube, roughly a foot in diameter. Water was running slowly through it about a third of the way up.

Karrott pointed. "Yes, see? Because we're so deep underground, they set this up so that water flushes stuff out constantly."

"Why doesn't the water fill it up all the way?" Garrett put down the plate.

"I'm guessing there's a flow gate where it comes in, open only enough that the level stays constant. It's pretty ingenious. A gnome must have designed it," Karrott said with obvious satisfaction. "The more interesting question is where it comes out, but I haven't been able to figure it out yet. Anyway, if you want to see your friends, you're going to have to go in there and push upstream to the next cell. That's where your guy is . . . but . . ."

"But what?"

"Well, the moment you go in, you're going to block the passage and severely restrict the flow. You'll have very little time before the pressure builds. I don't know what will happen then, but I'm sure it won't be pleasant."

"Not to mention that I'll be drinking shit the whole time." Garrett chuckled.

"There's that," Karrott agreed. "Sure you want to do it? I think the executions are pretty swift; I never heard anybody scream."

• • • • •

Garrett jumped into the hole. The water rose to accommodate him. "Here goes nothing!" he said, then lowered himself, letting his legs go downstream. He could feel clumps hitting his back. The water was now rushing around him, moving higher and faster than before.

The stench was nauseating. Garrett took a deep breath and closed his mouth.

He would give the rest of his memories to forget the next minute of his life.

The stream covered his head almost immediately, and he pushed slowly against the increasing pressure. The walls were slick with grime, and even though he wasn't trying to breathe, his biggest challenge quickly became to keep himself from gagging. His nostrils and ears filled with refuse-laden water. He could feel soft films of slime cling to his pores. He kept his eyes shut tightly as he felt his way, seeking the next hole up.

The tunnel was filling up quickly, and he fought the pressure inch by inch.

When his fingers finally found the bottom of the next wooden plate, the tube had filled with sewage. He pushed against it and pulled himself up as quickly as he could.

It was the second time in a short while that he felt like a cork being pulled out of a bottle.

• • • • •

"You made it!" Karrott announced as soon as Garrett opened his eyes. "Well done. I was curious to see what would happen if you didn't."

Garrett inhaled carefully through the corner of his mouth and wiped his face, which improved nothing. He blew out his nose loudly into the open hole and turned his head.

Aidan stood there in shock.

"Oh, hi, Aidan. Thought you could use some company."

"What . . . how?" Aidan blurted.

"Took the smelly route to pay you a visit. Karrott here tells me you're depressed. Figured you'd like a friendly face." Garrett smiled. "Look, Aidan, I've only known you for a short while, but that doesn't sound like the guy who saved my ass at Stormbridge. So . . . wanna figure out how we get outta here?"

• • • • •

Sollis looked dispassionately at the slime-covered Garrett as he emerged from the hole. She was sitting against the wall, her arms at her side, her fingers twitching slightly against the restraints.

He walked over to her, his eyes twinkling. "So what have we here?" He leaned to examine her collar. She winced at the smell. "Yeah, sorry, I'm covered in shit . . . maybe even some of yours," he said as he touched the device. It whirred slightly, and Sollis groaned. "Oops, sorry," he said, then bent down to examine her hands.

He rose up. "Look, Sollis, I don't know anything about magic, but the wrist guards look normal to me. Very well made, and they're locked and trapped, but not, you know, magical. Unlike this thing," he said as he pointed at her neck. "Do you want me to try and undo them? Just, like, blink twice for yes."

She blinked twice.

"Okey dokey," he said.

• • • • •

Several minutes passed as Garrett fiddled carefully with the bindings, swearing several times along the way. Suddenly, his head jerked backward. A tiny needle whizzed by his ear and lodged into the wall behind him. "Well, that took care of that," he said with satisfaction. A few seconds later, he stood up, holding a complex-looking glove in his hand.

"That's one!" he announced.

Sollis slowly brought her hand up, wiggling her fingers. She gestured for Garrett to step back. Karrott ran quickly to the door and slinked through the bars before turning back to watch.

They could see her tracing a faint magical sigil through the air. Then the sigil faded, its energy seemingly sucked into her index finger. She moved it slowly toward her neck. As the memory of the shock-wave flashed through his mind, Garrett involuntarily closed his eyes.

He heard a loud click.

"You okay there, Garrett?"

Garrett opened his eyes. The collar was on the floor next to Sollis, split in half. "Wanna help me with the other glove? I'm afraid I can't do anything to it with magic—it needs a burglar." Sollis's eyes twinkled.

A few moments later, the glove was off, and another needle had struck the wall. "I worked with these kinds of gloves as part of my training." Garrett stood back. "The needles are no joke. In training, they just coat them with an irritant, but normally it's lethal poison." He gestured at the broken collar. "I saw they put that thing on you when they arrested us. Does it stop magic?"

Sollis nodded. "Worse. It stops me from talking or even moving my head too much . . . wizards usually need to say something to do something. A head gesture might also be required. Turns out I can skip those parts for shock magic, just need my hands. I think because it was my first one, it's in my blood. Once you took off that glove, I shocked the collar off. Could have killed me, I suppose."

Garrett hugged her knees. "I'm so glad you're alive," he said.

"Me too, but in the name of the gods, move away. You stink!" she responded.

Garrett stepped back. "Yeah, I do." He giggled. "Listen, can you use that same trick to open the door?"

"Probably," Sollis said. "Can't hurt to try."

She traced another magical sigil before placing her hand on the doors' metal bars. The entire doorway shone briefly, and they could hear the metal snap. The door opened quietly. "I swear, this whole place smells like magic," she muttered.

"Yes, well, the trip I took to get here was tragic too. But we—"

"No, this whole place smells like *magic*." She stopped him. "It's in the background. I can sense it. Hell, I can practically taste it. It's wonderful. Wanna go get Aidan? I should be a little tired now, but my power is growing instead. It's the ambient magic. Will be no trouble forcing open another door."

"Yeah, let's go," Garrett said, fanning away the odor clinging to him.

"Ahem." They turned to Karrott, who had come back into the cell. "That was a neat trick and all . . . I'm definitely going to add it to my notes when I can write again. You don't mind if I take the collar, right? Good for research."

As Karrott picked up one of the bits, he turned to them and said, "You know . . . that thing you said about it smelling like magic . . . I think I know the source."

Sollis glared at the big rat. "Excuse me?" she demanded.

"Yes. There is lots of cool stuff down in the deeps, but the coolest, paws down, is the big stopper."

"The . . . what?" they exclaimed.

"The big stopper. Well, I don't know what they call it up top, but it's the thing that keeps the volcano from killing everyone. I think it's the reason this place exists—the prison came later."

AQUARIUM

ormek sat for a long while after Nyelle left, tears drying on his cheeks. He vaguely remembered refilling his cup a few times. He was therefore, he admitted, in a somewhat inebriated state when he felt the sensation.

There was no mistaking it.

He had to act.

Lormek stood up. "Ooph!" he exclaimed to no one in particular and sat back down quickly. His head throbbed and he winced. He took several deep breaths, then tried again, more slowly this time. The room wobbled, and he stabilized it by holding on to the table. Unfortunately, the table unexpectedly decided to move, and he crashed loudly to the floor.

"Nyelle," he murmured weakly. Then he remembered that she had left, even if he couldn't recall why. He felt a hand on his shoulder and swiped back at it, but his arm developed a life of its own and hit at the empty air. The invisible hand was joined by another. They moved under his armpits, and he tried to push them away but only ended up slapping himself. "Nyelle," he repeated as he was hoisted up to his feet.

"Take him outside," someone said. The voice sounded like someone he knew. The disembodied hands were distracting him as they half-lifted, half-dragged him in the direction of the door. Then he remembered. "Treena?" he asked.

"You've had a bit too much, Lormek," he could hear the familiar voice saying. "Don't worry, Stinky will take care of you, but you need some fresh air." He liked the voice and beamed proudly at his accurate recollection of the speaker's name. As Stinky carried him outside, he inhaled deeply, feeling the crisp evening air.

Then he passed out.

Sometime later, he woke up with his temples throbbing. The sun was well past its zenith, and the air was cool and fresh. *At least the ground isn't moving anymore*, he thought. Then he realized that the peculiar sensation was still present, and a warm, pleasant glow spread from his gut all over his body. He smiled and closed his eyes.

I'm so happy you're alive.

• • • • •

"Lormek."

"Go away," he mumbled and tried to turn away. Instead, he found himself falling down, and his face hit the ground. "Ow!" he exclaimed and sat up, rubbing his chin.

Nyelle stood over him, her arms crossed. The last rays of the setting sun were mingling with the colored lights of Kuuri and Anni, making it seem as if she had an aura. "So?" she asked.

"So what?" he croaked.

"Why did you call for me? They found me and told me you kept saying my name," she responded with measured coolness.

He rose shakily to his feet. "I'm really thirsty," he said. She didn't move. He shook his head gingerly, worried that it might start pounding again, and took a deep breath. "She's alive, Nyelle!"

"Who is alive?"

"Sollis."

"Wait . . . you mean . . . you mean you can feel her again?" Nyelle's face brightened.

"Can I please have some water?"

Nyelle handed him her waterskin. "Here, I just filled it. When did this happen?"

He took a long drink. "A little while ago. She just . . . popped . . . back into my consciousness. I don't know why, but she's alive. Oh, and Nyelle . . ."

"Yes?"

"How I reacted . . . you know . . . earlier . . ."

"Don't worry about it. I made a mistake. It's my fault."

"No, you don't understand . . . it wasn't what you said at all. It's just that . . . you know, when you said it . . . I was having a vision."

"A vision?" Nyelle's voice softened.

"Yes. An ugly one. I was drowning, and then I was covered in ants, and my mouth was full of sand. I'm really sorry. It wasn't about you, I promise. I really like you too."

"Oh," she said. After a moment she leaned in and draped her arm over his shoulders. "Come on, let's get you back inside. It's getting chilly, and I think you need to eat something."

· · · · ·

"The rest of the cells are empty," Aidan noted after Karrott left.

"Yeah, I guess six is plenty when nobody stays down here for long," Sollis said. "Come check this out. This must be where they get you to talk." In a larger cave were torture devices, including an iron maiden, a breaking wheel, thumbscrews, and flaying apparatus amongst others. Aidan shuddered. Even Garrett refrained from expressing his customary enthusiasm.

"Do they kill you in there too?" Garrett asked. "Karrott said he never heard anybody scream . . . which is weird, considering . . ." He made a sweeping gesture at the room.

"Let me check something." Sollis stepped into the torture cave. As she crossed the threshold, the sound of footsteps disappeared. She turned and said something. Aidan shook his head and pointed at his ear, and Sollis stepped back out. "Just as I thought. They have a sound barrier on the doorway . . . Cool magic, I'll have to try and replicate it sometime."

"Let's make our way out of here before one of us ends up on the wrong side of it." Aidan nervously pointed down the corridor. "Karrott said the tube's over there."

They rounded the corner and came across a circular area. There was a small table with a step stool next to it. Above, a large round opening beckoned.

"That must be it." Garrett pointed. Sniffing loudly, he added, "I should probably go last."

"Let's check it out." Aidan climbed up on the table. He peered into the hole and ducked back down. "Yup. It kinda spirals up and away. Pretty steep, but there's iron rungs every couple of feet . . . Sollis, can you listen for anyone coming down?"

Sollis concentrated for a few moments. "Far as I can tell, the coast is clear."

"All righty then. Let's do this." Aidan hoisted himself upward, disappearing into the hole.

• • • • •

"Thank you, Nyelle." Lormek sighed and pushed away his plate. "I needed that. My head isn't pounding anymore."

Nyelle smiled. "Well, to be honest, I'd never seen a dwarf drunk before . . . I didn't think it was possible!"

He felt his cheeks flush.

"So tell me—if you can feel Sollis again, do you have a sense of where she might be?"

Lormek closed his eyes for a few seconds. "Yeah . . . I think so . . . but it makes no sense."

"How do you mean?"

"Well . . . it feels like she's below us."

"Below us? Like, in the water?"

"I guess, yeah. And not very close, either."

"But she's alive? Not drowned?"

"Oh, no, she's definitely not drowned." Lormek nodded vigorously. "She's alive."

• • • • •

Aidan couldn't help but imagine there was a natural pathway laid within the mountain, and that whoever created the tunnel had followed it closely. He found himself daydreaming as he touched the smooth walls, wondering if rock could speak like wood.

Suddenly, it did!

Sollis, we know you're down there. We're trying to find you, it said. Aidan jerked his hand back. "Did you guys hear that?" he asked.

"Hear what?" Sollis asked from below.

Garrett, who was farther below, added, "Not me. What was it?"

"The wall just talked to me."

Sollis quickly understood. "Like wood, right? What did it say?"

Aidan repeated the message. Then he added, "I was feeling the rock, and it happened . . . a little different than I'm used to, but my hand had no trouble making out the words."

"That's gotta be Nyelle," Sollis responded. "Looks like they haven't given up on us. That's nice."

"Any way to send them back a message?" Aidan wondered.

"No, I can't do what she does. I can only listen." Sollis shook her head.

"How about a shockwave?" Garrett asked.

"Huh? What do you mean?"

"Well . . . a shockwave is a wave, right? And like Nyelle said, so is sound. So maybe you can send a shockwave of sound through the rock and the water?"

Sollis blinked and shrugged. She started moving her fingers in a complicated pattern, forming a faint sigil, which wrapped itself around her wrist.

Then she touched the rung above her.

• • • • •

"I sent it," Nyelle said. "Straight down, like you said . . . but Lormek, other than back in Corrantha City, I haven't tried to do anything like this. I'm used to seeing who I'm talking to and knowing them a little, and now I'm blindly talking through the mountain. You get that it's weird, right? I'm not even sure I'm doing it right."

"It can't hurt. Can you try a few more times? Just kinda spread it around a bit, go higher and lower."

"Sure," Nyelle sighed. "And then can we go to bed, please? It's been an exhausting day." These projections were a strange sensation; it felt like she was bouncing sound randomly off a surface, then pushing it further, amplifying it within itself to propel it forward through the water and volcanic rock underneath the inn.

Nothing happened.

"All right, I'm done." She stood up. "Let's go."

Lormek held his hand up. "Just give it a moment, okay?"

They waited a few seconds, hoping for some sign they'd been heard. Lormek lumbered out of his chair. "Oh well. Thank you, Nyelle. It was worth a shot."

In that instant, a strange sound permeated the atmosphere. It was barely audible, a quiet whisper emerging from below, and it rose rapidly up toward the ceiling. All the lights in the bar flickered. They glanced at each other.

"That felt . . . ," Lormek started.

"Just like the echo of a shockwave. Yes, I agree." Nyelle grinned. "I guess she did hear us after all."

• • • • •

The three escapees reached the top of the tunnel, which opened into a small flat area.

"Will you look at that?" They heard a voice and turned to see two men emerge from another tunnel, crossbows at the ready. "What have we here? A prison escape?" one of the men was saying. "That's a new one. Have you ever heard of someone escaping the prison?"

"Nope. Definitely a new one. I wonder how they got out of their cells." The other man turned to them. "We do appreciate letting us know you're coming though—whatever you did earlier came through here loud and clear."

The other guard moved to the side. Aidan noticed the guards were holding double-arrow crossbows. "Now do us all a favor and kneel with your hands in the air. I really don't want to kill you right now, but seeing where you just came from, it was going to happen anyway, and we really are excellent shots, both of us." He chuckled. "I just don't feel like cleaning up a mess." He sniffed and made a face. "Especially not yours."

Sollis winked at the other two and sank slowly to her knees while raising her arms. Puzzled, Aidan and Garrett copied her movement.

With her fingers playing an air tune, two ghostly flaming darts suddenly materialized in front of Sollis's hands. The guards' eyes opened wide, but they never had time to pull their triggers as the ghostly arrows flew with tremendous speed and buried themselves squarely in their chests. They dropped to the ground, and their screams of agony echoed around the walls of the small chamber as they died from a fire that consumed them from within.

Aidan was in awe. "Remind me to never piss you off." He clapped her heartily on the back.

Garrett was already running for the guards' tunnel. "Let's check it out!"

Aidan went to examine the bodies. He picked up one of the

crossbows and turned it over in his hands. "Decent. Although I can definitely make some improvements."

"Take one if you want, but our priority is to get out of here alive," Sollis reminded him. "Anything on them that we might be able to use?"

Garrett came back holding an apple. "It's a storeroom." He took a bite, chewing noisily. "Should check this other tunnel. Whatcha doing?"

"Was thinking we might search for keys."

Garrett knelt down next to him. "Here, let me." His hands worked as coins and other small items of value vanished, while he tossed aside useless odds and ends.

"This might be interesting." Garrett stood up. "Never seen anything like it before." The wooden object was a bit larger than his palm and shaped like a hexagon. A hole in the center that was shaped like a mouth was framed with thin metal. His finger traced the outline. "It's the same metal that's on the flying boxes, I think."

Sollis reached out her hand. "Can I see it?" She examined it closely, then held it up and inhaled deeply. "That's very nice." She giggled, and her face softened. Aidan and Garrett glanced at each other in surprise.

They could see her pupils dilating.

• • • • •

"Guys, you can't go in there." Treena came to stand behind them, hands on her hips.

"But why, Treena? We were supposed to meet with Bradd, but Stinky wouldn't let us through. What's going on?"

"I don't rightly know, Lormek. But I'm not paid to be nosy, and if Bhaven tells me to stay out and keep everyone else out too, then that's what I'm going to do."

"Bhaven said not to allow anyone in?" Nyelle asked. "Can I talk to him? He knows me."

"Hmm. Nyelle, you know I adore you, and I miss you singing up here. You always make the patrons spend more money. Tell you what . . ." Treena's expression relaxed. "I'll talk to him and make sure he sees you first thing in the morning."

"That's fair. Thanks, Treena." Nyelle started walking toward the second-floor stairs, then stopped short. "One thing, though. If our tall friend shows up, can you send her to our room?"

"You got it," Treena confirmed. "Now go and get some rest, and be down here at dawn. I'll make sure there's breakfast ready for you."

• • • • •

The other tunnel terminated at a door made of smooth stone without visible hinges. Garrett inspected it. "Wow, that's clever." He pointed. "See here? The door slides into the wall."

"But how do you open it?" Aidan asked.

"That might have something to do with it." Garrett pointed to the outline of a slight hexagonal depression set in the wall. Sollis held up the wooden piece they'd found. "Looks like it would fit."

She stood up. "It must be a key. Before we shove it in there, let me listen."

A moment passed, then she spoke again. "I have good news and bad news," she said.

"What's the good news?" Aidan asked.

"There isn't anybody on the other side," Sollis answered.

"And the bad?"

"It's because what's on the other side is water. If we open this door, I suspect the whole place will flood, and we will drown."

"That makes no sense. This has to be how they get in and out of here. I don't buy it."

Garrett examined the key more closely. "What do you think the mouth hole is for?" he asked, shoving his finger in the center.

The mouth snapped shut.

"Ow!" he cried and pulled his finger out with a bit of effort. It came out bloody. The mouth reopened. "Goddammit!" he swore. "I'm so sick of my fingers getting chopped off!"

Barely suppressing a laugh, Aidan took the device and, before Sollis could lunge to stop him, stuck it in the depression. It fit perfectly, then made a loud click as another door slid behind them, closing off the tunnel. The mouth snapped shut, then opened slowly, repeating the movement every few seconds.

Sollis looked at Garrett, whose face had developed a nice shade of crimson. "Did we miss something back there?"

"Uh . . . I'm sorry guys . . . I think I know what fits in the mouth."

"Yes?" Sollis crossed her arms.

"Well, you see . . . remember I was searching the bodies? One of them had a few bits of wood in his pocket. Seemed like he was a bit of a carver. I kept his folding knife but, uh, sort of discarded the rest."

"And?"

"Well, one of the bits didn't seem like anything. I figured it was something he just started working on, so I tossed it away." Garrett looked up. "Now I think it might have been the thing that fits in there." He pointed at the mouth. "I'm really sorry."

"Great. So now we're well and truly stuck. We can't go back, and we can't go forward. Might as well have stayed in our original cells." Sollis sighed. "I guess we'll just wait here until they find us." She plopped down and rested her head on her knees.

"Hey, Garrett, do you remember what the wooden piece looked like?" Aidan asked.

"More or less, yes. Why?"

"Describe it to me in as much detail as you can."

As Garrett explained, Aidan held the purloined crossbow. It creaked and groaned as the wood warped under his touch. Then they heard something snap, and the weapon broke apart and fell to the floor. Aidan opened his palm, showing them a wooden peg that matched Garrett's description.

"I make better bows." Aidan smiled. He stood up and stared at the others. "Ready?" He inserted the peg. They held their breath as the mouth snapped down. A second passed, and the mouth slowly opened again, letting the peg fall out. Aidan tried again with the same outcome.

"It's not a perfect fit." Garrett stood on his toes and examined the device closely.

"Right." Aidan gently nudged Garrett away, then held one hand to the wooden frame. He inserted the peg carefully for the third time and closed his eyes.

The mouth snapped shut, but this time, as Aidan's fingers made tiny movements against the device, they could see that instead of slowly opening back, it stayed shut, and its contours shifted ever so slightly.

They heard another loud click. Aidan stepped back. The device rotated into the wall, and they could feel the air pressure begin to drop.

"Oh! Take a deep breath, both of you, and hold it in! Don't speak! Now!" Sollis exclaimed, then held her breath. They could hear water moving behind the door. A few seconds later, it slid open quietly.

Behind it was a small tube leading straight up, with ladder rungs set to one side. It was wet, with water dripping off the walls. But what made it truly remarkable was that the tube was mostly transparent. They were some distance under the surface of the water inside the volcano's core; fish and algae were moving about. It was as if they were inside of a giant aquarium.

"It's so beautiful," Garrett said, his voice sounding flat and barely audible. Then he closed his mouth again, and fear came onto his face. He pointed at his chest. Aidan grabbed him and placed him high on the ladder, and Garrett scrambled upward with the other two following closely behind.

At the top, they moved onto another corridor. Garrett collapsed on the floor, opening and closing his mouth like a fish trapped on land. Aidan smacked the wall. They heard a click, and a door shut behind them to seal off the aquarium tube. Then the sound of flushing water could be heard, and air started flowing into the little chamber. A device like the one they had used below rotated onto the wall, clicked, and ejected slightly.

Another door slid open quietly ahead of them.

Garrett gasped, inhaled deeply, and started coughing.

"I told you not to speak, you idiot," Sollis said. "It was a low-pressure chamber, definitely of gnomish design. Ingenious. Filled with water unless it needs to be crossed. Looks like a good way of making sure that whatever needs to stay in there, stays in there."

Aidan reached toward the device.

Sollis stopped him. "No. I say leave it. I'm sure they have others, but it will be more confusing when they find it this way." She pointed forward. "My guess is we're under the inn . . . let's see where this comes out."

A short while later, they reached a vertical tube inside the bedrock. At the top was a circular hatch with a handle set in a groove along the outer edge. Aidan climbed up and tried pushing. Then he slid the handle and tried again. The hatch opened quietly.

They climbed into the room above.

It was the one where Bradd had recruited them to the Guild.

It was utterly demolished.

REUNION

"What the hell happened here?" Sollis wondered.

They had emerged at a spot previously covered by the plush, built-in couch facing the docks. The couch was split in half, showing how it had been constructed to hide the opening.

Art that used to cover the walls was smashed into pieces all over the floor. The rich velvet drapes were torn down, slashed, and shredded. The intricately patterned rug showed, with multiple blood stains everywhere, signs of a mighty struggle.

The great table was much worse for wear. Gashes were visible all across its surface, and it was singed badly in one corner. Aidan placed his hands over one of the gashes, tears streaming down his cheeks. "He hurts . . . a lot," he whispered.

Garrett tried the narrow door at the back of the room. It opened a little and stopped. "Something stuck behind," he grunted. Aidan joined him, and the door moved a bit more. Garrett reached through the crack. "Ooph!" he jerked his hand back.

It was covered in blood.

"There's a body." He peeked through the narrow opening. "Looks like a closet."

"A closet?" Sollis asked. "That's a weird place to put one."

"Yeah." Aidan examined the hinges. "I can ask the door to come out of its frame . . . what do you think?" He placed his hands on the frame and closed his eyes. After a few seconds, he tensed with the strain of holding up the now-unsupported door. "Done. You guys wanna help?"

Garrett and Aidan slid the door sideways. A body flopped into the room. Garrett leaned over it. "That's Bradd's bodyguard."

"Riiiight . . . or whatever Bradd's real name was," Aidan said. "I remember now, he stood by the wall when we had our meeting here . . . Sollis, come check this out."

"Sollis?" he repeated, and they turned to glance back at Sollis.

She wasn't there.

They rushed over and Aidan pointed at the floor. "Hatch is closed, which means she went back to the prison."

"What for?!"

"No clue." Aidan pulled open the hatch and shouted into the tube. "Sollis! Where are you going?"

They heard a faint reply. "Sorry guys! I have to do this!"

Garrett scrambled quickly down the ladder. "She's gone down already," he said when he came back. "I can't access the key on this end either, it's rotated back into the wall."

Aidan shook his head in frustration. "That's probably why she told me to leave it there. I will never understand the woman . . . we just escaped, and she wants to go back?" He gestured around the room. "Plus, it looks like we were very lucky to even make it this far."

"For sure." Garrett giggled. "Can you imagine coming up if there were people here? I think I'm beginning to understand how Karrott feels."

Aidan stood up. "You know what? Nothing we can do about it—me, I'd rather head out. Should we try the main door?"

Garrett raised his head to him. "I dunno, Aidan. Clearly something bad happened here, and we know there's Guild stuff all over the rest of this level . . . The Guild doesn't take shit lightly, and we're fugitives. Makes me a little nervous."

"You'd know, wouldn't you?" Aidan stared at him. "I just don't see any other way out, unless we break these windows . . . that kind of ruckus is sure to attract plenty of attention." He thought for a moment. "Let's at least go through the closet."

They went back for a more thorough examination. It was perhaps twice the size of a utility closet, extending behind and to the side of the door. Garrett stepped into the far end and examined the floor. "Oh!" He jumped up. "Aidan, there's a slit going right through the middle here! I think it's a trapdoor!"

"Hmm. Maybe it's an exit of some sort after all. I wonder how you open it? Can I have a look?" Aidan stepped inside. He leaned down to inspect the bottom. "Yeah . . . I can see it. Barely, but it's there."

"Yup, uh-huh," Garrett's voice made Aidan turn his face toward him. "I wonder what this does." Garret was standing in the doorway, his hand near the lower hinge assembly. He pressed on something.

The trapdoor snapped open, and Aidan tumbled down head first. Garrett heard a splash.

"Wait for me!" he shouted.

• • • • •

Aidan climbed onto the lower docks. Garrett, who had been clinging to his back, slid down and sat next to him. "Sorry, Aidan . . . you did really good getting us out. I never learned how to swim. I guess if you grow up in the Shallows, it's a thing that, like, everybody does, huh?"

"Will you, just for once, stop being so impulsive?" Aidan barely contained his anger. "Remember how you almost killed Sollis? We had no idea what was under the floor back there . . . you could have killed me!"

Tiny as he was, Garrett still shrunk visibly and melted into the shadows. Aidan could barely see him at all. "Okay, stop that, it gives me the creeps," he said in annoyance, and Garrett came back into full view.

"I'm really sorry, Aidan. I didn't know how it worked . . . but we were lucky, right? And you didn't die."

"Yes, we were, and no, I didn't." Aidan sighed. "It's a clever setup— the water is just a couple of feet under the trapdoor, and that little area is completely shielded from view. I imagine they use it to smuggle things in and out of the Shallows. Maybe even people." He paused. "I'm too tired to think about it."

"Where should we go? I don't feel like going back to the inn right now."

"Me neither. Hmm. I suppose we could try and sneak out to the beach . . . maybe a better option is the church. Lormek's dad takes care of all the homeless anyway. Just don't mention any of this, all right? Better that he doesn't recognize us."

"Yes, sir!" Garrett jumped to his feet and saluted. "Let's go!"

Groaning, Aidan stood up. "At least you smell better," he muttered as they both made their way slowly across the docks.

• • • • •

At sunrise, they made their way to the Steadfast Inn. Rajiv did recognize them and had kindly washed their clothes and dried them by the fire. They left him the coins that Garrett pilfered off the prison guards but skipped his signature turnip soup.

When they got to the inn, the bar was half full. Treena was there, setting up a table. "You're up early," she told Aidan.

"Morning, Treena."

Treena greeted them. "Your friends should be down in just a moment."

"Wait, what?"

"Your friends? You're here to see them, right? I got Nyelle the audience she asked for."

"Audience?" Aidan looked at Garrett in surprise. "Is Lormek here, too?"

"Ask him yourself when he comes down." Treena went back to the kitchen.

"Aidan! Garrett!" Nyelle rushed down the stairs. They hugged, and Nyelle stepped back. "It's so good to see you . . . where's Sollis?"

"It's a long story." Aidan sighed. "Where's Lormek?"

"Not feeling well. A strange delirium. He's been having these terrible dreams . . . he was fine last night, especially after he felt Sollis again"—Aidan raised an eyebrow at that—"But now it's like he's stuck in a nightmare. I couldn't wake him up. So where's Sollis?"

"She came up with us, but just as we were getting away, she ran back into the prison and locked us out." Nyelle opened her mouth, and Aidan added preemptively, "We have no idea either. We couldn't wait around."

Treena brought up two more sets of plates and cups. "I got you your interview, young lady." She winked at Nyelle. "He's speaking to an upper-shelver right now. She was sitting and waiting in the dark when I came down to open this morning. I overheard them shouting at each other earlier—but don't worry, you're next. In the meantime, why don't you have something to eat? Is Lormek coming down too?"

· · · · ·

"Another world? A metal called steel? And . . . what did you call them . . . nuts and bolts? Lormek's nanny is the King's Pope? What in the name of the gods have we gotten ourselves into?" Aidan was dazed.

"Not to mention two gold bars as a reward for that thing I found." Garrett laughed. "I guess almost losing a finger was worth it after all."

Nyelle smiled. "Sure seems that way." She placed a bunch of gold coins and the remaining bar on the table, and Garrett squealed in delight. "Anyway, Aidan, I also have a big surprise for you. Are you ready?"

"Wait, another surprise?" Aidan placed his hand over his chest dramatically. "My heart can't take it!"

"Ha. But I'm being serious. I kinda skipped the trip back from the city earlier . . . Lormek and I . . . we ran into a werewolf."

Aidan sat bolt upright. "A werewolf? For real? But . . . how are you still alive?"

Instead of answering, Nyelle reached inside her leather tunic and carefully pulled out a folded piece of cloth. She handed it to Aidan. "Whatever it is, it saved our lives."

Confused, Aidan unwrapped the small package. In it was a small, dull, silver-colored necklace with a tiny pendant shaped like the heads of three animals. His eyes grew wide and he gasped.

"Is this what I think it is?"

"Lormek and I believe so, yes."

"What is it?" Garrett demanded, trying to grab it out of Aidan's hand, who held it back.

"A talisman." Aidan whistled. "An actual goddamned talisman."

· · · · ·

"A magical prison with sliding doors? A talking rat? An aquarium? What in the name of the gods have we gotten ourselves into?" Nyelle teased.

Aidan grinned at her. "Don't forget the self-cleaning sewers. Garrett really liked those."

Garrett stuck his tongue out at him. "I'll go see Halley—er, Halleena—later, and we'll work out how to get you on Twoshelf so you can find your mom. I'm not sure what the rules are for escaped prisoners. I don't think they ever really thought about it." He grinned. "But my sister should be able to take you with her when she goes home."

"Good idea, Garrett." Aidan turned to Nyelle. "I'm still confused. So you're saying your real dad was the library guy? And your mom's alive? And she's married to that racist prick we robbed . . . what did you say his name was? Popeaide?"

"Albergino Frentenga. Yes, it seems that way. I still find it hard to believe. I mean, she's always been a bit . . . detached . . . in a way, but also very loving. Kind of a free spirit actually. It doesn't make any sense."

"Well . . . I don't mean it in a bad way, but . . . how well do you really know her?"

"Well enough to know that she isn't a racist! She's been around for a long time, and she never told me much about her youth—she said she was in some wars a long time ago and that she traveled all over the world, but many elves do that at some point because we"—here she paused for a moment—"they can."

Aidan squeezed her hand. "At least you know you're not sick."

"Just a half-breed!" Garrett chuckled. Nyelle glared at him.

"So what now?" Aidan pushed his plate away.

"Right now, I'm waiting to speak to Bhaven. What you said about the room being in that state explains a lot—that's probably why he's blocked access to that area. But I'm hoping that maybe he can tell us where we can find Bradd . . . or whatever his name is."

"Yeah. I know Bhaven too. My dad and I used to supply fresh game for his kitchen. We saw him a few times when we brought in more . . . exotic stuff. I stopped doing it after my parents died, but I'm pretty sure he'll remember me . . . maybe I'll join you?"

"Sure. No, you'll stay out here," she added quickly toward a disappointed Garrett.

Suddenly, a commotion could be heard from the back, the muffled sounds of people shouting. Treena hurried out from the kitchen and went through the back door. After a few moments, she returned. "He should be done soon," she said before heading into the kitchen.

They looked at each other, wondering what was going on.

A couple of minutes passed in silence. A door slammed. Then the back door swung open, and a tall hooded figure emerged from it, striding purposefully and powerfully past them.

Nyelle inhaled sharply and covered her mouth. Aidan and Garrett looked at her with raised eyebrows. She moved her lips silently.

"Are you all right?" Aidan asked.

As the figure reached the saloon doors, Nyelle stood shakily up on her feet. "Mom?" she whispered. Then she straightened and shouted, "Mom!"

The figure stopped.

"Mom!" Nyelle shouted again, tears streaming down her face. She rushed out, her chair falling. "Mom!"

The tall figure turned, removing her hood to reveal an elven woman. Aidan and Garrett were struck by her beauty. She had high cheekbones and slanted green eyes with a dispassion that spoke of age and wisdom utterly belied by her perfect, youthful skin. Even by elf standards, she was gorgeous.

As Nyelle ran toward her, the woman opened her arms in recognition, and the two of them came together in a long, warm embrace. Nyelle dug her face into her mother's shoulders, sobbing heavily, and she held Nyelle tightly and kissed her head.

"You're still alive!" her mother said after Nyelle calmed down. "I searched for you for so long but could never even find a trace of you."

"I thought you died in the fire!" Nyelle blurted and started sobbing again. "I couldn't find you or Dad . . . everything was burned to the ground! I . . . I ran away."

"Dad? Oh, you mean Yorros?"

"No, Mom! Dad! *My* dad! Yorros was my father!" Nyelle shouted. "I found his journal!"

Treena spoke softly behind Aidan and Garrett, "So, uh . . . he's ready to see her now . . . should I let him know it's no longer necessary?"

REVELATIONS FOUR-THREE

INTERLUDE: LORMEK'S HELLSCAPE

Lormek sleeps. Or at least he thinks he does. It's hard to sleep when he feels so much.

He sees Sollis, who stands nearby, smirking at him.

He holds his yearning arms out to her, but she's just out of reach. He tries to step closer but finds that he cannot move. Looking down, he discovers that his legs are trapped in the sand.

They're on a beach. He's sinking slowly.

He looks back up to Sollis, pleading.

She doesn't respond, and her grin only widens as she watches him.

"Help me, Sollis!" he cries, but she stays silent. He sees that her arms are crossed, and she appears relaxed. Perhaps even happy!

Happy that he is going to drown.

"Sollis?" he asks. Her eyes are so cold.

His heart beats faster, and he realizes that what he feels is not passion, not desire. It is fear. Fear—and hatred toward her, for dooming him to this. It is her fault that he is sinking in the sand, he knows it now. How had he missed that before?

Staring at her, unable to move, his hatred turns into something more, a white-hot rage like he has never experienced, never knew existed.

Never knew *could* exist.

Her loathing eyes are now boring straight into him. It enrages him further. He growls as his muscles tighten, and then he feels it: his feet are coming unstuck. She hasn't noticed.

Once he's free, everything happens quickly.

Somewhere inside of him, he knows it's wrong, but his anger is overwhelming. He can't stop himself from lunging at her, his hands locking around her fragile neck. He finds himself wishing that she would say something, maybe that she's sorry, or perhaps plead for her life, but she doesn't struggle. Her gaze bores into his soul as her life drains away.

He can feel her neck breaking under his powerful grip.

Time passes. Her body grows stiff in his hands.

The rage dissipates, replaced by sorrow.

"What have I done?" he screams.

A grief deeper than the bottom of the ocean washes over Lormek as he looks upon her beautiful silent body. His fingers are still locked around her neck.

He must atone! All he needs is simply to let the sands take him. Dropping her body, he steps back into the pit that had trapped him.

Preparing to die, he raises his face in a silent farewell.

He sees Sollis, who stands nearby, smiling at him.

• • • • •

"Sorry we took so long, you guys . . . we had a bit of catching up to do." Nyelle walked into their room. "I would like you to meet my mother, Enrielle."

Enrielle followed her inside. Garrett jumped up on a chair and extended his hand. "I'm Garrett!" He beamed. "And this is Aidan. He's a sourpuss!" Aidan shook his head and smiled.

"Yes, Nyelle told me about you. And presumably, this is Lormek?" As if in response, Lormek moaned in his sleep. "What's wrong with him?"

"We don't know, Mom. He was fine when he went to sleep, but he's been having strange dreams recently . . . and he hasn't woken up since last night. He moans like this every hour or so."

Enrielle sat down. "Where is the last one? Sollis, right?"

"How much did you tell her, Nyelle?" Aidan asked.

"Just the basics. She knows about the prison. Well, she already knew about the prison."

"Right. So Sollis went back into the prison. Garrett and I were with her, but she took us by surprise . . . she disabled the lock so no one could follow her." Aidan raised his palms. "We really have no clue why she'd want to do that."

"Why, indeed. I suppose you're aware that, as far as the Thieves' Guild is concerned, you're fugitives, right?" Enrielle gestured at Nyelle. "You too now, Ny-ny, because you're helping them."

Nyelle blushed at the use of her childhood nickname. "Is it true that you're married to Popeaide?" She sat down, then added hopefully, "I told them it couldn't be."

"Yes, it's true, honey."

"But how could you? He had this horrible book in his study . . . and it looked like he was writing it!" Nyelle was devastated.

"It's a marriage of convenience. Humans don't live very long. Gino wasn't always like this . . . but he started changing a little while ago. I suspect that he tried to do something he shouldn't have, and the experience has been slowly poisoning his mind."

"So are you in the Pope's organization too?" Garrett asked. "Lormek's dad runs the church here in the Shallows."

"Oh no, dear, not at all." Enrielle turned to him. "I work with the Thieves' Guild."

• • • • •

Sollis went to the storeroom first. As she anticipated, there was more than enough food, in ideal conditions for preservation. She never needed much to sustain her when she worked with magic; somehow, in a way she could never quite explain, magic itself provided nourishment.

She never had access to much magic. In this strange place, it was everywhere!

It permeated the pumice walls. With every step she took, she could feel it in her toes, the arches of her feet, and flowing up her ankles. Her mind was in a constant state of controlled ecstasy as her fingers found themselves moving, searching for patterns in the abundance surrounding her. Every breath meant another delicious whiff of the smell that had become her obsession ever since she first experienced the shockwave as a frightened child.

No better place for her to be.

No better place for her to die.

She closed her eyes and relaxed, allowing for as much time as she needed to adjust. Then she let her senses guide her. Keeping her eyes closed, she moved slowly, realizing she could see without looking. She climbed over the two dead guards, noting dispassionately that the smell of her cold fire darts was gone. Without stumbling, she climbed down into the tube leading to the prison, finding the rungs easily, as if she had been going through it her entire life.

Her magical blindvision was in sharp focus.

And like a tall, blond, and determined magic magnet, she headed toward its source.

• • • • •

At Enrielle's statement, Aidan and Garrett jumped out of their chairs, the former reaching for a dagger, the latter heading toward the window.

Enrielle laughed. "Don't worry, boys, I'm not interested in getting you arrested. These tribunals are usually arranged to make a political point or score a favor, not to seek justice. Once the point is made or the favor is scored, nobody cares anymore. Most people don't even know the prison exists. Even amongst those who do, few realize that most prisoners come out alive—it's just a matter of whether someone is willing to pay for them." She smiled. "It's not money that's needed to secure this kind of release."

The two relieved fugitives came carefully back to the table. "But we saw the torture chamber," Aidan said.

"Right. It's very impressive, isn't it? Tends to change the minds of even the most stubborn of people, if someone they care about is in a cell nearby." Enrielle paused. "Anyway, right now, there are much bigger issues the Guild's dealing with. So while your escape will be noted, since nobody's escaped the prison before, dealing with it won't be high priority. You have at least a couple of days to leave town."

"Umm . . . Mom, I don't think we want to leave."

"Wait, why not?" Enrielle was surprised.

"Well, we need to find out what happened to Sollis, for one thing. Also, Lormek's in no shape to travel. Like . . . he won't wake up, and he has a strange connection to her, so if we take him away, he might get worse or even die."

"Can't you drop him off with his father?"

"I suppose so, but . . ." Nyelle paused, struggling with her emotions. "Mom, I really care about him."

Everyone turned to her in surprise. Enrielle grinned. "Oh, the vagaries of youth! I was like you once. But you know, honey, we live longer than anybody else . . . by a lot. Oh, what am I saying? I know full well there's nothing I can say to change the way you feel."

Aidan looked at Nyelle, who nodded briefly. "Enrielle, we found a talisman. Maybe you can help us find someone who can figure out what it does?"

Enrielle leaned forward. "Can I see it?"

Aidan reached under his leather vest and carefully took off the talisman. Holding his palm out toward Enrielle, he uncurled his fist.

The talisman pulsated faintly, slowly.

Enrielle gasped and reached out. "Where . . . where did you find this?" she blurted. As her fingers neared it, the talisman jumped into her hand, its pulse fading as soon as she held it.

"It saved our lives. In Corrantha. A werewolf came after us . . . Mom? What's going on?"

Enrielle, who had settled back in her chair with eyes closed in deep concentration, suddenly opened them. She rose slowly and came around the table, kneeling beside Aidan, staring intently into his face. He stayed still, his hands resting on the table.

She touched his hand, tears filling her eyes. "Nylean?" she whispered. "But . . . how are you still alive? How is this possible?" Then, moving so swiftly that no one had a chance to react, she hugged an extremely confused Aidan tightly.

"My son!"

• • • • •

When Sollis emerged from the bottom of the tube, Karrott was there, apparently in anticipation of her arrival. He waited for her to step off the table. "You're back, huh? I knew we were kindred spirits. It's really interesting down here . . . so much to research!" He grinned, his rat's teeth gleaming in the dim light.

"Yes, very much so." Sollis started walking down the hallway. Karrott ran after her. "So what are we doing?"

She took a few more long strides, before stopping in front of the torture chamber. "*I* am going in here," she said and walked into it.

Interesting, Karrott thought to himself. *Very interesting.*

• • • • •

Finally, Enrielle let Aidan go and sat back on her knees, tears covering her cheeks. Nyelle held her hand to her mouth. Aidan sat stunned and motionless. Enrielle's finger traced his scar gently. "I thought you died at birth," she murmured.

"But . . . Mom . . . I don't understand . . ."

"Ny-ny, on one of my trips . . . I slept with a wild elf. I didn't realize I was fertile at the time. I was looking for this!" She held up the talisman, which had acquired its usual dull color. "Anyway, I gave birth to"—she squeezed Aidan's hand—"Nylean. In a clearing."

"That's the story you told *me* about *my* father," Nyelle murmured.

Aidan stood up and stepped back. "First of all, my name's Aidan. Second, my parents were Faergus and Isla, of the Shallows"—his voice broke at that, but then he continued—"And finally, I don't understand any of this at all, and I sure as hell don't like it!"

Enrielle stared at him for a long moment. "Those are human names, aren't they? You know they weren't your real parents? Maybe not when you were younger, but now?"

Aidan did not respond.

"You're, what now"—she stopped for a moment, doing mental arithmetic—"is it fifty-seven or fifty-eight? How would I know that?"

Aidan's shoulders started rocking slightly as his eyes got wet. "But then why did you leave me for dead?"

"Because I was heavily injured, and I didn't think this would be powerful enough to save both of us." She held up the talisman. "The fellow who made it was a bit of a jokester, and for whatever reason, the talisman didn't seem inclined to give me sufficient protection at that moment." She paused. "I had to make a choice."

"What are you talking about?" Aidan demanded.

"I was cornered by a werewolf right when I gave birth to you. Very unlucky, but the werewolf would have surely killed both of us. I was already on the verge of dying from a badly infected wound I took from a diseased goblin. So I had to leave you behind," she said calmly, having regained her composure. "But before I left, I placed this on your chest. It seems like the protection it declined to provide me was sufficient to keep you alive . . . I guess your parents—Faergus and Isla, you said?—I guess they found you in time to save you and they raised you."

"Wait . . . so you're, like, brother and sister?" Garrett swiveled his head back and forth between Nyelle and Aidan. "Can this day get any better?"

· · · · ·

Having examined the instruments of torture thoroughly, Sollis began carefully inspecting the walls of the cave.

"What are we looking for?" Karrott had followed her inside.

"A passage," Sollis said over her shoulder.

"A passage to where?"

Sollis stopped. "Look, rat, or garden gnome, or whatever you are, I appreciate your help in getting us out of here, I truly do. But right now, I need to find something, and I need to find it badly, and I don't think you can be of use." She resumed her search.

"Well, I suppose you're right. Still, if you're trying to get to the big stopper, then maybe I can help."

Sollis froze, then stared at Karrott in suspicion. He was licking his paws. "What do you mean, you can help? How?"

"See, I've been around here for a while. And I've sort of gone down every little nook and cranny. This place is very interesting . . . so full of magic, isn't it?" Karrott teased.

Sollis dropped to the floor and lowered her head to peer straight at the rat. "What could *you* know of magic?" she demanded.

"Oh, I just know about it, not feel it like you can. But like I said before, I do think the source is the stopper, and I think that's what you're looking for. Am I right?"

Sollis glared at him.

"Well, I only caught a tiny glimpse of it once and almost died because I'm just a little rat, but there is a way you can get down there if you want."

"And that way is . . . ?" Sollis spoke slowly and quietly.

"Through there." Karrott pointed toward the iron maiden. "But you'll have to put yourself inside and close it, and there's a trick to it."

"A trick?"

"Yes. You have to shift your weight in a peculiar way, and then, instead of getting impaled, you fall through a trapdoor. And it's underwater. And I think she also used some kind of magic."

"*Who* used magic?"

"The last girl who did it, maybe twenty years ago. But"—Karrott licked his paw again—"she never made it back."

"And how do you know all this?" Sollis stood up.

"I fell asleep in the device, and she entered it unexpectedly," Karrott answered. After a moment, he added, "Oh, and also . . ."

"Yes?" Sollis looked back at him.

"The girl—well, I suppose she was an important wizard or something—she also caused the volcano to erupt."

A DEGREE OF
SOCIAL SCIENCE

The reality of being on the lam gave them a sense of urgency. Thankfully, Enrielle seemed comfortable stepping into a leadership role and provided a calming voice. Aidan and Nyelle marveled at their newly discovered familial bond and were impressed by their mother's efficient command. For his part, Garrett was delighted to be along for the ride. He did little to contain his enthusiasm at the prospect of even more exciting discoveries.

They left Lormek in the care of his father and waited until Rajiv finished examining his son. "He's stuck in some sort of nightmare loop. I can keep him alive, but only as long as whoever is on the other side of the psychic link is alive too."

"It could only be Sollis," they told him and then had to explain.

Aidan and Nyelle described what they had witnessed around the campfire, what Lormek had shared of his dreams about Sollis, and how he could sense her like a ghost limb. Rajiv couldn't make sense of it. But to Enrielle, the concept of intertwined souls was familiar, which is how, for the first time in centuries, the real story of Port Kyber's founding was told.

A HISTORY LESSON

"You've all heard of Kenzer Kelstra? The founder of Kyber?" Enrielle started.

They all had.

"Well, he wasn't the only founder. Few remember today, but he had a partner and cofounder." Here, she looked meaningfully at Nyelle. "His name was Zacharias."

"What? The great bard? He founded Kyber?"

"They did it together."

"How do you know?" Nyelle demanded.

"Because I was there," Enrielle answered, a hint of a smile on her face.

Nyelle opened and shut her mouth several times. Finally, she spoke. "You *knew* him? In real life? But . . . when I told you . . ."

"Yes, I did know him. I knew him very well, actually. I'm sorry, Ny-ny, but this is ancient history, and there were lots of complications you wouldn't have understood when you were young. I just decided it's best to let you pursue your own path."

"Mom! How *could* you?"

Aidan squeezed Nyelle's hand. "Let her tell it to us now," he said quietly.

Enrielle resumed the story. "When I met them, Kenzer and Zacharias were already successful adventurers. They had spent years exploring the equator and the southern lands beyond and were putting together a company to go deeper into a remote area they referred to as the Underground Continent. I was about the age you are now, Ny-ny, but even though they had plenty of experienced volunteers to pick from, they chose me as one of the few to go with them. We spent several years there, and I doubt we saw much of it."

"What was it, exactly?" Rajiv asked. "I've never heard of it."

"A huge realm buried deep under the surface of the world. It's full of monsters and wonders like Corrantha's never seen. It's also extremely dangerous. To enter, you must travel down an active volcano during the brief interval while it is cooling off following an eruption."

"How does one do that without dying?"

"Ah. You've all heard of Kenzer, the great general. He was that. But history has forgotten that he was also a great magician. And not a wizard, either; he was a wildmage, like your Sollis, albeit an extremely powerful one. In fact, by the time we emerged from that realm, he had likely become the most powerful wielder of magic in the entire world. He got us in and out safely.

"The dozen of us who survived the trip became formidable in our own right. We were hardened by battle, survived against powerful magic, and . . . well, boneheaded. We felt like nothing could stop us. The incredible riches we brought back meant nothing because nothing could compare to the thrill of adventuring under the leadership of those two. But where could we go next? And so it was that we decided to venture into the Dark Spot."

"The Dark Spot?" Aidan asked.

"Yes. It was a place in Corrantha that nobody had ever succeeded in entering, though many had tried. Today, you know it as Port Kyber." Enrielle smirked. "Back then, it was completely inaccessible. The stone storms that mark its border today were bigger and in constant motion then, surrounding the peninsula. And if you somehow managed to survive crossing them, the whole place was covered in a dense cloud that would burn the flesh off any living being in seconds. The King of Corrantha back then, Anberg, formed the Magic Corps with the specific purpose of figuring out the secret of the Dark Spot. They were unsuccessful, even as most of the Corps died while seeking the answer."

Enrielle took a sip of water.

"We had a royal wizard in our company. He had decided to leave the college and seek adventure instead of joining the Corps. He told us he thought their mission was futile. His name was Talus, and if you've heard any of the silly stories about how some wizard enchanted the floor of the council chamber to make it float . . . it was all Talus, and the enchantment is nothing like what you've heard."

"That's funny," Garrett said. "I've heard him called so many names, but never Talus."

Enrielle confirmed. "Yes, and he was perfectly happy with that being the case. In fact, he was the one who seeded the name Zander as part of the false narrative that's being told today, centuries later."

"So what did he actually do with the floor of the council chamber?"

"I'll get to that, I promise."

"Zacharias was a form of wildmage as well," Enrielle continued. Nyelle was plainly shocked at hearing this. "Yes, Nyelle, he was a terrific bard, but that was just his occupation. He was, in reality, a soulmage, a kind of wildmage whose power is derived from their ability to manipulate sound in an unusual way. Souls have a special resonance, and soulmages can tune in to it and, through it, touch souls across all planes of existence."

"I've never heard of soulmages," Rajiv interjected.

"In the six centuries since then, there was only one more that I knew of. He served King Emmeka but died in the Underground Realm. There may have been others. Still, I strongly suspect that another one is alive today."

"Do you know who they are?"

"Well, yes. She's sitting in this very room," Enrielle responded casually.

Nyelle blinked as the realization hit her. "What are you saying, Mom?"

"Your path, your discoveries, and your experiences all point to it. Zacharias described the way he grew into his power . . . it was similar. Do you see why I couldn't tell you about it? He was clear that he needed to realize his talent on his own, in trying circumstances . . . like your encounter with the werewolf. The way he explained it to me, he only truly understood he could touch souls after learning every other sound first, even the quietest ones. That was when he realized that souls had their own unique sound."

Nyelle's mind went into overdrive for the second time in as many days as she found herself rearranging her understanding of the world. She thought about how she could shape and reshape sound to suit different people. The strange symbols in Zacharias's book that puzzled her for so long came into sharp focus, and for the first time, they made sense. She wasn't shaping sound for listening. She was doing it to match their souls.

Enrielle continued. "Zach and Kay worked together to reach the peninsula safely. Kenzer grasped the nature and severity of the divine wards, but it was Zach, the soulmage, who understood what they were there for. He didn't know what they meant, exactly, not until right before he . . . uh, died . . . many years later. But his intuition was correct. The stones, the flesh-burning fog, and the rest of the wards were a protective, divine barrier around powerful souls suspended in this plane, rather than a gate to keep others out. That part was just a convenient side effect. Initially, he thought it was a prison, but later he called it a 'soul crib,' which I always thought was a neat way of putting it."

"Suspended souls?" Aidan asked.

"Indeed, suspended here by a god. With their insights, Kay and Zach managed to make it all the way here, to the volcano, and discover the crystal buried inside it." Enrielle took another sip of water as everyone leaned forward. "Back then, there was no Kyber, only the volcano. And deep below the surface of its waters, they found this huge rock that shouldn't have been there. It was set on top of the mountain's enormous magma chamber, as if it were a cork. Kenzer said it was the only possible place for it due to the energy involved. Only a huge volcano like this one could contain it. The rock was a bit too large, which is the reason the gash exists. The god slammed it down while tearing apart the mountainside in order for the rock, really a massive six-sided crystal, to fit. The crystal was unlike anything they'd ever seen. The way Kenzer described it, it's like it was made of pure magic, and the energy contained within must have rivaled the sun's. Still does, I guess."

"Why would Kenzer, or Zacharias for that matter, tell you all this?" Nyelle asked suddenly. "What were you to them?"

"I was his lover." Enrielle smiled. "And Zach's. They decided that, since they loved me equally, they would share me. There was never any acrimony. I was glad for that because I loved them both equally as well."

She paused.

"The two of them experimented with the crystal. They were very careful and methodical, as they always were. I don't know exactly what happened, but one day, they showed up in our tent and showed me Kenzer's dagger."

Garrett snickered, and Enrielle flashed him a look of disapproval.

"It used to be iron—finely crafted, for sure, the best money could buy—but it had been transformed into something else. Something new. The metal was unlike anything else, but it hardened the dagger into the finest weapon we'd ever seen."

"Steel!" Nyelle whispered.

"Yes, I believe that's what it's called—how do you know?" Enrielle asked in surprise. When no answer was forthcoming, she continued. "They reforged our weapons and armor into steel. Then they built the original Shallows docks and made the first trip east to Decentea, returning with fruits and spices that Corrantha had never known before. Crossing the big chasm—folks didn't start calling it the Spasm until much later—was very dangerous back then, so after a couple of these trips, they partnered with the King to build Stormbridge. He provided the services of his engineers and the remainder of his Magic Corps, and our company brought in the materials. The stone was carved from the volcano while building Kyber, and the rest we brought back with us from the Underground Realm. Even with all these resources, it took over two years to build because of the stone storms. No matter how hard he tried, Kenzer never quite managed to shut them down."

"It must have been incredible to watch it being built." Garrett whistled.

"It was. And Kyber became just as incredible as a trading hub. So as soon as it was finished, King Anberg brought an army to take it."

"So what happened then? Surely the King won?"

"He would have, except that we had steel arms. That and our control of Stormbridge evened the odds. Most importantly, we were led by Kenzer. Magic Corps notwithstanding, wizards cannot engage in offensive magic like a wildmage can. And Kay had Zach by his side, a soulmage so powerful he could whisper to many souls at once. The King's army met fierce resistance and found itself rapidly demoralized, despite outnumbering us a hundred to one . . . we scared the hell out of them. By the time it ended, we had only lost the least experienced member of our group."

"Was that the Battle of Stormbridge?" Aidan asked.

"Yes. After that, Kay and Zach established Kyber as an independent city. They put together the council, except for the Grunt; that role was added a few centuries later. They started the Thieves' Guild as a way of making sure they stayed on top of everything that was happening throughout Kyber. They also put up the shelves, which brings us back to Talus and his enchantments." Enrielle turned toward Garrett. "He did something that highly trained wizards do very well. He masked the steel supports that Kenzer and Zacharias created to hold up the shelves with a permanent illusion so powerful everyone believes they're stone." She grinned. "Turns out steel is both created and repelled by the crystal. I suppose that in a way, the shelves do float, trying to get away from the crystal that made them—the stone is holding them at bay. How do you think the ships fly?"

Garrett jumped out of his chair. "I knew it!" he yelled. "I knew it, I knew it, I knew it! It's all made-up rituals, isn't it? The way it actually works has nothing to do with them!"

"Yes. Did you figure this out on your own? You're very clever. Of course, nobody will believe you. You know the Boxes Guild, the keepers of the boxes?"

Garrett nodded.

"It was founded with a set of complicated, precise rituals, starting when a guild officer is born. They involve a lot of strict training and extreme discipline. They really believe they are invoking a power that requires the right bloodline. The truth is simpler. Permanent dampening magic on the boxes is temporarily suppressed with a code phrase to allow their steel to carry a ship up the Elevator. I was with Zach and Kay when they came up with it . . . that was a fun night," she reminisced happily. "Anyway, Talus implemented the necessary magic once they dreamed up the idea. He was a genius. He also made several talismans, including this one." She placed it on the table.

"I don't get it," Aidan said. "How did they come up with this stuff? It's fantastic."

"Yes, it is. They took me down to see the crystal afterward, but when they were experimenting on it, Kenzer accidentally traveled in spirit to a place called Earth that is bound to the crystal. Apparently, Earth is where he picked up these notions. For example, the nuts and bolts, which inspired the creation of the shelf supports."

"Oh!" Nyelle exclaimed. "This Earth must be the other world Xephyna told us about when we brought her the nut. She's the one who told us it was made of steel."

"Sounds right. Kenzer also brought back the term Pope. He said it was how Earth people called unpopular religious leaders. Kenzer hated religion, especially as King Anberg's power was so reliant on it. So when he came back, he started calling Anberg the Pope in contempt. Later it morphed into its present meaning. Kenzer's distaste for religion is also why the volcano was never named; he didn't want people to start worshiping it, and because everybody wanted to please him, it became understood that it should never happen."

"Traveled in spirit? Like a ghost?"

"Something like that. Maybe he was hallucinating. But it gave him so many ideas . . . his power grew exponentially, and his energy, which was abundant before then, became intense. Luckily, he had Zach to support him and eventually meld with him when they ascended."

Enrielle waited patiently. After a few seconds, Nyelle finally spoke in a dazed tone. "Ascended? As in, became a god?"

"Why yes, honey. A god. Kenzer was powerful enough to ascend, but as he confessed to me the last time we slept with each other, it turns out that you can't do it on your own. That's the awesome, ultimate power a soulmage has. The power to guide a soul like this to its final impossible destination."

Enrielle sat back in her chair.

"Alas, it will consume the soulmage in the process. For a soulmage to serve as guide meant giving up their own soul and merging it with the guided. Which is what Zach did. His ultimate sacrifice, born out of his great love for Kenzer, allowed their souls to meld at the moment of ascension. Kenzer, with Zach forever by his side, joined the gods." She paused for a second, sat back in her chair, and crossed her hands in her lap. "I think you're quite familiar with him," she concluded. "You know him as Thor."

INNOCENT
BYSTANDERS

ollis used the abundant magic to form air into a bubble around her head. It would be enough to last her an hour if she stayed calm. Karrott said something, but his voice was suppressed; she realized she couldn't project her hearing outside the bubble.

Something to work on later.

Sensing her hesitation, Karrott ran into the iron maiden and pointed to several spots inside. Then he scampered out.

Sollis stepped inside the device. She twisted herself until she fit, then flattened herself as far away from its sharp spikes as possible and pressed on the areas Karrott had highlighted.

Here goes. She looked meaningfully at Karrott, and he moved outside her field of view. The iron maiden started closing. She could feel the spikes touching her skin and wondered if she had got it wrong and would end up being the first person to actually die in a device she had come to realize was mostly for show.

Then the floor gave way.

• • • • •

"Ready to go?" Enrielle asked.

"Yes," Aidan said. He turned to Rajiv, who was sitting by Lormek's bed. "Sir . . . I just wanted to say thank you."

Rajiv smiled, even while his face showed deep signs of worry.

They headed up the stairs to Humanridge and then on to Tradebay. There they mingled with the stream of porters carrying boxes of goods up from the Shallows docks to be sent overland to Corrantha.

When they arrived, Enrielle booked them onto a Frentrunner caravan that was set to leave shortly. The clerk recognized her and, sufficiently awed in the presence of such an important family member, she didn't question the presence of the other three. "Your friends will have to ride in the back with the boxes, ma'am," she apologized, looking down and shuffling her feet. "Our wagons are so full of travelers these days."

Enrielle placed a reassuring hand on her shoulder. "That means business is booming, and that's a good thing. You're doing well. Will you let the captain know that we should like to keep to ourselves at night?" she added, and the clerk ran away, visibly relieved.

Enrielle turned to them. "Make yourselves comfortable. I have to get something. I'll be back shortly. They won't leave without me." She left hurriedly.

"Remember the last time we headed out this way? I was hiding in a cart like this one. Feels like another life," Garrett said.

Soon they were on their way again.

• • • • •

Sollis took a moment to reorient. She was in another tube, except this one was fully submerged. She could feel herself passing through a magical threshold as she fell down. She guessed that it primarily served to keep the water from rising above the level of the prison floor, but sensed there was more to it. With no time to waste, she filed the mystery away for later.

As the hatch closed softly, the tube darkened. She was ready to invoke a light, but something made her stop. Sollis let her eyes adjust.

A dim aura of magic shone from below.

She swam.

The tube took several turns, following a path like a vein inside the volcano. The water was so warm that she wondered how it hadn't all evaporated.

She made one final turn and could see where the tube ended. Magic shone within the last stretch of tunnel in mesmerizing fashion, its yellowish and blue tints painting the rock into a kaleidoscope of color.

She inhaled deeply and screamed in frustration.

Her protective air bubble kept her alive, but it also kept her from smelling the magic.

• • • • •

"Everything all right, Nyelle?" Aidan inquired. The wagon was rocking slightly.

Nyelle, emerging from a deep trance, opened her eyes. "Yeah, I was thinking. If Mom's intuition is right, and I'm a soulmage, then maybe I can help 'Mek . . . if I can find his soul."

"Whoa," Garrett whispered. "That would be so cool!"

"Is that what you're trying to do?"

"No." Nyelle laughed. "I don't know what I'm doing. Right now, I'm trying to recall all the instructions Zacharias left behind for—I think—someone like me to find and figure out how to use them. Like, can I even perceive what a soul sounds like at all?"

"Any luck?"

"Not yet. But in the meantime, I'm learning that everything really does have a sound . . . even stuff that's supposedly dead. Like"—here she raised her eyes meaningfully toward her brother and touched the bench—"this."

"Yes. I hear it loud and clear. It's saying, 'Tell her it's naughty to listen in without asking permission,'" Aidan replied.

Garrett snorted at that.

"But seriously, yes. I always thought wood could speak to me because it has a . . . well, a soul, in a way. But I never thought about why I could hear it—does that make sense? It always felt like everyone could, if only they would listen."

Nyelle thought for a moment. "I can hear it, but I can't understand what it says. To me, it's just a unique sound wave. You can have a conversation with it. So maybe it's a different kind of soul magic?"

"I don't think so." Aidan laughed. "The whole idea of guiding someone to some manifest destiny freaks me out, sis."

• • • • •

Sollis emerged from the tube.

For a long moment, her heart stopped, and she forgot to breathe.

Stretching below her was the crystal.

Her first thought was that it was a massive volcanic stone that shone with the color of magic.

Crystal color.

Straining her eyes, Sollis could see its contours in the distance.

She resisted the temptation to revoke the air bubble just so she could catch a whiff.

From this distance, the crystal's surface was perfectly smooth. Staring at it, Sollis could not shake the feeling that it moved. She guessed it was made of something that existed beyond the physical realm. Closing her eyes, she tried to sense just how far and how deeply it extended, but the feeling that registered back frightened her, and she stopped. It was immeasurably, impossibly huge.

She longed to touch it.

Sollis recalled the six-sided room from her dream. But instead of a jigsaw puzzle, before her she now saw the crystal, growing ever closer as she swam. The images that resolved the puzzle now swirled lazily inside the crystal, and all she needed to do was touch it to finally see them clearly. Her hand reached out, and she knew that in just a few seconds, everything would finally make sense.

She sank further. The crystal's size made the rest of the world dissolve, and she forgot where she was. She recalled happier days, when she would sit at the edge of the cliffs overlooking the ocean, trying out new ideas with her fingers and feeling at one with the world. She knew her purpose, and it was simple—to make contact. She got ready to let her air bubble dissipate. Her heart beat faster. Closing her eyes, she extended her fingers as far as she could and smiled.

She was finally at peace.

• • • • •

"Oh!" Nyelle exclaimed.

Aidan and Garrett glanced up at her in anticipation, and Aidan spoke. "Figure something out?"

"Yes, I sure did! I'm super hungry! When are we stopping for camp?"

A couple of seconds passed in awkward silence, and they burst out laughing. "We're almost there," Garrett said after catching his breath. "Here, have an apple."

• • • • •

Sollis's hand almost reached the surface.

She opened her eyes and took a deep breath, then revoked her air bubble. She wouldn't need it anymore. Grinning as she sank slowly, she let the field of magic extend to her and engulf her.

Then, out of nowhere, something changed. *How rude!* She froze right above the crystal. The magic that only a second before had felt so comforting suddenly grew cold, colder than anything she had ever felt.

Annoyed, she tried to move but couldn't.

Then she understood.

She had been assessed, judged, and found lacking. An overwhelming sense of disappointment and rejection filled her entire being. *I need to be here! I want the answer!* She tried to scream, but her mouth filled with water, and the pressure of being so deep below the surface suddenly became very real.

Sollis started choking.

She was drowning in place, and her mind was filled with terror.

The last thing she remembered before her lungs collapsed was being punched in the gut.

By Lormek.

Then she blacked out.

• • • • •

"After we cross tomorrow, we're going to split from the wagons." Enrielle sat back. "I would rather get into the city more discreetly . . . they might still be searching for you."

"Yeah, I'm curious about that," Nyelle said. "When we left, Grinta said we were in danger, but she didn't tell us why. Do you know?"

Enrielle turned to her for a moment, then sighed. "I suppose it won't hurt to tell you at this point." She drew them closer. "The guards will respect our privacy, but just in case . . ."

"Some time ago, a series of reports started coming in about three individuals in the Shallows, each with a rare, even mystical ability—a wildmage, a soundshaper, and a woodspeaker. You might recognize them." Enrielle grinned. "Heck, one of them sounded so much like you, Ny-ny, that I went down to check whether it *was* you. I thought for sure you'd died in the fires. But a small part of me wanted to believe that somehow you survived. Unfortunately, I was caught in a big storm, lost my way in the Inner Shallows, and if your friend Lormek hadn't found me, I might not have survived that day."

"Wait, it was you who recruited Lormek?" Aidan laid down his bowl.

"Well, not directly, but the invitation came from me."

"But Mom, why would you be afraid in the tunnels? That's not like you. At all."

Enrielle exhaled heavily, and her face hardened. "It doesn't matter why; I'm not proud of it," she said firmly, and the others exchanged a glance. *Something happened,* they shared a thought. *Something important.*

"Anyway, the Guild decided to investigate, and the task fell to me. I assigned one of my charges, a military man by the name of Darryn, to set it up."

Nyelle jumped to her feet. "Darryn?"

Her mother gestured for her to stay quiet and to sit down. "Yes, Darryn . . . why, do you know him?"

"Oh, do I now. He came to me for years!" Aidan and Garrett gave her a questioning look, and Nyelle added, "Yes, exactly, for that. It was a good way to make a living, and I liked him. He was a simple man, but earnest, and sweet, and he loved my lullabies, even though I never shaped them for him. He offered to marry me at some point." She chuckled.

Enrielle raised her eyebrow. "The apple certainly didn't fall far from the tree," she remarked, before continuing her story.

"Darryn told me he assigned someone to deal with it and assured me it was handled. He said his guy made contact with the four of you—the three the Guild wanted to watch and Lormek. Darryn also said we had an agent embedded within the group . . ." She turned to Garrett. "Presumably that was you?"

Garrett shifted uncomfortably. Aidan patted him on the back. "It's okay, bud. We were there with you."

Garrett smiled at him, visibly relieved.

"It was otherwise a low-level matter, so I set it aside," Enrielle resumed.

"Darryn's man must have been Bradd," Aidan said. "Mom, do you remember the name of the guy Darryn hired, by any chance?"

Enrielle paused. "Yeah, his name was Hortus."

"Bradd is Hortus," Aidan murmured. "Go on."

"Well, what I didn't know—what none of us knew—was that Hortus was secretly working to undermine the Guild. And he did it under secret instructions from"—Enrielle lowered her voice to a whisper—"the Frentenga family."

They stared at her. "Wait a second. But aren't you *in* the Frentenga family?" Garrett finally asked.

Enrielle nodded. "Indeed. I had no idea that my dear husband and his family were involved in this conspiracy until very recently. Albergino's grandfather—Aurelius, the patriarch—is an old-time friend of King Emmeka. This is how Gino's brother, Bernelius, ended up as her Pope. The Frentengas don't give a rat's ass which religion runs supreme, but Emmeka has an agenda. Ever since she assumed the throne, she's been carefully working to weaken the hold of the Church on Corranthean politics. Especially when it comes to trade and economics. Kenzer would've loved her, I'll tell you that."

"Which church?" Aidan asked.

"Freyg's, of course. The real reason Emmeka claimed the throne is the trading houses have kind of had it with the Church. They see it as a force that keeps economic development at bay. She's been very loyal to her mission, so she remains King. The Church has tried many times to remove her, without success. She has many powerful allies. The Church has, historically, been the dominant force pushing for Corrantha to annex Kyber—ever since King Anberg lost the Battle of Stormbridge. Emmeka is the first King to change the narrative and treat Port Kyber as an important ally, and more critically, to truly reach out to Decentea. It's worked well for everyone. Everyone, that is, except the Church because it means their power is waning, and with that, so does their wealth. You can see it on the streets of Corrantha City, where people openly display symbols of many faiths . . . in particular, followers of Thor." Enrielle grinned.

"The Frentengas were all too happy to support Emmeka in her mission, but Aurelius saw this as an opportunity to realize his own secret wish—weakening the Kyber Thieves' Guild. He figured that if the Frentengas could wrest some of the Guild's control over Kyber's administration, then the Frentrunners could become the leading trading house of Corrantha. Maybe even rival Emmeka's Rocky Road Company."

"Sounds complicated. So how do we figure into all of this?"

"You don't, Nylean. You're just innocent bystanders. When Hortus was tasked with watching you, it was inconvenient for him. So he tried to get rid of you. I don't know the details, but I was informed by Darryn—once he caught wind of the conspiracy—that Hortus sent you on several fools' errands, like breaking into Gino's office. He hoped that you would implicate yourselves, a show trial would be held, and he wouldn't have to deal with you anymore. Darryn said that instead of getting caught like you were supposed to, you kept beating the odds. Hortus was apparently working directly with my husband. That's why Gino turned to his brother, Bernie, to handle you in the city. And how some of you finally got arrested. My guess is your friend Grinta caught wind of it and tried to warn you, but it was too late."

Enrielle paused.

"Is Darryn okay? I'd like to see him," Nyelle asked.

"He is and he isn't. That's why I came down to see Bhaven. After I relayed the plot to Prime, he sent a group to teach Hortus a lesson. Hortus managed to escape, but the room that hides the entrance to the prison was destroyed. That room meant a lot to Bhaven, and he's been demanding compensation and holding Guild property stored at his inn hostage until he gets paid. The Guild thinks he's asking too much . . . Darryn went down to beat some sense into him, but"—Enrielle was clearly enjoying this part of the tale—"good ol' Bhaven's much more capable than any ol' dwarf has any right to be. Darryn got himself captured instead. I came down to negotiate his release. Bhaven's tacked on a fairly sizable ransom and, as he told me, insult fees."

"How much are we talking about?"

"It's up to twenty thousand gold," Enrielle responded casually.

Garrett whistled. "That's a lot. Like, a lot a lot."

"It is, but the Guild can afford it, and my recommendation to Prime is they pay because I know Bhaven well, and he's not likely to budge. So they'd have to kill him instead. They might still do that, damn the consequences, and that's what I was trying to get him to understand, but like I said, he can be stubborn."

"Consequences?"

"Yes. Killing Bhaven will likely lead to a reshuffle of Kyber's power hierarchy. He's much more than an innkeeper and whoremaster. Which is why I think cooler heads will prevail."

"That's way over my head." Nyelle sighed. "What about your husband? And the Frentengas?"

Enrielle smiled. "Oh, I'm sure Prime and Aurelius will reach an honorable arrangement. My guess is Bhaven will get his money, but it will come from more than just the Guild. Gino is likely to be exiled from Kyber for a while. I honestly don't mind. He needs it, and I could use a break from him. As for me, I find all this invigorating! Reminds me of how much I used to love adventuring . . . so I hope you don't mind if I hang with you all for a while."

"Mind?" Nyelle cried as she hugged her mother. "It's the best thing in the world!"

THIRD TIME'S NO CHARM

INTERLUDE: THE LAST DREAM

Sollis lies on the beach.

The sun feels nice on her face, but she cannot open her eyes. She can't breathe either.

Oh, right. I drowned. The thought amuses her, and she chuckles.

She recalls her last moment of being alive. *That boy definitely packs a punch*, she muses. Then she remembers where she was and frowns. *I got so close . . . I have to find a way back!*

Sollis realizes that she can't move. She considers the irony of the moment and then recalls that she was never very good with ironies. Then the crystal comes again into view.

The pain is instant and severe. She tries to calm herself by breathing, remembers that she can't do that, and then just thinks about breathing instead, which feels awkward but calms her down. She thinks back to that last moment.

The crystal is beautiful and flawless, and it stretches forever. Tears fill her eyes, or at least, they should. Then she notices movement under the surface of the crystal. It's like a whirlwind but bigger. *Like a vortex,* the thought pops into her mind.

It appears to be made of two intertwined parts chasing each other endlessly.

The closer she gets, the more of the crystal comes into view. The vortex is constant and powerful, and the more she looks at it, the faster and more ferocious it becomes. *If it goes on like this, the crystal will break*, she realizes, and her thoughts shift.

Sollis finds herself staring into a dark void. Extending from below her is something that appears to be a rope but is made of energy and dark matter and antimatter. "I don't even know what those words mean," she mutters in confusion. She begins gliding quietly on the rope, slowly at first, and the crystal fades behind her, and she is floating out of the volcano. As her speed increases, she sees Kyber from above for a brief moment, then it is replaced by a view of the entire world. She sees the sun and the moons. She is accelerating so rapidly that soon everything becomes blurry; little dots of bright light become streaks. She feels herself flying through things—hot and cold and large and small. Some of them are so big that she is convinced they are entire worlds.

Then she slows down.

She is almost at the end of the rope, and there is a blue-and-white world ahead of her. As she descends, she is taken with awe. It is beautiful, with large land masses and towering mountains amongst huge blue oceans. As she gets nearer, she perceives that this world is full of people, and structures, and many metal wagons that move around quickly on the ground and in the air. Her mind tries to make sense of all the strange things around her and finds comfort in several bridges. One of them looks a little like Stormbridge but at an immense scale—it stretches for miles and miles, glinting white in the sunlight, connecting a small island with a much bigger land mass and continuing on the other side to a peninsula like Kyber's. The city at the end of the bridge shows the tops of extremely tall buildings. From above, some of them are surrounded by clouds and seem like they are floating amongst them.

Nyelle would love to see this! She recalls her friend's obsession with a library in the sky.

But the bridge isn't made of rock and diamond and jade. It is made of metal and—here she pauses until the term finally comes to her: *liquid stone.* Just like the tall buildings. One of them has a large eye on top.

The eye is staring at her.

Her consciousness snaps back to the crystal. Her fingers are about to touch it. For the first time, she notices the crack. It's only a foot long, but she somehow knows that the crack is extremely important and that it definitely shouldn't be there. Her eyes focus, and her heart races with alarm. The vortex inside the crystal is causing the crack to grow!

Then the crack shifts and it spells out a word, and Sollis crumbles, her entire being swallowed by the word. It shines in a fashion so heinous, so damning that her very existence is negated by its presence, and she knows it to be true, feels it to the core of her soul.

SHAME.

And so, when Lormek appears to punch her lights out, she smiles.

It's only what she deserves.

• • • • •

They woke up before dawn, and Enrielle let the caravan captain know they would walk the rest of the way. Then they peeled off and headed toward the south gates. There was no road around the city, so they made their way through the woods.

It was still early morning when they reached a forest clearing and sat down to have a quick bite.

"Last time we left the main road, we almost died," Nyelle said uncomfortably as they were getting ready to pack up.

Enrielle smiled. "Very unlucky. Surely there are plenty of wild animals, but being attacked by a werewolf is very rare this close to the city. If you go south a ways, it becomes far more dangerous."

"How does that phrase go?" Garrett asked suddenly. "About lightning striking twice?"

They followed his outstretched hand.

At the edge of the clearing stood a werewolf. Its eyes examined them, and it shook its head slowly, causing the hairs on its neck to move like a halo. It raised one of its massive paws toward them.

"Is that what I think it is?" Garrett whispered in awe.

"Yes," Enrielle replied as she jumped to her feet. "Do you have silvered blades?" she asked out the side of her mouth.

"Lormek and I talked about getting them after the last attack but never got the chance," Nyelle said. "Guys . . . it's the same one."

Aidan let his sword fall to the ground. He was trembling. "They took my bow and silver-tipped arrows when they arrested us. What do we do now?"

Enrielle pulled out a long, silvered dagger. "Hide in a tree." Then she turned to the wolf. "Last time we met, friend, I was severely injured. It won't be so easy this time." She twisted her dagger this way and that. In her other hand, she held the talisman.

It was glowing faintly.

Garrett bolted toward a large oak, but the rest of them didn't move. They seemed compelled to watch the scene.

The werewolf growled. Then, in the accent of an animal that had never spoken in any language, it pointed at Aidan and said, "*Cub*."

"Go already! Why are you standing there?" Enrielle hissed at them. Nyelle edged toward the end of the clearing and closed her eyes. She was sensing the vibrations around her, of the sun and the foliage and the ground and many little critters running away as Garrett scrambled up the tree as high as he could go.

The soundscape became visible in her mind.

Her eyes still closed, Nyelle could hear Enrielle's heart beating calmly, steadily, and sense the tautness of her muscles as they prepared to spring into action. She could hear how Aidan was frozen in fear, his heartbeat so fast it might stop. His respiration was shallow and irregular. His muscles were whining faintly as if about to shut down. The talisman whirred, coming off to Nyelle as content, almost disinterested. That was odd. Diving into the sound, she realized that the talisman perceived little danger and trusted its bearer.

Nyelle wondered how a talisman could think.

Then, still in sound vision, she examined the werewolf. It made a deep, predatory growl. She saw the sound clearly, and it was so much more; it was a rich and complex rumble, deadly and beautiful. It showed her the pain of defeat, of escaped prey, of an incredible disappointment. It communicated the abiding hurt of traumatic loss, and also desire, a longing so deep and lasting that it verged on insanity. It spoke of a hatred forged in decades of memories.

She realized it was directed at the talisman.

She opened her eyes in shock.

• • • • •

"I found her this morning. She washed up on shore—maybe a ship went off course and fell prey to the rocks. She's still alive."

Sollis could feel someone lift her up gently and carry her away. She tried to speak but couldn't muster the strength. Even opening her eyes was too herculean a task, so she just concentrated on breathing.

"Thank you for coming to get me. I know this woman." She heard the voice coming from her carrier. It was a safe voice, one she knew from somewhere, and it made her happy.

Then she blacked out again.

• • • • •

The talisman shone with a faint white light, much weaker than the one Nyelle remembered from their previous encounter. She tried to concentrate on creating another sound fist to punch the werewolf but found that she was too distracted by the richness of her sound vision. Frustrated, she took several deep breaths and tried to focus.

"Begone, beast!" Enrielle shouted at the werewolf. She moved rapidly, her dagger making incisive movements through the air as she held the talisman forward.

The werewolf leapt. His direction took Enrielle by surprise, and she misjudged his trajectory. Instead of jumping at her, he aimed at the talisman she was holding. His powerful jaws closed on it, and his momentum took him away, tearing the dagger out of Enrielle's hand where she had struck his side. He screamed in agony as he landed, and Nyelle's concentration broke as she found herself empathizing with the pain of his soul.

The werewolf stood up shakily. Light smoke rose from the wound where the dagger had lodged. It was clearly burning him from the inside, but the massive creature's eyes spoke of a determination that could not be easily overcome. The talisman shone brightly now, even as most of its light was contained inside the werewolf's mouth. They could all see his neck muscles bulging hideously, as he slowly, painfully tightened his jaw with an immense effort, his humanlike eyes filling with tears.

Then they heard a sharp crack.

The light stopped shining, and the werewolf, panting, opened his jaw and let the darkened pieces of the talisman fall to the ground.

The sound of the talisman breaking finally snapped Nyelle into focus. It was a sound like she'd never heard before. Not just snapping metal, but the sound of magic and power beyond the material, at the very edge of existence. Something she now knew was real, but never before knew how to hear.

It was the sound of a soul.

"I'm so sorry, brother," Nyelle whispered. She knew exactly what she needed to do.

• • • • •

Sollis found herself lying in a meadow. It was a perfect day, sunny and warm, with a few clouds floating overhead. The grass underneath her felt comfortable and inviting, and everything smelled crisp and wonderful. Sheep were grazing nearby, and their coat was so perfect and so soft that she couldn't help but reach out to touch one of them. It felt softer than anything she could imagine, and she sighed in satisfaction. Then she felt something against her skin and looked down to see a sweet ladybug crawling lazily. The ladybug glanced up at her.

"You're going to be fine," the ladybug said, and Sollis smiled. "Drink some of this."

Sollis opened her eyes.

The ladybug transformed into Rajiv's face. He was holding a steaming mug to her lips. His touch was gentle, and his eyes were caring and kind. "Oh good, you're awake. This will help you feel better. You almost drowned."

Sighing, memory of the beautiful meadow fresh in her mind, she took a sip.

It tasted bland.

• • • • •

Nyelle, her eyes shut tightly, seized the soul of the powerful amulet. It was afraid, alone, and confused. Forged with a singular purpose, it had nowhere to go and no more reason to exist.

She found the trembling anchor of the little spirit and guided it across the clearing toward Aidan. Aidan's soul was resonating in fear. But the underlying sound wave had another quality.

A quality that matched the little one she was guiding.

She brought Aidan's frightened soul and the talisman's lost one together.

It took but a split second, and then the souls merged.

Nyelle opened her eyes. Enrielle had started to circle the werewolf, aiming to drive home the dagger still stuck in his side. The werewolf was circling as well, preparing to strike, secure in the knowledge there were no more weapons that could hurt him.

Then everyone stopped and stared at Aidan.

He transformed right before their eyes. One moment, he was standing there. Then he was surrounded by a white aura, which grew so bright he was lost from view. A moment later, the aura dissipated, and standing there instead of Aidan was a second, smaller werewolf.

The new werewolf had a shining scar running down the left side of its face, and it was grinning. Then it spoke in Aidan's voice.

"Step back. I'll take care of him. With that knife in his ribs, he doesn't stand a chance."

• • • • •

Finally strong enough to rise to her elbows, Sollis noticed Lormek in a nearby bed.

"Is he all right?"

Rajiv shook his head.

"Physically, yes—and I can keep him alive even if he doesn't wake up. But something ails his soul, and it leaves him unconscious."

"Let me try." Sollis walked on wobbly legs across the room.

"Hey there, buddy . . . are you all right?"

Lormek moaned. She squeezed his hand.

Lormek's eyes snapped open. He jerked his hand back and scrambled away, pressing himself into the corner and babbling incoherently. His eyes were full of fear.

Rajiv came to his side quickly. "At least he's up." He pulled Sollis away gently but firmly. Lormek calmed down a bit. "Better you stay away from him until we figure out what's going on."

• • • • •

Wolf-Aidan stood over the bigger werewolf's lifeless body. Then he reached down with his mouth and slowly but carefully pulled out the silvered dagger. He winced as the base of the blade touched his lip and hastily dropped it on the ground.

"I believe this is yours." He looked at Enrielle. "Boy, the silver really does burn."

Nyelle ran to him and hugged him deeply, burying her face in his mane. "I'm so sorry, Aidan! I had no choice."

"It's all right, sister. I kinda like it, honestly. And if you hadn't done it, I'm pretty sure we would have died."

Garrett climbed down from the tree. "Can someone explain what the hell just happened?"

Nyelle stood up and pointed at the dead werewolf. "When he broke the talisman, I could hear it. It was different than anything else in the world." She turned to her mother and grinned. "But you told me about soul magic. I've been thinking about all the stuff in Zacharias's book, and I somehow understood the talisman had a soul."

"Whoa," Garrett whispered. "Really? An object with a soul?"

"A very limited one, with an explicit purpose. Zacharias had a term for it. He called it a soul spark. I didn't understand what he meant. I do now."

"Oh, Talus," Enrielle murmured softly. "What did you do?"

"Anyway, when it broke, I guess its purpose ended. It was going to dissipate. But at that moment, I heard Aidan's soul scream and realized they resonated with each other perfectly. So I did the first thing that came to mind—I brought them together. It made them both . . . happy."

"It shone!" Garrett exclaimed. "I saw it. His scar shone right when the thing broke."

Nyelle shrugged. "I really don't have a good way to explain it. But it seems like when they joined, the talisman's soul conferred a form of its power on Aidan. It's like the talisman carried over its most recent experience. I guess that's why he became a werewolf."

"And because I started off as Aidan and not an animal, I carry all my own experiences and memories into my wolf form . . . just like Karrott."

Enrielle stepped forward. "I do believe this is the very same were-wolf that attacked me when you were born, Nylean. Looks like it carried a grudge for all these years. I'm glad it's over. Let's get moving, though. For what it's worth, with a pet wolf, we have a much better chance of getting into the city at the south gate."

THE SOUL CRIB

"We'll head straight to the Royal College," Enrielle said as they approached the south gate. Garrett was riding on Aidan's back, clearly enjoying himself.

"Mom, you never actually told us why we're coming here other than letting things cool down in lava town." Nyelle flashed a withering look at Garrett who snorted at her little rhyme. "But we didn't have to go all the way to Corrantha City."

"We need to see Xephyna."

"The adept? Why?"

"Just trust me. There is something I want to show her . . . good day to you, my good man!" she hailed the guard whose post they'd just come to.

The guard's eyes locked on Aidan. "A wolf?"

"Yes!" Garrett gave Aidan's scruff a vigorous rub. "He's my pet, and I love him so much!" The guard raised an eyebrow as Aidan growled.

Nyelle couldn't hide her smile. "Hey . . . he's *our* pet, not just yours."

"Fine!" Garrett leaned down and wrapped his hands around Aidan's neck. "But I'm the only one who can ride him!"

Aidan shook vigorously, in the process throwing a laughing Garrett to the ground.

The guard sighed, then turned to Enrielle. "There's been recent rumors of a werewolf so we're being a little careful." He pointed at a sign posted behind him. "Those are the rules, but what they say is keep to yourself and don't cause a bother, and you'll be all right. It's one silver apiece to enter." He gestured at her jacket with its embroidered Frentrunners symbol. "Do you know your way around?"

Enrielle handed him the money. "Yes, we're familiar."

"All right. Go ahead. And do yourselves a favor—watch the wolf! People can get skittish."

• • • • •

It was midmorning by the time they arrived at the Royal College. Nyelle was struck again by the magnificence of the building. *I wonder if they have more of Zacharias's writings*, she found herself thinking. *I'd like to visit the library someday.*

Enrielle faced no trouble gaining entry. She was well known after a decade of attending social functions as a member of the Frentenga family. Even when she went unrecognized, Nyelle noted that all it took was for her mother to flash a smile at most anyone and they would respond favorably. *I know so little about you, Mom.* She felt embarrassed. *I hope you'll tell me more once this is all over.*

They waited in the meticulously maintained college gardens. The morning glow gave everything an otherworldly feel. Aidan stayed quiet so as not to cause alarm were he overheard speaking, but he did force Garrett to walk. Garrett in turn stuck his tongue out at him before giving him a hug. Even in wolf form, Aidan was taller than the gnome, and they found themselves laughing at the strangely comical gesture.

Eventually, they were shown to Xephyna's office.

Just as messy as the last time, Nyelle noted to herself.

• • • • •

"So many guests!" Xephyna jumped off her chair and rushed over. "Oh, and look—a werewolf! What's your name, werewolf?"

"Aidan," he answered hesitantly. "But . . . how did you know? I've stayed silent the whole time to make sure everybody thought I was a house wolf."

"It's all in the eyes." Xephyna bobbed her head vigorously. "And if you're here and not eating everybody, then it's easy to conjecture that you were taken as a humanoid . . . elf or half-elf, I'm guessing? Anyway, that doesn't happen very often! You must have some resistance to the dire toxin . . . mind if I take a sample of your blood?"

"No need. How I became a werewolf was not . . . the usual way."

Xephyna cocked her head. "Not the usual way? Now, that's interesting! You weren't bit by a direwolf?"

Enrielle intervened. "It's a long story, Xeph, and we'll be delighted to share it with you afterward, but please, at this moment, we need your assistance."

"Right, right." Xephyna turned to Enrielle. "Sorry about that. A friend of mine was doing research into were-ing—right where you came from actually, in Port Kyber. He left his research notes with me before he disappeared. He's the one who first proposed the mechanism through which were-ing occurs, and the link to dire critters. Very interesting."

"Was his name Karrott, by any chance?" Garrett asked.

"Why yes! Do you know him?"

"Aidan and I, uh, met him recently." Garrett grinned.

"Oh, that's just excellent news!" Xephyna clasped her hands in joy. "I was so worried that he ended up doing something silly like getting himself bit in order to check his theories! He's such a clever one, Karrott, but not very careful."

"Yeah . . . I can assure you, he's still both of these things."

"You must tell him to come visit me," Xephyna continued enthusiastically. "His theory seems right on the money! I've spent a bunch of time trying to poke holes in it, and I have some ideas about how we can go about proving it."

"Oh, I don't think that will be necessary." Garrett chuckled. "From all we could tell, he's proven it pretty conclusively."

"Even better news!" Xephyna turned to Enrielle again. "So, what did you bring me?"

Enrielle pulled out an ornate scroll case. "I've had this since . . ." She paused, took a deep breath, and continued, "Since the Battle of Stormbridge." Aidan bared his fangs as the rest of them gasped. "It's written in that strange language. I know you're the foremost authority on it."

"English?" Xephyna looked up at her.

"I believe so. It was written by Zacharias. I . . . kept it . . . but . . ." She took another deep breath. "I never mentioned it to anyone." She lowered her eyes. "Please be careful with it. He told me it was an important finding he made before . . . before he left."

Xephyna accepted the scroll case. "Wow . . . from way back in the wars, huh?" She inspected it gingerly. "Is it preserved by magic?"

"I think so. I opened it a few times in the first couple hundred years, just to look at his writing. The parchment appeared fresh."

"All right then." Xephyna strode toward a corner desk. "Give me a couple of hours, and I'll get this translated!"

• • • • •

After a time, Xephyna came to invite them back into her office. She had arranged chairs and a rug for Aidan to lie on. Then she climbed on a stool, cleared her throat, and started reading aloud.

The Soul Crib, by Zacharias

When we came upon the peninsula, it was immediately clear that it was protected by a god. And not just any god; the divinations were clear, that this was done by XLTL, the supreme deity, the one sometimes known as X. After Kenzer found a way to travel past the flying stones and through the flesh-eating fog, we delved deep into the volcano, and there we discovered the huge crystal, the soul crib itself. I have written much about how it was made from materials both exotic and unknown, and of its unusual abilities such as transforming metal. And also of its purpose, as a container of souls; not a prison, but a safe house.

Here, I note my most important discovery. With this knowledge, Kenzer will attempt the ascension, and as I guide him, my own soul will be lost. I write this in foreign tongue, intuited from walking the soul bridge, in the assurance that it will not be casually understood except by an inquirer of sufficient skill and mental acuity.

Let me, therefore, lay bare my conjectures.

The crib has been here for a long time. My best guess is forty, perhaps fifty thousand years; long before the humanoid races came to populate the world of Corrantha.

There are three souls contained within. Two are of mortal creatures, the nature of which I cannot establish with certainty. When I attempt to infer from the echoes of their resonance their prior material form, they appear to my mind as reptilian. It is extremely difficult to gain a better understanding, as they are dormant, suspended in an eternal dream, and protected by the soul crib. But I suspect that, fantastically, they might be dragons somehow escaped from the Underground Realm.

The third is unlike the other two; it is awake, but only barely. It exists in the crib for a singular purpose and has been given just enough of a spark to fulfill that purpose. This soul is immortal in nature. Having considered this at length, I propose that it is a celestial, an immortal who is not a god. The question remains—why should it be in the crib with the others?

What is its singular purpose?

Here, I stand on shakier ground, and my conclusions cannot be verified except by going on the journey with Kenzer.

Here, then, is my theory: this third being is a guardian. It was placed in the crib by X to ensure that the other two remained dormant. Like a cloth covering, it is not aware of this purpose, only of its need to exist, and yet its very existence protects the contents of the crib. I sometimes wonder what terrible thing the poor immortal creature must have done to deserve this punishment, to lose its agency and its place in the heavens. But the ways of the gods are not for mortals to question.

All three souls are fed by the energy of the crib, and from all I can tell, this can continue for millions of years without trouble, for the crib has two unique properties: first, it is so dense and made of materials so exotic that its energy might exceed that of the sun. Second, the soul bridge attached to and hanging off its edge traverses many worlds. Thus it feeds from the magma underneath and across the soul bridge, the combined energy keeping it intact.

I shudder to think of what would happen should the crib crack and break—it likely will collapse under its own weight and will then destroy this world and all the worlds connected to it via the soul bridge, by pulling them into itself. Which must be why X has commanded the celestial guardian to inhabit it; so long as the guardian remains within, such horrible damage cannot accrue, for the guardian's presence will ensure that the crib stays intact.

And why should the most powerful of deities go to so much trouble?

Now I arrive at the most fanciful aspect of my theory. If I am right, then Kenzer will ascend, and I shall be able to satisfy myself that I was correct; if I am wrong, then we shall both be extinguished forever. Either way, in your diligence by reading this essay, you will possess an important clue that I, sadly, cannot have.

Like Kenzer, these two mortal souls were aiming to travel to Celestia. But unlike Kenzer, they were battling each other, and in this, they failed themselves. Perhaps they needed a soulmage, or perhaps neither was ready to accept the need for one to lead, the other to follow. I judge by the sheer power inherent in this remarkable device, the soul crib, that X admired their attempt, but that they were about to destroy each other with their arrogance. X thus suspended judgment of their conflict and let the issue rest for a moment. The gods do not share our sense of time, and maybe X has simply not yet decided how to deal with the matter.

And so they shall slumber until he turns his mind to them again.

This conclusion is supported by all the facts that I have gathered. Both Kenzer and I are preparing to stake our very souls on it.

"Oh, wow," Garrett whispered softly.

"Are you all right, Mom?" Nyelle asked.

Enrielle, whose cheeks were covered in tears, nodded. "Yes. It's just that . . . it has been so long." She sighed deeply, wiping her tears. "Zach was a truly remarkable person."

"But this is surely a fantastic discovery!" Xephyna shouted. "I know you'll want this back," she said as she handed the scroll case back to Enrielle. "But I'm going to keep a copy I made for my records. All right?"

Enrielle assented, her face expressionless.

Nyelle broke the silence. "Wait a second . . . this looks like . . ." She was pointing at a painting sitting on Xephyna's desk, depicting the gnome standing inside her lab. She pulled out the portrait of her mother and Albergino Frentenga. "It looks like this! Do you know how they're made? They appear so real."

Xephyna took a quick glance at it. "Yes, it's called paintography, and this is a paintograph." She handed it back. "The school of wizardry spent decades working on it before coming up with the right process. The idea came a long while ago through a wildmage who traveled on the soul bridge. The Magic Corps can make them now. They've recently become fashionable amongst the big trading houses. I just got this one . . . I didn't have to pay for it." She beamed at them.

Then as realization dawned on her, Xephyna faced Enrielle. "But you should know all that, right? Since you're in it."

Before she could answer, Aidan pawed at the floor. "Did you feel that?"

They looked at him in surprise. A second later, a slight tremor shook the building.

"Whoa. What was that?" Garrett exclaimed.

"Didn't you tell us this happens when the volcano erupts?" Nyelle asked.

"Yes! But it shouldn't be happening again so soon!" The adept ran over and rummaged through a pile of papers, then picked one and held it up. "The next suboceanic eruption shouldn't occur until seventy to one hundred and twenty years from now!"

Shouts of panic could be heard outside.

"Come with me!" Xephyna started running. They followed her up a spiral staircase, joining others from all over the college. They emerged at the top of one of the towers and ran to the guardrail. Xephyna pushed through the crowd, climbed on a stone bench, and pointed. "Look!"

In the distance, over Kyber the clouds shone with the color of magic.

"Uh oh," Garrett said to no one in particular. "Should we head back now?"

CRISIS

Enrielle commandeered a Frentrunner fastwagon. As soon as he realized who his passenger was, the driver, a fellow named Muetell, was visibly awed. He did all he could to make her happy—even if it meant letting the wolf, which clearly made him nervous, sit in the back of his wagon. The horses were also skittish but calmed down after Nyelle spoke softly to each of them in turn.

"What did you say to them? Do you speak horse now?" Garrett asked after the wagon started moving.

"Not really, but I do speak 'soul.' I found their fear, calmed it down, and encouraged them. Now that I know what to search for, souls are easier to locate—at least when it comes to animals. They don't hide theirs like we do."

Aidan whispered so as not to alert the driver. "That truly is remarkable, sister. I am very grateful that you figured it out when you did . . . we wouldn't be here otherwise."

"I am too." Nyelle stared at Enrielle. "Mom, what do you think is going on?"

Enrielle's eyes were closed. She was clutching the scroll case in her lap. "Mom?"

Sighing, Enrielle opened her eyes. "I'm sorry. His voice came through so clearly in his writing . . . I still miss him and Kenzer very much." She sighed again. "When I last came searching for you, I felt them . . ." She hesitated. "That's why I couldn't find my way in the tunnels, Ny-ny. It was such a shock when I suddenly felt their presence . . . I lost myself in it."

Nyelle squeezed her mother's hand. "You mean when Lormek found you?"

Enrielle nodded.

"Wait! That's when Lormek said he got his calling, right? The same afternoon?" They turned to stare at Garrett. "Well, his calling came from Thor, didn't it?"

Enrielle nodded again. "Yes, you're right. Thor blessed him, and because I have—had—such a strong connection to . . . Thor . . . I felt his presence in the moment. I was deeply grateful for it, but you see how it really was unexpected. I didn't understand what happened. Or maybe I wasn't ready to acknowledge it. But I do now."

"Huh. That's pretty cool, being touched by a god like that," Garrett said enviously.

"Or in your case, just being *touched*," Aidan growled.

• • • • •

In accordance with Enrielle's instructions, Muetell drove as hard as the horses would go. They reached the Kyber trail's furthest camp at dusk. It was a small area, somewhat secluded from other spots. Along the trail, they had noted several caravans that seemed to have stopped and reverted direction back toward Corrantha City, and no travelers at all were coming from Kyber.

As they were setting camp, Muetell looked nervous, smelling the air.

"What is wrong, my good man?"

"It feels like a storm. We left without delay or planning, m'lady. With your permission, I should like to go and speak to one of the drivers over there." He pointed toward the nearest campsite. Enrielle nodded, and he mounted a horse and rode away.

He came back some time later. "The news is not good, ma'am. There are rumors of a stone storm that began this morning and hasn't abated since." He was clearly uncomfortable. "I've never heard of such an event—the storms are fierce, but they last but an hour at most. I find it difficult to believe, as did the driver over there, but some caravan captains have turned back already to avoid it."

"I mean, if it's true . . . I wonder if it could be related to the clouds we saw," Garrett said, then added for Muetell's benefit, "from the tower in the college. The clouds over Kyber were shining."

Muetell stared at him. "I never heard of anything like that either. Should we go back?"

"No," Enrielle said. "We will continue forward in the morning and assess the situation when we arrive. We really must make it into Kyber quickly—hopefully by tomorrow night."

"Of course, ma'am. I shall retire for the night, then. Must be well-rested for the morn, it will be stressful." Then, looking at Aidan, he said, "I s'pose it's good we have your wolf. I heard of werewolf sightings 'round here recently . . . we're in the most vulnerable spot on the trail."

Garrett chuckled. "No worries about that, Muetell. My pup here can take on anyone, even a werewolf!" Nyelle rolled her eyes and Aidan bared his fangs as the driver turned away muttering under his breath.

· · · · ·

They were on their way at first light.

In a couple of hours, Muetell slowed the wagon's pace. "This seems to confirm it; there are no wagons leaving for Corrantha City, which means none from Kyber made it out yesterday." He gestured to the empty campsites. "What shall I do, m'lady?"

Enrielle thought for a moment. "Do continue. Maybe the storm quieted by now."

The driver hesitated. "If so, there will be a mighty awful backup at Stormbridge." He urged the horses to pick up their pace.

It wasn't to be.

As they turned the final bend of the trail leading to Stormbridge, they saw it. The horses stopped and whinnied, and Muetell turned and said, "Some sight this is, ain't it? Shall we turn back? This is a fastwagon and you're a light load—we'll be at city gates right after nightfall."

The wind from the storm's fury was only a breeze at the top of the hill. Ahead of them, past the fence and tollbooths, they could see where the storm grew. Constant eddies built and dissipated, tossing around small stones and clumps of dirt. But it was the Spasm and Stormbridge itself that drew their attention.

The scene was at once majestic and vertigo inducing. The waters of the Spasm seemed to be swirling at least a hundred feet above ground, yet somehow remained over the bridge as if constrained by invisible walls. And in the swirling waters they could see them—the boulders flying, some of them so big their wagon was small by comparison. The stones floated over the Spasm, and every so often, one of them would hammer Stormbridge.

"Whoa." Garrett gasped. "That's . . . awesome."

A huge boulder struck the side of the bridge. The sound of the crash reached them, a wave that washed over them in anger even at this distance, followed a moment later by the ground under the wagon shaking slightly. The horses neighed, and only Muetell's expert handling kept them from bolting. He turned to Enrielle. "Ma'am, we have to go!"

Enrielle shook her head. "No. We shall disembark here. You go back to Corrantha City, my good man." She gestured for the rest to step off the wagon, and reaching into her jacket, handed him something. "Show this to your company captain—it's a commendation."

The driver stared at her in astonishment. "Are you sure?" She smiled. "Yes, ma'am. As you wish." He turned the horses and drove away.

"So what now?" Nyelle asked.

"Let's get as near as we can." They exchanged skeptical glances, and sensing their discomfort, Enrielle urged them on. "Remember, I was here at the edge of exactly this kind of storm before, only fiercer . . . and there was no bridge then."

"Oh, right," Garrett muttered. "With Kenzer and Zacharias." Enrielle was already walking briskly toward the gate, where a single guard standing within the open door of the tollbooth was staring at her in disbelief.

• • • • •

They stood at the edge of the stone storm.

"It should be howling, yet it isn't," Nyelle said. "I've been trying to understand why."

Another huge boulder hit the bridge, and they waited for the tremor to pass.

"It's a divine storm, not a regular one," Enrielle told them. "All the stone storms since Kenzer undid the barrier have been weak, minor echoes of the original . . . like the chasm itself retained a fragment of its initial purpose to safeguard the soul crib, and occasionally a memory would discharge for old times' sake. But this . . . this feels like the original barrier. If so, then something made it come back."

"So what do we do? It's not like any of us are wildmages or ready for ascension." Aidan's ears were flapping in the wind. "Even in wolf form, this thing scares the hell out of me."

"I don't know." Enrielle turned toward them. "I just wanted to be near it again. There is a special feeling that comes from being so close to the divine . . ." She seemed wistful.

The only sounds were those of the stones flying in the wind. It made for an unnatural rumble, as if a great beast was hungry.

"Look!" Garrett pointed toward Stormbridge.

They followed his gaze.

A small magical aura slowly became visible. It was indistinct at first. As it neared the edge of the bridge, it grew and eventually took a roughly humanoid shape.

One of a ridiculously tall woman.

She walked toward them.

• • • • •

It took Sollis a couple of minutes to get to them. "Hey, you guys. I was wondering if you were going to come by. Was gonna look for you in Corrantha City. Is that Aidan?" She pointed. "Did you get bit by a direwolf?"

"Yes, it's me. And no. It's a long story. We'll tell you later."

Sollis looked toward Enrielle. "And who might you be?"

"My mom," Nyelle said. "And, well . . . uh . . . his too." She pointed at Aidan, who responded with a wolfish grin. Sollis raised an eyebrow.

"Where's Lormek?" Nyelle asked.

"With his father. Umm . . . he's sick."

Nyelle couldn't hide her disappointment.

"*Excuse* me!" Garrett shouted. "How did you come through this . . . insanity?" He gestured at the chaos in front of them.

"Oh, that." Sollis turned and glanced back at the stone storm. "I was pondering how to make it through, and it just came to me, honestly. Think of it as a parallel ethereal pathway across Stormbridge. I've been learning and my power has been growing. A lot. I have much to tell you . . . but let's do it on the other side, okay? We really need to get back to Kyber."

"We can't go through *that*!"

"Don't worry, just stay close to me. Nothing will hurt you as long as you're inside my bubble—it will mostly feel like a normal crossing."

• • • • •

When they emerged on the other side, frustrated travelers gathered there erupted in alarm. Ignoring the frenzy they caused, Enrielle again commandeered a Frentrunner barouche from amongst the many waiting for the storm to abate. Once the two merchants that had hired the barouche realized who she was, they happily accepted the quadruple fee refund and her promise of a favor. Enriclle impressed upon the driver the need to ride without stopping for the night.

By the time they'd caught each other up, it was dusk. Kyber was a few hours away.

"So what's with the shining clouds?" Garrett asked. "Is it from the underwater crystal?"

"It has to be," Sollis responded. "It's leaking magic. That's why everything in, around, and over Kyber has this glow. I can feel it everywhere—I've been able to experiment so much in such a short time. It's also roused the monsters from the Deeps. The militia has been busy fending them off in the tunnels. The Lieutenant has called in all available forces to the Shallows—they set up base at the docks, took it over entirely, the Steadfast and Lassy too. And the church."

"All of them? That's like a thousand people."

"Nearly all—all routes in and out of the city except the main tunnel are closed, and they are keeping a skeleton crew in critical areas. The Stairway is still open too, but nobody cares."

"I'm still amazed that you managed to get so close to the crystal . . . ," Enrielle said quietly. "When Kay and Zach did it . . . they said only a very special and powerful kind of wildmage could even try. When they took me down to see it—from a fair distance—I could sense it trying to repel me. It wasn't pleasant, almost like being punched in the gut."

Sollis stared at her. "Punched in the gut?"

"Yes." Enrielle returned her stare. "Why? Is that important?"

"It might be. When I got near, that's how it felt before I blacked out. I've been replaying the moment in my mind—it seemed like everything was going fine and then suddenly the crystal decided that . . ." Here she paused for a while and blushed. "I wasn't ready. So it rejected me."

"That sounds a lot like being repelled. Other than Lormek delivering the punch like you told us, which can't be literally true, did you notice anything else?"

Sollis sat back. "Well . . . I didn't think it was important until just now. The last thing I saw was a small crack on the surface. Not large—a couple of feet or so. But it did look out of place."

"You think that's what's causing all the trouble?" Garrett asked.

A few seconds passed with Sollis deep in thought before speaking in a grave tone. "It might be. And if so, then I suspect the world is about to end."

They turned to her in shock.

"Think about it," she continued. "It all makes sense now. Remember my puzzle dream I told you about? When I got near the crystal, I think I saw them—the souls trapped inside of it, and I'm sure those were the people from my dream. It also fits with the description of the soul crib you just told me about. But the thing is . . ." She paused.

"Yes?" Enrielle prompted.

"There were only two souls inside. Not three. If the one that's missing is the guardian . . ."

"Then according to Zacharias, the entire thing will collapse unto itself and destroy the world," Nyelle finished the sentence.

"Multiple worlds!" Garrett said enthusiastically.

Sollis looked at him in distaste. "If the guardian is gone, then the magic may be leaking through the crack I saw, which might also explain why the mountain is waking up and the divine stone barrier is back."

"Maybe the crack is how the guardian escaped. How much time do you think we have left, Sollis?" Aidan murmured.

Sollis shuddered. "I have no idea, but this is starting to feel like a serious crisis . . . and I can't imagine we have very long."

"So how do we find this guardian, or a different one who could do the job?" Nyelle asked, but nobody had an answer.

REVELATIONS FIVE

The magical glow provided eerie illumination at night, and as light from the moons Kuuri and Anni filtered through it, their images splintered unnaturally. Even standing a mile away at the main tunnel entrance, they could see the buildings that dotted the mountainside silhouetted in a dim red aura, and the few torches carried by those who hadn't fled shining with a blue flame. Inside Tradebay Tunnel, the glow refracted off the walls in crazy patterns, with colors mixing and bouncing off each other. It was mesmerizing.

The tremors that shook the mountain every couple of hours also made it disorienting.

When they arrived at Tradebay, Enrielle had to go back to her official duties. She hugged Nyelle and Aidan, then patted Garrett on the head, causing him to giggle. She shook Sollis's hand. "Go figure this out," she said. "I know that I will see you again."

Then she left, and they headed down to the Shallows. On the way, Aidan transformed spontaneously back into his humanoid form. Luckily, it happened in a quiet moment when no one saw it take place. "Looks like I know when my threedays are now," he commented casually.

Oddly, the clothing and equipment he had on him reappeared with the transformation.

• • • • •

The Shallows docks were overrun by the Kyber militia. It was a madhouse of activity, and the group quickly agreed to head toward the Church of Tranquility.

When they got there, it was full of injured militiamen.

Once they managed to convince the officer in charge to let them through and found Rajiv, he was unusually haggard. "I've been treating them so they can return to the front lines. Freyg has stayed with me, but I can feel her irritation with my constant requests; it is not pleasant." He sighed before adding, "No time to take care of anybody else."

"Is the situation really that bad?" Nyelle asked.

"It seems that way, dear child. The Deeps monsters are relentless, I'd even say desperate. I keep telling the officers it sounds like they're afraid of something and simply trying to escape, but no one will listen to me." He sighed again. "Soon enough, I fear I will no longer be able to heal our wounded. What will happen then?"

"Can't Lormek help?" Aidan asked. "He can heal, we saw him do it."

"He could and he would, were he able. But he is in a state. They've granted me the courtesy of one private room, and that's where I'm keeping him."

"What's wrong with him?"

"I wish I knew, for then I could heal it. He seems normal, except always very tired. He eats little and cannot bring himself to leave his room. And"—he looked up at Sollis—"when she is near, he panics." Two more soldiers were carried through the door on makeshift stretchers. "Excuse me. I have to go tend to them." He squared his shoulders and left hurriedly.

Sollis looked at her friends and shrugged. "I have no idea why. When I woke up here, he was still stuck in that nightmare, and my voice snapped him out of it. But now he's scared of me. It's very strange."

"Wait a second," Aidan said. "Didn't we establish your souls are linked together?"

"We did?" Sollis seemed confused.

"Yeah, when you were down there by yourself, Rajiv did some divination and told us you were connected, but he couldn't understand it. Your *souls* were connected." Aidan stared meaningfully at Nyelle.

"Right. I remember his words now," Nyelle responded. "He actually said that Lormek's soul was intertwined with somebody else's, and we assumed it had to be yours, Sollis."

"Why?"

"Because he's been feeling you like a ghost limb," Nyelle said softly. Sollis looked at her with genuine surprise. "It's why we knew you were arrested before we found out it was true. Lormek sensed it when they . . . when they muzzled you. He collapsed when it happened. We never discussed it with you because . . . well . . . it was pretty awkward."

"Oh." Sollis sat next to the altar. "So . . . he wasn't *just* being weird then." Nyelle shook her head. "I guess it could also explain why I saw him punching me out of the crystal."

"Do you think you could figure it out, Nyelle?" Aidan asked.

"I can always try. Sollis, are you okay with me doing . . . my thing? My new soul thing?" Nyelle eyed Sollis, whose hands shook slightly in her lap. The wildmage nodded.

Nyelle moved next to the room where Lormek was staying, opened the door slightly, and peeked inside. They heard her soft whisper projected toward them across the crowded room. "Looks like he's asleep." Then she leaned against the door frame and closed her eyes.

• • • • •

A couple of minutes later, she was back to share.

"Took longer than I thought. I know what to search for, but it was easier with Lormek since he's the only one in the room. Here . . ." She gestured at the room full of casualties and sighed. "So many vessels reflecting the agony of their souls."

"Vessels?" Aidan asked.

"Yes, right, I guess that's how it comes across to me now. Souls are tied to the body like . . . like a bird in a custom cage. The body is a container. It keeps the soul happy and fed, and each body is tied to one soul . . . am I making sense? That's also how, say, a soul spark can live in an object, like with the talisman—the object is the vessel—but the soul gives it awareness."

"Wait, hold on. Are you saying the talisman was . . . alive? I didn't quite catch that before."

"After a fashion, yes. I can't explain it better—Zacharias did, and even I couldn't understand his book until recently." She turned to Sollis. "Anyway, I can tell that there's a connection between the two of you. But . . ."

"But what?"

"It's . . . complicated. I can see the link, but it looks . . . off. Like you two are dancing around each other, rather than being tied together. I don't understand it. And then . . ." She paused again. "Then I can also see that your soul is connected elsewhere."

"Elsewhere?"

"Yes. I tried to follow but couldn't . . . I was blocked by something."

Garrett, who had kept quiet until now, spoke up. "Ny-ny . . ." He ducked under Nyelle's hand as she tried to slap him for using her childhood nickname. "Okay, Nyelle." He laughed. "But seriously. You're saying that you can see the soul of Sollis is connected to Lormek's, but not exactly, and then to something else, but you can't say where the other connection goes?"

"That's about the size of it."

"No wonder she's messed up!" Garrett pointed at Sollis. "I'm dizzy hearing about it!"

Just as he said it, the volcano shook again.

• • • • •

The grueling pace of a forced march and the shock of current events had exhausted everyone, and they decided to rest until dawn. Sollis stayed in the main room to keep away from Lormek. She claimed she didn't need much sleep anyway; the surges of ambient magic were apparently sustaining her in some fashion. Her discomfort around Lormek was evident.

Rajiv came into the room to take a nap, palpably exhausted. He slept on a small cot at the foot of Lormek's bed. When he got up, Aidan, whose body was still adjusting to being a werewolf and who hadn't slept at all, could see just how much the man had aged.

Aidan also noted that, just as his elven eyes allowed him clearer vision than he might otherwise have in wolf form, so did his wolfin eyes give him the ability to see in the dark in his elven form. After Rajiv left, he prepared a simple breakfast for the others.

"Good morning," Lormek said as they were finishing their meager repast.

"Lormek!" Garrett jumped on the bed and gave him a long hug. The rest came over.

Nyelle held Lormek's hand, and he smiled warmly. "We have so much to tell you."

• • • • •

"Wow, that's quite a story." Lormek nodded appreciatively. "Hard to wrap my head around it." He stared at Aidan. "Are you really a were-wolf now?"

"Yes, but because of the way I became one, I think I'm also a little different than the typical werewolf. I'm not sure how yet. I'm able to carry all my stuff with me when I'm in my other form, for one thing. It somehow comes back when I turn elven."

"Well, I'd have expected that you'd be able to control the transitions." Aidan stared at him. "Wait, you haven't thought about it?" Lormek was surprised. "If you got your were-ing from the talisman, which was made by a wizard, then the whole thing should be less . . . chaotic than with the disease, no? It's how divine magic works, in a sense—if you know how to ask for it, and the god deems you worthy, then it happens, but it isn't predictable. With a wizard, I'd expect the power to be structured and come from within. Have you tried it?"

Aidan stood in shocked silence for a second, then closed his eyes. A little later, his image grew indistinct, surrounded by an aura that quickly turned too bright to see through. Then it dissipated and wolf-Aidan stood there instead. "Well, I'll be." He wagged his tail before changing back. "I just realized that my transformation last night wasn't spontaneous at all—I did it subconsciously because we were heading down here, and I didn't want to scare people." He beamed. "Now that I know how to do it, I'm in full control. Thank you, buddy!"

Lormek laughed. "You're welcome, I suppose, although it seemed pretty obvious." He looked back at Nyelle. "How's my dad doing?"

She shook her head. "Not so great, 'Mek. He looks utterly spent."

"I need to help him!" Lormek tried unsuccessfully to rise. He was deeply embarrassed. "I don't know what's happening to me . . . I feel fine, but when I try to move, my muscles feel like they're stuck." He sighed in frustration.

"How do you mean, stuck?"

"Like . . . I'm being held down somehow. Or maybe a better way to describe it is I don't want to get up. It's very hard to explain."

"Like the ghost limb," Garrett whispered. "I wonder if they're connected somehow."

"What did you say?" Nyelle turned to him.

"Just that maybe those two things are connected. You know, Lormek being able to sense . . ." Garrett glanced furtively at Lormek for a second before resuming, "Her . . . when she's gone, and him feeling held down right now. You know, because he's afraid of her," he added by way of explanation.

Nyelle seemed to go into a trance.

"Oh, it's her turn now, is it?" Garrett murmured.

• • • • •

Opening her eyes a little while later, Nyelle smiled. "That was very clever, Garrett. I've discovered something."

"What?" Lormek asked. "Is it going to help me get out of this bed?"

"Maybe." Nyelle turned to the others. "Remember I told you I saw Lormek's and Sollis's"—she made sure to hold Lormek's hand tight as fear came into his eyes—"souls were intertwined, but not exactly? That they were dancing around each other? What Garrett said gave me a different perspective, and now I understand it. 'Mek, your soul is not afraid of Sollis. It's trying to leave your body, which is why you're so lethargic. Her soul is . . . defending itself."

"From *what*?" Lormek asked in exasperation.

"From *your* soul taking over *her* body."

"Oh," Aidan whispered. "Like what we saw near the campfire."

"Yes, I think it was already happening then. It's not everything I saw, either." Nyelle stopped to rearrange her thoughts. "Now that I've figured out the soul dance, the rest of it falls into place. I still can't see where the other anchor for her soul goes, but for a moment, it almost appeared like Sollis *wanted* it to happen."

At that moment, Rajiv opened the door, holding a steaming mug. "Is he awake?" he asked. "Oh, good. Here, son, drink this. It should allow you to move around a little."

• • • • •

"So you can choose to control your transitions?" Rajiv asked Aidan a few minutes later, after they quickly filled him in.

"Yes, turns out I can."

"Then, my boy, may I suggest you volunteer to help these poor soldiers? In your wolf form, that is. Those monsters are still coming strong, and we need to hold the line or Kyber will be overrun."

"I hadn't thought of that. Yes, of course. Why don't I come with you?"

Nyelle rushed over and hugged Aidan closely. "Stay safe, brother," she whispered as her fingers brushed his scar. "I can't stand to lose you." Aidan stepped back and wiped her tears away. "Don't worry, sis. I'll be fine. If I could handle the other werewolf, I can handle some Deep Shallows monsters." He smiled affectionately. "You have the more difficult job."

Then he and Rajiv left the room.

Lormek carefully lifted himself from the bed. "I need to go and clean up." He smiled. "And . . ." He hesitated. "I think I can stand to be next to her now. Sollis." As he said the name, he shuddered visibly. He looked at Nyelle. "Somehow when you told me about what you saw . . . it felt like a weight lifted inside my head. I'm still . . . afraid . . . but not like before." Then he slowly left the room as well, leaving Nyelle and Garrett behind.

Nyelle sat down. "Quite a pickle, huh?" She stared at the gnome.

His head was cocked to the side at an unnatural angle.

"What's wrong, Garrett? Are you okay?"

He didn't answer. Then his eyes shifted, and she found herself irresistibly bound by them; her entire being was transfixed by what felt like the entire world—no, bigger than that, the universe—contained in his glance. *Multiverse*, she found herself thinking calmly, even as the rest of her brain was screaming at her in downright panic. *And all of time and space.* She felt lost, without material or spiritual boundaries.

Why am I not freaking out?

Then his eyes cleared, and his head relaxed. "Yeah, I'm good. Totally mystifying, right?"

The sound of his voice gave her senses license to catch up, and she jumped out of her chair, shaking and pointing at him. "What was *that*?"

"Umm . . . what was what?" he asked in confusion.

"Your eyes! The thing you just did! What was it?"

"Umm . . . I don't know what you're talking about. Are you sure you're all right?" He stepped closer and she moved quickly behind the table, keeping it between them. He stopped. "You look really scared."

At that moment, her overwhelmed brain reached its capacity to process. Her last conscious thought before she fainted was, *Screw that.*

SCATOLOGICAL WINDMILL
(SHIT, MEET FAN)

"Yeah, man, she just looked at me funny like she was scared of me and said I did something with my eyes. Then I asked her if she was all right, and she fainted! I swear I was just standing there," Garrett pleaded.

Nyelle lay in bed, with Lormek sitting next to her. Sollis stood at the other end of the room, carefully avoiding him. Garrett sat at the table together with Rajiv, who had come back after seeing Aidan off to help fight the monsters.

"One of you is always down for the count," Rajiv observed. "Truly, I wish I understood what we're dealing with. Freyg . . . I'm afraid I've been asking a lot of her. My divinations . . . they stopped working a while ago. I can still heal physical wounds, but I don't know how much longer." He sighed deeply and gestured toward the bed. "It's sad. She's a sweet girl."

Lormek, his face pale and his shoulders drooping, made his way over slowly and sat next to Nyelle. He held her hand and closed his eyes, muttering softly. A shallow aura extended from his hand toward her. Lormek was breathing heavily, his chin down to his chest.

Nyelle's eyes flew open.

• • • • •

Once the happy cheering subsided, Nyelle explained.

"So what happened was I saw Garrett's eyes change, and then it was like I lost all sense of where and when I was . . . like I became an insignificant part of . . . of everything, all at once." She squinted at Garrett with suspicion. "Are you sure you didn't do anything?"

"I didn't, I swear! I didn't feel any different either."

"Maybe I imagined it then. All this soul magic stuff has been coming fast and heavy . . . my subconscious must have assembled and expressed it in some weird fashion. Still, something good came out of it."

Nyelle grinned. "While I was passed out, I think I figured out part of the puzzle, and it's going to blow your minds."

They leaned in.

• • • • •

"'Mek, remember what you said? How you never had memories from your childhood? Not even vague ones? And how you've always felt disconnected and never entirely comfortable in your own vessel—uh—body?"

Lormek nodded.

"And all those dreams you had . . . wasn't there a theme?"

"Yes. I want to touch her, then she wants to kill me, then she laughs at me for dying, then I want to kill her," he recited in a strained voice. With obvious effort, he lifted his gaze. "Sorry, Sollis. It's been driving me crazy."

She smiled at him. "Don't worry, I've had my own crazy dreams."

"So anyway," Nyelle continued, "between his dreams, the apparition Aidan and I saw at camp, the divination we got from you"—she tilted her head toward Rajiv—"and my own examination of the soul connections, it finally dawned on me that there's a simple explanation."

"There is?" Garrett asked in surprise.

"Well, maybe not simple, but straightforward. Now that I have a grasp on the bigger picture of how souls work, the answer presented itself. It occurred to me after the out-of-body moment I experienced with Garrett. That shift in perspective gave me the last clue." She breathed deeply. "You see, 'Mek . . . I think you were born with the wrong soul."

In the shocked silence that followed, she had an insight. "Oh, and maybe you, too, Sollis, although I'm less sure about that. Your soul never came across to me quite the same as his does."

"I was born with the wrong . . . soul?" Lormek said weakly.

Nyelle nodded. "It explains everything, and it all fits. Your soul is anchored to your body, of course, but it's a more tenuous connection than anybody else's. I initially thought you were suffering from some terminal disease and that your soul was barely holding on, but I was wrong; it's trying to get away. And . . ."

She paused for effect, and her eyes twinkled.

"For all I can tell, it wants to reanchor. Into, uh, Sollis." She paused again. "Look, I know it sounds terrible, but I honestly feel relieved. It finally all makes sense." She leaned back.

"Relief?" Lormek blurted. "Are you *mad*? You're telling me that my soul hates me so much that it wants to leave my body and take over hers? What does it even mean? What if it . . . what if I succeed?"

"Yeah, I'd like to know that too," Sollis said. "What would happen to my soul? Would it go into his body?"

Nyelle sighed. "I don't know the answers. But it feels good to understand the problem."

Rajiv, who had been quietly listening to this exchange, suddenly asked, "Do you believe that their souls have been transposed?"

"I don't know, but it's plausible."

"But that doesn't make sense, does it?" Rajiv continued. "Didn't you tell us that"—he gestured at Sollis—"her soul was bound else-where, too? If they were transposed, wouldn't her soul simply be connected to his body, like his soul is connected to hers?"

"Good point," Nyelle murmured. "I wish I could see the other place yours is attached to, Sollis. But I can't—it's like I'm not *allowed* to follow it."

"How do you mean exactly, not allowed?"

"It's hard to explain. Right now I can see everybody's souls if I focus—generally, it looks like you'd expect, with each soul anchored tightly to one vessel. Lormek's soul is anchored to his body, but it's a weaker link—it wishes to be elsewhere, and all signs point to that 'elsewhere' being Sollis. But Sollis . . . her soul is trying to be in three places at once. It's anchored to her; it's intertwined with 'Mek's soul; and it has another anchor. That last anchor is the strongest of the three actually. But when I try to follow it, I run into a . . . kind of wall, a spiritual soul barrier."

"Is it on another plane? Is that why?"

"No." Nyelle shook her head. "I'm certain it's on Corrantha. Which is frustrating because I should be able to follow it all the way through once I grab hold of the soul thread."

The room fell into an awkward silence. Rajiv excused himself to tend to injured soldiers.

Then Garrett spoke up. "I know it's not a body, but it occurs to me that there's one place around here you might not be able to go. The crystal."

•　•　•　•　•

"That's an incredible idea," Nyelle said after a little while. "But it's certainly possible for a soul to be bound to an object, like with the talisman."

"Yes, it would make sense," Sollis said quietly. "I am clearly connected to it in some way—even though it rejected me earlier."

"But assuming that it's true, what does it mean?" Lormek asked. Then he yawned. "I'm really exhausted, please forgive me." He immediately started snoring softly.

Nyelle turned to Sollis. "Remind me, when you were rejected—you said that you imagined Lormek pushed you out, right?"

"Right," Sollis said.

Nyelle thought for a moment. "If your souls are intertwined, then maybe he's pulling you back to him instead? Your brain could be interpreting things it can't make sense of, like mine did with Garrett. Heck, it's even possible it's happening in reverse—you can't exchange souls with him because you're held in your body by the crystal."

"So I'm stuck between them?"

"I guess."

"It doesn't solve the 'guardian' question though," Garrett said. "Remember? From Zacharias's essay?"

"Oh, right, I forgot about that." Nyelle sighed. "This is really confusing."

A strange sound came from Sollis's direction, and they turned their heads toward her. She somehow appeared taller than ever before, and her face was both reassuring and unsettling. Her eyes glinted with magic. "I know," she said . . .

"I am the guardian."

• • • • •

"I can't believe it took us this long to figure it out." Nyelle laughed.

"Yeah, seems totally obvious now that you said it." Garrett examined Sollis.

"Right? I'm embarrassed that I didn't connect the dots earlier. It fits perfectly, like a jigsaw. But I still don't understand what it means. Clearly, I'm not the guardian in a physical sense—that would be absurd."

"For sure," Nyelle said. "But your soul may be that of the guardian's."

"Then how come I don't remember anything other than my life? Like, this guardian creature has supposedly been around for thousands of years," Sollis mused.

"Tens of thousands is more like it," Garrett pointed out. "And it is—well, you are—immortal, so it could be millions of years for all we know."

"So how come I don't have any sense of all that time?"

Nyelle spoke again. "Didn't Zacharias write that the guardian's powers were restricted within the crystal? Your memories might have been wiped. It sounds awful, but for an immortal being, maybe it isn't so bad. What does time mean to an immortal?"

"It also said I was being punished for something horrible. But I get your point. And if my memories were wiped when I was placed inside the crystal, then perhaps they were wiped again when I was taken out of it. Which probably means that my existence now has an explicit purpose. I wonder what it is . . . and why I couldn't go back into the crystal to accomplish my original task, whatever it was."

"Complicated."

"What's complicated?" Lormek asked. They turned to him. He yawned and rubbed his eyes. "Sorry, I . . . find it hard to stay awake."

"Any ideas?" Nyelle asked after filling him in.

He returned her gaze. "Actually, yes . . . I think so . . . but . . ." He sighed and squared his shoulders. "All right. Let's say that Sollis was the guardian in the crystal, then was ejected from it through the crack she saw. Sollis, didn't you tell me that magic couldn't create something out of nothing?" She smiled in affirmation. "The guardian clearly didn't have a material form at that point. It would have needed to find a form to occupy, right?"

"Oh! Of course! I would jump into the nearest available body!"

"Exactly. So you pop out of the crystal and let's say a baby is born in that exact instant nearby, so there you go. Maybe its intended soul hasn't fully anchored to it yet. Does this sound like something that could happen, Nyelle?" She also indicated her assent.

"So," he continued, "this means that something had to happen to that other soul. Is it possible that it too jumped ship, so to speak?"

"That would be some domino chain." Garrett chuckled.

Lormek turned toward him.

"But it could end with the other kind of readily available body. Remember that my dad found me lying on the beach. He thought I was dead. What if I actually *did die*? My—or my body's—original soul would depart, and the body would begin to decompose. But what if another soul occupied it at that very instant? What if that was the soul that was displaced by the guardian?" He took a deep breath. "It would explain everything, wouldn't it? Why I have no memories before the moment my dad found me. Why I was behaving like a baby even though I was already a child—this new soul had to catch up. It really would explain everything. And . . ."

"And it would also explain why your souls are intertwined, and why yours is drawn to her, because her body should be yours," Nyelle finished for him. "That's . . . remarkable."

Sollis whispered something but none of them could quite make it out.

"Did you want to add something, Sollis?"

With downcast eyes, Sollis took several deep breaths to calm herself. Then, in a deeply pained voice, she said, "Shame."

• • • • •

Having relayed the very last bit of her last dream, the part she had kept to herself, Sollis touched her hair. "So what happens now?"

"If you went back into the crystal, then I suppose his soul would try to jump back into your body . . . I might be able to guide it. But as long as you're kept out . . . then I dunno."

"The shame stops you from entering the crystal because you failed in your task, right?" Garrett asked.

Sollis nodded.

"And yet we don't know how you failed exactly. But to figure it out, you need to find a way back into the crystal?" Nobody responded. "That's quite the paradox. But maybe having knowledge of the paradox will allow you back inside? It would be a pleasingly ironic way to resolve the challenge." He chuckled.

Sollis shrugged. Suddenly Garrett gasped and rushed over to her. "If you succeeded . . . it means you'd be gone!" His eyes filled with tears. She hugged him back. "I think you're right," she replied quietly.

As if to underscore the moment, the volcano shook longer and harder than before. The door flew open, and Rajiv came inside. "It's getting worse out there. The bay waters are heating up, and the shelves are shaking as if they are trying to pry themselves off the volcano. The vibrations are especially bad near the arch, and the dome on the viewing platform broke. It's closed off, but all the guards are fighting down here, so they weren't stopping anyone from going on it. They kept the council chamber's ceiling open to avoid it crashing down. Someone was mad enough to make their way on the viewing platform and fired a crazy shot into the council. They hit the Prime! Then the shooter jumped off the arch. So . . . have you made any progress? If the crystal breaks and the volcano erupts . . . the town and everyone in it will be gone in a flash."

"Worse than that, we think," Nyelle said. "Much, much worse."

Rajiv raised his eyebrows, and Lormek came over to explain. "Dad . . . we are going to try and save Kyber, but . . . just know . . . even if it looks like I'm gone, I may still be here in a different way." His father read his face, but said nothing, and Lormek hugged him deeply. "I love you, Dad." Rajiv returned the hug. "I love you too, son. I have to go back to help, even if it's hopeless." Then he departed.

Another tremor shook the church, and screams split the dawn. "To the beach?" Lormek suggested. "Seems like the easiest route to the crystal." As they got up to leave, he mused, "Funny. If all of this is true, then in a way, the beach is where this all started, and where it will end. It almost seems like a prophecy."

"There's no such thing as prophecies, silly!" Garrett yelled as he ran toward the door. "Come on, let's go save the worlds!"

THE
Book
OF
Trials

38

FOUR

idan met them in the tunnels. "The whole place is warming up and we had to retreat toward the surface." He grinned. "I never imagined how much fun I could have being a were-wolf . . . it's even better than using my bow!"

"How's the militia holding up?" Lormek asked.

"Not great. We've lost more than two hundred to the monsters, and at least as many are incapacitated. Your dad has done a great job treating the injured, but he can't keep up. And the recovered soldiers come back less . . . enthusiastic. I'm worried about morale. There are some deserters already. Tell you what, though." He turned to Nyelle. "Darryn is down there and he's something else. I mentioned you were my sister and he's been with me every step of the way. Refuses to get treatment, either, says his injuries are minor and he'll fight until he can't. Never seen anybody so brave!"

Nyelle hugged her brother. "He's a good man, and very loyal. Keep him alive, okay? I know I broke his heart, but he was always very sweet to me."

Aidan brushed back Nyelle's hair and stared at her fondly. "Don't worry, sis, I'll keep an eye on him." Then he transformed into a wolf. "All right, I have to go back. I hope the plan works!" he shouted as he ran into a side tunnel.

In an uncharacteristic move, Kyber authorities made the exit toll-free for refugees, even from the lower shelves. As a result, the beach was deserted.

There they made their first attempt.

Even the constant ocean inflow was not sufficient to stop the volcano's bay waters from warming, as if slowly boiling on a stovetop. Or in this case, atop a small sun in the form of an entirely improbable crystal.

Confident in her newfound purpose as guardian, Sollis dove in.

A few minutes later, she materialized out of thin air on the beach. She started speaking before realizing she still had her protective air bubble on and flicked it away so they could hear.

"Water's definitely getting warmer. I also noticed another kind of barrier. It's like a dome that sits above the crystal, masking it from view, making it look like a deep dark hole. I can't tell if it will block other living things from crossing—I'm allowed past, but I can sense a tingle. I tossed pebbles at it, and they went through, but the fish won't—they stay above or below. I was repelled again when I tried to touch the crystal, but I was prepared this time, so it didn't knock me out. Looks like there's magic involved that I didn't think was possible, because I found myself here without any sense of having traveled."

"Why would it be impossible?" Garrett asked.

"Because teleportation is the elimination of something in one place and recreating it in another. Elimination is easy, but recreation would violate the way magic works. I'll figure it out if we live through this."

"If we live through this, you won't be with us any longer," Lormek pointed out.

"I suppose there's that. I wish I had my immortal memories—that would help answer a lot of questions."

"So what is the next step?" Nyelle asked. "We knew it wasn't going to be easy. I tried sensing your soul from here, Sollis, but I was cut off, probably by the barrier. Your soul just disappeared. Can you extend your bubble to me? If I can get through with you, then maybe I can follow you all the way to the crystal to understand how your soul can transition into it."

Sollis considered it. "I can do it so long as you stay close, like when we crossed Stormbridge. That's another limit I discovered. Anything I do doesn't stick if I'm not around. I think that's the biggest difference between my magic and that of a wizard, actually. Mine can be more powerful and varied—I can do almost anything I can think of—but it's tied to my presence. A wizard like Talus could create effects that stay forever, like the shelves or the flying boxes."

"I have no intention of straying." Nyelle laughed. "All right, guardian, do me good."

With Nyelle following Sollis, they made their second attempt.

The others were waiting for them to materialize when Sollis's head popped out of the water. "Help me! Quick!" They jumped in and hauled Nyelle's unbreathing body onto the beach. "Lormek, do something now! She's drowning!"

Confused, Lormek leaned over Nyelle and placed his hands over her chest. A magic-tinged aura appeared, and they held their breath. Then she heaved and started coughing up water. After she regained her composure, the two women explained what happened.

"We went down to the barrier, and I crossed it. Nyelle was following me closely, and we tested that being a couple of feet apart wouldn't break the air link. But as soon as I crossed, I could feel the bubble shrinking . . . I crossed back and there she was, struggling—I got her out as quickly as I could."

It was Nyelle's turn. "Sollis disappeared at the barrier. Everything was going fine—it does seem foreboding when you get close, the darkest of dark voids. Even the idea of trying to make progress is terrifying, so there's got to be some sort of mind-impacting magic at play too. The only reason I was even able to try was because I was focusing on her soul. Then she crossed, and all of a sudden, all the links severed—the air bubble was gone, her soul was gone, and I panicked. I do remember her coming back and grabbing me before I blacked out."

As she finished talking, the volcano shook violently, and they could hear the sounds of crashing in the distance. Sollis cocked her head in the direction of the volcano's caldera. "It sounds like the shelves are starting to disintegrate."

"That sounds pretty bad," Garrett said. "And I guess this is probably not good, either." They followed his gaze. The stone storm shrouding Stormbridge had extended over the ocean and was orbiting Kyber. "I recall something about another barrier, the flesh-eating fog covering the peninsula . . . I wonder if that's next," he lamented.

"Is there another way for us to get closer to the crystal?" Nyelle asked.

Garrett and Sollis exchanged a look. "Why, yes, there is," he answered, his voice picking up again. "Let's go to prison!"

FIVE

Garrett ran through the tunnels as fast as his little legs could carry him.

The air grew muggy. His progress was slowed by makeshift blockades, fallen debris, and a constant stream of injured soldiers. He could hear the battle from below; it sounded like it was getting worse. The lines of defense were being pushed upward.

Eventually, he emerged at the Outer Shallows and headed toward the docks. There he stopped, caught his breath, and disappeared.

Crossing unseen would have been challenging on a normal day. It was nigh impossible when the docks were crawling with Kyber militia. But Garrett was no stranger to impossible feats of stealth. His Guild training stood him in good stead as he tiptoed, skipped, and jumped a circuitous path toward the Steadfast Inn, relying on every ounce of his ability to melt into shadows and make himself unnoticeable.

Even so, he was almost caught a couple of times. But Sollis, who was listening in to his progress, relayed his predicaments to Nyelle, and she in turn projected phantom noises that provided just enough distraction for Garrett to slink away.

As he sneaked past the inn's saloon doors, he heard Nyelle whisper. "We're at the spot, Garrett. Take your time . . . but don't take too long. The water's warming up. We're slowly roasting, and Sollis can't figure out how to keep us cool. The crystal is messing up her magic."

Several patrons tiredly eyed the saloon doors, wondering what had set them swinging.

"I'll be right there," he muttered and moved rapidly. The bar floor was converted into a makeshift headquarters. Treena and her staff tended to everyone. The Lieutenant was there, directing the futile effort to save the town from the Deeps monsters. He was pale, and Garrett noted that his arm was in a sling, and he was leaning on a makeshift crutch, his leg amputated above the knee. Garrett wondered if Rajiv could restore lost limbs.

He made it to the hallway and down the stairs to the room where it had all started. It had been cleared of debris, and its bare walls and lack of trimmings made it feel like a huge underground cave, in stark contrast to its original luxurious setting.

It took Garrett but a short moment to trigger the trapdoor in the back closet. Sollis, Lormek, and Nyelle immediately burst through it.

"Ouch and ouch again," Nyelle said. "A few more minutes and my skin would be peeling off!"

"Yes, it wasn't pleasant," Lormek agreed. "But we aren't burned . . . yet."

The handle on the outer door rattled, followed by a heavy knock.

"Who's there?" someone shouted.

Garrett smiled sheepishly. "I guess I locked it when I came in."

More angry knocks followed. "Open this door at once!" someone shouted again. They could hear a muffled conversation and departing footsteps.

"We don't have much time. I already opened the hatch," Garrett said and pointed toward the floor opening that led to the aquarium and the prison below. "Go!"

The others descended hastily. Nyelle went last, and Garrett quickly closed the hatch over her head. "I'll stay and make sure they don't follow for at least a couple of minutes," he whispered urgently. "Good luck!"

• • • • •

They rushed to the aquarium.

"So how do we get past this thing?" Lormek asked. "Didn't you guys say it needed someone on the other side?"

Sollis confirmed, "Yes, it does." She pointed toward the floor. "Nyelle, do me a favor and project a message to the bottom of the tube—it's roughly twenty feet down from here—and a similar distance in the same direction we're heading."

"A message? What should I say?" Nyelle glanced at Sollis in surprise.

"Just say 'do it now.'" Sollis held an aquarium key in her hand. "Make it loud."

"Whatever you're doing, do it quickly," Lormek whispered. "I can hear them opening the hatch."

Nyelle blinked, then shrugged and projected her voice. Sollis attached the key to the matching wall plate. A second later, the plate rotated and disappeared.

• • • • •

A middle-aged gnome was waiting on the other side. "I see you brought some new friends with you." He chuckled, then extended his hand. "I'm Karrott."

As they greeted him in turn, Sollis said, "These are the other two, Nyelle and Lormek. Thank you for sticking to our agreement, my friend."

"Of course! That's why we made it, in case everything goes awry. It was a good plan. I guess I can still be useful in my gnome form."

Lormek looked at Karrott. "You're the talking rat from the prison?"

Karrott responded cheerfully, "I was about to unrat, and Sollis thought she might need a backup plan, so she asked if I'd wait here. Usually, I head out of the prison while I'm in my gnome phase, but there isn't anybody else here right now . . . and it sounded interesting! Judging by the shaking and rise in ambient temperature, I guess something is happening."

"Yes, *something* is definitely happening. Not that we could keep you away. You're welcome to join us," Sollis offered Karrott, "but it's likely we're all going to die."

Karrott returned her gaze. "Dying while learning is the best way to die!"

• • • • •

They entered the torture chamber.

"By the gods." Nyelle eyed the various instruments. "Seems . . . efficient."

"Aye," Lormek said. "Also, I wonder why this place stays cool."

"There are layers of protective magic around this chamber. It's the closest we can get to the crystal without being underwater." Sollis gestured at the floor. "The soul barrier runs right under here—I didn't know what it was, but I felt it when I went through the first time."

"How did you do *that*?" Nyelle stamped the floor a couple of times with her boot.

"Through there." Sollis pointed at the iron maiden. "Don't worry, if you know how, you won't get hurt."

A second passed in stunned silence as Lormek and Nyelle examined the massive torture device and then turned back at Sollis. "Oh, sure, why not?" Nyelle said finally. "Won't be any crazier than anything else that's happened today. So what do I need to do?"

• • • • •

That was their third attempt. It ended quickly.

After receiving an air bubble from Sollis, Nyelle stepped inside the iron maiden, making sure to push against the pressure points. Sollis triggered the mechanism and closed the device carefully.

"Ow! No, ow, no, take me out, take me out!" They heard Nyelle shrieking from inside. Sollis yanked open the door.

"What happened? Didn't the floor drop?"

"It did!" Nyelle climbed out. "And I found myself sitting on the surface of the water—which is butt-burningly hot, by the way—but somehow not falling in."

"Wait, how come you're not injured from the spikes?" Lormek asked.

"They back off before piercing your skin." Nyelle rubbed the backs of her thighs. "It's scalding."

"Oh. It makes sense that they would retract," Sollis murmured. "See, when I went through, I just barely felt them before I fell in the water."

They looked at each other as they considered the challenge.

"Can you travel there ethereally?" Nyelle asked. "Maybe I can join you that way?"

"No, I tried it. The barrier stops me from crossing that way."

"It seems like you two have something in mind." Lormek raised his eyes toward Sollis. "I thought the goal was for Nyelle to examine the crack to help you understand how to enter the crystal. Sounds like you have another idea."

Nyelle took Lormek's hand in hers. "Yes. Sorry, 'Mek. I think we both realized along the way that I need to be her soul guide."

"Her guide? But if we're to believe Zacharias, then it means . . ."

Nyelle turned her eyes down.

"*No!*" he yelled and jumped between her and the iron maiden. "I won't let you!" Tears were streaming down his cheeks. "She's . . . she was never even supposed to be here . . . but you are, and . . . and I won't lose you! I won't!"

Karrott, who was standing forgotten in the corner, cleared his throat. "This may be the wrong moment, but might I inquire as to the nature of this conversation? It sounds rather intriguing, and . . . well . . . who knows? Maybe I can help."

TWO AND THREE

They spent a few precious minutes sharing their findings and conclusions with Karrott.

"I get it. The only physical body that can pass is Sollis, but Nyelle needs to be there to figure out why Sollis can't get back into the crystal." Karrott thought for a moment. "Didn't you say that Nyelle is a . . . 'soulmage,' was it? Why can't she join Sollis in spiritual form?"

Nyelle stared at him in astonishment.

"By the gods, he's right! I've been thinking about this all wrong . . . if I can see everybody else's souls and their anchor points, then I should be able to see my own too. It never even occurred to me. And if I can see it, I can manipulate it, like I did with the talisman!"

"Looking inside ourselves is always the hardest," Sollis whispered.

"What are you talking about?" Lormek, still barring them from the iron maiden, demanded.

Nyelle turned to him. "Sollis is going in, and I'll join her by loosening my own anchor and attaching my soul to hers. You know we have to do this, 'Mek. And we don't have much time." Lormek gave her a look that was at once so loving and so hurt that it brought tears to her eyes. "Please, 'Mek. Let's not make it harder than it needs to be."

Karrott cleared his throat again. "Umm . . . excuse me . . . I think it is still perhaps the wrong moment, but I wanted to point out a couple of things." He smiled awkwardly. "First, you don't know that you'll make it this time either."

They agreed that he was right.

"More importantly," he continued, "if you don't make it, then somehow Nyelle's soul will need to reattach to her body, otherwise it might dissipate entirely. And if her body has already stopped living due to the departure of her soul, then her soul might fail."

Nyelle stared at him. "Shit, you're right. So what do we do?"

Lormek stepped reluctantly away from the iron maiden. "I think I know how to handle that. I can ask Thor to help me keep your body in stasis while you travel with her. But, Nyelle . . . please promise me you'll come back. Don't go into the crystal together."

Nyelle bent to hug him for a long moment. "I will, 'Mek. I want to come back," she whispered. Then she turned to Sollis. "Are we ready to try it?"

And so began their fourth attempt.

With Nyelle's soul riding shotgun, Sollis created another protective bubble and entered the iron maiden. When they emerged above the crystal, Nyelle was so awed that she forgot she was only there in spirit and flinched involuntarily. Even for Sollis, the changes were surprising. The crystal had truly come alive, the two souls within moving at impossible speed. Their frantic auras charged the crystal to radiate blinding flashes of magical energy. Their gyrations were slowly widening the crack; it had grown dramatically and extended across half the crystal. Sollis realized it was getting near the point of breaking.

They could see the magma rising below.

As they neared the crystal, Nyelle focused on the soul threads. She guided Sollis toward the infinitely tiny soul anchor where the crack began. "Clearly," Sollis noted dryly through their spiritual link. Nyelle could feel her sarcasm. Otherwise, it seemed simple; once Sollis knew where the soul anchor was, she just had to touch it and let her soul through. Nyelle concentrated in preparation for returning to her body; she could just about feel it, and Lormek's caring presence devotedly hovering over it.

Then everything went wrong all at once, and she barely had the presence of mind to guide both of them to reappear in the room above.

· · · · ·

"What happened?" Lormek asked, removing his hands from Nyelle's midsection.

The women stood up. "Just like before," Sollis said, "I very nearly got in, then got punched in the gut. Though we ended up here instead of the beach . . . you did that, right Nyelle?"

"Yes. And I saw something important. You weren't punched out. We were pulled back here, to 'Mek. It was, well, crystal clear—there's something you two have to deal with before Sollis is allowed back into the crystal."

They stared at her in confusion. She shrugged. "Just telling you what I saw."

Sollis stared at Lormek. Then her face showed deep remorse as she was hit with a sudden realization. "Oh, Lormek, I'm so sorry. As the guardian, I . . . took over your body when I came out of the crystal. That must have been . . . painful."

As she said it, Lormek started crying openly.

"I don't know what my immortal self intended," Sollis continued. "But it surely had no grasp of what it means for a soul to lose its vessel right when it's getting anchored to it. I cannot possibly imagine how devastating it must be to live your entire life in the wrong body. I'm really, really sorry." She went to her knees and embraced the weeping dwarf.

"Is it working?" Karrott, who seemed to materialize from thin air, whispered in Nyelle's ear. She shook her head slowly. "Almost. So that's what her shame was about. Not for failing in her task, but for stealing his vessel. Her soul is trying to disengage and free up the body for him to come back into it, but he won't let her leave."

Lormek hesitantly raised his arms and returned the embrace. He cried even harder, and Sollis shocked everybody, herself most of all, by crying as well.

Lormek gathered himself and mumbled, "I know, Sollis, I know." He sniffed loudly and took a step back from the comically tall, miserable human with her funny ears.

"Thank you, Sollis. I mean it. I . . . like my body now. I'm used to it. It's . . . it's the only one I've ever known." He sighed deeply. "I'm going to keep it. And . . . I forgive you."

A powerful wave of energy swept over everyone in the small room.

"You're free, Sollis!" Nyelle shouted. "That was it! 'Mek had to forgive you for taking his body from him!"

Sollis and Lormek ignored her, their eyes locked in a silent exchange. The moment lingered as they held each other's hands, their fingers crossed together. Then they slowly let go.

Sollis turned to Nyelle. "I think we should try it again."

They set up the same way, with Lormek keeping Nyelle's body in stasis, and Nyelle's soul riding shotgun.

That was their fifth and final attempt.

It went smoothly. Almost disappointingly so, considering. At the very end, when Sollis reached down toward the crack, Nyelle prepared herself, anticipating the need to reanchor both of them back into the room and to Lormek. But this time she made the trip alone, secure in the knowledge of their success. They floated gently the last fraction of an inch, the wildmage touched the crystal, and Nyelle was gone.

It seemed the right moment for me to reveal myself.

ONE

"Hey, Is," I said as I froze time and restored all their memories.

"Oh, hi," *They* responded after they took a moment to reintegrate. "Say, X, I'd like to stick to female pronouns for a while. I . . . grew fond of them recently."

"Of course, Is. That has always been your special quality. The immortal with mortal emotions. You are, after all, why I wrote this story, and why I devised the test for you and put you in the crystal to guard the dragons."

She considered it for a moment. "Right. It was never about choosing between the two—neither of them was worthy on their own, were they?"

"No. Not until they became one. Still, a shame to waste such power . . . rarely do mortals grow so powerful that they can join us."

"It was all about my emotional capacity then. You know, you could have told me that, X." When I didn't respond, she continued. "Then again, if you did, there would be no test, and they would destroy each other. I'm curious—did you want them to succeed?"

"I think it's something I learned from you, Is. All of us did. The idea of boredom. It's the sort of thing mortals suffer from, isn't it? I figured their struggle would be interesting to watch. And if the dragons could work it out—if one would agree to serve and guide the other's soul so they could merge and join us in Celestia—then we might enjoy it." I paused. "Judging by Thor, I think I was right. Thor's a total revelation, Is. So much fun! Freyg's decided to let Thor shape this world's faith for a while. They seem pretty invested in it."

"Do Thor think of themselves as one?"

"Yes, otherwise they wouldn't have made it to Celestia. Though come to think of it, they do use the male pronouns a lot, like you do the female. They . . . uh, *he* gets so wonderfully excited by being a god, even if he's still such a very small one. The old pantheon is getting a little jealous—which is also distinctly mortal. Look at what you've done, Is!" I laughed.

She projected the image of her mortal body smacking its forehead. "Damn it, X! It finally occurred to me why my mortal parents named me Sollis—you gave them the idea!"

I grinned. "It was apparent. You're a Solar, and your name is Is, so *Sol-Is* suggested itself. Speaking of which, you were a bit enthusiastic about it all, no? You couldn't possibly have known that you were forcing your human body to grow . . . but what made you stop?"

"Whether I knew it consciously or not, at some point it was . . . apparent." She laughed. "But I get your point." She thought for a moment. "When you put me in the crystal, I wasn't being punished, was I? I realize it now. You wanted to see if I could use my compassion to get the dragons to cooperate."

"And also get you out of the way for a bit," I admitted. "That's why I had to take all your memories, Is . . . or at least I thought so back then. These mortal emotions you have, like compassion . . . they're a new thing. New things can make us nervous. We—well, some of us, anyway—don't like new things." I paused. "Now I realize perhaps I didn't need to do that."

I shared the true and full story with her.

"You really are a terrible liar . . . and for that matter, storyteller." She laughed again.

"I didn't think I was *that* bad." I felt offended, which I took a moment to cherish. Being in the presence of Is is always a powerful learning experience. "And it was fun to tell this tale, even if my grasp of emotions is limited. Once the five of you learned to trust each other, I didn't have to narrate things much anymore and instead just recorded what you were saying . . . from that point you wrote your own story."

"*Our* story? Really? What about your deceptions . . . like, there were never any wizards in the Shallows? Why did you even make up that one, X?"

It was my turn to laugh. "It wouldn't be as much fun If I let everyone know the innkeeper was the wizard Talus and not merely the dwarven Bhaven."

She considered this. "Hmm. And since she's the only one who knows his secret, you twisted the tale of Enrielle to fit your narrative needs. She was never anybody's whore, and definitely not his. I imagine Talus absolutely adores her."

"That *was* my biggest ruse," I admitted. "I enjoyed it! And I wasn't lying. Their bond is very strong. Enrielle did help Talus build the reputation of the place. She spent decades seducing so many because of how badly she missed Thor—or rather, Kenzer and Zacharias. I just pretended that she and the wizard didn't know each other. Really, all I did was change a few words in their conversation. She nearly told all of you the truth herself."

"That would have been fitting. Sadly, it never worked out for her, did it? It's impossible to get over being god's lover, let alone the two halves of one. It's too big a void to fill." Is paused. "I see now. Talus is very old. She's going to lose him soon, and she knows it. She was

practically a child when they recruited her. Talus is her last living connection to them. I feel sorry for her, X."

What Is could feel was well beyond my grasp.

"Do you think they figured out the rest?"

"Who? The mortal audience? Does it matter?" I retorted. "In time,
they might. Or they will grow old and die."

"You do realize they will be reading this part too, don't you?"

"Of course I do, I'm the one writing it. I'd like to think they're
enjoying it."

"I'm sure they are. Many of them get very excited when they read
or hear stories written by gods. It makes them feel close to the divine.
Like what Enrielle felt in the tunnels when Lormek got his blessing.
But do at least tell the truth about the ones they care about."

I projected a sigh. "All right, Is. You understand mortals much better than any of us do. So let me start with the healer since you brought
him up. He is actually a wildmage, but he doesn't know it. He's very
earnest, and his voice is strong, and Thor was a little too eager to
get involved with him—even a bit careless. It takes a while to adapt
to being a god, and the boy is a remote descendant. Thor's blessing
didn't work, but wildmages can emulate divine magic very well up
to a point, and the healer is absolutely convinced of his nature, false
though it might be."

"That explains a few things."

"The soundshaper is destined to be *his* soul guide, which she
already suspects. But she believes him about being a healer and that, of
course, would make it impossible for her to serve as his guide. Divinity
is guided by us, not driven by the mortals. It makes her feel lost, but
she's stubborn and will stay with him until she finds an answer. In the
meanwhile, he's going to grow in power, so long as he overcomes his
shame. Speaking of which, that's one emotion I hope we never catch
back home!"

"Do you think they can end up ascending like Thor?"

"Perhaps. They are very immature, and the healer will need to realize his true nature. If they don't die first, it will take them a few centuries to figure it all out. I'll be watching. It could be entertaining! Regardless, like Kenzer and Zacharias, these two are very compatible, and also like them, will be great lovers."

"What about Aidan?"

"The woodspeaker? You really need me to spell it out?"

She waited.

"Fine. He's also a wildmage, in his own unique way. A first of his kind. The soul spark he ingested through the talisman transformed him in more ways than just into a werewolf. There has never been one who could combine the chaotic magic and the orderly before."

She raised an ethereal eyebrow.

"Oh, you are such a delight, Is! All right. Yes, I did in fact guide Garrett a few times."

"Just a few times? It was you at the bridge, wasn't it? And on the stairway? And when he made poor Aidan take a dive? And all those other places where he did or said something that was downright dangerous or merely outrageous, yet somehow nudged us forward?"

"Not *all* of them." I chuckled. "He's perfectly capable of getting into trouble on his own."

"And Garrett being your mouthpiece is why you didn't flesh out his origin story like you did with the others. I see that now. It would have made things too complicated. But it was definitely you that Nyelle saw that scared her so much."

"Yes, of course. It seemed timely to intervene in a more obvious fashion, although I may have gotten caught up in the moment."

She smiled. "You really are getting emotional, X. So what now? Are you going to take my memories away again?"

"No. I realize it was a mistake. It's hard enough with the dragons in the crystal—we've kept them in suspended animation. They're just as stubborn as they ever were and just as determined that only one will ascend. I understand it better now. Your compassion is the thing that might make it possible for them to solve their conundrum, but without your memories, how could you have compassion? The inevitable conclusion is that emotions and memories are tied together like two parts of a god."

"Yes, that's how it works, X. Memories store emotions so as to better guide mortals as they go about their lives. They need both. I do too."

"Is, it means you're going to have to stick around down here until they ascend, or until you tell me they're never going to. Are you okay with that? No going back to Celestia."

"That's kind of you, X. See? You actually care about me."

She was right. "True," I mused. "How fascinating."

"But I meant it. Don't worry about me, X. First of all, I have memories of being the spark in the crystal, and that was pleasant, and it's going to be so much better if I have all my other memories too. Also, the soul bridge allows me to visit many places, now that I know how to use it. The first place I'll go is this Earth. It's so full of feelings!" She whooped. "There may be more feelings when the people there read this story. And I can easily keep the crystal whole for as long as it takes, even if my attention isn't always focused on it."

"You are like *them* as much as you are like *us*," I noted.

"I know, X."

I'm not sure, but I think she was happy.

"Also, because I will have all my memories, I would be able to communicate with the other four if they came to see me—I suspect they will, once they realize who they truly are. Especially Lormek and Nyelle. I think it's inevitable I will meet them again."

She paused. "If the dragons ever figure out how to meld their souls and complete their journey—I'll stay down here, X, to make sure the crystal doesn't collapse. I grew to like this place and all its people and their feelings. I'd like to keep it safe."

"Safe?" I asked in surprise. "But it doesn't matter if it's gone. I can always recreate it for you, Is. Recreate all the places. It will only take an instant."

"But I wouldn't want you to. It's something you won't be able to understand, X, but emotions and memories become fused through time, and when it happens to a lot of mortals over a very long period . . . it creates history. And history is full of really amazing feelings."

I considered it.

"All right, Is. I guess you've earned the right to determine your own fate. You've even earned the right to change your mind, if you like, once the situation with the dragons is resolved. I think I might come to visit you. I find that I'm quite"—I paused to savor the unusual sensation—"fond of you."

She beamed, and I restored time and let her go into the crystal.

42

EPILOGUE . . . ISH

Once Is returned to the crystal, things turned around quickly. The crack healed and the agitated volcano calmed itself with a submarine eruption. The massive stone storm that surrounded the peninsula quieted shortly after that. The monsters, no longer threatened by eruption, went back to their deep lairs. Repairs began immediately, and Kyber slowly returned to normal.

The Prime died from the sniper's shot, leaving behind a leadership vacuum. When the assassin's body was pulled from the ocean, it turned out to be Hortus with Aidan's bow slung on his back. He also wore a pair of glider wings, which were shredded to pieces by flying stones. In the ensuing power struggle, Enrielle applied her unique, deep knowledge of Port Kyber and the Thieves' Guild and became the new Prime. She thought of it as a fresh kind of adventure and would spend several decades running the Guild and serving as Kyber's head of government.

Under her guidance, a historic formal alliance was signed with King Emmeka, much to the dismay of the Church of Freyg.

After his heroics defending Kyber in its time of need, serving as its last line of defense, Aidan became a folk hero. Once the previous Lieutenant succumbed to his injuries, Aidan was offered the commission but declined it. His suggestion of promoting Darryn to the post instead was approved unanimously. Neither of them realized that Enrielle, as the new Prime, made sure the appointment was confirmed; she was pleased with Darryn's role in unearthing the conspiracy against the Guild.

And her daughter liked him.

Aidan and Garrett then took to adventuring. The sight of the gnome riding the werewolf became common folklore. They would visit Kyber every so often, and those in the council chamber would stare in astonishment as the werewolf walked in, shook the gnome off his back, and casually transformed into his elven form.

Rajiv, who almost died healing a thousand soldiers, spent weeks in recovery, tended to by his son. During that time, Lormek took over Rajiv's duties and discovered that he could do even more for the needy than his father ever did, albeit in new ways. He added staff and trained them in the ways of Thor. The renamed Church of Ascendance grew just as important as the inn, the library, and the whorehouse. After he recovered, in recognition of his impressive logistical skill in Kyber's hour of need, Rajiv was appointed as the new Grunt. He spent the last years of his life practicing compassion in Kyber's internal administration. For one thing, nobody ever again fell to their death off the Stairway.

Nyelle stayed with Lormek, and they finally admitted they were in love. They lived for a while in a little house her mother owned in Greenpark District. A few years later, they had a child. They named her Solace, in honor of their immortal friend who saved the world by choosing to forever watch over it, alone. After Rajiv passed away, Lormek handed off running the increasingly influential Church to his most promising disciple, and their little family took off to track down Lormek's roots. It turned out he came from Clan Tallgrass. Their elders remembered him and honored him with the title of "Diplomat," which had belonged to his birth father. They eventually set up a small trading company, the first in northern Decentea. That led them to travel to many places, including the South. And in the South was where Lormek finally discovered that he was not a healer after all.

Is stayed in the crystal, taking care of two fiercely combative soul dragons, and patiently waited for her four friends to visit her. I'm still not sure why, but she seems to enjoy the whole thing. A benefit of having her full awareness means she cannot be ejected again by incompetent wizards or their greedy masters causing the crystal to crack. I wonder if she ever figured out who it was that ended her reality so rudely back when our story began—even if, in retrospect, they did her a favor.

I never told her, and she never asked me.

Then again, I know how much she likes puzzles.

That's it. There's nothing more to tell. With that, I have come to understand that mortals enjoy closure, so I'll sign off in the same way that he did much earlier in the story, in a moment when he didn't act as my mouthpiece.

And so, without further ado . . .

Garrett, out.

ACKNOWLEDGMENTS

D&D played a role in my intro as an immigrant to the USA.[1] Two decades later, in the prendemic[2] era, I started a new D&D campaign.

To me, setting up a coherent series of encounters—the baseline for any campaign—is the least interesting aspect of being game master. Instead, I presented my players with three options of published adventures, and they picked one.[3] Still, no matter the source

---

1   Now here's a cool interview question to ask me.

2   Pre-pandemic. Footnotes are fun—let's have more!

3   It's called *Legacy's Wake* and has some very cool mechanics (like D&D cinematic sequences). You should definitely buy it. Feel free to reach out for notes on how to run it even if you don't want to completely change it like I did (I hope I don't regret this). This also serves as my first thank you to Chris, Derek, and Warren, creators of the module.

material, by the time I'm ready to roll, it will have been recrafted with new story arcs, non-player characters, hidden relationships, and red herrings—all in service to my players, who to my mind, must feel like the most important people in the world.

It's their story, after all.[4]

Then COVID shut everything down. We transitioned to video conferencing, but I couldn't adjust; so much of my style depends on being able to read the table.

It was the worst game I ever ran.

Still, I found myself on COVID time and started writing a novel. It took their characters—our heroes—into a fresh setting. It had a new, complicated storyline; too much for a game where players will inevitably derail anything not bolted down, yet perfect for a book. But as best I could, I kept intact their individual voices as I heard them around our virtual gaming table. It also incorporated a couple of our top shared moments, like the Aidan scene near Stormbridge.

I wrote the book for myself, with no thought of getting it published. Then I started sharing it. The die was cast when I decided to do a series of recorded public readings of my first draft manuscript,[5] and Alisson, whom I did not previously know, joined in. By the time it was done, I asked her professional opinion as a creative writing teacher, and her emphatic response could best be summarized as *this has to be in stores, dum-dum.* Thank you, Alisson, for your support along the way and everything else too. To paraphrase J. D., You are a lady and a scholar.

A massive thank you to Willow (Sollis nee Sollys), Dan (Aidan nee Aodhan nee "A Dan"), Shayan (Lormek), Lauren (Nyelle), and Corey (Garrett). I hope that getting your characters' names immortalized this way is as fun for you as it was for me.

------

4   This sentiment is echoed in the book (see if you can find it).

5   Quite literally as it was getting finished. There is a sad, lonely YouTube channel where they are all posted.

Thank you to the late Gary Gygax and Dave Arneson for D&D itself; I met the two in Gencon 2000 where they signed my Player's Handbook. It is my most treasured gaming book on account of that memory. And to all the giants who inspired my writing. I can't possibly name everyone, but Harry Harrison, Orson Scott Card, Douglas Adams, and Terry Pratchett are up there; their styles made a significant impact on this tale. *The Crack in the Crystal* pays homage to different authors and their stories; for example, *Gone Ghost* is a reference to *Gone Girl*. Some are rather more obvious than others. And in a meta sort of way, I am thus honoring *Ready Player One*.

Thank you, Mia, my love. I cannot imagine I'd ever feel confident enough to make this happen without you. Plus you had to hear the raw version in fits and starts, which means you gave me incredibly valuable feedback—and never got to really enjoy the story. Hopefully, reading it now, it makes more sense.

Thank you, Greg, for inspiring me to launch the public readings, and Idan and Sharaine, for hosting so many of them, even though the readings were open to anyone, strangers included. Thank you to Corey and Rich and Dan, for helping with tech and answering my call to put on your hacker hats and go seeking plot holes in the original manuscript. My "real job" in cyber paid dividends . . . because they did find a few holes that you get to avoid.

Thank you to my vast beta testing group who experienced the story in different versions and didn't throw up (except in that one place where, appropriately, a few gagged). Mara, Mary, Christina, and Hamid, it was a wonderful experience for me to have private, individual read-throughs with you. I learned so much through observing your reactions in real-time.

Thank you to all the agents who said no when I was initially trying to get this published. I learned from those rejections, and there's a small chance that you will have collectively done me a great favor. Thank you to the amazing team at Greenleaf who gave the book such an enthusiastic thumbs-up and helped work out the kinks; Lindsey, your delight filled my heart.

346 • THE CRACK IN THE CRYSTAL

And to be 100 percent cliché about it, thank YOU. My biggest goal is to bring a bit more joy to the world. Feels like it needs it. Thank you for taking the journey with me. I hope you find it joyful.[6]

—BARAK

---

6   Now say "joyful journey" in a Jersey accent. See? It's already happening!

ABOUT THE AUTHOR

Barak grew up dreaming of being in the creative arts. Instead, he faced the choice of being a doctor or lawyer; the Jewish stereotype jokes write themselves. After being accepted to medical school and realizing what it actually took to become a real doctor, his inner lazy fair (which is *such* a dad pun he insisted it be pointed out) recoiled in horror and he went into engineering instead.

Graduating from the Technion in Israel, he embarked on a cyber-security career, and later became the world's first "virtual CISO." If you're reading *this* book, then it is (mostly) irrelevant, as is the fact that he wrote a few books on the topic of cybersecurity. He also built a couple of companies and along the way proudly adopted the title given to him by his own staff: Pretty Lil' Princess.

That's what "PLP" stands for on his LinkedIn profile.

His passion for the arts, though, never wavered.

The unusual final twist in *The Crack in the Crystal* has been percolating in his mind for a long time, looking for a story anchor. When one finally showed up, Barak spent several ecstatic months crafting the narrative around it, hoping that when it came time for the big reveal, he would find a way to do it justice. He was thrilled that during the extensive period of beta testing, not one person managed to figure it out before it happened.

Getting it right only took a day's long medicine journey on a heroic dose of magic mushrooms.

Barak loves books that skew happier, with humor, clever dialogue, unexpected twists, and fewer meandering descriptions of the specific shade of a particular banana. He therefore prefers *The Hobbit* to *Lord of the Rings*; couldn't get through *Game of Thrones* even back when it was only three books; adores the *Stainless Steel Rat* series, which he strongly believes deserves a streaming conversion; and is emphatic that *The Hitchhiker's Guide to the Galaxy* is.[1]

Barak lives with Mia of the two hands and Gidget, Pippa, Ziggy, and Dingo, each of the four paws. His offspring, Joshua and Karma, are out adulting, but they do visit sometimes, to which he always eagerly looks forward.

He hopes his story brings you joy, and if so, he says, then it is enough.

---

1   Yes, just like that.